An Amish Year

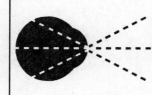

AN AMISH YEAR

FOUR AMISH NOVELLAS

BETH WISEMAN

THORNDIKE PRESS

A part of Gale, Cengage Learning

GALE
CENGAGE Learning·

Farmington Hills, Mich • San Francisco • New York • Waterville, Maine
Meriden, Conn • Mason, Ohio • Chicago

GALE
CENGAGE Learning®

LIBRARY OF CONGRESS CATALOGING-IN-PUBLICATION DATA

Names: Wiseman, Beth, 1962-
Title: An Amish year : four Amish novellas / Beth Wiseman.
Description: Large print edition. | Waterville, Maine : Thorndike Press, 2016. |
    ©2015 | Series: Thorndike Press large print Christian fiction
Identifiers: LCCN 2015039134| ISBN 9781410484918 (hardback) | ISBN 1410484912
    (hardcover)
Subjects: LCSH: Large type books.
Classification: LCC PS3623.I83 A6 2016 | DDC 813/.6—dc23
LC record available at http://lccn.loc.gov/2015039134

Published in 2016 by arrangement with Thomas Nelson, Inc., a division of HarperCollins Christian Publishing, Inc.

Printed in the United States of America
1 2 3 4 5 6 7 20 19 18 17 16

CONTENTS

ROOTED IN LOVE

To Jenni Newcomer Cutbirth

GLOSSARY OF LANCASTER COUNTY AMISH WORDS

ach — oh
bruder — brother
daed — dad
danki — thank you
dochder — daughter
Englisch — non-Amish person
gut — good
haus — house
kaffi — coffee
kapp — prayer covering or cap
kinner — children or grandchildren
maedel — girl
mamm — mom
mei — my
mudder — mother
nee — no
Ordnung — the written and unwritten rules of the Amish; the understood behavior by which the Amish are expected to live, passed down from generation to generation. Most Amish know the rules by heart.

scrapple — traditionally a mush of pork scraps and trimmings combined with cornmeal, wheat flour, and spices. The mush is formed into a semisolid congealed loaf, and slices are then pan-fried before serving.

Wie bischt — How are you?; Howdy

ya — yes

CHAPTER ONE

Rosemary crossed her legs, folded her arms across her chest, and tried to focus on the bishop's final prayer as he wrapped up the worship service. Saul Petersheim was making that a difficult task. She'd made it clear to Saul that she was not interested in dating him, but the man still gave it his best shot from time to time.

"He's doing it again," Rosemary whispered to Esther. "Smiling and staring at me."

Her best friend grinned. "Are you ever going to give that poor fellow a break and go out with him?"

"We've been through all this, Esther. Saul and I dated when we were sixteen. It didn't work out then, and it wouldn't work out now." Rosemary clamped her mouth closed when she realized that Bishop Glick had stopped talking and was staring at her, along with most of the congregation. She could feel the heat rising from her neck to her cheeks, so she sat taller, swallowed hard, and didn't breathe for a few seconds.

"See, Saul even gets me in trouble at worship service," Rosemary said once the bishop had recited the final prayer and dismissed everyone. She stood up, smoothed the wrinkles from her white apron, and shook her head.

Esther chuckled. "You're twenty-one years old. I think you're responsible for your own actions at this point."

Rosemary sighed as they waited for several of the older women to pass by before they eased into the line that was forming toward the kitchen. "I guess. I just wish Saul would find someone else," she whispered as she glanced over her shoulder toward him. "Someone better suited to him." The words stung when she said them aloud.

"Saul only has eyes for you." Esther smiled. "And I don't understand why you won't give him another chance. It was five years ago." Rosemary bit her bottom lip, tempted to tell Esther the whole story. But every time she considered telling her friend the truth, she stopped herself. There was once a time when Rosemary couldn't picture herself with anyone but Saul.

All the men had gone in the other direction toward the front door, most likely to gather in the barn to tell jokes and smoke cigars while the women prepared the meal. Rosemary shrugged. "It just wouldn't work out."

Esther picked up a stack of plates from the counter and shook her head. "I don't understand you, Rosemary. Saul is one of the most desirable single men in our district. The fact that someone else hasn't already snagged him is mind-boggling." She nudged Rosemary's shoulder. "But I really do think he is holding out for you."

"Well, he is wasting his time." Rosemary picked up a pitcher of tea and followed Esther out the kitchen door and onto the porch. As they made their way down the steps toward the tables that had been set up in the yard, Rosemary commented to Esther that the Lord couldn't have blessed them with a more beautiful day. She wasn't going to let thoughts about Saul ruin it.

It seemed like spring had arrived overnight following a long winter that had seen record-low temperatures in Lancaster County. The Zooks were hosting church service today, and their flower beds were filled with colorful blooms. Rosemary glanced to her right at the freshly planted garden, then sighed, knowing how disappointed her mother

15

would be if she were still alive. Rosemary hadn't planted a garden in four years. She'd tried to maintain the flower beds, but even that effort had failed.

She'd filled up most of the tea glasses when she saw Saul walking toward her. She swallowed hard. All these years later, Saul still made her pulse quicken.

"You look as pretty as ever, Rosie." Saul pushed back the brim of his straw hat, then looped his thumbs beneath his suspenders. There was no denying that Saul was a handsome man with his dark hair, deep-blue eyes, and boyish dimples. He had a smile that could melt any girl's heart. Aside from her father, Saul was the only other person who called her Rosie, and a warm feeling filled her when he did. But she'd never tell him that.

Rosemary looked up at him and forced a smile, wishing things were different. "*Danki,* Saul." She turned to walk away, but he was quickly in stride with her. "Can I help you with something?" she said as she continued to walk toward the house. She kept her eyes straight ahead and masked any facial expression.

"*Nee,* just going inside." He scratched his chin. "And trying to figure out how long it's been since I asked you out. Wondering if I

16

should try again."

Rosemary stopped midstep. She glanced around to see if anyone was in earshot, and after waiting for one of her brothers to jet past them, she said, "I-I just don't think it's a *gut* idea for us to date. I'm very busy trying to run a household full of boys and take care of *mei daed*." She locked eyes with his, knowing she'd do better to avoid looking at him altogether.

"Did I hear hesitation in your voice?" He grinned, and Rosemary's knees went weak. Saul wasn't just nice looking, he was also well respected within the community and known to have a strong faith. He was sure to be a good husband and provider since he ran a successful construction company. He'd taken over his father's business when his father never fully recovered from back surgery. But there were two reasons Rosemary wasn't going to get involved with Saul. And one of them was walking toward them. Her five-year-old brother stopped in front of her, his face drawn into a pout.

"I can't find Jesse or Josh." Abner stared up at Rosemary.

"They're around here somewhere." Rosemary straightened her youngest brother's hat, making a mental note to cut his blond bangs when they got home. "We'll be eating

17

soon, and neither Jesse nor Joshua is going to miss a meal."

Saul squatted in front of Abner. "Anything I can help you with, buddy?"

Abner shook his head. *"Nee."*

Rosemary looked down at her feet for a moment. Saul was born to be a father. She'd watched him with the *kinner* in their district over the years. The man was loving and kind to anyone he came in contact with. She needed to get away from him before she threw herself into his arms or said something she'd regret. She held up the empty pitcher and focused on Abner. "I've got to go refill this and help get lunch on the table. Don't go far." Then she turned to Saul, and a sadness weighed so heavy on her heart, she couldn't even force another smile. "I have to go."

Saul scratched his chin again as he watched Rosemary walk away. Most days, he wondered why he continued to pursue her since she always turned him away. But every now and then he would see something in her beautiful brown eyes that made him think he might still have a chance. Or like today . . . he was sure he'd heard regret in her voice.

Sighing, he turned and headed back to the barn. As he pulled open the door, the

18

stench of cigar smoke assaulted him. He'd never cared for this recreational activity that some of the men practiced. It used to be reserved for after the Sunday meal, but somewhere along the line, a few of the men began having a smoke before they ate. Saul enjoyed the jokes and company of the other fellows, but considering John Zook had already lost one barn to a fire, Saul was surprised he allowed smoking in his new one. The men were already walking toward the door, so Saul turned around and they all made their way to the tables.

Saul took a seat at the table beneath a large oak tree, mostly because Rosemary's father, Wayne Lantz, was sitting there. Wayne was a leader, a fair man, and someone Saul had always looked up to. Saul wouldn't be surprised if he became bishop someday. He was also the first person on the scene of any emergency and available whenever a neighbor had a crisis. Saul glanced toward the Zook barn. On the day of the barn raising, Wayne had spent more time working than any of the other men. And even after his wife died four years ago, he continued to do for others.

"Any luck with that *dochder* of mine?" Wayne's face was void of expression as he picked up his glass of tea, then took several large gulps.

Saul had never been sure if Wayne approved of his pursuing Rosemary. "*Nee.* She still won't give me the time of day." He reached for his own glass, took a large drink, and hoped that his answer had sounded casual enough.

One corner of Wayne's mouth lifted into a subtle grin. Saul wasn't sure if the man was impressed with Saul's persistence or if he was happy that Rosemary wouldn't have anything to do with him. Wayne was quiet.

Rosemary walked up to the table carting a full pitcher of tea.

She'd stolen Saul's heart the summer they'd both turned sixteen. That was the year she had blossomed into a woman, and the maturity fit her perfectly, both her figure and her personality. She'd been full of life, always laughing, and a bright light wherever she went. Saul was pretty sure she'd stolen a lot more hearts than just his that summer. He was blessed to have dated Rosemary for three months. But then one day after worship service, she'd broken up with him without giving him a good reason why. Through her tears, she'd mumbled something about the two of them not being right for each other, and she'd run off before Saul could get a better answer. She'd refused to

20

talk about it in the months that followed.

Then her mother died the following year, and everything changed. She withdrew from everyone, and responsibility swallowed her up as she tended to her father and siblings. But Saul had seen the woman Rosemary was meant to be.

She walked around the table topping off glasses with iced tea, and when she got to her father, she set the pitcher on the table, then brushed lint from the arm of his black jacket. Wayne glanced at her and smiled, and in a rare moment, Rosemary smiled back. She left the pitcher on the table before she walked away, not one time glancing in Saul's direction. The six other men at the table were deep in conversation about a new buggy maker in town, an *Englisch* man who was building the buggies cheaper than anyone else. Saul was only half-listening when Rosemary's father leaned closer to him.

"I'd tell you to give up, but I'm guessing that isn't going to happen."

Saul shook his head and grinned as they both watched Rosemary walk across the yard to the house. *"Nee."*

Wayne ran his hand the length of his dark beard that was threaded with gray. He didn't look at Saul, but kept his eyes on

Rosemary as she walked up the porch steps.

"Will be a blessed man to win her heart." Wayne kept his eyes on his daughter. "She's so much like her *mudder,* though. Hard to tell what's going on in her head." He turned to Saul, and the hint of a smile formed. "But she will be well worth the time invested if you are that man."

Everyone had thought Wayne Lantz would remarry quickly after his wife died. Widowers and widows were encouraged to marry another as soon as possible. But Edna Lantz had been a fine woman. Saul figured Wayne was having a hard time finding happiness with someone else.

Even though Rosemary never did tell Saul why she broke up with him so suddenly, he couldn't imagine spending his life with anyone else. He'd tried to bring up the subject from time to time, but it had just put even more distance between them. But realistically, how long could he go on pursuing her?

CHAPTER TWO

Rosemary was giving the kitchen rug a good thrashing against a tree on Monday morning when a buggy turned into the driveway. Squinting against the sun's glare as it peeked over the horizon, she watched as Katherine Huyard slowed down and stopped. Rosemary bit her tongue, reprimanded herself for allowing ugly thoughts to creep into her mind, then put the rug down in the grass and walked toward the buggy. Katherine stepped out toting a basket that was most likely filled with fresh vegetables from her garden.

Rosemary glanced at the healthy weeds she was growing within what used to be a fenced garden, determined not to let Katherine get under her skin. The first few times Katherine brought vegetables, Rosemary had been grateful that she didn't have to buy them in town. But now Katherine came at least two times a week, and the woman

23

made Rosemary feel inferior. Her tomatoes were the biggest and tastiest Rosemary had ever had. So were her cucumbers, zucchinis, squash, melons, and spinach. And Katherine was always dressed in a freshly ironed dress and apron. Even her *kapp* looked just pressed, and there wasn't a hair out of place. Rosemary blew a strand of her own wayward hair from her face as she took her wrinkled self toward Katherine. She waved, hoping the visit would be short.

"Your *daed* told me at worship how much he's been enjoying my vegetables, so I've filled the basket." Katherine flashed her perfectly white teeth as she handed Rosemary the produce. It seemed Katherine was always smiling. Rosemary wondered how that could be. Katherine had lost her husband to cancer a year ago. It had been four years since Rosemary's mother died, and only recently did her father show any signs of joy.

"*Danki,* Katherine." Rosemary accepted the gift, knowing her father and the boys would be grateful. "Would you like to come in for *kaffi* or tea?"

"*Nee.* I've got some mending to do for *mei* nieces and nephews. I try to help Ellen as much as I can."

For a few seconds, Katherine's smile

faded and she got a faraway look in her eyes. Rosemary never knew why Katherine and her husband, John, didn't have any children. Rosemary was about ten years younger than Katherine, who was in her early thirties. In a flash, Katherine's smile was back. Rosemary wondered what it would be like to switch places with the woman for a day, to have no one to tend to but herself. Even though Rosemary longed for a husband and children of her own, having even one day to herself sounded like heaven.

"Anyway . . ." Katherine bounced up on her toes, then glanced around the yard. "I just wanted to get out this morning to enjoy the beautiful weather and drop off these vegetables."

Rosemary looked around. In addition to the eyesore that used to be a garden, the flower beds were overgrown, the yard needed mowing, and Abner had left toys all over the place. There just wasn't enough time in the day to take care of everything. "*Ya*, okay. Well, *danki* again for these." She lifted the basket as she managed a small, tentative smile.

Katherine looked around again, and Rosemary shifted her stance. "I'm a little behind on my outside chores."

Katherine shook her head. "Not at all. I

think everything looks nice." She gave a quick wave and turned to leave. Rosemary had to give her credit. She almost sounded sincere.

She walked back to where she'd laid the kitchen rug in the grass, gave it a final slap against the tree, then headed inside with the rug and veggies. She was thankful that Abner, Jesse, and Joshua were all in school. But school would be out for the summer in a few weeks. The older boys would likely help *Daed* tend the fields, but Abner would be in her care all day long, which would slow her down even more.

As she pulled out a chair and sat down at the kitchen table, she wondered why she was allowing bitterness to consume her. Her mother had died, and these responsibilities were God's will for her. To tend to her family and to have very little time to herself — and certainly no time for a relationship.

The sooner Saul found someone else and got on with his life, the better for both of them.

Saul got his brother lined up first thing in the morning on Lydia Jones's house. The *Englisch* woman wanted her entire downstairs painted. Saul thought it was an awful color, a dark burgundy that made the house

26

look even smaller than it was. But Joel was the best painter he had on his six-person payroll. He'd dropped off the other four fellows at another *Englisch* home where they were putting in laminate floors. He'd been blessed to have plenty of work the past few months, but after these two jobs, he didn't have anything else lined up, which was a little worrisome.

"Why would anyone paint the inside of their house this color?" Joel finished covering a hutch by the door with plastic as he eyed the one wall he'd painted last Friday.

Saul shrugged. "I don't know. But it's her *haus.*" He quickly inspected the work Joel had done last week. As usual, it looked good. Joel was only sixteen, but he was a perfectionist, and Saul was thankful he could leave him in a customer's home, knowing his brother would do a *gut* job.

"I'll be back for you at five." Saul maneuvered around furniture that he and Joel had moved to the center of the room. "You'll probably have half of it done by then." He sighed and stretched out the tightness in his back. Some new job opportunities needed to come up by the end of the week.

A few minutes later he was pulling onto Lincoln Highway and heading toward Bird-in-Hand. He had a few errands to run this morning, but he'd barely stepped out of his buggy at the market when it began to pour. He hurried to tether his horse, then took off running across the parking lot. He tipped the brim of his hat down in an effort to shield his face from the heavy pelts. He wasn't paying attention when he rounded a big blue van and slammed right into another person, hard enough that it brought them both down onto the rock-solid cement. He felt his arm sliding across the pavement, but he was more concerned that the person he'd slammed into wasn't moving.

Wayne Lantz. Saul's heart pounded in his chest as he reached over and touched Rosemary's father on the chest. The older man was flat on his back with his eyes closed.

Rosemary threw a twenty-dollar bill over the seat before she jumped out of Barbie Beiler's gray van. The *Englisch* woman was yelling that Rosemary didn't owe her anything for the ride when Rosemary slammed the door and raced up to the front of the hospital, dodging puddles along the way.

Soaking wet, she dripped across the white tile until she reached two women behind a desk. They quickly pointed her in the direction of the emergency room. She only had a few details, but she knew her father had been in an accident in the parking lot of the Bird-in-Hand market. A stranger had shown up at Rosemary's house, an older *Englisch* woman in a banged-up white car. She'd said that she was at the market when an ambulance pulled into the parking lot. Rosemary's father had been taken to the hospital in Lancaster. A young man with him had given her Rosemary's address. Even though Rosemary didn't have any reason to doubt the woman, she'd held out hope that maybe it wasn't her father who had been injured.

A few minutes later, a nurse escorted her through some double doors. The lump in her throat grew as she walked. She was worried about her father, but as the smell of the hospital filled her nostrils, she was also reminded of all the time she'd spent here with her mother. *Dear God, please don't let my father die too.*

The moment she cried out to the Lord, she felt guilty. She hadn't shown much appreciation for God's grace lately. If anything, her bitterness had pulled her away from Him. Just the same, she said another prayer for her father.

As she followed the nurse behind a curtain and into a small room, she was shocked to see Saul standing at *Daed*'s bedside. She hurried to her father's side and edged Saul out of the way.

"Daed." She leaned closer to him and put a hand on his arm.

"What happened?" Before he could answer, she turned to the nurse, who was writing on a clipboard. "How is he?"

"He's going to be just fine," the tiny woman with silver hair said. "The fall knocked him out for a short time, but no concussion." She raised her eyebrows and pointed with her pen to the end of the bed. "That broken ankle will keep him down for a couple of days, but we'll send home some crutches so he can be mobile when he's ready. It's not a bad break, but he still needs to stay off of it as much as possible so it heals properly."

"Daed, what happened?" She eased Saul even farther out of the way, wondering why he was here, but more concerned about her father. "Did you slip on the wet pavement?"

"It's *mei* fault." Saul took off his hat and rubbed his forehead. "I didn't see him, and when I got on the other side of a parked van, I ran into him."

Rosemary sucked in a breath and held it, while bringing a hand to her chest. She let it out slowly. "You hit *Daed* with your buggy?"

30

"That might have been better," her father said as he grinned. "Might not have hurt as much as the body slam." He laughed out loud, and Rosemary looked at the nurse, who smiled.

"He's not feeling much pain at the moment. You know, the medication."

Rosemary studied her father for a few moments, and once she'd decided that he was all right, she turned to Saul. "What in the world were you doing that made you run into *Daed* hard enough to knock him down?" She waved a hand toward the end of the bed. "And to break his ankle?"

"*Ach, dochder,* settle down." Her father shifted his position as the hint of a smile left his face. Instead, he groaned slightly, closing his eyes for a couple of seconds. "It was just an accident." Once he had repositioned himself, he nodded to Saul. "Saul's got a pretty nasty scrape on his arm."

Rosemary noticed Saul's bandaged arm for the first time, and a twinge of guilt coursed through her for not seeing it sooner. She'd been so worried about her father, and even though fear had fueled her snappy comments to Saul, no one was to blame for this accident. She just wasn't sure she'd survive if anything happened to her *daed*. It had been hard enough losing one parent.

31

"*Ach,* it's okay, Wayne. Not much to it." Saul held up his left arm, which was wrapped in gauze and tape. He lowered his arm, then his head. "I'm just so sorry."

Rosemary's feet took on a mind of their own, and before she knew it, she was right next to Saul. Now that she knew her father was going to be okay, a part of her longed to tend to Saul as well. Instead, she forced herself to turn to the nurse again. "Can my father go home?"

"Yes. But he won't be comfortable riding in a buggy. Do you have a driver?"

Rosemary sighed, wishing she'd asked Barbie to stay. "*Nee,* but I can get one." She reached into her apron pocket and pulled out a piece of paper with Barbie's phone number. "Can I use your phone?"

Saul stood quietly at Wayne's bedside while Rosemary called for a driver. It didn't take an overly smart man to know that Rosemary blamed him for the accident. Blame he was willing to accept. He should have been watching where he was going. At least they would both fully recover. Saul's cousin hadn't been so lucky five years ago when a car plowed into his buggy, leaving him without the use of his legs. The smell of this hospital reminded him of when he went to visit his cousin in Ohio following his accident. He shook the thought away as another worry came to mind.

"Wayne, were you able to finish your planting?" Saul held his breath as he waited for an answer. Wayne usually planted acres of alfalfa. If he wasn't done, Saul would have to finish it for him.

"*Nee.* But almost. We'll make do."

Saul sighed as he shook his head. "*Nee,* I'm going to finish the planting for you. It's the least I can do. If I'd been more careful, watched where I was going . . ."

Wayne eased himself up in the bed, which, judging by his expression, was a tedious task. His pain medication didn't seem to be keeping him comfortable. "Now, Saul, don't you worry about it. You have a business to run."

Saul thought about how he didn't have any jobs lined up for the following week. He hoped something would come up, at least for the sake of his employees, but he had to make this right. "I'm free next week. I can come finish up the planting in the fields, and . . ." He glanced at Rosemary and thought about the weeds growing where her mother used to have a garden. He'd noticed it the last time the Lantzes held worship service. He wondered if Rosemary

33

had gotten around to putting in a garden. "And I can put in a vegetable garden if Rosemary hasn't had time to do that."

"Nee!" Wayne actually lifted himself to a sitting position. "That is not necessary, Saul. I won't have you doing that. Jesse and Joshua can finish the planting in the fields, and we've gone without a garden for the past four years."

Rosemary hung up the phone. "*Daed,* Jesse and Joshua should not be on the plow by themselves. They're not old enough to be left unattended." She turned to Saul, and he couldn't help but smile. She was fearful for her brothers' safety — as she should be — but she'd also just invited Saul into their lives, intentionally or not.

"*Nee, nee.* I'm not having Saul work our land. This was an accident and no one's fault." Wayne scowled, shaking his head.

"*Daed*'s right about the garden. We've gone without one for a long time. But we do need the planting finished." Rosemary sighed as her eyes met Saul's, but she quickly turned to her father. "*Daed,* it's just not safe for Jesse and Joshua to be on the plow by themselves." She shook her head. "Too many accidents happen out in the fields."

Wayne didn't say anything, and Saul knew

34

it was hard for him to let another man finish where he'd left off, but Wayne was wise enough to know that Rosemary was right.

"I can start Monday. Beginning next week, I don't have any construction jobs. If we still don't have any jobs by the time Monday comes around, I'll bring my crew and we can knock it out fast."

Wayne looked up at Saul and ran his hand the length of his beard. "Hmm . . . the more I think about it, I do like the idea of you putting in a garden."

Rosemary took a step toward the hospital bed, her face drawn into a frown. "*Nee, Daed.* I'll get to it."

Wayne's left eyebrow rose a fraction. "When, *mei dochder*?" Then he shifted in the bed to face Saul. "Rosemary has her hands full with the *kinner.* It would be nice to have a garden, and I think once it's in, Rosemary will be able to maintain it. But I will only allow this if I pay you a fair wage for doing it."

Saul shook his head, but before he could argue, Wayne added, "That's the offer. And if I was a man without any work lined up for the following week, I'd take it." He gave his head a taut nod.

Saul felt his face redden, and he avoided Rosemary's eyes for a few moments, but he had to know her reaction to this plan, so he glanced her way. Her eyes were cast toward the floor, her arms folded across her chest. It looked like she was holding her breath.

Saul looked out the window and rubbed his chin, then glanced back at Rosemary. He wasn't sure . . . but he thought he saw her smile.

It was just enough to give him hope.

"It's a deal. I'll see you first thing Monday morning."

CHAPTER THREE

Rosemary helped her father out of the hospital bed and into the wheelchair the nurse had brought, wishing it was anyone other than Saul who would be spending time at their home. But she figured she would stay inside and avoid him. In the end, the planting would be done, and she'd have a garden. And that would put an end to Katherine showing up with her vegetables. Rosemary would have her own garden. And if Saul did things right, maybe she'd have vegetables to be proud of.

Saul pushed the wheelchair until they were outside the hospital. Barbie lived in Paradise, so Rosemary knew it wouldn't take her long to get back to the hospital.

"Wayne, is there anything else I can do for you?" Saul hung his head for a moment before he looked back at her father.

Daed shook his head. "I can tell I'm not going to like those things."

He nodded toward the crutches Rosemary was carrying. "But it could have been worse, and I wasn't watching where I was going."

"It was my fault," Saul said again. They all started moving toward the circular drive when Barbie pulled up in the van. It was still sprinkling, and as Saul helped her father into the front seat, Rosemary was thankful the area was covered by an awning. She realized that Saul would need a ride home too.

"We will drop you at your *haus* on the way." Rosemary opened the sliding door and climbed into the van, then scooted to the far side. Saul just nodded, and they were all quiet on the way to his house. After a while, Rosemary shifted her eyes to the right to peek at Saul. No smile, and his boyish dimples weren't visible. He was staring out the window. "Joshua and Jesse can help you in the fields and with planting the garden, but it won't be till late afternoon since they're in school most of the day and have chores." Rosemary waited until Saul turned her direction before continuing. "So, I don't know how much time they'll have."

Saul smiled, but just barely. "*Nee,* I'll be able to do it."

After a few minutes, Rosemary swallowed hard and asked, "How's your arm?"

Saul offered her another weak smile. "It's fine."

Rosemary's father looked over his shoulder. "It's a nasty case of road rash. I heard the nurse say that. I also heard her say it was real important that you take the antibiotics they prescribed." He turned back around and spoke to Barbie. "Can you stop at the pharmacy before you drop Saul? The boy needs his medication."

"That's a *gut* idea. *Daed,* you have prescriptions too." Rosemary leaned forward and put a hand on his shoulder as Barbie turned the corner, nodding that she'd heard.

"I'm not taking those pills for pain. Made me feel all loopy." He scowled as he shook his head.

Rosemary glanced at Saul and wondered if he was so quiet because he felt bad about everything or because he was in pain. She bit her lip for a few moments. "Does it hurt?" She was directing the question to Saul, but both her father and Saul answered no at the same time. Rosemary suspected that neither of them was being completely truthful, and as Saul flinched, Rosemary wondered how he was going to finish planting the alfalfa and get a garden put in with his arm in such bad shape.

"We've gone without a garden for a long

time." Rosemary kept her eyes straight ahead as she spoke. "Maybe just finish the little bit of planting *Daed* has left and don't worry about the garden."

Saul glanced at her but then looked forward. "*Nee,* I'm going to get the garden put in too." He flinched again, and Rosemary wondered if this was about needing the money. She knew that was why her father had changed his mind about having Saul put in the garden. *Daed* saw an opportunity to have a garden for the first time in years, but he also saw a chance to help someone.

"If that arm gives you trouble, Saul, I don't expect you to do either of those jobs," her father said. "Katherine Huyard keeps us supplied with fresh vegetables. And she doesn't have any chickens, so I try to make sure she always has plenty of eggs." He twisted around. "That reminds me, Rosemary, I want you to pick out one of the goats to give Katherine. She's been mighty *gut* to us, and her only goat died last week. She loves to make soap from goat's milk, like your *mamm* used to do."

Rosemary was quiet. She thought about not seeing Katherine so often once the garden was finished. For the first time, she wondered what Katherine's life must be like. Lonely, she decided. No matter her bubbly personality, Katherine was bound to miss her husband. They'd been married a long time, at least ten years.

Rosemary was sure she'd let her own bitterness affect her attitude lately. Just because she was unhappy, she surely didn't wish that on others. She tried to recall the last time she laughed and couldn't. One word always came to mind. *Cheated.* God had taken her mother much too soon. And Rosemary had no time to herself amid taking care of her father and brothers. As much as she loved them all, she often found herself wondering if happiness would ever come her way. She glanced at Saul again. And the same word surfaced. She'd been *cheated* out of a relationship with the one man she'd wanted to be with.

When Barbie parked at the pharmacy, Rosemary offered to go in and get both of their prescriptions. The men both nodded, and Saul said to let him know how much his cost.

Once Rosemary was in line at the pharmacy, she asked the woman in front of her what time it was. She'd already called Esther and left a message, telling her what had happened. And she'd asked Esther to meet the boys at the house after school if they were still at the hospital. But it looked like

41

Rosemary and her father would be home in plenty of time. She would ask Barbie to get word to Esther.

Thirty minutes later, her father was asleep in the front seat and they were pulling into Saul's driveway. It was a beautiful home, a big place that had been in his family for three generations. The farmhouse looked freshly painted, and so did the white picket fence surrounding a lovely garden. All the flower beds were filled with colorful blooms. Rosemary felt a pang of jealousy but quickly stuffed it away. She didn't want to be that kind of person. Maybe someday she'd figure out how to balance her time well enough to have a lovely home, an organized household, and flourishing flower beds. She thought about Katherine. *And freshly ironed dresses, aprons, and kapps.* But she sat taller, smug with the idea of having her own garden soon. The price was having Saul around for a week. Maybe the Lord was angry with Rosemary to put such temptation right outside her own front door. She cringed, knowing that wasn't how God worked. And despite her feelings for Saul, Rosemary knew it was a temptation she would have to resist.

Elizabeth Petersheim shielded her eyes from the drizzle as she hurried down the porch steps and across the yard. She was at the van when Saul slid the door open.

"I've been worried sick. Your father got the message you left at the shanty, but not until an hour later." Elizabeth's eyes drifted to her son's bandaged arm. "Are you in pain?"

"Nee." Saul stepped out of the van, and Rosemary wondered if he'd been given pain medication at the hospital. He winced as he stood, and Rosemary's father awoke and rolled down his window.

Elizabeth and *Daed* exchanged greetings, and Elizabeth asked how he was feeling. "I will be just fine. *Danki,* Elizabeth." Her father turned to Saul. "I was running just as hard and fast as you were. This wasn't anyone's fault. Just an accident. But I appreciate your offer to finish the planting, and it will be nice to have a garden again."

Rosemary saw the look in her father's eyes, the faraway gaze he got when he was thinking about her mother.

"I'll be there next Monday after we finish the job we're working on this week." Saul was holding his injured arm now, his mouth tight and grim, like he might be gritting his teeth. "Stay off that ankle as much as you can for a few days before you start using the crutches, like the doctor said." He reached into his pocket, pulled out some money, and handed it to Barbie. She argued and tried not to accept it, but in the end, Saul convinced her to take it. Gas wasn't cheap these days. He'd already paid Rosemary for his prescription.

Elizabeth latched onto Saul's arm. "*Danki* for bringing him home, and Wayne, please let me know if you need anything. Take care." She gave a quick wave as she tugged on Saul's uninjured arm. "Let's get you out of the rain."

It was endearing the way Elizabeth nurtured her grown son. Rosemary assumed those maternal feelings must hang on forever, no matter how old your children got. Rosemary wanted nothing more than a houseful of children. And a husband to help rear them. She looked at Saul. He waved, and just before he turned to leave, Rosemary saw him clench his jaw. She had no doubt that Saul was hurting much more than he'd let on. She waited until they were almost home before she said anything.

"*Daed,* I'll make time to plant the garden. Maybe Saul can just supervise Jesse and Josh on the plow."

Her father twisted to face her. "I know you have way too much to do, *mei maedel.* I don't think I've ever pushed you about

44

that garden. Besides, it sounds like Saul could use the money if he doesn't have any work lined up for next week. I'm sure Katherine will keep us stocked with vegetables until our garden starts producing." *Daed* smiled. "It's a *gut* arrangement, trading eggs and a goat for her produce. But even after our garden is flourishing, I'll continue to invite Katherine to gather eggs for herself. No need for her to bother with chickens when we have such a plentiful supply of eggs."

Rosemary was quiet as she pondered exactly what it was about Katherine that she didn't like. Yes, she was a bit jealous that Katherine always seemed to have herself together and be so organized and cheerful. Rosemary knew good and well that jealousy was a sin, but even as she made a mental note to work on it, something else about Katherine bothered her. Something Rosemary couldn't quite put her finger on.

Saul went straight to the bathroom and sat down on the side of the tub, cradling his arm as he bit his bottom lip to keep from crying. Whatever they'd given him in the hospital before they treated his wound had worn off, and it felt like his arm was on fire from his elbow to his wrist. He'd turned

45

down the prescription for pain medication, thinking it would slow him down and make him sleepy. Right now, all he wanted to do was sleep. He would take the antibiotics like the doctor said and hope he healed quickly, for sure by next Monday when he needed to start work at the Lantzes' place. He would spend the rest of the week mostly supervising and give his arm a break.

He'd seen a softer side of Rosemary, and as much as he looked forward to the possibility of spending more time with her, it was going to be a challenge to get the work done unless his arm was much better. He jumped when someone knocked on the bathroom door.

"Saul, are you okay? *Mamm* said you hurt your arm. Do you need anything?" His sister was the caregiver in the family, even more so than their mother. Saul could remember when Lena was younger and she'd told everyone that she was going to leave the community to go be a nurse or doctor. At some point she'd given up the idea, and two years ago she got baptized. But she was born to tend to others.

"I'm okay, Lena."

"I'm going to help *Mamm* get supper started. You holler if you need anything."

Saul waited until Lena's footsteps got

farther away, then he pulled his arm close to him, and for the first time since he was a young boy, he cried. The doctor had told him that it was a nasty wound, but he didn't realize how bad it was until the pain medication wore off. He'd made a point not to watch the doctor cleaning and bandaging it. Saul planned to tend to it himself and do his best to help out the Lantzes. He was thankful he'd hurt his left arm and not his right.

Rosemary had acted a little like the girl he remembered and the young woman he'd fallen in love with years ago. Compassionate and loving. She wasn't the spirited, happy person she used to be, but Saul was committed to peeling back the layers of sadness that had consumed her since her mother died. He couldn't imagine that kind of pain, to lose someone so close. But surely the old Rosemary was in there somewhere, and he wasn't going to stop searching. He dabbed at his eyes, glad no one was around to see him like this. He dreaded having to change the bandage on his arm tomorrow. Maybe he'd let Lena do it after all. For now, he just wanted to rest. Despite the aroma of something delicious wafting up the stairs, Saul walked to his room and eased down onto the bed. He would rest for just a bit before supper.

CHAPTER FOUR

Monday morning, Rosemary finished scrambling eggs and making *scrapple* while her father and the boys sat patiently at the kitchen table. Over the past week, her father had gotten used to his crutches and was getting around pretty well. Katherine had been to the house every day, bringing not just vegetables but also pies, casseroles, and loaves of bread. And in exchange, she'd picked up some eggs and accepted one of their goats. They had a dozen of the animals, so they wouldn't miss one.

She hadn't had a chance to chat with Katherine much, and that was okay. Her father usually met her at her buggy, then together they went and gathered eggs. Rosemary was thankful for Katherine's help, and even though she felt inferior, Rosemary was working to shed any bad feelings about the woman. Katherine had good intentions.

Rosemary put the bowl of eggs on the

table and sat down. After they bowed their heads and prayed silently, her father pointed his fork at both Jesse and Joshua.

"Saul will be here today to finish up the planting and to start a garden for your sister. If he doesn't bring his crew with him, get your chores done after school, then see if you can give him a hand." He looked down and scooped up a forkful of eggs.

Jesse and Joshua both frowned as they glanced at each other.

At eleven and thirteen, both were at an age when they'd sometimes argue, but though they didn't look happy, neither said anything. Little Abner didn't seem to have a care in the world as he lathered up his biscuit with way too much butter. Abner had been spending a lot of time with their father. *Daed* would often sit on the couch and read, his foot propped up on the coffee table. He'd start each morning saying how useless he felt, but when Abner crawled up on the couch and snuggled in next to him with a book, both soon had big smiles on their faces.

Katherine usually came around late in the afternoons, mindful to come and go before the supper hour. Rosemary knew she should invite Katherine for supper every now and then since the woman would most likely go

50

home and eat alone. But would she find the inside of the Lantzes' house as untidy as the outside? She'd never known her father to be sloppy, but now that he was couch-bound most of the time, he'd started leaving his glasses and plates on the coffee table. Books would pile up on the floor and end tables, and this morning he'd spilled coffee on the counter and hadn't cleaned it up. Rosemary was happy to take care of her father, but other things then got pushed aside. She glanced at the wood floors in the kitchen that desperately needed sweeping.

"I don't want peanut butter and jelly," Jesse said as he inspected the contents of his lunch pail.

Rosemary knew it wasn't his favorite, but she'd run out of lunch meat, and she was on the last of the groceries. She needed to make a trip to town. Jesse was a picky eater, and most of what Katherine brought, he wouldn't touch. "Well, it will have to do for today." She opened the refrigerator and stowed the butter. Jesse stormed off, letting the screen door in the living room slam behind him.

Once the boys were off to school, she finished the breakfast dishes and wiped down the counters and stovetop. She'd just reached for the broom when she heard a

51

buggy coming up the driveway. *Saul.*

She looked out the window as Saul tethered his horse to the fence, but then stepped out of sight when he came toward the house. The doors were open, as were the windows, but it wouldn't cool down until after sunset. She pulled a handkerchief from her apron pocket, dabbed at her forehead, then put it back. By the time she reached the living room, her father was on his crutches, pushing the screen door open. Rosemary waited until Saul was inside and her father was finished explaining what was left to do in the fields, then she asked about Saul's arm. It was still bandaged from his elbow down to his wrist.

"Much better," he said, barely smiling. "And it will just be me doing the work. We ended up getting a pretty big painting job the end of last week, so my whole crew is working on that. It might take me a while since I'll be working by myself."

Daed scratched his forehead as he leaned most of his weight on one crutch. "Saul, if you need to supervise your employees, or . . ."

"*Nee, nee.* They'll be fine. I've got plenty of people on the job site, so this works out *gut.*"

Daed nodded. "Hopefully Josh and Jesse

can give you a hand after school."

Abner walked up to where they were standing in the living room and tugged on Rosemary's blue dress. She glanced down at him. "What is it, Abner?"

"Is Katherine coming today?"

Rosemary glanced at her father, but he was busy readjusting his crutches and didn't look up. "I guess. She comes by most days."

"Gut." Abner walked over to the couch and sat down. She hadn't been giving Abner much attention lately. There'd just been so much to do. Sometimes Abner walked to the chicken coop with their father and Katherine to collect eggs.

"Well, I'll get to it." Saul tipped the brim of his hat, then turned to leave.

"Dinner is at noon," Rosemary said as he closed the screen door behind him.

Turning back around to face her, Saul said, "Lena packed me a lunch, so I can just eat in the fields and get right back to work."

"I won't hear of it." *Daed* pounded one of the crutches against the wood floor. "It's mighty hot already for May. You'll need a break from the heat and a *gut* meal in your belly."

Saul nodded, glancing at Rosemary with a slight grin. "I'm sure whatever Lena packed won't be nearly as *gut* as Rosie's cooking."

Rosemary felt the flush rising up her neck to her cheeks, but before she could acknowledge the compliment, Saul had turned around and was heading down the steps. Having him around for the next week or so was going to be torture. She planned to stay busy, even though no amount of chores was going to completely rid her mind of him.

She spent the rest of the morning trying to get the kitchen spick-and-span in between running loads of clothes through the wringer and hanging them on the line to dry. When she'd pinned a load of towels to the line earlier, she'd seen Saul guiding the horses and plow across the far stretch of land. Now as she took down the last load from the line, she didn't see him anywhere. She was walking back to the house when she heard him call her name. She stopped and turned around, balancing the laundry basket on her hip. Her father was right. It was hot for this time of year. She ran the sleeve of her dress across her forehead and squinted from the sun's glare as she waited for Saul to reach her.

"I'm going to finish planting today, then tomorrow I'll get started on your garden. Do you have a tiller, or should I bring one from home?"

Rosemary shifted the laundry basket to the other hip as she thought for a moment. "I think we have one. I'll check with *Daed* to make sure it still runs." She glanced at his arm. "So, you said it's much better?"

"Ya." Saul was staring at her, and she hated that she could feel herself blushing again.

"I'll be serving lunch in just a few minutes if you want to wash up." She nodded toward the pump on the north side of the house, but Saul didn't move. Then he took a slow step toward her and leaned closer. Rosemary couldn't breathe. As his face neared hers, she fought the panic pounding in her chest. Even though he towered over her by several inches, he was hunched down enough that he could easily kiss her. Saul was the only man she'd ever kissed, and even though it had been five years, she could still recall the heady sensation his kisses brought on and the tenderness of his touch. She should put some distance between them and not do anything to lead him on. The logical part of her brain told her this since they couldn't have a life together, but instead she barely parted her lips and thought about how often she'd dreamed of this moment.

Saul reached up with his right hand and

swatted at her prayer covering. She dropped the clothes basket and brought a hand to her head. "What are you doing?"

"Sorry!" he said when Rosemary jumped. "A bumblebee was crawling on your *kapp*. Lena got stung by one last week, and it swelled up to the size of a walnut. She was miserable for days."

"Danki," she said softly as she leaned down and picked up the laundry basket, glad her freshly folded towels hadn't spilled onto the grass. She turned and hurried to the house without looking back. Her heart was still pounding, and she was weak in the knees. There was no doubt in her mind that she would have let Saul kiss her. He would have felt the love she had in her heart for him. It had been hard enough to walk away from him when they were teenagers. She'd cried for two weeks. It would be even harder now. She needed to be careful not to get too close to him since she wasn't sure she could trust herself.

Saul ate as much of the cheesy salmon casserole as he could. Neither his mother nor Lena ever made salmon, so it should have been a nice treat. It tasted wonderful, and he'd known for years that Rosemary was a good cook, but his arm was throbbing to the point that he felt a little light-headed. She'd been watching him during the meal, and he wondered if she thought he didn't like the meal, even though he'd commented a couple of times about how good it tasted. By the time she put dessert on the table — a raisin crumb pie — Saul was sweating like it was over a hundred degrees. It was warm, but a nice breeze blew through the screens, and it wasn't hot enough for him to be perspiring this much. He dabbed at his forehead with his napkin. Again. Then he ate some of the pie, but couldn't finish it.

"Everything was really *gut,* Rosie." He laid his napkin across his plate, hoping she wouldn't notice how much was left. Wayne and Abner excused themselves and went into the living room, so Saul stood up, and sure enough, the room spun a little. He hoped Rosemary didn't notice the color draining from his face as he headed toward the back door.

"Saul."

He swallowed hard and turned around, lifting an eyebrow *"Ya?"*

She walked toward him and cupped his left arm in her hand. Saul flinched, then noticed that fluid was draining through his bandage. He hadn't let Lena change the bandage in three days, for no other reason

57

than it hurt. Saul thought of himself as pretty tough — until it came to blood or wounds. Then he was worse than a five-year-old.

"This looks terrible." Rosemary gently cradled his arm in her hands. "Did you bump it or something while you were on the plow?" Saul looked down at the yellowish color oozing through his white gauze, and he silently prayed for God to not let him pass out. He eased his arm away from Rosemary. Under other circumstances, he would have basked in the tenderness of her touch, but his feet were failing him. He quickly sat down in a kitchen chair and forced a smile.

"It's okay. Really."

Rosemary shook her head. "It is *not* okay. Wait here." She left the kitchen and passed through the living room toward her father's room, but the door was shut. Either he and Abner were napping or *Daed* was reading Abner a story. Either way, she didn't want to disturb them. She hurried upstairs to her bathroom and found her first-aid kit. With three brothers, she had doctored her fair share of wounds. When she returned to the kitchen, Saul's face was pasty white.

"Are you going to *faint*?" She raised an

eyebrow, and Saul grunted.

"Of course not."

Rosemary wasn't so sure as she sat down in a chair beside him and gently raised his arm to have a closer look. "Has your *mamm* or Lena been tending to this, changing the bandage?"

"Uh . . . *ya.*"

Rosemary frowned. "I think we need to take this bandage off and have a look."

"It's fine. Really. And I've got lots of work to do."

"You won't be getting any work done if you don't take care of this. I'm going to change the bandage for you. Did the doctor in the emergency room give you any medications to take?"

"I've been taking antibiotics."

Rosemary reached for a small pair of scissors in her first-aid kit. "I'm going to snip this tape, then change your bandage."

Saul pulled his arm away. "*Nee.* No need. I'll have Lena change the bandage when I get home."

"Then go home now." Rosemary put the scissors back in the box. "I can't. I want to get the alfalfa in the ground today. I'll take care of it this evening."

Rosemary put her elbows on the table, rested her chin in her hands, and twisted slightly to face him. "Saul Petersheim, you are white as these walls, and you look like you're about to pass out."

He shook his head, grinning slightly. "*Ach, nee.* I don't know why you think that."

"Then let me change the bandage. I think you're afraid."

Saul grunted again. "I'm not afraid of anything." He stood up. "Now, I'm going to get back to work."

Rosemary watched him teetering, and she didn't want Saul ending up in the hospital on her watch. "I'm going to get *mei daed.*" She stood up, folded her arms across her chest, and looked up at him. "You're not well enough to be out on that plow. Maybe you can supervise Jesse and Josh when they get home from school, but you're not going back out there."

"I'm a grown man. I think I know when I'm well enough to work and when I'm not."

"Then let me have a look at your arm."

"*Nee.*" Saul turned toward the door, pulled the screen wide, and wobbled down the porch steps. Maybe he was running a fever. She followed him but stopped on the bottom step as he hurried across the yard.

"I'll go out with you Saturday night if you come back here and let me have a look at your arm." Rosemary brought a hand to her

60

chest as she squeezed her eyes closed for a few moments. When she opened them, Saul was walking toward her. *What was I thinking?*

He stopped in front of her, smiled broadly, and held out his arm. "Here you go."

Rosemary huffed, spun around, and went back into the kitchen. She could hear Saul following. "You know, I shouldn't have to bribe you to get you to take care of yourself."

"You change your mind already?"

She pulled out a chair and pointed at him. "Sit." She sat next to him. This was all she needed . . . to have yet another person to take care of. She could be cleaning the kitchen floors right now. But this was Saul, and when she felt him trembling as she snipped the tape and unwound it from his arm, she said softly, "I'm going to be very gentle, okay? And if I do something that hurts, you just tell me."

Saul nodded but turned his head the other way. She recalled the time Jesse had borrowed an *Englisch* boy's skateboard and taken a bad fall. Rosemary wondered if Saul's arm would look anything like that. Jesse had slid across the concrete on his left knee, and it had been a real mess for a while. But Jesse was only nine at the time

61

and had been much braver than Saul was being now. And she hadn't had to bribe Jesse to let her tend to him.

She glanced up at Saul, and it was impossible not to feel sorry for him. He was still white in the face, and his arm was shaky. Rosemary was a little afraid of what she might see. As she began to unwrap the dressing, Saul's breathing sped up. This was surprising to her, that he was so fearful. In every way, he'd always appeared confident, as if he had no fear.

"Are you okay?"

"*Ya*. Sure." He tried to smile but avoided looking at his arm, and Rosemary wasn't convinced that he wouldn't keel over right there at the kitchen table. She took off the last of the bandages. Saul cringed.

"It's not bad. It just needs to be cleaned up. I'll put some topical antibiotic on it as well." Rosemary spoke in a slow, calm voice, even though she was shocked by what she saw. He was missing several layers of skin, and the last thing he needed to be doing was plowing or putting in a garden. The wound was clearly infected.

Rosemary doctored him up and put on a new bandage. If he was this much of a baby, she figured he probably hadn't let Lena change the bandage in days.

"All done." She gave him back his arm. "You really need to change this bandage every day." She stood up, and he did too. "No more working here, though, until your arm is healed. You don't want to get dirt in that wound. We've gone without a garden for this long — we will be just fine. And Katherine will keep us stocked with veggies."

"I think I can finish planting the alfalfa today, then I can start on the garden tomorrow." He glanced down at his arm, then up at Rosemary, smiling. "Your touch is as tender as I remember."

Rosemary swallowed hard and looked down. By going out with him on Saturday night, she was going to send him the wrong signal.

When she didn't respond, his smile faded. "I'll probably just bring our tiller from home. We've got a really *gut* one."

Rosemary nodded and Saul walked outside. Obviously he wasn't going to heed her warning to take it easy the rest of the day. She stood on the porch step and watched him walk across the front yard until he disappeared behind the barn. All the while, visions of them together on Saturday night swirled in her head.

What have I done?

CHAPTER FIVE

Saul showed up the following morning with the tiller on a small trailer he'd hitched to the back of his buggy. Finishing the alfalfa proved to be a large task. He was glad that Jesse and Josh had shown up after school. Even though Saul had already completed the planting, the boys took the draft mules to the barn, brushed them down, and got them stowed for the evening. Everything was going well at the job site, and the crew was staying busy, so he didn't want to pull anyone away to help him with the garden. His arm wasn't as sore, but he was embarrassed about his behavior in front of Rosemary. What kind of man would accept a date as a bribe? He planned to let Rosemary off the hook today.

It was midmorning when Rosemary walked out to the garden area. Saul had cleared most of the weeds with the tiller, but he was pulling the ones against the fence with his hands. When she got closer, he saw that she was wearing working gloves.

"I told you that you cannot get that wound dirty." She put her hands on her hips. "I'm going to help you with the garden, even though this whole project is nonsense. Why grow vegetables when you can buy them in town?"

Saul used his good arm to swipe his forehead before beads of sweat trickled down his face. "There's nothing better than using the land that the Lord gave us to grow food to nourish our bodies." He walked closer to where she was standing on the other side of the white picket fence. A fence that needed a fresh coat of paint. "It's a *gut* feeling to watch the fruits of our labor become whole." He smiled as he eyed his progress so far.

Rosemary shrugged and sighed deeply. "*Ach,* well. I'm never going to share your passion for gardening, but I'm going to help you so it will get done faster. And I'll do the dirty work, like planting the bushes, so you don't get dirt in your wound."

Saul laughed. "*Bushes?* We're not planting bushes. We're going to plant seeds."

Rosemary tapped a finger to her chin for a few moments. "Katherine is already getting lots of produce from her garden. Are you sure we have time to start from seed?"

"There's still about two weeks of planting season left, really right up until the end of May. And it won't take as long as you think before you have your own red, ripe tomatoes and cucumbers and . . . anything else you might want." He paused and glanced around. "I want to get the rest of the weeds cleared first, the ones up against the fence." He looked back at her and shook his head. "But I don't need you to help me."

Rosemary opened the gate that led to the other side of the picket fence where Saul was standing. Her father was at the kitchen table with bills and receipts scattered all around. Paperwork he said he'd let fall behind. He'd encouraged Rosemary to go outside and help Saul since both Jesse and Josh had stayed after school for a class project.

"I'm going to help you anyway." She wiggled her fingers inside the gloves that had belonged to her mother, then squatted down and started pulling the tall weeds by the roots. As she tossed the first handful over the fence, she couldn't help but recall how pretty this place had been at one time. But that fond memory clouded quickly as she focused on her mother and how much she missed her.

Rosemary looked up. Saul was just standing there watching her. "I said I'm going to help, but you've got one *gut* arm to help, no?" Grinning, she tossed another handful of weeds over the fence.

Saul narrowed his eyebrows and shifted his weight, still staring at her. "You don't have to go out with me Saturday night."

Rosemary avoided his gaze and tugged at another group of weeds. "I know I don't *have* to." She should have just said *okay* and left it at that, but she was wondering why he was giving her an out. "You've been asking me for years." She shrugged, not looking up as she latched onto another cluster.

He squatted down beside her, and with his good arm, he yanked about four times the amount of weeds as she had, then tossed them over the fence. "And there's nothing I want more than to go out with you. But I want you to want to. Not because of a bribe or anything."

Rosemary's heart was beating faster than normal. "I do want to." She couldn't look at Saul, afraid she'd get lost in his eyes. Their date was all she'd thought about for the past few days. Memories of the summer she'd turned sixteen were fresh in her mind, but she was resolved not to get too close to him. But if he wanted to kiss her at the end of the night, Rosemary was going to let him. Then walk away. Like she'd done before.

"Why did you do it?" Saul sat down in the dirt, and when Rosemary looked at him, he said, "Why did you break up with me when we were kids? It was a long time ago, so can you tell me now? Because I've always wondered. I thought we were so happy, and . . ." He shrugged, and as Rosemary had feared, she was lost in the depth of his big blue eyes.

"I-I just . . . it just wasn't working out." She reached for another patch of over-growth, but Saul put his hand on top of hers.

"Did I do something?"

"Nee." She took her hand back. She couldn't tell him about the conversation she'd overheard that night. He would think she was as selfish and shallow as she felt. But it would most likely stop him from pursuing her. Maybe after their date she'd tell him. She wanted — needed — just one kiss. She felt like she was sixteen years old again with every emotion she'd had back then rising to the surface. Her eyes welled with tears.

"Rosie, don't cry."

When she bit her lip and didn't speak, Saul racked his brain, thinking back five years. He could picture them kissing beneath the big oak tree behind the Millers' house that day. Everything had been perfect. But not long after the meal, she'd found him, and they'd gone behind the house again. Saul had thought she wanted to sneak in a few more kisses. Instead, she'd broken up with him, giving him a lame excuse about not wanting to settle down with one person yet. But she'd cried through the entire conversation, and Saul never bought into it.

He'd tried to get over her by asking other girls out, hoping that one of them would measure up to his Rosemary. But every time Saul could feel himself getting close to someone, it was Rosemary's face he saw, and he always pulled back. She'd held his heart back then. And she still did. He lifted his shoulders and dropped them slowly. "Whatever I did, I'm sorry. I never would have done anything intentionally to make you unhappy. So I guess you're just going to have to tell me."

Rosemary's heart ached, but there was no way she could tell him what fueled her decision to break up back then. She was still holding on to the same reasoning now, although as she gazed into Saul's eyes, she knew that being around him Saturday night was only going to make things harder. As much as she longed for his touch, even one kiss, she needed to take this opportunity to back out.

"You didn't do anything back then, Saul." She sat down and folded her legs beneath her, plotting how to avoid a lie but still not tell the truth. She shrugged, her eyes locked with his. "I just changed my mind."

"You changed your mind?" His voice was curt. Not that she blamed him. "You just changed your mind about wanting to date me? Did your feelings just . . . *change*? I mean . . ." He shook his head. "I don't get it."

Rosemary opened her mouth in an effort to say something that would make sense to him but still stay short of the truth. She bit her tongue, knowing that she needed to talk to Esther. She'd been keeping this secret to herself for a long time, and while Esther might think she was wrong in her decision, it seemed safer to run the truth by her friend before she fessed up to Saul. She lifted herself up, pulled off her gloves, and brushed the dirt from her apron.

Her heart was heavy, but she forced the words out of her mouth. "I guess we really shouldn't go out Saturday night."

Saul stood up and just stared at her for a few moments before he leaned down and picked up his gardening spade, shovel, and a pair of work gloves lying in the weeds. Then he turned and walked out of the gate, even though it was still early in the day. Rosemary left the garden area and slowly inched her way toward him. Surely he wasn't leaving.

"I'm not feeling well." He tossed the items in the small trailer he had hitched to the buggy. "Tell your *daed* that I will be back tomorrow."

"Saul?" Rosemary walked up to him and touched his arm. "I'm sorry."

He eased away from her and readied his horse. Then he opened the door of the buggy, but before he got in, he looked at her, an expression on his face that Rosemary couldn't read.

"You don't have to worry about me asking you out anymore." He hung his head for a few moments, then looked back up at her. "It's always been you, Rosie. The only woman I've ever wanted to be with. But a man can only take so much." He paused, shaking his head again. "I don't know why we broke up when we were teenagers, and it's already starting again. A few minutes ago, you said you *did* want to go out with me, and you've already changed your mind. I want to be with someone who is sure that they want to be with me. I was hoping we'd have a chance to spend time together, but you're right. It's not a *gut* idea."

As Rosemary watched him direct the buggy down the driveway and onto the road, a tear slid down her cheek. *It's always been you too, Saul.*

CHAPTER SIX

Rosemary spent the rest of the day weeding the garden, her self-inflicted punishment for the way things had ended with Saul. He was right. She did change her mind about him. A lot. Some days she thought she could get past what she'd overheard his mother saying that day, but other days . . . it was just too much to bear.

She pulled her gloves off and stared at her dirty hands. Dirt had gotten in her gloves, and her fingernails were a mess. She even had two blisters. *Guess I deserve it.*

Her father was sitting in the rocking chair on the front porch when Rosemary climbed the steps. She fell into the other rocker and leaned her head back.

"*Mei maedel,* I don't know why you did all that work. Saul said he was coming back tomorrow, no?"

"*Ya,* he'll be back." *And I guess I'll stay away from him.*

73

"You didn't say what was wrong with him earlier. Was it his arm?" *Daed* closed the newspaper he'd been reading.

"I'm not sure."

Her father shook his head. "He had no business taking on this project with his arm like that."

Rosemary thought about how Saul would probably be working on the garden for at least another week Or maybe not. She'd noticed that he seemed to be taking his time, but that could have been due to his arm. Either way, she wouldn't be surprised if he picked up speed after what happened today. She looked up in time to see Katherine turning into the driveway. She lifted her tired body out of the rocking chair.

"I'm going to let the oven heat up while I take a bath. Where's Abner?"

Her father stood up. "He was in his room coloring when I came outside." *Daed* smoothed his beard with his hand and waved to Katherine. "What time will the other boys be home?" he asked before she walked in the house.

"I told them to be here in time for milking and chores, so pretty soon. And I'll check on Abner before I take a bath." She paused. "*Ach,* and, *Daed,* if it's okay, I'd like to take the buggy and visit Esther later.

I won't be home late."

Her father nodded, so Rosemary went inside, glanced at the clock on the mantel above the fireplace, then hurried upstairs to bathe. She wasn't sure how Esther would take Rosemary's news, but her friend would be honest. Esther had come into her life right around the time Rosemary's mother died, and they'd hit it off instantly. Esther's mother had died three years before that, and Esther had been the only person who understood what Rosemary was going through. But Rosemary hadn't ever told her about Saul. She'd come close, especially when Esther questioned her about him.

She peeked into Abner's room on the way to the bathroom. Her youngest brother had a small red suitcase filled with crayons and coloring books that *Daed* had picked up at a rummage sale a few weeks earlier. Abner was busy at work, so Rosemary scurried to the bathroom at the end of the hallway.

Always rushing. But today it was her own fault for letting guilt make her feel like she needed to give Saul a jump-start on the garden. No matter the circumstances, she could tell Saul was hurt, and that had never been her intention.

She was pulling her dress over her head and running the bathwater when she remembered she was out of shampoo. Her mother had always made their shampoo, but after she'd died, it was easier to purchase it in town — like the veggies — and she'd left a new bottle on the kitchen counter. She turned off the bathwater, lowered her blue dress, then ran downstairs. Supper was going to be late if she didn't hurry, and while she'd completely lost her appetite, she had a houseful of boys who'd be hungry come four thirty. She grabbed the shampoo from the counter and turned to go back upstairs when a movement outside caught her eye. She rolled her eyes when she saw her father and Katherine heading toward the barn. *I'll never be as perfect as her.*

As she watched them nearing the barn, Rosemary thought maybe she was being unfair to Katherine. The woman had been nothing but polite and generous. But when her father and Katherine stopped outside the barn and began kissing like teenagers, Rosemary grabbed her chest and gasped.

Her father had invited Katherine to stay for supper and then insisted that Katherine not help Rosemary prepare the meal, even though she'd offered twice. "*Nee,* you're our guest," her father had said both times.

Our guest and your girlfriend. Rosemary

had already calculated that Katherine was at least ten years younger than her father, and she couldn't stop thinking about what the woman's intentions were. As upsetting as it all was, this new knowledge had kept her thoughts from straying back to Saul, at least. This was what Rosemary had been unable to put her finger on.

"Everything looks lovely." Katherine's green eyes twinkled as she spoke, and she barely looked at Rosemary before she turned to *Daed* and grinned. So *that's what all the veggies, casseroles, and egg exchanges have been about.* Katherine could walk right into a ready-made family and take over. No one was going to replace their mother, especially not someone who was only ten years older than Rosemary — no matter how much pressure it would take off of Rosemary.

It took everything she had, but Rosemary forced a smile. "*Danki,* Katherine. Glad you could join us." She glanced at her father as she set a bowl of mashed potatoes on the table, fighting the frown that was settling on her face. *A little young for you, Daed.* While it was customary for widows and widowers to remarry, her father had already gone four years, so Rosemary had assumed he had no desire to remarry. And why did it have to be

Katherine?

After the blessing, *Daed* reminded the boys about manners when they dove into their food like they hadn't eaten in a month of Sundays. Once everyone had a plateful, it got quiet, and Rosemary began to think about Saul. And the look on his face when he left, knowing that she'd put an end to his pursuing her. That should have made her feel good. One less thing to worry about.

Instead, it made her want to cry. She couldn't wait till after dinner when she could go to Esther's and talk with her about everything.

Her father had an extra helping of shoofly pie, and Rosemary was pretty sure he just didn't want Katherine to leave yet. They kept glancing at each other like they were love-struck teenagers, and Rosemary wondered how she hadn't suspected anything before.

Finally, Katherine left, and Rosemary peeked out the window. Her father had the good sense not to kiss Katherine good-bye out by the buggy. Who knew if the boys could see from the living room?

She quickly cleaned up the kitchen and headed to Esther's. Fifteen minutes later, Esther's father greeted Rosemary at the door and motioned for Rosemary to go on upstairs. Esther was an only child, and she had a huge bedroom upstairs. Rosemary knocked. "Esther, it's me."

Her friend answered right away, wearing a white nightgown, and her dark-brown hair hung to her waist. "You're already dressed for bed? It's not even dark yet."

On most nights, Rosemary didn't even get a bath until after sundown. She had to help Abner get settled in, and despite the mess they always left, she'd usually let Jesse and Josh bathe first. It would be nice to be tucked in early and have time to read a book.

Esther shrugged. "Nothing else to do."

Rosemary bit her bottom lip, realizing it must be lonely for Esther much of the time. She walked to the double bed and sat down. Esther sat down beside her.

"What's wrong?" Esther pulled one leg underneath her as she twisted to face Rosemary.

Rosemary took a deep breath. "I told Saul I'd go out with him Saturday night." Esther's face lit up right away. "But then I changed my mind and told him I didn't think it was a *gut* idea." Rosemary closed her eyes for a few moments and shook her head. "Everything got all messed up, and I can tell he's mad, and it's — it's just a mess."

Esther frowned as she folded her arms across her chest. "I don't understand you, Rosemary. And I'm not surprised he got mad. He's been wanting to date you for years. Then you say yes, then you say no."

"I know, I know," Rosemary said. Her pulse quickened. "I love Saul. I really do. And I always have. But . . ."

Esther raised an eyebrow. "What? If you love him, why haven't you gone out with him all this time?"

"Promise me that you won't hate me or think I'm a horrible, shallow person," Rosemary said.

Esther reached for Rosemary's hand and gave it a quick squeeze.

"There is nothing you can tell me that would make me think less of you."

I don't know about that. Rosemary lowered her head for a moment, then looked up at her friend. "Saul and I had been dating about three months when I overheard a conversation between Saul's mother — Elizabeth — and a visiting cousin." She paused, reflecting on how she felt when she listened in on the private conversation. "I know this is going to make me sound awful, but . . ."

Esther reached for Rosemary's hand

again. "What did you hear?"

Rosemary took another long breath and closed her eyes. "Saul can't have *kinner.*" She opened her eyes, and Esther's straight face was hard to read. "And I want *kinner,* Esther. I want a large family. And a life with Saul wouldn't include that."

Esther was quiet for a few moments. "Rosemary, I don't think you're awful, and I don't think any less of you. If anyone understands about wanting a large family, it's me. I'd do anything to have some siblings, and whenever I get married, I want lots of *kinner* too. So I don't judge you or think badly of you."

Rosemary threw her arms around Esther's neck. "*Danki,* Esther. I've been so afraid to tell you."

Esther eased away. "I'm guessing Saul doesn't know that you know . . . that he can't have children."

"*Nee.* I forced myself to walk away from the relationship when we were sixteen, thinking we were young and that I'd find love with someone else." She took a deep breath, then blew it out slowly. "But I don't think I will. It's always been Saul, and it seems so unfair that I can't have him *and* the big family that I want."

Esther just nodded, and Rosemary wished

she'd talked to her a long time ago.

"My heart hurts, Esther. I don't know what to do now." Rosemary realized this was the first time that she had ever considered sacrificing a houseful of children to be with Saul. She recalled the expression on his face, the sharp tone of his voice. There had always been a level of comfort in knowing that Saul stayed in pursuit of her. A few times, she'd worried when he'd started dating other girls. She'd never wanted to commit to him, but she hadn't wanted anyone else to either. She was ashamed she felt this way.

"Are you sure you heard correctly?" Esther tucked her other leg beneath her, then scratched her forehead.

"*Ya.*" Rosemary remembered the words exactly and the way they stung. "I was walking past where Saul's *mamm* and Naomi were talking, carrying Abner on my hip. He was about a year old, and he still used a pacifier. When he spit it out of his mouth, I leaned down to pick it up, and that's when I heard Saul's name. I lingered. His mother's exact words were, 'It has been very upsetting for us to learn that Saul won't be able to have *kinner.*' "

"And you never asked him about it?" Esther began braiding her hair off to one side.

"*Nee*. Because he'd know I broke up with him because of that, and that would make me look awful. Plus, I didn't want to embarrass him."

"You're not awful, Rosemary. You just know what you want."

Rosemary tried to smile. "Do I?" She wanted to tell Esther about her father and Katherine, but she'd probably shared enough with her for one night.

Saul was staring at the ceiling. He'd lain down before it got dark, and now his room was pitch black. After he'd left Rosemary's, he had checked on his crew, then come home to sit in his room and pout like he was sixteen years old again. He'd gone downstairs for supper but excused himself early.

He'd spent all this time believing that Rosemary was the girl for him. Now he would have to readjust his thinking, even though he wouldn't be getting over her anytime soon.

Lena had changed his bandage earlier, and even though his sister was gentle, all Saul could think about was Rosemary's tenderness. He'd thought it was his calling to find the Rosemary he'd once known, the happy girl with a playful spirit, the girl who drifted away from him one day without any explanation. Then her mother died, and any hint of playfulness disappeared overnight.

He was wide awake when he heard his cell phone vibrating on the nightstand by his bed. He mostly used it for work, but he always kept it on vibrate out of respect for his father, who was against the use of any phone in the house. Both his parents still walked a half mile to the phone shanty when they needed to make a call. Saul picked up the phone and saw that it was after ten o'clock. He recognized the number.

"*Wie bischt,* Katherine? Something must be wrong if you're calling this late."

"*Nee,* not really." She paused. "But maybe."

Saul eased himself up in the bed and fluffed his pillow behind him. "What's wrong?" He'd formed a friendship with Katherine after her husband died. They shared a love of gardening, and Saul had a love for Katherine's pineapple cherry crisp. After Katherine's husband was gone, she was so lost that she'd busied herself doing for others — sharing her vegetables, taking neighbors meals, and helping her sister with her children. She'd become like an older sister to Saul.

"I think Rosemary saw me and Wayne

84

kissing out by the barn. We were so anxious to see each other that I'm afraid we didn't use much caution. The older boys weren't home, and Wayne said Abner was upstairs in his room, but I'm worried Rosemary might have seen us. She was even more standoffish than usual."

Just hearing Rosemary's name caused his heart to beat faster. He'd spent so much time loving her, he didn't know how to stop. "*Ach,* well . . . maybe it's time for her to know how you feel about her father."

Katherine was quiet for a few moments. "I don't know. I love that man so much that I feel like it's written all over my face, but we wanted to wait until closer to October or November before we shared our news. We haven't set a firm date, and we will still have to publish our wedding announcement."

Publishing usually happened four to six weeks prior to a wedding, when the bishop announced the engagement to the congregation during Sunday worship service. Based on previous conversations he and Katherine had had, Saul was pretty sure Rosemary wouldn't be happy about the news, whether she heard it now or a couple of months from now.

"She's going to have to find out sometime." Saul yawned even though he didn't feel sleepy.

"*Ya,* I know. I just didn't want her to find out like that. And I was hoping that she and I would grow closer, but she seems to resent me at every turn. I mean, she is always nice and polite, but I can tell that it's forced. I never would have thought I could love another man again, but I do. And I love his family. I feel very *gut* about all the boys, but it's Rosemary I'm worried about."

"I'd offer to talk to her, but I'm so angry with her that maybe that's not the best thing."

"Angry? For what, that she still won't go out with you? That's been going on for years."

Saul told her about the events of the day, his heart still heavy. "If she cared about me half as much as I care about her, she would have gone out with me a long time ago. She would have given me an explanation about what went wrong when we were younger. I'm just tired of the whole thing."

"Oh dear." Katherine was quiet, and Saul felt a little guilty for shifting the conversation to his problems.

"Not a problem. I'll just finish the garden like I promised Wayne. And I'll leave her alone."

"I don't believe that for one minute. Love doesn't just go away overnight, and I've heard you say on many occasions that Rosemary is the only woman for you, and that you'd keep trying until she could see that and love you in return."

Saul sighed. "I know. I'm just irritated."

"Saul, life is too short for regrets or to take anything for granted. If you really love Rosemary, don't give up. Things happen on God's time frame, and maybe there's a reason that you two didn't get together when you were younger. Pray hard about it, and I will too."

"I will be praying for you too, Katherine. Might the Lord's will be done for both of us."

After he hung up, he still couldn't sleep. Katherine was as good a woman as he'd ever known, and Wayne was a fine man. She'd be a good wife to him and mother to his children. But he could see where Rosemary might feel as if her toes were being stepped on. He wished they were closer so he could talk to her.

For now, praying would have to be enough.

CHAPTER SEVEN

Rosemary watched from the porch as her father stowed his crutches in the backseat of Katherine's buggy before he hobbled to the front seat. Then they both waved as Katherine pulled away. Katherine had offered to take him to the market today. Rosemary knew good and well that her father was capable of taking himself. He'd already done so several times. She shook her head, disappointed that she hadn't seen the truth before. Everything Katherine had done for their family was only in an effort to win over her father. And apparently, she had succeeded.

She sat in the rocker on the front porch for a while, glad that school wasn't out yet and the boys were gone, glad that her father had left, and wondering what things would be like between her and Saul today, assuming he showed up. But when she saw his buggy pulling up the driveway, her stomach rolled, and she jumped from the chair and went into the house. She stayed to the side of the window and peeked a few times. Once he'd tethered his buggy, he hauled the tiller to the garden.

For the next two hours, she tried to stay busy. She got the floors cleaned, made a grocery list, and tidied up her father's bedroom. But not once did she pass through the living room without looking out the window toward the garden. Saul was a hard worker, and no matter what had happened, the man was easy on the eyes. He'd always been handsome, but for the first time since they were teenagers, she was envisioning a life with him. A life without children. Could she be happy, just the two of them?

She stood at the front door for at least five minutes before she started toward the garden. Her heart was heavy about Saul, and about the thought of Katherine becoming her stepmother, which just seemed outrageous. She wanted to be happy for her father, but she was having a hard time wrapping her mind around the fact that he must be in love with Katherine. Rosemary knew her father pretty well, and she didn't think he'd be behaving so carelessly unless he really loved Katherine. Thank goodness the boys hadn't seen any of their public affection.

Saul stopped tilling when Rosemary neared the gate. The man was dripping in sweat. *I should have at least brought him something cold to drink.*

"*Wie bischt?*" Rosemary tried not to cringe, unsure if Saul even wanted to talk to her. He wiped sweat from his face with a rag that was tucked in his pocket.

"*Ach,* it's going *gut.*" He paused, the hint of a smile on his face. "Mighty warm out here, though." He pointed to a thermos lying nearby on the ground. "Finished that up already."

Rosemary took a step closer, until she was right on the other side of the fence. "If you'll hand me your thermos, I'll fill it up with iced tea."

"*Danki,* that would be great."

Rosemary stood there a few moments, curling her toes in the grass beneath her bare feet, feeling the awkwardness. No matter the situation, she couldn't see herself with anyone but him. *Is this Your plan for me, Lord? Am I to sacrifice my dream for a large family to be with Saul?*

"How's your arm?"

"Much better. *Danki.*" He stood looking at her. Rosemary wondered if he felt half as

90

awkward as she did. Maybe he just wanted her to go away.

"I'll go then and let you get back to work." She smiled, then turned to leave.

"Rosie?"

She stopped, turned around, and waited, her heart still pounding as hard as it was when she came out the front door. *"Ya?"*

Saul scratched his chin for a moment and grinned. "I thought you were going to help me."

She swallowed hard. "Uh . . . I . . . uh, I mean, you said your arm was better." She shrugged and looked down at the grass. "And after yesterday, I was thinking you probably didn't want me around." She looked up, knowing she sounded pitiful. But she felt pitiful.

"It's better, but that doesn't mean it doesn't hurt and that I couldn't use some help."

She stared at this handsome man standing on the other side of the fence, the one who had stolen her heart when she was young. His boyish dimples, beautiful blue eyes, and broad shoulders made her feel a bit weak in the knees, and with clarity, she could almost feel his lips on hers as they'd been five years ago. And she longed to feel them again.

"Okay." She pointed toward the house.

"My gloves are inside. I'll get them when I fill up your thermos."

Saul smiled and said, "I'll be here."

Saul watched her for a few moments before he started back to work, Katherine's words replaying in his mind. *"Maybe there's a reason that you two didn't get together when you were younger."*

Saul had prayed about it last night. He'd worked hard at being mad at Rosemary, and her wishy-washy behavior was frustrating. But he loved her, a fact he couldn't deny. He did miss the Rosemary he knew at sixteen. *I wonder if I'll ever see that girl again.*

His arm was throbbing. He'd known that pushing the tiller would be the hardest part of this job, but he was almost done, and then he could start planting the seeds. For Saul, that was the best part of putting in a garden. Though gardening was normally women's work, Saul had been in charge of it at his house for years. His mother and Lena would water and maintain it, but Saul laid the seeds in the soil, a process that made him feel closer to the Lord. He finished tilling just in time to see Rosemary pass through the opened gate toting his thermos and her gardening gloves.

"Here you go." She smiled as she handed

him the thermos, and Saul wished he could pull her into a hug. It would be more than enough for now. But the ice still felt thin, and he wanted to step softly.

"Danki." He chugged down half of the thermos, put the lid back on, and blew out a breath. "I needed that."

She folded her hands in front of her. "As you know, I've never put in a garden. I used to help *Mudder* when she was alive, but even then, I didn't like it, and I'm sure I was more hindrance than help."

"Come and see." He pointed to a large bag he'd brought and motioned for her to follow him. He kneeled down, and she did too. "We are late into the planting season. Some plants tolerate root disturbance and it's *gut* to start early. Broccoli, Brussels sprouts, cauliflower, eggplant, and even tomatoes should be planted before now." He turned to her and smiled. "But we're going to plant tomatoes anyway. And there are some veggies that don't like to be transplanted that do well when you direct-seed them. We're late on those, too, but they're cold hardy, like corn, beans, and peas."

Rosemary sighed and shook her head. "Gonna be a long time before those little seeds become vegetables."

93

Saul chuckled, which felt good in light of everything. "You might have to keep accepting vegetables from Katherine for a while. She's told me how much she enjoys her visits with your family." He paused. "And during one of our conversations, she even seemed a little disappointed that I was putting in a garden for you."

Rosemary frowned. *I bet she is.*

Saul was busy sorting through the seeds and putting them in piles. Rosemary wondered how often Saul and Katherine talked. Maybe Katherine was hitting on all the single men in the community, not just her father. Maybe she preferred men ten years older or ten years younger.

One thing she knew for sure — her father's heart was involved, and if Katherine's intentions weren't exclusive to *Daed,* she needed to know. As much as she would like Katherine out of the picture, she didn't want her father hurt. Accepting Katherine into their lives was the lesser of the evils, as long as she wasn't making herself available to other men.

"Are the two of you *gut* friends, you and Katherine?" Her stomach flipped, and she was suddenly afraid of the answer.

Saul stopped his seed sorting and looked up at her. "*Ya,* we are very *gut* friends.

Katherine is a wonderful person. Any man would be lucky to have her."

Rosemary swallowed hard, surprised that Katherine was a contender for Saul's affections after all the energy Saul had spent chasing Rosemary over the years. Jealousy was a sin, but Rosemary was experiencing it. Again. And both instances had one thing in common: Katherine. Everything about her rubbed Rosemary the wrong way, and the thought of Katherine and Saul together was even more disturbing than Katherine being with her father.

"I saw Katherine kissing *mei daed*." The bold statement was fueled by jealousy, and as soon as she said it, she regretted it.

Saul didn't look up from sorting the seeds, but he grinned. "Or maybe you saw your *daed* kissing Katherine?"

Rosemary folded her arms across her chest. *Hmm . . .* He didn't seem a bit bothered by the news. "It's very inappropriate for them to be carrying on like that. I mean, what if the boys had seen?"

Saul stood up, brushed dirt from his pants, then shrugged. "I don't think the boys would have cared. I think they like Katherine." Rosemary walked closer to Saul. "How do you know so much about Katherine and *mei* family?"

Saul shrugged. "I told you. Katherine and I are *gut* friends. She loves gardening, so we started out sharing gardening tips, and the friendship just grew from there." He paused, swiping at a bee that was buzzing around him. "And she brings us lots of food. I'm especially fond of her pineapple cherry crisp."

Rosemary walked closer to him, close enough that she could see the tiny scar above his right eyebrow. She'd forgotten about it until now. She remembered when Saul got hit in the forehead with a baseball bat when they were young. He was playing catcher, and Levi Esh had swung the bat a little too close and nailed him in the forehead.

"Katherine brings food to your family?"

"Ya. And *Mamm* and Lena take things to her too. It's called *sharing."* Saul winked, then tore open a package of seeds with his teeth.

"I share. All the time." *Forgive me, Lord.* It was a tiny lie. She'd been so busy feeling sorry for herself and tending to the household that she hadn't made much time to do for others. She reached for the package of seeds that Saul was getting ready to rip into. "Give me that. You're going to break a tooth." She peeled back the top of the package and wondered why Saul had used his teeth. "There aren't many in here," she said. It would be winter before these seeds produced any vegetables, and they would probably freeze over. *By then, Katherine might be living with us, and then she can take care of the garden.*

She pushed the thought aside, and when Saul squatted down in between two rows of freshly tilled dirt, Rosemary did too.

"We've been lucky that it hasn't rained. It's best to plant in dry soil, fertilize, and then water like crazy when you're done."

Rosemary watched Saul lay out the seeds, spacing them perfectly with a steady hand. You would have thought he was performing surgery or that his life depended on the exact placement of each tiny seed. His expression was stern, his mouth tight, and his eyes completely focused on the task.

"These are fast growers. The large-seeded ones usually are, like this squash." He delicately dropped the seed in, pushed on it, and looked up at her. "They'll root pretty fast." He wiped his brow. "That's the key. We want them rooted well. Then you'll just have to water them *gut* every day."

While Rosemary didn't relish the idea of adding another task to her chore list, she had to admit, she'd be anxious to see the first signs of growth, and Saul's passion for gardening was almost contagious. Almost.

They finished the row of squash, then Saul walked to the other side of the garden where he'd left a brown backpack. He came back holding a tiny flag with the word *Squash* written on it. He stuck it in the ground. "There. The first row is done."

They both stood up, and Rosemary felt something slither beneath her bare foot. Without thinking, she jumped and threw her arms around Saul's neck. He swooped her up as she screamed. Nothing scared her more than snakes. She buried her head in his chest and clung to his shirt with both hands as he cradled her in his arms.

"Is it gone?" She held on tighter. "Please tell me it's gone!"

Saul held her even closer. "You're okay. It's all right." He spoke softly, tenderly. "It was a tiny grass snake." He eased her down on the ground, then burst out laughing. "No bigger around than a pencil, and not much longer."

Rosemary playfully slapped him on the arm. "It's not funny!"

But the more he laughed, the larger her smile grew, and before she knew it, she was bent at the waist laughing just as hard as he was, and thinking how dumb she must have seemed. It felt good to laugh. Saul stopped before she did, and when she faced him, he was staring at her.

She struggled to get control of herself, and finally she said, "What? Why are you looking at me like that?"

"There she is."

Rosemary turned in a circle, looking all around before she turned back to him. A slight smile was on his face, but his eyes were serious and locked with hers. "Who?" she asked.

"The Rosie I remember."

CHAPTER EIGHT

By Friday, Saul was exhausted from planting. It took every ounce of patience he had to go so slowly. A garden this size could have been finished days ago, but things on the job site were going well, and he was stretching out his time with Rosemary for as long as he could. It had been a wonderful week, and they'd talked and been silly. But the old and the new Rosemary still came and went, and Saul could tell that something was weighing heavily on her. Sometimes she'd put distance between them, often going back in the house early, saying that she had chores to finish. He still wasn't sure where he stood with her, and neither had mentioned anything about going out on Saturday.

He looked up midmorning and saw her coming across the yard. She smiled and waved, and Saul decided he was going to officially ask her out on a date since things had been going so well. "Are you still working on that garden?" She giggled as she came through the gate, and Saul's heart warmed.

"It takes a keen understanding of how to plant properly." Saul walked toward her as she drew closer, and it took everything in his power not to pull her into his arms. It had been torturous to be around her all week. In a good way.

She glanced around. "Looks like we'll finish today."

Saul wasn't sure, but he thought he heard a bit of regret in her voice. "I think so."

She reached over and touched his arm. A tingle ran up his spine, and he reminded himself not to just grab her, that it might ruin everything if he spooked her. "I see you're down to a much smaller bandage. Your wound must be healing nicely."

"*Ya.* I've even been changing the bandage myself instead of bothering Lena with it."

Rosemary laughed. "I know that was a big step. I've never seen a man who was such a baby about an injury."

Saul could feel his cheeks turning red. "*Ya,* I know." He paused, rubbed his chin. "Rosie . . ." He took a deep breath. "Would you still like to go out with me tomorrow night?" He swallowed and held up one hand, palm toward her, and avoided her eyes. "I'll respect whatever you say." He waited a few moments, then looked up and steadied his gaze as he met her eyes. "This will be the last time I ask." He stepped closer.

She kept her eyes on his, her expression not giving away what her answer would be.

He waited, his heart still thumping.

"Well," she finally said, smiling. "You have waited a long time for a date."

"*Ya.* I have."

"Under one condition."

Anything. He cocked his head to one side and waited for the terms.

"You have to finish the garden by yourself today. That will give me time to prepare tomorrow's meal for *Daed* and the boys, something they can easily heat up. None of them knows how to cook."

"It's a deal." He knew he could have the rest of the seeds in the ground in a couple of hours, but he was willing to stretch it out, hoping she'd come visit with him during the afternoon.

Rosemary reached into her pocket and pulled out a small white nylon bag, stared at it, then looked up at him. "Can we plant this somewhere?" She took out a seed, and Saul immediately knew what it was.

"A passionflower seed." He turned it over

in his hand, wondering which species it was. He knew that some passionflowers grew wild in much of the southern United States, but others were a bit harder to root.

"Mae Kauffman gave this to me. She remembered that it was *mei mudder*'s favorite." Rosemary reached over and touched the seed, her finger brushing against his, which seemed intentional. "Will it grow?"

Saul gazed into her eyes, not wanting to disappoint her. "I think so. But we should plant it in a pot until it sprouts, then it should be planted on the south side of the house." He pointed to one of the barren flower beds. "Over there would be *gut.*"

Rosemary had a faraway look in her eyes. "That's exactly where *Mamm* used to have a passionflower. But like everything else around here, I let it die."

"That will be a *gut* place for it. Do you have a pot we can put it in? It will need lots of water to make sure it establishes strong roots."

"*Ya,* I'll go get one." She bounced up on her toes for a moment before she took off toward the house.

Saul couldn't wait until tomorrow night.

After supper, the boys went outside to finish their chores. Rosemary finished cleaning the kitchen, then took the opportunity to spend some time alone with her father. He'd been quiet the past couple of days, and Rosemary had noticed that Katherine hadn't been by. "Saul finished the garden today," she said as she sat down beside him on the couch. He had his foot propped up on the coffee table, and he was reading the Bible.

"Gut, gut." He didn't look up as he turned the page. "It will be nice to have fresh vegetables of our own."

Rosemary wondered what that meant. Would he be glad not to have Katherine bringing veggies anymore? Would Katherine already be living here, so it would be her garden anyway? She slouched against the back of the couch, crossed one leg over the other, and kicked her foot into action.

"Daed, is anything wrong?"

He turned another page and still didn't look up. *"Nee.* Why do you ask?"

"I don't know. You're just quiet."

"Ach, just tired of this foot, of the inconvenience." He pushed his gold-rimmed reading glasses up on his nose, and neither spoke for a few moments.

"I haven't seen Katherine in a couple of days," she finally said as she uncrossed her legs and turned to face him. She thought again about what nice things Saul had said about Katherine.

Daed took his glasses off, set them on the end table, and closed the Bible. He reached for his crutches, then slowly pulled himself up. Rosemary rose also, offering him a hand, but he shook his head. He took two steps toward his bedroom and didn't turn around when he said, "I don't suspect we'll be seeing much of her anymore."

He closed his bedroom door behind him, and Rosemary just stood there, staring at her father's closed door. There was no mistaking the sadness in his voice. The decision to stop seeing each other must have been Katherine's idea, and Rosemary wanted to slap the woman silly for hurting her father. She walked to his bedroom door, lifted her hand to knock, but then just softly placed her palm against the door. *Whatever happened, Lord, please give him peace and wrap Your loving arms around him.*

Rosemary had been praying more lately, and with each heartfelt prayer, she found herself reestablishing a relationship with God that she'd come close to abandoning. Once she'd started to shed some of the bitterness she'd been feeling, it was easier to see God's will. She was beginning to believe His plan for her didn't include children, but

He was giving her a chance at love, and Rosemary could no longer fight her feelings for Saul.

Before she could move forward with her own life, she would have to make things right for her father and Katherine. Katherine had tried so hard to be nice to Rosemary, and Rosemary hadn't behaved very well in return. But would Katherine really have ended the relationship because of Rosemary's attitude? She doubted it. But something must have happened . . .

Saturday morning, Rosemary awoke excited about her date with Saul, but she was worried about her father. He had slept late this morning and said he didn't want any breakfast. In her lifetime, Rosemary couldn't recall her father ever skipping a meal, except for once — the day *Mamm* had tried a new dish, and everyone in the family learned that *Daed* didn't like liver and onions. None of them did, except for Jesse. He'd eaten the leftovers for two days.

She made Jesse and Josh promise to keep an eye on Abner, and once she'd checked on her father, she hitched the buggy and headed to Katherine's. Her mind was awhirl with various scenarios. The one in the forefront was that Katherine had broken up with her father because of Rosemary's attitude toward her, although Rosemary had never been outright rude to the woman. Or maybe Katherine had found someone else, someone younger maybe. Either way, her father was suffering, and she was going to find out why.

Katherine's yard was perfectly maintained. *Of course.* Beautiful blooms in all the flower beds and a lush garden three times the size of the one Saul had put in for her family. The yard was freshly mowed, and the white clapboard house looked newly painted. Two cardinals were perched on the porch railing, and butterflies were plentiful. It looked like one of the paintings she'd seen at an *Englisch* shop in town.

She took a deep breath before she knocked, surprised that Katherine didn't have the door open, welcoming the breeze through the screen. She glanced around, and none of the windows were open either. Katherine's buggy was here, but maybe she had gone somewhere with someone else. She rapped on the door, and when no one answered, she was about to turn and leave when she heard footsteps.

Katherine opened the door a few inches and spoke to Rosemary through the screen. "Rosemary, what are you doing here?" She suddenly pulled the door wide. "Oh *nee* . . . is it your father? Is he all right?" Katherine brought a hand to her chest as her eyes grew round.

Rosemary was too stunned to speak at first. Katherine didn't have her *kapp* on, and her red hair was in a loose bun on top of her head, with lots of escaped strands sticking to her tearstained face. Dark circles hovered underneath swollen eyes, and her dark-green dress was wrinkled like she'd slept in it.

"*Daed* is fine." Rosemary leaned closer. "Can I come in?"

Katherine pushed the door halfway closed again. "Now isn't a *gut* time, Rosemary. Please forgive me." She started to close the door, but Rosemary yanked the screen door open, then gave the door a gentle push.

"What's wrong? Did you and *Daed* have a fight? I know about the two of you, and *Daed* seems just as sad as you are. What's going on?" Katherine opened the door wide and stepped aside so Rosemary could enter.

"I had a feeling you knew about us." Katherine walked ahead of Rosemary toward the living room, so Rosemary followed. After Katherine raised the two green shades on the windows facing the road, she lifted the panes and a welcome breeze wafted into the room. Katherine sat down on the couch and motioned for Rosemary to sit near her. Katherine looked a mess, but the inside of her house was equally as beautiful — and clean — as the outside.

"I saw you kissing out by the barn," Rosemary finally said. Katherine reached for a tissue from the box on the coffee table, blew her nose, and nodded. "That's what I thought."

Rosemary studied Katherine for a few moments, more confused than ever. "Who ended things? *Daed* seems just as upset as you are. What happened?"

Katherine covered her face with her hands, crying and mumbling. Rosemary couldn't understand her, so she waited, then asked again, "What happened?"

Katherine moved her hands, folded them in her lap, and sat taller. She didn't even try to stop the tears from pouring down her cheeks. "I love your *daed* with all my heart. I never thought I'd love again after *mei* husband passed, but the Lord blessed me with a second chance. Or so I thought." She cried harder, and Rosemary wasn't sure that she should ask what happened again, but she did. And after a few more sobs, Katherine finally started to talk.

"We had planned to be married in October

or November." Katherine quickly looked at Rosemary, but when Rosemary just nodded, she went on. "We were tired of sneaking around, especially from you and the boys." She hung her head. "I'm sorry about that. We both just wanted to be sure that it was a love to last the rest of our lives before we shared the news." She started shaking her head and crying again. "And I thought it was."

At this point, it was becoming obvious that her father had been the one to end the relationship. "So *Daed* called off the wedding?" Katherine nodded and blew her nose again. Rosemary couldn't remember seeing such sadness since her mother died. "Why?" she finally asked. *Dear Lord, please don't let it be because of me, the way I acted, or anything I did.* Guilt wrapped around Rosemary and she knew that whatever Katherine's answer was, she wasn't feeling very good about herself.

Katherine gazed into Rosemary's eyes, and Rosemary stopped breathing and braced herself.

Katherine smiled. The kind of sad smile that makes the heart hurt. "He said he didn't feel that he deserved a second chance, and that marrying me would be dishonoring your *mudder*."

"That's ridiculous!" Rosemary was relieved that blame hadn't been placed on her, but also shocked. "Of course he deserves a second chance. He's a wonderful man." She shook her head. "*Mei mudder* would want him to remarry. That's what the *Ordnung* encourages."

"And . . ." Katherine flashed the same smile, and Rosemary knew what was coming this time. "He knew that you didn't like me, so that was a problem too."

Rosemary lowered her chin, now fighting her own tears.

"Katherine, it's never been that I didn't like you." She cringed at the lie, but she didn't want to hurt Katherine further. *Forgive me, Lord.*

Katherine raised her arms, then let them fall into her lap. "Then what was it? I would like to know." A tear rolled down her cheek. "I always tried to be nice to you. I love cooking and doing for others, but I started to wonder if you thought I was overstepping my bounds with you. I just wanted to help." She waved her arm around the house. "Perfectly clean. All the time. Do you know why that is?"

Rosemary didn't say anything, just swallowed.

"Everything is always in order because I

111

have more time on my hands than I know what to do with. When there isn't anything left to do, the loneliness sets in, and I used to start missing John." She smiled. A real smile this time. "Then your father and I got close, and I was filled with hope about the future. It didn't take long for me to fall in love with him. I thought that I could be like a *mudder* to Abner since he didn't know his *mudder*. And I'd hoped to be a *gut* friend to the boys. And to you. I've admired you so much over the years." Rosemary's eyes grew wide, but before she could question Katherine, she went on. "Such huge responsibilities you have, tending to an entire household, your father, the boys . . . and to be so young."

Rosemary couldn't speak. She was suffocating with guilt, and even though she should shed the emotion, she didn't think she could.

"So, why don't you like me?" Katherine frowned, still crying.

Rosemary took a deep breath, not wanting to lie again. "It's just that . . ." She let out a heavy sigh. "You were . . . uh . . . always so *happy.* So organized and perfectly put together." She paused. "I guess I always felt inferior." Rosemary squeezed her eyes closed, cringing. When she opened them,

Katherine started laughing.

"*Danki* for giving me something to laugh about. I'm so tired of crying." She shook her head and chuckled again. "Really? That's all it takes is a happy, organized person to offend you? Well, I assure you, I hadn't been happy for a very long time until your father. And I never wanted to make you feel inferior. I only ever wanted to help." She covered her face with her hands again as though she were hiding.

Rosemary knew she'd go home and talk to her father about this, but right now there was only one thing on her mind. She reached for Katherine's hand. "I'm sorry, Katherine."

"*Danki.*" Katherine looked up and sniffled. "Edna was a wonderful woman. I'd never try to replace her. I'd be happy to come in second."

"That's not what I meant." Rosemary paused. "*Ya,* I am sorry about you and *Daed,* but I meant . . . I'm sorry for the way I treated you. I'm ashamed of myself." She looked away, blinked a few times.

Katherine squeezed her hand. "I forgive you, Rosemary. Please don't feel shame. It's the devil's sword."

Rosemary let go of Katherine's hand and stood up. "I'm going to talk to *mei daed,*

113

see if I can make him understand how worthy he is of your love, and I'll be praying for you both."

Katherine threw her arms around Rosemary's neck. "*Danki.* I would spend the rest of my life loving him."

The embrace lasted several seconds, and Rosemary wondered how she'd ever misread this woman. She knew how. She'd been wallowing in her own dark place, walking a path away from the Lord, and resenting those who seemed to have it all. Rosemary couldn't have it all. But she could have Saul. She hoped.

She was almost out the door when Katherine touched her arm. "One more thing." She paused, dabbed at her eyes with a tissue, then smiled. "Saul loves you very much. He always has. And he would make a wonderful husband and father."

Rosemary smiled. "I know." She hugged Katherine again before she left, surprised that Katherine obviously didn't know that Saul was unable to have children.

Chapter Nine

Rosemary was glad to see her father up and about when she returned from Katherine's. He was sitting in one of the kitchen chairs reading the newspaper.

"Where'd you run off to this morning?" He took off his reading glasses, and he had the same dark circles under his eyes that Katherine had.

Rosemary pulled off her black bonnet and hung it on the rack by the kitchen door. "I went to see Katherine."

Her father stiffened. "It's not your business, Rosie."

She eased a chair out and sat down. "*Daed,* she's a *gut* woman who loves you very much. Allow yourself to be happy." *Something I haven't done myself.*

"How long have you known?" He scratched his nose but didn't look at her.

"Not long."

"I didn't think you cared for her." He

sighed and reached for his cup of coffee.

"I didn't know her, *Daed.*" She waited, but her father was quiet.

"She just made me feel . . . inadequate. But I was wrong, and I can't stand to see you upset."

Her father pushed his chair from the table, locked his crutches underneath his arms, and moved to the living room. Rosemary followed.

"Don't you want to talk about this?"

He didn't turn around as he headed toward his bedroom. "This isn't your business," he said again before he closed his bedroom door.

Rosemary stood on the other side of the door, tempted to burst in and make him listen to her, but she knew her father, and that wouldn't work.

Well, I'm going to make it mei business. She walked back to the kitchen, grabbed her bonnet, found her black purse, and headed out the door. A plan was working in her mind, and she knew she'd need Saul to help her.

Saul took extra time readying himself Saturday evening, and he even dabbed a splash of aftershave on his face, something Janet Murphy had given him after he'd

116

helped her do some yard work. The *Englisch* woman didn't know such luxuries were frowned upon. It was the first time he'd used it. He didn't want to offend anyone, but he was hoping to get close to Rosemary tonight.

By the time he got to her house, his heart was racing. He hoped that Rosemary's idea didn't backfire on her, but he was glad she'd included him in the planning. All day, he'd relived the three months they'd had that wonderful summer. He'd spent the past five years hoping for another chance with her. They seemed to be moving in the right direction, and he'd been praying that tonight would go well.

Wayne answered the door when Saul knocked.

"Glad to be having you for supper, Saul." Wayne shook his hand, then eased his crutches to one side so Saul could move into the living room.

"Glad to be here," Saul said as he shook his head. "How much longer on those crutches?" He sighed, knowing that everything had happened according to the Lord's plan. If he hadn't plowed into Wayne, he never would have planted their garden and gotten a bit closer to Rosemary. But it was still hard to watch Wayne hobbling around all because Saul had been in such a hurry.

"Not too much longer. I'll be happy to get rid of these cumbersome things. Poor Rosie has been taking up the slack, taking care of things I can't do." He chuckled. "Like that poor *maedel* doesn't already have enough to do."

Rosemary walked barefooted into the room wearing a dark-maroon dress and black apron. She was smiling from ear to ear, and Saul winked at her. He wanted to tell her how beautiful she looked, but not in front of her father.

"The boys aren't here tonight," Wayne said as he motioned for Saul to sit in one of the rocking chairs across from the couch. "Ben Smoker's folks picked all three of them up for a sleepover." He shrugged. "Kind of last minute, if you ask me, but the boys were happy to go spend time with their friends. I think I heard mention of a late-night volleyball game." He sighed. "Them Smokers got that place lit up like a baseball field, enough propane to blind a person." Saul was glad that the Smokers had helped with the plan by taking the boys. And he was glad to see Wayne chuckling. Rosemary had told Saul how down her father had been.

"Supper is almost ready. You men chat

118

while I finish up." Rosemary smiled and headed back to the kitchen.

Wayne and Saul engaged in small talk, but occasionally Wayne's attention would drift, and it was clear that his thoughts were somewhere else.

Saul kept glancing toward the window.

Rosemary did her best to keep the beef casserole warm, hoping that Katherine would show up soon, before her father hobbled into the kitchen and saw four place settings laid out. She leaned against the counter, tapping her foot on the wood floor, hoping she hadn't crossed a line. She was glad that Saul had agreed to the plan, even though she'd sensed a tiny bit of disappointment in his voice when she'd told him. Rosemary was looking forward to some alone time with Saul as well, but she couldn't stand to see her father so upset. Or Katherine. She cringed, knowing how much she'd misjudged Katherine. She was hoping this whole thing wasn't a mistake, but when she heard her father say from the living room, "I wonder who is pulling in the driveway during the supper hour," she knew it was too late. Rosemary hurried out of the kitchen and walked into the living room just in time to see Saul opening the screen door.

119

Katherine looked beautiful in a dark-green dress and black apron, all perfectly pressed, but Rosemary no longer held that against her. She glanced down at her own black apron and swiped at a smudge of flour.

"Hi, Katherine. Come in," Rosemary said as she eased up to where Saul was standing. She took the dish Katherine was carrying and whispered, "*Gut, gut.* You brought the pineapple cherry crisp like we talked about."

It had taken a lot of convincing for Katherine to agree to come for supper, and she didn't exactly mention to Katherine that her father didn't know about the invitation. Rosemary turned to her father, who was now standing with one crutch under his arm. She tried to read his expression, wondering how mad he was, but the instant twinkle in his eye let Rosemary know she'd made the right decision.

"Hello, everyone." Katherine's eyes were still swollen from crying, but they sparkled just the same when she looked at Rosemary's father.

"Supper is ready, so let's all move into the kitchen." She carried the dessert Katherine had brought and put it on the counter. *Guess I'm going to need to learn how to make this since Saul loves it* so *much.* As soon as she had the thought, she hoped she wasn't being too presumptuous. She could easily visualize a life with Saul now, and there wasn't any reason that they couldn't adopt children someday. She knew several Amish couples who had. She touched her stomach with one hand and briefly thought about never feeling a new life growing inside her. But it had been five years, and she was still as in love with Saul as she'd ever been. Would it really have been fair to marry someone else, someone who would always be second to Saul?

She turned around as they all moved into the kitchen, just in time to see that Katherine and her father weren't the only ones with a twinkle in their eyes. Saul winked at her again, and somehow she knew that everything was going to be all right. For all of them.

During the meal, Saul ate like he was eating for two grown men, but both Rosemary's father and Katherine picked at their food. Rosemary had hoped that after a few days without seeing Katherine, perhaps her father had changed his mind. She caught Katherine sneaking glances at *Daed*, but her father was a tough one to read. She hoped she hadn't misread his earlier expressions. *Daed* had always told Rosemary that it was hard to tell what was going on in her head, the same as it had been with her mother. But Rosemary had always thought that it was her father who was often the hard one to read.

"Please let me help you clean this up," Katherine said when Rosemary began clearing the table.

Rosemary thought about the last supper Katherine had with them. "That would be *gut. Danki.*"

Katherine began running soapy water in the sink while Rosemary continued clearing the table. As she reached for her father's plate, she cut her eyes in his direction and held her breath. When he winked at her, she relaxed. *Everyone is winking tonight.* She smiled at him, and after the kitchen was clean, Katherine excused herself to the bathroom, and following the plan, Saul walked out to the porch.

Rosemary whispered to her father once they were alone, "Time is too short. I know you love Katherine, and *Mamm* would want you to be happy. God is giving you another chance at love, at happiness." She paused, studying her father's guarded expression. "I've been wrong about Katherine, and she loves you very much." Her father opened his mouth to speak, but Rosemary beat him to it. "And I know you love her."

Katherine walked back into the kitchen, and Rosemary hurried out the door to the porch. *Daed* had to know this was all a setup, but she prayed that he could rid himself of any guilt and be happy with Katherine.

"Well, they didn't say much to each other during supper. Do you think they'll get back together?" Saul stood up from the rocker. "It's hard to tell what your father is thinking, but he couldn't hide his happiness when he first saw Katherine at the door."

"I know." Rosemary walked to where Saul was standing. She had so much more on her mind than her father and Katherine, even though that was important to her. "*Danki* for going along with my idea. I'm sorry we didn't get to go out to supper like we planned."

Saul edged closer. "Then I guess you still owe me a date." He smiled, and as a gentle breeze swept across the porch, Rosemary caught the scent of something spicy. Saul gazed into her eyes, and she knew what was coming. They'd waited five years, and it was hard not to have regrets, but if things had happened any differently, they might not be together now. God always had a plan. On His time frame.

"*Ya,* I guess I do still owe you a date."

Rosemary squinted from the late-afternoon sun rays dipping beneath the porch rafters, and Saul instantly moved slightly to his left to put her in his shadow.

"Well, I'm pretending this is a date, and I know what happens at the end of a date, or what I've always prayed would happen when I finally got to take you out." As he leaned down, his lips met with hers, and Rosemary felt sixteen again, sharing her first kiss with the man she'd always thought she would marry.

"Give me the chance, Rosie, and I'll spend the rest of my life loving you and making you happy." Saul kissed her again, and she decided there would be no more worrying about children. God would provide if it was meant to be.

They both jumped when the screen door creaked and Katherine and her father walked onto the porch. Katherine was smiling, which was enough for Rosemary.

"Shame on you for being so tricky," her father said in a stern voice as he pointed a finger at Rosemary. But then his expression broke into a smile, and Rosemary made her way to where he was standing to hug him. "I love you, *Daed.*"

"I love you too, *dochder.*" He kissed her on the cheek before he eased her away and moved toward Saul, and as the men stood chatting, Rosemary walked over to Katherine.

As they shared a hug, Katherine whispered, "*Danki,* Rosemary. I will always love your father and be very *gut* to him. I'll be a *gut mudder* to the boys too." She stepped back, latching onto both of Rosemary's hands with hers. "And I promise not to step on your toes. It's still your *haus,* and I'll fit into whatever role you would like."

Rosemary smiled as she squeezed Katherine's hands. They hadn't formally announced it, but based on Katherine's comments, Rosemary knew the wedding must be back on. "Nonsense. It will be your *haus,* and . . ." She paused, smiling as she looked over at Saul, then she leaned closer to Katherine. "I think Saul and I are going to make up for lost time, so it might be your *haus* sooner than you think."

"*Ach,* Rosemary. I'm so glad. He's always loved you, since you were both sixteen."

Rosemary took a deep breath, basking in the hope that she felt, the love in her heart that had always been there — in hiding — for Saul.

"I thought we were going for a walk," Rosemary's father bellowed, then gave a hardy laugh. "Where's *mei maedel?*"

125

Katherine bounced up on her toes, kissed Rosemary on the cheek, then ran to the man who would be her partner. When they had passed through the yard and toward the open fields, Rosemary watched the man who would be *her* partner moving toward her.

He kissed her again, and Rosemary counted the many blessings of the evening.

Saul nodded toward the maroon pot at the far end of the porch. "Sometimes it takes a while for a passionflower to root, but once it does, it can thrive for years with nourishment and love."

Rosemary's heart was fluttering as she listened. Her mother had told her the same thing years ago. Their passionflower had thrived for a long time. But Rosemary had let it die after her *mamm* passed. But she had a second chance with this one and was going to make sure to nurture it so it would stay rooted in love for a lifetime.

Just like she planned to do with Saul.

"I've missed this." Saul kissed her again but then eased away. "Rosie, I'm fearful to bring this up and ruin the moment . . ." He took a deep breath. "But one thing is going to continue to haunt me. Can you tell me why you walked away before?" He paused, but spoke again before she could answer.

126

"Because I don't want to make the same mistake again."

Rosemary swallowed back the lump in her throat. "It was never anything you did. I've been just as afraid to tell you the truth as you were to bring up this subject. Probably more so."

"You can tell me anything, Rosie. It won't make me love you any less."

He loves *me. But will he still after I tell him the truth?*

She looked down, but Saul gently cupped her chin and brought her eyes to his. "There's nothing you can tell me that will cause me to walk away."

"I don't know about that," she said softly.

They were both quiet, and Rosemary leaned up and kissed him on the mouth, just in case it was the last time she'd be able to. She lingered for a while, but she knew she owed him an explanation.

She eased away and took a step backward, but kept her eyes locked with his.

"I-I always wanted *kinner.*" She lowered her eyes for a few moments, then looked back up at him. "And I just couldn't imagine not having a large family. I know. It was self-ish. I should have known that our feelings back then would have been enough to sustain us, but I just couldn't imagine my life without children." She closed her eyes and waited, but when Saul didn't say anything, she slowly looked up at him. "Please say something."

He took off his hat, scratched his forehead, then put his hat back on. "I want a large family too. We used to talk about that when we were together back then."

"*Ya*, I know we did." She moved closer to him, praying that he'd understand. "I was young, and I thought that if I walked away from you, I'd find someone else whom I would love just as much, someone who could have children." She shook her head. "But there's never been anyone else, Saul. Only you."

He was quiet for a few moments, then he rubbed his cheek and chuckled. "Rosemary . . ." He shook his head. "What in the world are you talking about?"

Rosemary bit her lip and tried to calm her breathing. "I know you can't have *kinner*. One day I overheard your *mamm* talking to her cousin Naomi who was visiting. I heard them saying you couldn't have children." She paused and hung her head again. "I'm so sorry. I don't know if you can forgive me. I don't blame you if you can't." She gazed into his eyes. "But I love you just as much now as I did back then. Maybe more.

And we can either adopt *kinner* or the Lord will provide if it's meant to be. I just know that I want to be with you." She held her breath. "If you'll still have me."

Saul's expression was blank, and a tear slipped down Rosemary's cheek. *I've lost him.*

"Let me make sure I understand," Saul said. "You broke up with me because you thought I couldn't have children?"

She nodded as another tear slipped down her cheek. "I'm sorry." Saul leaned over, hands on his knees, and started laughing.

"I'm really not sure whether to laugh or cry." He straightened and pulled himself together. "Rosemary, as far as I know, I'm quite capable of having *kinner*. You overheard *mei mamm* and *mei* aunt Naomi talking about Saul Bender, a cousin. He was in a bad accident back then, and his injuries left him unable to have children."

Rosemary stopped breathing. "What?" Her mouth hung low for several moments as she let this news soak in. "Do you mean that we wasted — I wasted — five years?" Her chest hurt. "It was bad enough that I left you because of it, but for it to not even be true?"

Saul didn't say anything, just shook his head.

Rosemary was sure that this was the most bittersweet moment of her life. And was Saul going to walk away from her?

"Why didn't you just ask me?" He reached his hand out to her, but she backed away as she was swallowed up by regret.

"I don't know." She buried her face in her hands and started to sob. "I'm an awful person. We could have been together all this time."

Saul pulled her close to him and held her tight for a while before he eased her away and kissed her on the forehead, then on the cheek, then his lips met hers. "If anything had happened any differently, we might not be together now. It was God's plan for things to work out this way."

"How can you say that? Aren't you angry? At me? At God?"

"Rosie . . ." He reached for her hand and walked her to the shade of an oak tree in the front yard. They sat on the grass, and Saul brushed back a strand of her hair that had fallen forward. "If we had gotten together back then, how do you think your *daed* and *bruders* would have done on their own after your mother's death? Maybe your father would have been so busy raising the three boys, he might not have noticed the spark between him and Katherine. My

130

sweet Rosie. Everything happens on the Lord's time frame. Not ours." He pulled her close and kissed her tears. "We can't have regrets. We are exactly where we are today because of every event that has led us here. I just want to be with you. I love you, and I always have."

Rosemary buried her head in his chest, then looked into his eyes. "I love you, too, and I always have."

Saul grinned. "And I don't know of any reason why we can't fill a house with lots of *kinner.*"

Saul was right. Carrying the burdens of the past would only weigh them down. As she sat up and watched her father and Katherine walking toward them hand in hand, Rosemary knew that they were exactly where God meant them to be.

DISCUSSION QUESTIONS

1. Rosemary ends her relationship with Saul because she believes he can't have children. Have you known couples in this situation? If so, was it a deal-breaker?

2. Years later, Rosemary changes her mind and knows that she wants Saul as her husband, even if that means they will never have children. Do you think that Rosemary changes her mind, in part, because she is older and more mature? Or has enough time gone by that she realizes she won't find anyone she loves as much as Saul?

3. Several scenes in the story are filled with large doses of miscommunication, and things could have turned out very differently had all truths been on the table. But, as mentioned in the story, things happen on God's time frame, and by the end, all the characters are where they are meant to be. Are there instances in your life when

you met resistance, only to have things play out much better than you could have imagined?

4. In a lot of ways, Rosemary and Katherine are alike. Can you name some of the characteristics they unknowingly share?

ACKNOWLEDGMENTS

To my husband, Patrick, and my family and friends — thank you for your continued support on this amazing journey. And as always — God gets the glory for laying these stories on my heart.

Many thanks to everyone at HarperCollins Christian Publishing. I'm a lucky gal to work with such a fabulous group of people, and I'm blessed to be able to call you all friends.

To my agent — Natasha Kern — a huge thank you for your career guidance and friendship. You are just a supercool person!

It's an honor to dedicate *Rooted in Love* to Jenni Cutbirth, a woman whom I admire. She's someone who has more strength than she ever thought possible — a necessary trait when you find out that your two-year-old daughter has cancer. For a year, I watched Jenni go back and forth to the hospital, sometimes staying for days at a time for her daughter's chemotherapy and radiation. A *year.* I was exhausted just hearing about her routine, and I jokingly appointed myself "President of the Jenni Fan Club." But all joking aside, my dear Jenni . . . you are amazing. And Raelyn is a blessed little girl to have you as her mommy. May God always shower you and Raelyn with His blessings.

A Love for Irma Rose

To Larry Knopick

PENNSYLVANIA DUTCH GLOSSARY

ab im kopp — off in the head; crazy
ach —oh
daed — dad
danki — thank you
Englisch — non-Amish person
fraa — wife
gut — good
haus — house
kapp — prayer covering or cap
kinner — children
maedel — girl
mamm — mom
mammi — grandmother
mei — my
mudder — mother
nee — no
Ordnung — the written and unwritten rules of the Amish; the understood behavior by which the Amish are expected to live, passed down from generation to generation. Most Amish know the rules by heart.

141

rumschpringe — running-around period when a teenager turns sixteen years old

sohn — son

wunderbaar — wonderful

Wie bischt — How are you?; Howdy

ya — yes

Jonas glanced around the small cemetery, sprigs of brown poking through the melting clumps of snow. Sunshine beamed across the meadow in delicate rays, as if God were slowly cleaning up after one season, in preparation for the next. Soon it would be spring, Irma Rose's favorite time of year, when new foliage mirrored hope for plentiful harvests, when colorful blooms represented life, filled with colorful variations of our wonderment as humans.

"I love you, Irma Rose. I've loved you since the first day I saw you, sittin' under that old oak tree at your folks' house, readin' a book. You musta been only thirteen at the time, but I knew I'd marry you someday."

— FROM *PLAIN PROMISE,* BOOK THREE IN THE DAUGHTERS OF THE PROMISE SERIES

CHAPTER ONE

1957, FIFTY-THREE YEARS EARLIER

Jonas clutched the reins with sweaty hands, his fingers twitching as he waited for Amos Hostetler to blow the whistle, signaling the start of the race. He glanced to his right and scanned the crowd, at least fifteen onlookers — including Irma Rose Kauffman. This buggy race down Blackhorse Road was more than a friendly competition. More than just a group of Amish kids enjoying their *rumschpringe* on a Saturday afternoon.

He peered to his left at Isaac Lapp's flaring nostrils, knowing that his rival for Irma Rose's affections wanted to win as badly as he did. Jonas knew that pride was a sin, as Isaac surely did, but when it came to Irma Rose, Jonas figured Isaac's thoughts were as jumbled as his own. Jonas had been waiting to court Irma Rose for three years, since right after his father died. He recalled the way she lit his soul at a time when his grief threatened to overtake him. And now that she was sixteen, her parents were allowing her a few freedoms. Buggy races were looked down on by the elders in the community, but the young members of the district still gathered at the far end of the road most Saturdays to see who had the fastest horse and buggy.

"That ol' horse of yours ain't gonna be able to keep up with Lightning." Isaac smirked from his topless buggy, the type used for courting. Jonas hoped he never had to see Irma Rose riding alongside Isaac.

"*Ya*, well . . . we'll see about that." Jonas kept a steady hand on the reins while he and Isaac waited for the spectators to start loading into their buggies. They would wait about ten minutes, until everyone reached the finish line down by the old barn at the far end of the King property. Then Amos would blow the whistle to start the race.

Jonas sat taller, raised his chin, and tried to ignore that his own horse chose this moment to relieve himself. Bud was a fine animal. And fast. But Bud pooped more than any other horse around, and always at the wrong time, as if he was showing off. Or just trying to irritate Jonas.

Luckily the whistle blew before Isaac had

time to make a joke, and Jonas slapped the reins. *"Ya!"* Within seconds, he was several yards ahead of Isaac, squinting as the late-afternoon sun almost blinded him. But he kept pushing Bud, anxious to see Irma Rose standing at the finish line, hopefully cheering him on.

Competition was against the *Ordnung* and everyone knew it, but there was a certain thrill about being victorious, even though deep down, Jonas knew God wouldn't approve. As he crossed the finish line two buggy lengths ahead of Isaac, God wasn't the one on his mind. As he pulled back on the reins, he looked to his right, searching the crowd standing in the grass on the side of the road.

Bud was completely stopped — and relieving himself again — when Jonas finally located Irma Rose. Even though the women in his district all dressed similarly, Irma Rose was easy to spot. She was tinier than most of the women, with dainty features. Loose tendrils of golden hair framed her face from beneath her *kapp,* and if a man was lucky enough to attract her gaze, he could feel her green eyes searching his soul. Even though she was petite and flowerlike, she had the perfect balance of femininity and strength. But she wasn't even looking toward the road. Instead of watching Jonas whup Isaac in the race, she was standing way off to the side of the crowd, smiling and seeming to enjoy the company of someone who threatened Jonas's potential courtship with Irma Rose way more than Isaac or anyone else. Jake Ebersol.

Irma Rose hung on Jake's every word. He was so wise and knew more about Scripture and the teachings of the *Ordnung* than anyone she knew. He was only nineteen, but he had the mind of someone much older. When Jake Ebersol spoke, people listened. And it didn't hurt that he was quite handsome. His big brown eyes peeked from beneath sandy-blond bangs cropped high on his forehead, and his face was bronzed from his work outdoors. Jake was tall and muscular, his suspenders tightly fitted atop his blue shirt. He was everything an Amish girl could want.

"I'd love to go with you to the singing next Sunday." Irma Rose blinked her eyes a few times, unable to control her reaction to his invitation as a smile spread across her face. She'd been waiting for Jake to ask her to a singing since she'd turned sixteen last month. She loved when someone hosted a singing for the young people in her district, a time for fellowship, prayer, and singing. And best of all, it was a time to socialize without adults hovering nearby.

"Gut, gut." He pushed back the brim of his straw hat, smiling, then he brushed a clump of dried dirt from his britches. Several of the men who were standing too close to the race had been splattered with mud.

Irma Rose snuck a peek at Isaac, who was standing a few yards away. He'd been staring at her most of the day. She'd known for a long time that he was interested in courting her, and he was nice enough . . . but in her mind, there was only Jake. She offered Isaac a quick wave before she turned her attention back to Jake. A smile lit his face again, and she was basking in the moment when Jonas Miller walked up.

"I won. Ol' Bud came through for me." He smiled as he looped his thumbs beneath his suspenders, which were not doing a very good job holding up his britches.

Irma Rose hoped Jake would make pleasantries with Jonas so she didn't have to. Jonas was wild and reckless, and Irma Rose could often smell the lingering scent of cigars when she was around him. He was the same age as Jake, and while Jonas was handsome in his own way, he was certainly not Irma Rose's type.

"It was a *gut* race," Jake said, smiling. "Congratulations on the win."

Irma Rose was thinking about sitting next to Jake in his buggy on Sunday and wondering if he'd kiss her at the end of the night. She became aware that Jonas was speaking to her.

"Did you ask me something?" She blinked her eyes a few times, then brought her hand to her forehead to block the sun.

His firm mouth curled as if always on the edge of laughter, and Irma Rose found it unsettling. As his dark eyes raked boldly over her, she felt her cheeks reddening, the way they always did around him. He caused a tingling in the pit of her stomach that made her uncomfortable. Jonas was tall, but unlike Jake, he was thin, like he hadn't yet grown into his height. Jonas had the biggest feet she'd ever seen, and she'd heard that Mr. Tucker at The Shoe Barn had to order his black leather loafers from another state. Jonas took a step closer to her, and she noticed the stubble on his jawline. It seemed that no matter what time of day or night, he was never quite clean-shaven. Maybe because his hair was as black as a starless sky.

"I asked what you thought about the race." Jonas's smile grew and so did the funny feeling in Irma Rose's stomach.

150

She lifted her chin. "I don't think such competition is necessary." She shrugged and smiled back at him. "It's just silly." She turned to Jake, wishing he'd reach for her hand — something to let Jonas know that Jake would be courting her. Or at the least, taking her to the singing next Sunday.

"I'll be back," Jake said as he pointed to his right. "*Mei* sister is yelling for me." He extended his hand to Jonas. "Congratulations again. Bud is a fine animal."

Irma Rose glanced around, looking for a way to escape being caught in a conversation alone with Jonas, but everyone seemed involved in their own conversations. She twisted the tie on her prayer covering, hoping Jake would return soon. And that Jonas would mosey along.

"I was wondering . . ." Jonas grinned as a river of sweat flowed down both sides of his face. ". . . if you'd like to go with me to the singing on Sunday?"

Irma Rose pulled a hand-stitched handkerchief from the pocket of her apron and dabbed at the perspiration beading on her forehead. She cleared her throat, her heart hammering against her chest. She hated that he had this effect on her. "*Nee,* I can't," she finally said, fighting the knot rising in her throat. "I'm going to the singing with Jake."

151

Jonas took another step closer, his tall build casting a protective shadow over her, shielding her from the setting sun behind him. July had never felt so hot. "I think you should go with me instead."

Irma Rose stepped back as she tried to get control of her uneven breathing. "I just told you . . . I'm already going with someone else." She turned away to find Jake.

She could feel Jonas's eyes on her as she rushed away. Blotting her forehead with her hankie again, she picked up the pace.

Jonas took a step to go after her, but stopped himself. He rubbed the stubble on his chin and took a deep breath, knowing he had to make Irma Rose see that they were meant for each other. Jake Ebersol was a likable fellow, a pillar in the community, and everyone thought he'd follow in a long line of footsteps and become a deacon or bishop someday, like his father and grandfathers. But Jake wasn't the right guy for Irma Rose. Jonas had watched her for three years. She had a fire for adventure. He'd watched her jump from the highest peak into Pequea Creek, and she could run faster than any girl he knew. She could swing a baseball bat and knock a volleyball over the net with ease, and her laughter stole his breath.

Irma Rose was beautiful. Great with the *kinner* in the community. And she was going to be the mother of his children.

She just didn't know it yet.

CHAPTER TWO

Irma Rose sat with her girlfriends — Hannah and Mary — at the soda shop, as they did every Tuesday after they went to the market. They all shared a strawberry malt at the counter while watching the television — knowing their parents wouldn't approve.

Hannah's father would be particularly upset, whether it was their *rumschpringe* or not. He'd ground her for sure if he knew. Irma Rose was an only child, and her parents wouldn't be happy, but they weren't as strict as Hannah's. Most likely, Irma Rose would just get a good talking-to. Unless, of course, they caught her watching something inappropriate — like Elvis Presley or Jerry Lee Lewis. Then there would be trouble. As for Mary, she always said her parents had more children than they could keep up with — fourteen — so she figured her chances of getting caught were slim.

Today, the sound on the television was

turned down so low they could barely hear it, and the daytime soap opera *As the World Turns* was on, which didn't interest the girls much.

"I hope it doesn't rain on the way home." Mary leaned forward and slurped from one of the three straws. "We should have brought one of the covered buggies."

Irma Rose glanced out the plate glass window facing Lincoln Highway and toward the dark clouds in the west. They'd ridden into the town of Paradise together in Hannah's topless buggy. She looked down at the floor beside them where their few grocery bags were. "*Ach,* I've got flour in my bag. That won't do well in the rain."

"We'd better go." Hannah reached into her pocket for some coins. It was her turn to pay for the malt. She was waiting for change when the bell above the door rang, drawing their attention to a tall Amish man walking in.

Mary gasped, then covered her mouth with one hand. "It's Jonas Miller," she whispered.

Irma Rose sat up straighter and quickly looked away. Mary fancied Jonas — although Irma Rose couldn't understand why. Mary said he was rough around the edges, but that all he needed was a *gut fraa* to tend

155

to him. Irma Rose was pretty sure he needed more than that. She cut her eyes in his direction. For starters, he needed a haircut and, as usual, a shave. And someone in his house needed to mend the missing button on his blue shirt. Irma Rose could already smell the stale stench of cigar, yet a brief shiver rippled through her.

"*Wie bischt,* ladies?" He stopped right in front of Irma Rose. "Have you reconsidered going with me to the singing next Sunday?"

Irma Rose glanced at Mary, whose expression immediately fell, and she wanted to smack Jonas for hurting her friend like that. Didn't he suspect how Mary felt about him? "I already told you . . ." She took a deep breath as the pit of her stomach churned. "I'm going with Jake."

Jonas's edgy grin crept up one side of his face. "I was just making sure you hadn't changed your mind."

"*Nee.* I have not." She forced a thin-lipped smile. "Maybe Mary would like to go with you though."

Mary hung her head as her face reddened, but she quickly lit up when Jonas said, "Sure. Mary, do you want to go with me on Sunday?"

Irma Rose felt her pulse beating in her throat as she watched Mary nod. Mary was a quiet girl, pretty with wavy brown hair and rosy cheeks. She had big blue eyes and long lashes that she was batting at Jonas.

"We have to go." Irma Rose stood up from the stool, leaned down, and began gathering her share of the bags. "*Danki,* Mr. Weaver," she said to the soda shop owner, who waved and nodded.

"Here comes the rain." Hannah pointed at the window that ran the length of the soda shop. "Your flour isn't going to make the trip home in my topless buggy." She turned to Jonas. "Since you brought a covered buggy, can you cart Irma Rose to her *haus* so her flour doesn't ruin?" She nodded toward the window, and Irma Rose looked in that direction. Jonas's buggy was parked in front of the store, Bud tethered to the hitching post. Jonas's buggy was easy to spot. It was the only one with bullet holes in it. There were all kinds of stories floating around about what happened, but Jonas would never confirm or deny any of them.

Irma Rose clutched her bags to her chest. "*Nee.* It will be fine."

Mary spoke up too. "Hannah's right. You should let Jonas carry you home."

Looking down at the five-pound bag of flour, Irma Rose considered her options. Riding two miles in the buggy alone with

Jonas, or showing up at home with wet flour and having to endure a lecture about reading the weather forecast in the newspaper before heading to town. "Fine," she said stiffly as she lifted her eyes to his.

Jonas tipped the brim of his straw hat toward Mary. "And I'll see you on Sunday."

Irma Rose pursed her lips and said goodbye to Hannah and Mary. Jonas picked up the bag of flour, then Irma Rose followed him to his buggy carrying a brown paper bag of groceries. They placed the items in the backseat, then Jonas offered his hand to help her into the buggy. Ignoring the gesture, she heaved herself onto the bench seat and folded her hands in her lap.

Jonas had barely closed the door on his side when the rain started in earnest. He clicked his tongue and set the horse in motion, and Irma Rose prayed silently that it would only be rain and not a storm. Not only was she frightened of lightning and thunder but sometimes the horses got spooked, and they were going to have to cross Lincoln Highway to get home.

She was particularly worried about Hannah and Mary, and she could see her friends getting soaked in the topless buggy. "Can you follow Hannah and Mary to Mary's *haus* before you take me home?"

158

Jonas began crossing Lincoln Highway behind Hannah. "*Ya.* Planned on it." He turned to her and grinned. "Someone forgot to check the weather."

She ignored him for a few moments, then turned to face him. "What were you doing in the soda shop, anyway?"

He didn't answer at first, concentrating on getting across the highway safely. Once Bud was trotting behind Hannah's buggy and away from the traffic, he turned to her. "I was looking for you."

"I don't know why," she said dryly as she rolled her eyes, aware of how close they were in the small buggy.

Jonas smiled but didn't say anything. Either he was the happiest man on the planet, or he just liked to make her uncomfortable.

They were quiet as both buggies made their way down Black Horse Road in the pouring rain. Irma Rose needed a distraction, something to keep her from focusing on the flashes of lightning up ahead.

"That was nice of you to ask Mary to the singing." Irma Rose kept her eyes straight ahead, knowing she was fishing for information. Would Jonas say that he'd had to settle for his second choice? *And why does that matter?*

"Mary is a sweet *maedel.*" He wasn't smiling anymore, and his jaw tensed as he strained to see through the windshield. The wipers were working hard, but it was still difficult to see.

Irma Rose jumped and covered her eyes when she saw a rod of lightning not too far ahead. *One, one thousand . . . two, one thousand,* then BOOM! She pressed her hands against her ears and fought the tears forming in the corners of her eyes.

"That was close," Jonas said in a whisper, then she felt a hand on her arm. "Are you okay?"

She pulled her hands from her ears, nodded, and bit her trembling lip.

"Don't worry, Irma Rose. I'll get you home safely."

His voice was so strong and determined that she believed him. She was relieved when she saw Hannah and Mary turn into Mary's driveway. She knew Hannah would wait to leave until the storm was over.

Another bright burst of light shone ahead of them, and she wondered if maybe they should ride out the storm at Mary's house, too, but by the time she thought to suggest it, Jonas had Bud in a good trot and was passing Mary's house. Irma Rose's heart was pounding in her chest, and with one

160

loud, thunderous boom after another, she fought the urge to cry.

Then Jonas shouted, "Bud!" He pulled back on the reins so hard the horse's front feet came off the ground; the horse waved his hooves in the air until Jonas stopped pulling on the reins and they were at a complete stop.

"That was close!" Jonas let out a long breath and stared at the tree lying across the road in front of them.

"Should we go back the other way?" Irma Rose had both hands on the dash as she peered through the rain. Then she turned around and, in the distance, could see water starting to flow across the road in front of Mary's house, an area that flooded easily.

Jonas slammed a hand against the dash of the buggy, causing Irma Rose to jump.

"I should have left you at Mary's," he said, shaking his head.

"You couldn't have known that a tree would fall in front of us." She paused, turning to look at him. His forehead was creased, but she covered her ears when another bolt of lightning flashed up ahead with a quick, thunderous follow-up. Jonas put an arm around her and pulled her close, and Irma Rose buried her face in his chest.

"Everything's okay, I promise. The lightning is still a ways off, and it's moving to the east. We'll just have to wait here a little while." He rubbed her arm, and she could feel his heart beating against her ear. She knew hers was pounding twice as hard, but the nearness of him gave her comfort. And something else. Something she wouldn't examine until later.

She lifted her face to his, gazed into his eyes, and tried to figure out what it was about Jonas that left her feeling light-headed. He slid a finger along her cheek, pushing back a strand of hair, and for a few seconds, she was sure he was going to kiss her. She quickly wrenched herself away, straightened her *kapp,* and took a deep, cleansing breath.

"I think the rain is easing up." She stared straight ahead but eventually turned to face him. He was grinning again — that irritating, all-knowing quirky smile. "What's so funny? Why are you looking at me like that?"

"I almost kissed you." He paused, his smile fading as he gazed into her eyes. "And one day, I'm going to marry you."

Irma Rose's jaw dropped as she turned to face him. "You are *ab im kopp!* And arrogant. You think everyone wants to be with you! You've always been like that, Jonas Miller." She chuckled. "I'm not one of those

162

people."

"Whatever you say, Irma Rose." He smiled again, winked at her, then turned and looked over his shoulder. "The water's going down." He eased Bud around until the buggy faced the opposite direction. The rain had all but stopped, and when they got closer to the small stream of water moving across the road, it was easy to see that it wasn't more than an inch deep, and Bud easily got them safely through it.

She couldn't look at him, so she kept her eyes on the road in front of them as they passed Mary's house. Jonas took an alternate route to Irma Rose's house. When he finally pulled into her driveway, she knew she had to thank him for the ride, but she wasn't about to look at him. *"Danki."* She pulled on the door to open it, but he caught her arm, causing her to stop breathing for a moment.

"Go with me to the singing on Sunday. Please."

She eased her arm out of his grip and released her breath. "I'm going with Jake." She opened the door, stepped out, then turned to face him. "And you're going with Mary."

Jonas watched her walk up the porch steps,

open the door, and go inside her house. She didn't turn around. After a few seconds, he eased Bud into a light trot and headed for home.

He'd known Irma Rose was the one for him when he first met her three years ago, and he suspected that she'd felt that spark too. Even though she'd been too young for courting at the time, it was easy for him to envision the woman she would become someday. Jonas's father had just died, and despite his strong faith, he was struggling to find joy, even just a reason to smile. Irma Rose had been sitting in the grass, reading a book. When she looked up and saw him, she closed her book, her cheeks filling with color. She was soft-spoken but confident as she told him about the book she was reading, and he'd listened to the gentleness of her voice, even though he had read this same book nearly a dozen times, as recommended by his father. And when she'd tenderly lifted a baby grasshopper into the palm of her hand, coddling it as if it were a newborn baby, something inside of Jonas changed forever. He would wait for her.

But he was going to need to do something extra special to convince her to give him a chance. Jake was stiff competition. All this time, he'd been worried about Isaac. And somehow Jake had snuck up and stolen her affection.

When he got home, he settled Bud in his stall, then set to work on all the chores he'd missed while he was out. As he dumped a bucket of feed into the pigpen, he thought about what he would have done if anything had happened to Irma Rose. *Thank You, Lord . . . for getting us home safely.*

After he'd tended to the pigs, he took to milking the cows. That's how it was when you had all sisters and no father. His *mamm* and four sisters took real *gut* care of him, so he tried to make sure they had everything they needed and that the farm was kept up the way his father would have wanted. He didn't really have time to be chasing after a *maedel.* But Irma Rose wasn't just any girl.

He'd almost finished his late-afternoon chores when Missy came running out of the house. His four-year-old sister was a bundle of energy. She most likely was coming out to tell him what was for supper, that it was ready, or maybe just to fill him in on her day. He tried to be a father to her as much as a brother. His other sisters were a little older, and he was thankful for that, for his mother's sake. At least they were able to help *Mamm* with laundry, cooking, and tending to the many tasks it took to keep

165

things running smoothly.

Mae was ten; Annie, eleven; and Elizabeth, thirteen. Jonas's father used to jokingly tell Jonas, "It took us six years to have Elizabeth. I reckon the good Lord thought you were plenty a handful on your own back then." Jonas smiled as he recalled memories of his father.

"*Mamm*'s sick!" Missy screamed, and because of the tears in her eyes, Jonas was already moving toward her. He scooped her into his arms as he hurried to the house.

"Now, now. What's wrong?" Jonas's heart was pounding as he picked up his pace.

"Elizabeth said to come get you. *Mamm* is throwing up red. What's wrong with her, Jo Jo?"

He set Missy on the porch steps and ran into the house. He didn't know what he'd do if the Lord saw fit to take his mother too.

CHAPTER THREE

Irma Rose huffed as her mother packed a variety of baked goods to take to the Millers' house. She leaned against the kitchen counter and folded her arms across her chest, sighing heavily.

Mamm added a loaf of bread to the bag. She paused and looked over her shoulder at Irma Rose. "Why are you giving me fits about taking this to the Millers? I told you that Sarah Jane is going to be in the hospital for a while, and I'm sure the girls and Jonas have their hands full in her absence. That little *maedel,* Missy, isn't even five yet, and without a father, I know they will need some help. Their oldest girl is only thirteen."

Irma Rose thought the name Sarah Jane was the prettiest name she'd ever heard. *I'm going to name my daughter that someday.* She couldn't wait to be a mother, and for a few moments, she allowed herself to imagine a life with Jake and lots of *kinner.* "I know," she finally said as she chewed on a nail. Maybe Jonas wouldn't be there when she made the delivery.

Mamm handed her the bag of pastries, breads, and cookies. During the summer, they tried to do all of their baking early in the day, but the kitchen was still stifling. "Tomorrow I'll send a casserole or something easy for them to have for supper. But I know Widow Zook took care of their supper for tonight."

Tomorrow? Was she going to be carting food to the Millers every day? Guilt nipped at her for having the thought. Of course she wanted to do what she could to help their family. Jonas would probably be working in the fields anyway.

Ten minutes later, she pulled into their driveway. She loved the Miller homestead. Not only was it pristine but it had just the right mix of wide open fields as well as areas that were slightly wooded, keeping the house and other structures out of view from the road. Once you laid eyes on the home and property, it took your breath away, especially this time of year. Sarah Jane and her daughters had filled the many flower beds with colorful blooms, a reminder to Irma Rose that her own beds needed sprucing. The house always looked freshly

168

painted; she knew Jonas could be credited for that. Since his father had died three years ago, Jonas had worked hard to keep the property up. Wild and reckless, yes. But not lazy.

As she tethered her horse, she tried to figure out what it was about Jonas that bothered her so much. She always came back to the same conclusion. He made her feel uncomfortable because he assumed she had feelings for him that she didn't have. He acted like he knew her better than she knew herself. His arrogance put her on edge. She carried the bag through the plush green grass, wishing she was barefoot so she could feel the warm dewy blades tickling her toes. She knocked on the door and waited. A few moments later, Elizabeth answered the door with Missy standing beside her.

"*Wie bischt,* Irma Rose. Come in." Elizabeth swung the door wide and stepped aside so Irma Rose could enter the living room.

Since all of the Miller girls were younger than Irma Rose, she didn't know them all that well. But the age differences hadn't been the only reason Irma Rose avoided coming here if she could, and she'd been doing so for the past three years. Ever since Jonas showed up at her house while she was sitting underneath a tree reading a book. He'd struck up a conversation with her after returning a serving bowl to her mother, and not only did her hands get clammy that day but she'd stuttered while talking with him, something she'd never done. And after only a few moments, she'd broken out in a rash on her face. At thirteen, she'd been sure she was allergic to Jonas Miller. She didn't break out in hives around him anymore, but her hands still became sweaty sometimes.

"*Mei mamm* sent some baked goods to help out while your mother is in the hospital." She handed the brown paper bag to Elizabeth. "And she said she would send supper for tomorrow night." She leaned down and said hello to Missy.

"*Ach,* this is so kind. *Danki.*" Elizabeth smiled, but Irma Rose saw the black circles underneath the girl's eyes. It had to be a lot of work taking care of this huge place and three younger sisters. Irma Rose suspected Mae and Annie spent half a day at summer Bible school, like most of the *kinner* that age, so that left Elizabeth home alone with Missy while also taking care of everything else. Even after just a couple of days, the schedule looked to be taking a toll on Elizabeth. And the poor girl must be so worried about her *mamm* too.

"I was just making Missy a sandwich," Elizabeth said as she headed back toward the kitchen. "Can you come in and visit a few minutes?"

Irma Rose followed Elizabeth and Missy across the spacious family room, and just before they rounded the corner to the kitchen, Irma Rose heard someone cough, but it was too late to turn back.

"Please tell your *mudder danki,* but there is no need to send supper tomorrow." Elizabeth smiled as she nodded to the kitchen counter, filled with bowls and casserole dishes. "I'm still trying to fit everything into the refrigerator. But I'm very grateful for all of the kindness everyone in the community has shown our family."

Guilt gnawed at Irma Rose again because of the relief she felt over not having to return tomorrow. She avoided Jonas's eyes as he stood up from the kitchen table. His dark hair was flattened on top of his head, like he'd just taken off his hat, and after a few moments, her eyes drifted to his. "*Wie bischt,* Jonas." She held her head high, determined not to let him get the best of her today. She glanced at her hands, then back at him. "I'm sorry to hear of your *mudder*'s illness."

"*Danki.*" He smiled slightly, the familiar

dark shadow across his jaw. Maybe he just needed a better razor. "Irma Rose . . ." He scratched his head for a moment. "I think it's best that I not go to the singing on Sunday. Will you be seeing Mary? Might you be able to get word to her?"

"*Ya,* I can go by her —"

"*Nee,*" Elizabeth interrupted. "The *Englisch* doctor said *Mamm* is going to be okay." She glanced at Irma Rose. "She has an ulcer in her stomach, a bad one." Elizabeth turned back to Jonas. "But she might even be home before Sunday afternoon. Don't cancel your plans with Mary. I can take care of things here."

Jonas took in a deep breath and blew it out slowly. "I don't know . . ." He looked down at the floor, then back up at his sister. "But if she's not home, I'd be here to help you."

Elizabeth shook her head, frowning. "I can do this, Jonas." She glanced at Missy, who was busy sneaking a cookie from a tin on the counter, then looked back at her brother. "I'm old enough to take care of everything."

Irma Rose wondered if that was true, but she stayed quiet as they waited for Jonas to respond. He finally nodded, and Elizabeth began slathering a slice of bread with peanut

172

spread. She waited for Elizabeth to get out the homemade cheese spread, but instead, she stacked on a bunch of pickles before slapping the other slice of bread on top.

Jonas laughed. "It looks terrible, *ya?*"

Irma Rose pulled her eyes from the sandwich, looked at Jonas for a moment, then glanced down at her hands. She turned to Missy and waited for the little girl to finish praying silently, then flinched when Missy took a big bite.

"Can I make you a sandwich, Irma Rose?" Elizabeth didn't look up as she slathered another piece of bread with more of the peanut spread. Followed by more pickles.

"*Nee. Danki,* though." Irma Rose swallowed hard. Just the thought of eating that sandwich caused her stomach to rumble a warning.

Elizabeth put the other slice of bread on top of the pickles and handed the plate to Jonas. He took a large bite, swallowed, and smiled.

"I said it *looks* awful, but it's *gut.*" He took another hefty bite and winked at Irma Rose. She pulled her eyes away as her heart thumped against her chest.

"I guess I should be getting home. Please let us know if you need anything, and I hope that your *mamm* will continue to be on the mend."

Jonas almost knocked his chair over as he stood up, still chewing the last of his sandwich, which he'd practically inhaled. "I'll walk you out."

"*Nee.* No need." She gave a quick wave to Elizabeth before she hurried out of the kitchen. She'd almost made it to the front door when Jonas edged up beside her and pushed the screen open.

She didn't look back as she made her way across the yard toward her buggy, but she could hear Jonas's big feet tromping through the grass behind her.

"Irma Rose."

She stopped a few feet from her buggy and slowly turned to face him. *"Ya?"*

Jonas scratched his forehead and knitted his eyebrows. "Do you think it's wrong of me to take Mary to the singing? You suggested it, but it wonders me if maybe it ain't right."

Irma Rose didn't want to see Mary get hurt, but the situation was becoming awkward. "And — and why is . . . that?" She tried to avoid his dark eyes peering down at her, but she felt like a piece of metal drawn to a huge magnet. If she ever let herself get too close to him, she might be stuck with

174

him. Forever. And that thought terrified her.

As he inched closer to her, she took a step backward, recalling the moment in his buggy when he admitted he'd almost kissed her. And even more wildly inappropriate, him saying he would marry her someday.

"You're the person I want to date. Not Mary. But if you really don't want anything to do with me, then I'll do my best to get to know Mary better."

She blurted out the first thing that came to mind, and she spoke through a slight chuckle. "So much for marrying me, *ya?*"

Right away, she felt the color drain from her face, but there was no taking it back, so she faked a smile before turning to leave. He was on her heels again, and this time he latched onto her arm before she could get in her buggy.

She shook loose of his hold. "Go with Mary to the singing. Date Mary. She likes you, Jonas. And — and . . ." She searched her mind for a way to tell him that he just wasn't right for her, but there was no kind way to do so. "I'm dating Jake. He's the man I'll marry someday." She folded her arms across her chest.

The only thing she was sure of was her uneasiness when she was near Jonas, and she couldn't live her life feeling like that.

She'd no sooner had the thought when she remembered how safe she'd felt with him during the storm, the gentle way he'd held her, the tenderness in his voice, the feel of his heart beating against her ear. She held her breath and waited to see if he would argue, but instead he was quiet, his expression masked.

He took a long, slow step backward, lifted his hand to his forehead to block the sun, and said, "Okay." He kept his eyes on her as he took a couple more steps, but when he turned around, his pace quickened as he went up the steps and disappeared into the house.

Irma Rose couldn't move for a few moments as she pondered exactly what it was that she wanted from Jonas Miller. She didn't want to be with him, but she wasn't sure she wanted him with anyone else either.

Jonas towel-dried his hair, tossed the towel on the floor, and sat on his bed. He raised the flame on the lantern, then opened his copy of *The Rawhide Kid,* sure his mother would blow her top if she knew he'd snuck the comic book into the house. Especially since it was about a heroic gunfighter from the nineteenth century who was unjustly wanted as an outlaw.

He opened the book and started where he'd left off, but he couldn't concentrate. Something about taking Mary to the singing on Sunday just didn't feel right. He had to assume that Irma Rose was telling the truth, that she intended to marry Jake Ebersol someday. The thought caused him to shiver. But if that were the case, then it would be best for him to get to know Mary better. Jonas had known for a while that Mary fancied him. She was a sweet girl, a pretty *maedel* who was a bit quiet for Jonas's liking.

Tossing the book to the end of the bed, he lay down. The room was stuffy and humid, and he was already sweating again. Summer was *Mamm*'s favorite time of year, and she never seemed bothered by the heat that settled over Lancaster County. Jonas preferred the sharpness of a cold winter. Maybe because it allowed for more time in the house, a fire in the fireplace, and extra family time. It wasn't the same without his father, but he enjoyed the togetherness and reading to the girls more during that time of year.

He closed his eyes, trying to envision himself and Irma Rose with a family of their own. But he was having trouble concentrating on that as well. He was worried sick about his mother, and for the hundredth time, he begged the Lord not to take her. The doctors had said she'd be just fine, but that's what they'd said about his father too.

Chapter Four

Irma Rose walked into the Lapp basement with Jake at her side. About fifteen teenagers were gathered around a table of food in the middle of the room. Once everyone was full, they'd likely break off in small groups at first to chat, then someone would suggest a song. This was the only time they would be able to harmonize since it wasn't allowed during worship service. Irma Rose loved to sing songs that glorified God.

She scanned the room until she saw Isaac. She was glad to see him chatting with several girls on the other side of the room. As she continued to look around, she noticed something in the corner of the room was covered with a sheet. It wasn't hard to tell that it was a radio. One of the large, box types from the 1930s or '40s. No one would speak of it, but plenty of families kept a radio hidden from plain view. Mostly transistor radios these days, but some folks held on to the older models. They'd say it was for listening to President Eisenhower talk about world events, but Irma Rose's mother had said some women she knew admitted to listening to variety shows. Irma Rose's family had never owned a radio.

"I'm going to go talk with Isaac for a minute. Be right back." Jake smiled at Irma Rose before he walked off. She greeted several friends hovering around the food, then reached for a chocolate-chip cookie before she scanned the room. Her eyes landed on Mary. Her friend was alone in the corner of the room, munching on a whoopie pie.

Irma Rose sidled up to Mary. "Where's Jonas?"

"I have no idea." Mary spoke with her mouth full, and before she had even swallowed, she stuffed another chunk of the dessert in her mouth. "He never showed up, so I rode with Jacob and John."

Irma Rose glanced around the room and saw Mary's two brothers standing away from the table of food and talking with two girls whom Irma Rose thought might be a bit too young to be here. "Hmm . . ." Jonas wasn't dependable; she'd add this to her list. "Awfully rude of him."

Mary finally swallowed the last of the pie.

"Maybe it's his *mudder*. She's not well. She's in the hospital."

"*Ya*, I know." Irma Rose felt bad that she'd assumed the worst about Jonas without considering the situation with his mother. "I hope everything is all right."

"Me too."

"He still should have gotten word to you." Irma Rose looked around again until she saw Jake. He winked at her, and after a few minutes, he cozied up beside her. Mary excused herself and said she was going to get another whoopie pie.

"Didn't she just eat one of those?" Jake whispered to Irma Rose as he nodded toward Mary.

"*Ya.* Mary has always liked pies and cakes. But I'm not really one to talk. I have a sweet tooth too."

Jake grimaced. "I'm not much of a sweets eater."

Irma Rose nudged him gently. "*Ach*, I bet you'd eat my shoofly pie. *Mamm* says I make better shoofly pies than *mei mammi* did."

Jake shrugged. "*Nee.* I'd rather have something salty, like a pretzel."

Irma Rose rocked from heel to toe a couple of times, searching her mind for something to talk about. She'd waited a long time for Jake to ask her out, and now

181

that she was sixteen, she'd hoped they would become a couple. Taking a girl to a singing was almost as good as announcing to the world that you were dating. But when Jake didn't offer up any conversation either, her mind became preoccupied with Jonas. *I hope he is okay.* She hoped his mother hadn't taken a turn for the worse.

She pulled a handkerchief from the pocket of her apron and dabbed at the sweat starting to bead on her forehead. "I'll be glad when summer is over and it cools down. And I can't wait until the first snow after that. I love to make snow angels, then curl up in front of a fire and drink hot cocoa."

Jake frowned as he shook his head. "Not me. I'll take summer over winter any day."

Irma Rose had thought she'd feel different standing here with Jake. She tried to talk to him about a book she was reading, but he said he didn't do much reading. He wasn't much of a talker either.

By the end of the evening, her emotions were all over the place. For more than a year she'd waited to be old enough to date. But her first date hadn't been at all what she'd hoped for. Jake was handsome, polite, hardworking, and would make a wonderful husband and father one day. But as he pulled into Irma Rose's driveway at the end of the night, another word came to mind. *Boring.*

Now, as he walked her to her front door, she worried he might try to kiss her, and she wasn't sure how she felt about that anymore.

"*Danki* for taking me to the singing, Jake. I had a really nice time." That wasn't a lie. She'd enjoyed talking with everyone, and Ida Lapp was one of the best cooks in their community, so the food had been wonderful. She looked up at Jake and smiled. In one swift movement, he leaned down and pressed his lips to hers. As only their lips touched, Irma Rose stood frozen. Should she put a hand on his arm? Why wasn't he cupping her cheek or the back of her neck? She'd heard that's how it was done. Her discomfort bordered on painful, and when Jake finally pulled away, Irma Rose reached up and dabbed at her lips.

Jake stood taller, looped his hands beneath his suspenders, and grinned as if he'd just set Irma Rose's world on fire. As if fireworks would burst into the sky at any moment. He winked at her again, but instead of finding it endearing, she fought a frown. She halfway expected him to start beating his chest triumphantly. Waving, he left her standing on the front porch. If that was how kissing was done, she didn't know what all the excitement was about.

Irma Rose walked onto the front porch the following Friday, then bounced down the steps and into the yard. It was a beautiful summer day, and she decided to deliver some freshly baked cookies to the Millers. But she was on a bit more of a mission than she cared to admit to her mother. Yesterday, at the malt shop with Mary and Hannah, Mary said she'd never heard from Jonas and that Sarah Jane Miller was still in the hospital. "No one has laid eyes on Jonas in almost a week," Mary had said.

Irma Rose wondered if members of the community were still taking food to the family, so she'd told her mother she would make a delivery. Mostly, she wanted to find out where Jonas was hiding.

When she pulled into their driveway later that morning, she noticed his buggy sitting alongside two others the family owned. She knocked on the door, and Elizabeth answered.

Irma Rose's jaw dropped when she saw the girl. No *kapp,* and not even a scarf over her head. Her blue dress was a wrinkled mess, and she had a smudge of flour on her chin.

184

"*Wie bischt,* Irma Rose?" Elizabeth brushed several strands of hair from her face. "Would you like to come in?" Her voice was almost a whisper, and Irma Rose hesitated but finally stepped across the threshold. "Please excuse the mess," Elizabeth added and then sighed.

Mess? Irma Rose gulped. This was much more than a mess. It was a disaster, with toys everywhere, a half-eaten sandwich on the coffee table next to a spilled glass of orange juice, and at least two piles of clothes sitting on the couch waiting to be folded.

Elizabeth nodded to the clothes. "Mae and Annie will help me with those when they get home. They're at a friend's house. I could tell they were worried about *Mamm,* and I thought some playtime might distract them from their worries." She picked up the overturned glass and blotted up the spilled juice with a clean towel from the pile.

"I brought you some cookies." Irma Rose eyed the rest of the room. Muddy shoes in the middle of the floor, and it looked like someone had walked across the living room in them.

"*Danki.*" Elizabeth accepted the bag from Irma Rose and rushed to the kitchen. Irma Rose followed her, stepping over two pots in the entrance to the kitchen, with a large metal spoon nearby. Maybe Missy had been playing the drums. Irma Rose couldn't even see the countertops. But instead of an overabundance of food like the last time Irma Rose visited, there were dirty dishes, an opened box of crackers, spilled coffee, and a platter of pastries that were a tad green on the edges.

Irma Rose remembered when her grandmother died. For a while, everyone took meals to her grandfather, but after a time, the visitors stopped coming. Maybe no one realized that Sarah Jane was still in the hospital. Irma Rose wished she'd brought more than just cookies. "Where is Jonas, Elizabeth?"

"Um . . . what?" Elizabeth faced the counter and began gathering dirty dishes and putting them in the sink. Irma Rose walked to her and gently latched onto Elizabeth's arm until the girl turned to face her.

"Where is Jonas?"

Elizabeth's eyes filled with tears. "I-I can't say."

Irma Rose's heart flipped in her chest. "Where is Missy?" She realized she should have asked that as soon as she saw the living room.

"Missy is upstairs napping." Elizabeth sniffled. "Are you going to tell anyone that

186

I've let things get in such a mess?"

Irma Rose began rolling up the sleeves of her blue dress. "*Nee.* I'm going to help you get all this cleaned up."

"*Nee, nee.* I can do it." Elizabeth straightened, still sniffling. "I just got behind on my chores."

Irma Rose scratched her forehead for a moment. "Do you not *know* where Jonas is?"

"Um . . . that's not what I said." Elizabeth turned away from her and picked up two dirty glasses at the far end of the counter.

"You said you can't say. So, what does that mean? That you know where he is and won't tell me? Or you can't say because you don't know?" Irma Rose stared at Elizabeth until Elizabeth looked her in the eye. "Tell me, Elizabeth."

"I told Jonas I wouldn't tell anyone." She covered her face with her hands for a few moments before she wiped her eyes and looked back at Irma Rose. "Please don't ask me again."

Elizabeth was so upset that Irma Rose just nodded. "Can I go check on Missy?"

"It's just as messy up there."

"It's okay." She hurried up the stairs and spied on Missy, who was sleeping soundly. She walked back to the kitchen.

For the next two hours, Irma Rose helped Elizabeth clean and put the house back together, and when they were finally done, Elizabeth made them both a glass of tea and they sat down at the kitchen table.

"Much easier with two people doing it," Irma Rose said as she smiled at Elizabeth.

"*Ya. Danki* so much, Irma Rose. I've been staying up late finishing chores from the day before. I overslept this morning, and everything just piled up on me. But I'm sure I'll be able to keep up now."

Irma Rose sipped her tea. "Do you know when your *mudder* will be home?"

Elizabeth shook her head. "We thought she would be home last weekend, but the doctor said she was bleeding inside her stomach, and now she has some sort of infection too. She would be so upset with me if she knew the *haus* was like this, and that you saw it this way." Her eyes rounded as she shook her head. "I've been going to see her every day; that's another reason I got so behind around here. I never stay long because I worry about the girls being alone, especially Missy. I sometimes bring her with me to the hospital."

Irma Rose chose her words carefully, wondering exactly how sick Sarah Jane was. "Did they give you a time frame, a day she

188

might be coming home?"

"*Nee.* But when I went to see her yesterday, she looked much better and said she was feeling better. I hope she'll be able to come home soon."

Irma Rose couldn't stand it anymore. "Elizabeth, you must tell me where Jonas is. Even if he told you not to. This is too much responsibility for you."

Elizabeth covered her face with her hands again. "I promised I wouldn't."

"Jonas would want you to tell me if he knew that you were having such a hard time. When is the last time you talked to him?"

Elizabeth uncovered her face, sniffled, and swiped at her eyes. "When he called me last Friday."

"Was he okay?"

Elizabeth nodded. "*Ya.* I think so."

"Where was he?" She waited, her heart thumping in her chest. "Where was he, Elizabeth?"

Elizabeth's eyes filled with tears again. "Jail."

CHAPTER FIVE

"You have a visitor," the young jailer said as he put a key in the lock, then opened the door. Jonas stood up from the soiled mattress in the corner of his cell where he'd been sitting.

They exited the cell, Jonas getting in step beside the man.

"Personally, I don't think it's right for an Amish girl to be in a place like this, but I reckon it's your business." The guard, dressed in all black, didn't look much older than Jonas.

Elizabeth was the only person who knew he was here, and Jonas didn't want her in a place like this either. He glanced down at his orange slacks and shirt, thankful the jailer hadn't put handcuffs on him. They'd let him keep his black loafers, but they'd taken his straw hat. "I'll tell my sister this isn't a *gut* place for her to visit," he finally said as they rounded the corner toward the front of the building.

"The normal place for visits is down the hall, but there's a plumbing problem down there, and we got repairmen working on it." They walked around another corner. "I seriously doubt that your sister is going to try to slip you a nail file in the box of whoopie pies she brought." He turned to Jonas and grinned. "Which are mighty good, by the way."

"Elizabeth is a *gut* cook."

The guard stopped and faced Jonas, narrowing his eyebrows. "Elizabeth? This woman said her name was Irma Rose." He scratched his head. "Maybe she is here to break you out after all, if she's giving a fake name." The man chuckled.

Jonas's heart thumped against his chest as he looked down at what he was wearing again before looking at the guard. "I don't want to see Irma Rose. She's a friend, but I don't want her to see me like this."

The guard laughed again. "Friend, I'm not sure what you're wearing is any worse than the getup you wore when you came in, but suit yourself." The guard spun around and took two steps, but Jonas didn't follow. This might be the only time he'd get to hear how his mother was. Irma Rose might have information. And as much as he didn't want

Irma Rose here, it was probably better than Elizabeth, if for no other reason than Irma Rose was older than his sister.

"*Nee.* I need to speak with Irma Rose."

The guard shrugged as he walked back to Jonas, and they took a few more steps to a door on the right. The man let Jonas walk in first. There was a table and two chairs in the middle of the room, and that was all. Except for a box of whoopie pies and Irma Rose.

"This is normally where we interrogate people, but it'll do for now. You've got ten minutes, and we can see you through that two-way mirror over there."

Jonas didn't look away from Irma Rose as the guard spoke. Her eyes were teary and she stood up as he walked closer. He wanted to run into her arms. He wanted to cry.

"Is my mother okay?" He folded his arms across his stomach, feeling like he might throw up.

"*Ya, ya.* She's much better. She doesn't know you're in jail. Elizabeth didn't want to worry her." Irma Rose blinked her eyes a few times. "Are you okay?"

Jonas nodded, fighting the urge to run around the table and into her arms. "*Ya,* I'm okay. But why . . . ? How — how did you know I was here?" He looked down, then back up at her. "I'm sorry for you to see me like this." He motioned for her to sit down, and he did the same.

Irma Rose had planned what she was going to say during the ride to the jail. Her hired driver had wanted to chat and seemed particularly curious why an Amish girl would ask to be taken to the county jail. Irma Rose had answered politely, but she'd also stayed busy trying to script her conversation. And now, with Jonas sitting in front of her, she couldn't recall any of her thoughts, so she asked the question heaviest on her heart.

"What did you do?" She brought a hand to her chest, drew in a breath, and held it.

Jonas hung his head for a few moments before he looked back at her. "Are Elizabeth and the girls all right?"

Irma Rose nodded.

Jonas slouched into his chair and leaned back, sighing. "I'd rather not say."

Irma Rose let out the breath she was holding and dropped her hands to her lap. She sat taller and spoke to him in the firmest voice she could muster. "Jonas Miller, you listen to me . . ." She started to tell him about the disarray at his house and how much trouble Elizabeth was having, but

193

then she thought about Sarah Jane in the hospital, and the expression on Jonas's face was one of genuine pain. There was no half smile, and his dark eyes were moist. The whiskers on his face were more than just a dark shadow, almost a beard.

"I asked for a razor, but no one brought one," he said, as if reading her mind.

Irma Rose leaned forward in her chair, frowning. "What did you *do*?" She'd only known one Amish person who'd gone to jail, and it had been a case of mistaken identity. "Do they think you are someone else?" Hope filled her at the thought, until Jonas shook his head. "Then what?" She raised her shoulders, left them there, then let them fall when Jonas looked away.

Jonas scratched his scruffy chin, squinting. "If I tell you, you gotta promise not to get mad."

"I won't get angry," she said quickly, hoping it was a promise she'd be able to keep.

"Well . . ." He cringed. "There's this guy named Lucas. He's *Englisch*." Jonas paused and locked eyes with Irma Rose, as if waiting for a reaction. Irma Rose knew *Englisch* people, so this didn't seem odd. "He's a fine Christian. A *gut* man. He's about my age, maybe a year older, maybe twenty or so."

Irma Rose let out an exaggerated sigh.

"And . . ."

"And he's got this car, a Chevy 210 Delrey." He paused, the familiar half grin returning. "And it's real fast, Irma Rose. He special ordered it; it's a powerful machine. I've watched him race it before at a little place on the outskirts of Paradise." His smile grew. "And he was going to race it against Andy Smith. I don't expect you to know him. Smith is a common name, but anyway . . . Andy has a Pontiac Bonneville, and it's fast, too, and . . ."

"Jonas!" Irma Rose slammed a palm on the table. "Did you hear that man say we only have ten minutes?"

Jonas lost his animated expression right away. "Lucas was racing Andy, and Andy asked me if I wanted to ride along. And I did. The police came. I didn't know there was beer in the back of Lucas's car. I got arrested because I'm underage and drag racing. And here I am." He shrugged before a big smile filled his face. "Remember, you said you wouldn't be mad."

Irma Rose slowly lifted herself out of the chair and raised her chin, choosing her words carefully. "I'm not mad, Jonas. I am disappointed in you. Your mother is in the hospital. You've left poor Elizabeth by herself tending to the house and your

195

younger sisters. All because of your silliness with things that go fast. You are irresponsible. Couldn't you have just paid a fine?"

"The fine is over a hundred dollars. I can't get that kind of money, and I didn't want to worry *Mamm* while she's in the hospital. They told me I could go to jail for two weeks instead. So that's what I decided to do. I know *Mamm* will find out when she gets home and I'm not there, but I didn't want this news to hinder her recovery. I figured she'd be home by now. And I talked to Elizabeth about it. She said she'd have no problem handling everything." He paused, searching her eyes for approval, but Irma Rose just looked away, knowing she had to tell him the truth. "The other guys chose to pay the fine," he added.

"Elizabeth is having a very hard time. The children are all fine, but it's a lot of work. She's very tired. And the house . . ." She chewed on her bottom lip, not sure how much more to say. It wouldn't change the situation. "I will help Elizabeth until you are freed. Annie and Mae are still going to Bible school at the Stoltzfuses' *haus* in the mornings."

"I will make this up to you, Irma Rose. I don't know how, but I will. Tell Elizabeth I'm so sorry."

She rolled her eyes as Jonas stood up. "I have to go." She turned toward the glass window, wondering if people were listening to their conversation or just watching them. She turned back to Jonas. "We are not going to tell anyone about this." She hurried to the door, leaving the box of whoopie pies on the table.

"Irma Rose?"

She waited while Jonas walked toward her. He stopped in front of her, and she dabbed her forehead with a sweaty hand, despite the coolness in the room. "What?"

"Everything that happens is God's will, part of His plan."

Irma Rose grunted. "Jonas, I can't think of one reason why the Lord would have you leave your family in a time of need because you did something stupid. God also gives us free will to make *gut* choices."

Jonas nodded toward the table. "*Danki* for the whoopie pies. The food isn't *gut* here."

"At least you have air conditioning." Irma Rose lifted an eyebrow before she moved toward the door. She knocked just as someone was pulling the door open.

"I told the kid to just pay the fine," the young man dressed in the black uniform said. "Seems weird to be holding one of your kind in the county jail."

Irma Rose lifted her chin and brushed past him, wondering how she was going to keep this secret without telling a lie. And when did it become her responsibility to clean up Jonas Miller's messes? But that's what she was going to do. By the time she returned to the Miller farm later that day, she had come up with a plan.

Elizabeth and Missy greeted her at the door, and even though there was a hint of lemon cleaner in the air, a pungent smell hit Irma Rose as she stepped over the threshold. "Elizabeth . . ." Irma Rose sniffed the air. "What is that smell?"

Missy ran to a pile of faceless dolls in the corner. She had them all sitting in a circle. Next to the dolls was a replica of a Captain Kangaroo Tasket Basket, a box filled with different-shaped blocks that fit into the shaped holes. Irma Rose had seen the toy in an *Englisch* store display. Although this model didn't have the words *Captain Kangaroo* etched into the side of the box. She wondered if Jonas had made it for Missy.

But before she could mention it, Elizabeth motioned for Irma Rose to follow her to the kitchen. "Missy, we'll be in the kitchen. You stay in here with your dolls."

"Missy had an accident," Elizabeth whispered. "That's never happened until this past week. It's happened four times since Jonas has been gone. I just cleaned her up. I didn't realize the smell was lingering." She walked to the open window in the kitchen and raised it even higher. "Sorry."

Irma Rose leaned against the kitchen counter. "I'm sure Missy is wondering about Jonas and also worrying about your mother."

"I've been taking Missy to the hospital when Mae and Annie are at Bible class. I thought it would help her to see *Mamm*, but sometimes they are drawing blood while we're there, or *Mamm* looks like she might be having some pain. On those days, Missy seems scared. I was trying not to disrupt Annie and Mae's schedule any more than I had to, but I guess I need one of them to stay home with Missy while I visit *Mamm*."

Irma Rose tapped a finger to her chin. "Okay. Here's what we will do. I will come over at eight o'clock each morning. I can tidy things up and do some baking while you go visit your mother. Unless it upsets Missy even more not to go to the hospital, she can stay here with me while you're gone."

Elizabeth gave her a blank stare. "Why are you doing this?"

Irma Rose was surprised that no one in

their community had offered to help Elizabeth, but then, folks didn't know that Jonas was away. "Because I want to help your family."

"But you . . ." Elizabeth paused, biting her lip. "You don't really know us all that *gut.* I mean, we've grown up in the same place, but we haven't been around each other very much."

Irma Rose had been asking herself the same question. "You need help, and since I'm an only child, it doesn't take nearly as much work to run our household. *Mamm* will be fine if I'm gone part of each day."

"That's nice of you." Elizabeth smiled. "Jonas was right."

Irma Rose suddenly felt warm all over as she raised an eyebrow and tried to appear casual. "About what?"

"He said that you are loving and kind, that you are *gut* with children, and that you go out of your way to help others."

Irma Rose felt her face reddening as she shook her head. "*Ach,* I don't know how he knows all that."

"But he does!" Elizabeth stood taller, smiling. "Anytime he talks about you to others, he tells stories. One is about the time you went to Widow Zook's *haus* every Monday for six months to do her laundry." Elizabeth chuckled. "And we all know Widow Zook is a bit cranky." She lifted a finger. "*Ach,* and he also tells people about the baby bunnies you found, how you hand-fed each of them with a bottle. And . . ."

Irma Rose was hearing part of Elizabeth's recollections, but mostly she was thinking about Jonas. How irresponsible and reckless he could be, how he always smelled of cigars — how he just wasn't right for her. Maybe she needed to give Jake another chance, though she really didn't want to. Or maybe Isaac? She focused on Elizabeth again when she heard her name.

"*Danki* again, Irma Rose."

"You're welcome. But there is one more thing." She paused. "We don't want to lie, but we don't want people around here to know about Jonas going to jail. We need to say something that is truthful, but also keeps his whereabouts a secret."

"What about 'Jonas is away on business'? I heard an *Englisch* man say that once." Elizabeth smiled from ear to ear. It was the first time Irma Rose noticed how much Elizabeth looked like her brother.

"Then that's what we will say. 'Jonas is away on business.' "

Irma Rose wasn't sure that was the best solution, especially since Jonas's "business"

201

was farming, but she couldn't come up with anything better.

CHAPTER SIX

Irma Rose's mother put a loaf of cinnamon-raisin bread in the bag that Irma Rose was taking to Elizabeth the following morning.

"It's nice what you are doing for the Millers, going there to babysit Missy and help tend to the house. I suspected it might be too large a job for Elizabeth and those younger girls. Is Jonas helping out inside while his mother is away?"

Irma Rose swallowed hard, putting the plan to the test. A plan that now seemed ridiculous. "Jonas is away on business."

Mamm scratched her forehead. "What kind of *business* would take him away?" She stuffed her hands in the pockets of her apron, frowning. "The Millers make a living working the land."

Irma Rose stared at her mother, determined not to lie. She snapped her finger. "Oops. I forgot something upstairs." She left the room and darted up the stairs, hoping that by the time she returned, her mother would have forgotten the question. *This is going to get tiresome.* She grabbed her small black pocketbook, thankful she really had forgotten something. She wasn't going to let Jonas's shenanigans shove her into a pit of lies.

"So, what kind of business?" *Mamm* asked the moment Irma Rose walked back into the kitchen.

"Just business. Bye!" She grabbed the bag, kissed her mother on the cheek, and didn't look back as the screen door closed behind her.

Jonas stared at the pale yellow blob on the plate in front of him. He'd never missed his mother's cooking more than right now. He pushed the food around with a plastic fork, afraid to taste it, but too hungry not to give it a try. It resembled eggs but didn't look like any he'd ever seen. Up until now, his breakfasts in the jailhouse had consisted of either half-frozen waffles or a bowl of mushy cereal. His mother made the best dippy eggs cooked over easy, but these were over-cooked, bland, and tasted old. Jonas loved the eggs they had at home with dark-yellow yolks fresh from their hens.

He forced himself to swallow, then eyed

the only other offering on his plate, a piece of toast that was burnt, no jam or butter. He wished he hadn't forgotten to grab the box of whoopie pies Irma Rose brought yesterday. The guard confessed that he and two other men ate them. After a few more bites, he set the plate on the floor beside one of the cots in his cell. He picked up the Bible he'd asked for when he first arrived, and he gave the next hour to God. He was closing the Good Book when he heard a commotion down the hall. Lots of screaming and carrying on. He stood up when the same guard, whom he now knew as Peter, stopped at Jonas's cell, toting a young man in handcuffs.

"Jonas Miller, meet Theodore Von Minden the third, your new roommate." Peter unlocked the cell and the man's cuffs, then gave him a gentle push before locking them both in. Jonas closed his Bible, stood up, and waited for the man to stop screaming and cursing at the guard. Finally, Theodore turned to face Jonas. He threw his hands up in the air.

"You have got to be kidding me!" He spun around, grabbed the metal rails, and shook them. "Hey! I can tell by this guy's stupid haircut that he's Amish. You can't leave me in here with this religious freak!"

Peter strolled back up to the cell, grinning. "Oh, I can, and I am. Now quit all the yelling and screaming. There's a price to pay for that, so shut your mouth. Even your rich daddy can't help you now."

Jonas didn't move. Theodore yelled a string of curse words as Peter walked away. After he appeared to have exhausted himself, he hung his head, then seemed to remember that Jonas was in the cell with him.

"What are you looking at?"

Swallowing hard, Jonas had a better understanding of why his people tried to stay away from the *Englisch*. Jonas had heard curse words before, but never so many of them strung together at one time. He shrugged, towering over Theodore. "Just wondering if anyone tended to your wound." Jonas pointed to a trail of blood running down the side of Theodore's face from his eyebrow. His blond hair was cut short, parted to the side, and shone with a mixture of hair gel and dried blood. He was short and skinny and wore the same kind of orange slacks and pants as Jonas. Except Theodore was wearing a pair of fancy tan loafers.

Theodore reached up and touched his head, cringing and cursing again. Then he walked over to the only other cot in the room and sat down. "Do me a favor, will you?"

Jonas nodded. "*Ya.* How can I help?"

Theodore pulled a handkerchief out of his pocket and pressed it against his head. "Do me a *favor,*" he repeated in a strained voice. "Just don't talk to me."

Jonas sat down on his cot, picked up his Bible, and started reading, seriously wishing he'd had enough money to pay his fine. He wasn't sleeping. The food was terrible. And using the toilet in the corner was humiliating. Now he'd have to share this space with an irritable young *Englisch* man. He buried his head in the Book, but he could feel Theodore's eyes blazing a hole through him.

"It amazes me how you people buy into that bunch of bull."

Jonas didn't look up until Theodore sprang from the bed and knocked the Bible from Jonas's hands, causing it to fly across the cell. Jonas stood up and clenched his fists at his sides, fighting the urge to smack the guy. It wasn't their way, but . . . *Give me strength, Lord.* He calmly went and picked up the Bible, returned to the cot, and flipped the pages to find where he'd left off, this time keeping a tighter grip on the book. Theodore stood in front of him, and Jonas braced himself. When Theodore's arm swept down in front of him again, this time Jonas latched onto his wrist.

"Don't do that." Jonas let his eyes slowly drift upward until they were locked with his new cell mate's.

"Or what? You gonna hit me?" Theodore grinned. "Your people don't do that. I grew up in Pennsylvania. There isn't much I don't know about your kind." He wiggled loose of Jonas's hold. "So, what are you going to do?"

Jonas's blood was boiling as he stood up, and once again he asked the Lord for strength. "You might have grown up here, but you don't know everything about our *kind*. And you don't know *me*." Jonas said it with just enough intent to hopefully confuse the guy, and he breathed a sigh of relief when Theodore went back to his cot and sat down. *Like dogs marking our territories,* Jonas thought briefly. He set the Bible on the floor, then lay down, not completely sure that Theodore wouldn't start pushing him for a fight again. Jonas had only been in a fight one time, and it had been with another Amish boy when they were both about ten years old. Amos King wouldn't stop pulling Mary's hair that day, and eventually Jonas had shoved him, which led to a full-blown fight on the playground. Jonas was pretty sure that's when Mary developed a crush on him. It had won Jonas a trip to the woodshed when he got home. He'd endure a hundred trips to the woodshed for spanking just to have his father back. He sighed, knowing *Daed* would be disappointed in him for being here. Like Irma Rose.

A few minutes later Theodore spoke again. "So, what are you in for? It's not every day you see an Amish man in jail."

Jonas opened his eyes. "Drag racing and alcohol in the car."

Theodore burst out laughing. "Well, ain't that something."

Jonas closed his eyes again but finally asked, "What about you?"

"I robbed an old lady and stole her purse. She beat me over the head with her cane, thus the blood."

Jonas sat up and stared at Theodore, wondering how he was going to keep from hitting this guy. It must have shown on his face.

"Relax, fellow . . ." Theodore held up a palm toward Jonas. "I'm just joking." He shook his head, frowning. "Man, I have some issues, but I would never rob anyone, especially an old woman." He grunted. "Yet you believed me." He pointed a finger at Jonas. "And you know why? Because that's the way we are. Humans believe the worst about each other. People at their core are untrusting, selfish, and mean. Even if we really aren't like that, people will just assume it. So you're doomed from the start." He pressed the rag to his head again, scowling.

"I believed you because you said it was so." Jonas wasn't sure what to say as he recalled Jesus saying that the truth will set us free.

Theodore grinned but shook his head.

Jonas wasn't sure the truth was going to set this guy free, but he owed it to Theodore — and God — to try to educate Theodore. "But the fruit of the Spirit is love, joy, peace, patience, kindness, goodness, faithfulness, gentleness, and self-control. Scripture doesn't say anything about people being born untrusting, selfish, and mean."

For a few long moments, Theo just stared at him. Finally he spoke. "I know all that. I didn't say we were *born* that way. But if people drill it into our heads enough over the years, I guess it just becomes true." Theodore tossed the bloody handkerchief on the floor near his bed. "I hope my father rots in hell."

Jonas was quiet for a few moments. It wasn't his place to minister to this man, so he went back to his original question. "What did you do to get in here? Were you in a fight?"

Theodore chuckled, then flinched and reached for the bloody rag nearby on the floor, placing it to his eyebrow again. "I guess you could say that. My pop was beating the snot out of me, and it's taken me seventeen years to fight back, but today I finally did." He shrugged. "And here I am."

Jonas ran his hand the length of what was becoming a beard. "That doesn't seem fair, that you're in jail for defending yourself against an abusive father."

"Bingo, Jonas Miller! You're the grand-prize winner today!" Theodore clapped his hands hard and loud. "You just hit the nail on the head. Life isn't *fair*! But when your father is Theodore Von Minden the second, the wealthiest and most powerful man in the state of Pennsylvania . . . well, let's just say you don't punch him in the face, no matter the circumstances. It can get you an assault-and-battery charge."

Wonderful memories flooded Jonas's mind, recollections of his father. He never would have struck Jonas in anger, and Jonas credited his father — and God — for helping to mold him into the man he was, or at least the man he hoped to be when he stopped doing dumb stuff. "I'm sorry for your troubles," he finally said.

"It's the hand I've been dealt." Theodore pulled back the rag, looked at it, then put it back against his head. "And this time, it was the hand with his college ring that met with my head."

Jonas was quiet.

"Your pop ever hit you?" Theodore locked eyes with Jonas.

"*Nee.* I mean no. Not like that. We got spankings, but . . ."

"Yeah, yeah. I know all about the perfect life of an Amish person."

Jonas thought for a moment. "I'm not so perfect since I'm in here."

Theodore laughed. "True. I guess even the Amish love a good race and having a few beers."

Jonas had never had a sip of alcohol in his life, but he let it go.

"So, how long you in for?" Theodore kicked off his loafers and tucked his legs underneath him on the small cot.

"Two weeks. I've already been here a week. What about you?"

He stretched his legs out and rested his socked feet on his shoes, grinning. "I'm here

212

as long as my father thinks I need to be here. He'll convince the district attorney to drop the charges when he's good and ready. But I'll tell you this . . . the moment I'm out of here, I'm getting my hands on whatever money I can, and I'm leaving this godforsaken place. I hope my disappearance at least embarrasses him. He won't care if I'm gone, but he'll want to keep up appearances."

"Where will you go?" Jonas could understand Theodore wanting to run away from his father, but he suspected the guy was running from more than just that. "What about your mother?"

"I have no idea where I'll go. My mother's dead. Anything good left in me, I got from her."

"My father died three years ago. But my Father in heaven is always with me."

"See, that's the thing about you religious types. At the end of the day, it's always about God. He's responsible for everything." He pointed to his head. "Which means He is responsible for my father hitting me hard enough for me to see stars."

"Theodore, that's not how it works. Our Lord wants us to be healthy and happy, and He gives us free will to —"

"Stop." Theodore held up a palm again.

"First of all, only my father calls me Theodore. My friends call me Theo. That's what my mother called me, too, and even though I highly doubt you and I will be friends, for the sake of our time stuck in here together, I'd appreciate you just calling me Theo." He paused, took a deep breath, and blew it out slowly. "And as for your rubbish about God and free will, do you really think that it was by choice that I was born into the life that was forced on me? No, sir. Not my choice. And if your God wanted me to be happy and healthy, He should have stepped up to the plate long before now."

Jonas sat quietly. *Not my job to minister to this man.*

Theo made a noise similar to a growl. "I'd do just about anything for a smoke."

"Me too."

Theo laughed. "Oh, stop the presses. Since when did the Amish start smoking?"

Jonas grinned. "I don't smoke. I just like to puff on a cigar every once in a while. I don't inhale. I like the way it smells and tastes though."

"Well, my good man, I must inform you. That is *still* a form of smoking."

They both turned their attention to the bars of the cell when they heard someone approaching.

214

"Well, I'm glad to see you two haven't killed each other," Peter said as he pulled keys from his pocket. "Jonas, your girlfriend is here again today."

"She's not my girlfriend." Jonas smiled. "Yet."

"Well, if she keeps bringing food every day, I'll be rooting for her to win the role. She always offers us some. Which, by the way, sorry we finished off your whoopie pies, but you left them in the interrogation room. Today she brought a shoofly pie. Not very original, but I've always been a fan of that Amish staple." He motioned with his hand for Jonas to step out of the cell, then he locked it behind him and led Jonas in the same direction as the day before. As much as Jonas wanted to see Irma Rose, he hated that it was under these circumstances, and he felt his stomach churn, hoping she wasn't bringing him bad news about his mother. Maybe *Mamm* was home from the hospital by now.

As he walked quietly alongside Peter, he fought the shame that was threatening to engulf him, promising God that he was going to work harder at being a better man.

CHAPTER SEVEN

Irma Rose sliced the pie with the pocket-knife the nice guard named Peter had given her. *They are very trusting in the jailhouse,* she thought as she handed the guard a slice, the same man as yesterday. In her mind, if she were extra sweet to the people who worked here, they would be nicer to Jonas. She owed that to Jonas's mother. Sarah Jane was still in the hospital, and she would want someone tending to her son. But when Jonas walked into the room, she admitted to herself that coming here wasn't just about doing the right thing for Sarah Jane Miller.

"I don't know if you should be coming here, Irma Rose," Jonas said after Peter left with his slice of pie. "Is my mother all right?"

"*Ya.* Elizabeth went to see her this morning, and I stayed with Missy and did a few things around the house while Mae and Annie went to Bible school."

Jonas put his hands flat on the table and hung his head. "I should have found a way to pay the fine. I thought *Mamm* would be home way before now." He looked up at Irma Rose. "I don't like you coming here," he repeated. "I love you for doing all this, but this is not a *gut* place for you."

Love? It should have rattled her, but instead, she was pretty sure she heard angels singing somewhere in the heavens. Whatever this infatuation was for Jonas, she needed to move past it. She'd thought that if she forced herself to be around him, maybe the clammy hands and pounding heart would go away. Now she was hearing choirs of angels.

"These are all things you should have thought about." She smirked as she handed him a plate with pie on it. He set it back down on the table.

"I told you, I will make it up to you somehow."

"I won't be by tomorrow unless there is news about your mother. Even though it's Sunday, I'll visit Elizabeth tomorrow morning to make sure everything is okay. There's no church service so I'll offer to stay with Missy so Elizabeth can take Mae and Annie to visit your mother. But I have a lunch date after that."

"Date?" He folded his arms across his chest.

"*Ya.* With Jake. It's our second date. We went to the singing, remember? The one you were supposed to take Mary to." No need to tell Jonas how the first date with Jake had gone.

"How was the date?" He looked her in the eye. "Please tell me Jake didn't kiss you."

You had to ask, didn't you? "That's none of your business."

"Ugh." Jonas lowered his head and gently hit his palm on the table. "That means he did."

Irma Rose avoided his eyes as she recovered the shoofly pie with plastic wrap. "This is mostly for the guards. So they'll be nice to you."

"You're bribing the jailers, kissing Jake Ebersol, and . . . what else are you up to, Irma Rose?" The hint of a smile played across his face, but the mischievous sparkle in his eyes made Irma Rose go weak in the knees for a moment, and all she could focus on was Jonas's mouth as she wondered if kissing him would be more enjoyable than Jake's kiss had been.

"I'm going to lunch with Jake," she said in a snappy tone, as if to convince herself it was the right thing to do. Just because their

218

first kiss hadn't been everything she'd expected, maybe the second one would be better. But as she wound around the table, Jonas stepped in front of her and leaned down.

"I almost kissed you once in the buggy."

"If you try to kiss me in here, they're going to keep you locked up and throw away the key." She hurried toward the door and knocked hard until the guard came and let her out. She didn't look back as she hurried to where her driver was parked, with a quivering lower lip, clammy hands, and a swirling in her stomach that she loved and hated.

Despite his circumstances, Jonas had a bounce in his step as he walked with Peter back to his cell. He wasn't happy that Irma Rose would be having lunch with Jake, but he'd seen a playful fire in her eyes today, and he knew she wasn't just coming here to bring sweets and give him updates about things at home. At least he hoped he'd read her expression correctly. He needed that hopefulness to get through the next few days. Especially now that he had such a cranky cell mate. This time, he'd remembered to grab what was left of his pie.

"She seems like a sweet girl," Peter said as

he unlocked the cell and let Jonas back in. Jonas nodded, then tiptoed to his side of the small room and sat on the cot, thankful that Theo was curled up on his cot, facing the wall. Surely the noise from the gate would have prevented Theo from sleeping, but Jonas was just glad that he was quiet. He felt badly for Theo, for the life he'd lived, and he made a mental note to pray for his cell mate.

"How was your conjugal visit?" Theo rolled over and faced Jonas.

"My *what*?"

"Never mind. How was your visit with your girlfriend?" Theo sat up and rubbed his eyes.

"I already said, she's not my girlfriend. But I hope she will be one day. I hope she's my wife someday."

"Wow. You've got everything all planned out."

Jonas shrugged. "*Nee,* not everything. But I know I want Irma Rose in my life." He paused, nodding at the covered pie dish he'd set on the bed beside him. "There's three slices of shoofly pie left if you want a piece."

"Not a fan of molasses, but thanks." Theo scratched his cheek. "Is Irma Rose a common name among your people?"

"*Nee.* Not really. There are a few women named Irma, and even more named Rose or Rosie, but there's only one Irma Rose that I know of." He smiled. *My Irma Rose.*

"Hmm . . ." Theo continued to stare at Jonas. "I once knew a girl named Irma Rose. It was before we moved to Lancaster. I met her when we lived in Hershey, around three years ago. Maybe a little longer. She was a year or two younger than me, but wise beyond her years." He paused as he leaned against the cement wall that his cot was pushed against. "I was fourteen at the time, but I'll never forget her."

Theo seemed to drift away for a few minutes, just staring into space. Jonas was glad they were having a normal conversation without yelling and cursing.

"The first time I ever saw Irma Rose was when she was sitting under a tree at her house," Jonas said, recalling his own memories. "She was reading a book, and I was running an errand for my mother, returning a casserole dish. I knew Irma Rose was too young for me at the time, but I waited three years for her. I never dated anyone else. I watched her grow from a pretty girl into a beautiful young woman. And not just on the outside."

"She must be pretty special to come visit

you in a place like this. Especially since she's Amish. Most Amish girls I've known wouldn't be caught dead here." Theo chuckled. "Maybe she just comes for the air conditioning since you backward people don't have that luxury."

"How is it that you are so familiar with the Amish?"

"I told you. I've lived in Pennsylvania my whole life. You people are everywhere." Theo grinned. "Before my father reached the level of success he has now, he and my mother ran several small inns in Hershey. We had a few Amish gals who came and cleaned the rooms. After my mother died, Pop sold his businesses and we moved to the city of Lancaster. He built hotels, ultimately making him worth more than most people could spend in a lifetime." He paused, slapping his hands to his knees. "But I'm here to tell you, money isn't worth the paper it's printed on if it can't buy you happiness, and I assure you . . . happiness costs more than I've got. But it'll be enough to get me out of Lancaster County."

Jonas scratched his scruffy chin again as his pulse picked up. "This might sound far-fetched, but . . ." Jonas waited for Theo to look at him before he went on. "Irma Rose lived in Hershey before she moved to Paradise, which is where I live. She was twelve or thirteen when they came to Lancaster County."

Theo sat taller as his jaw dropped. "Your Irma Rose is *my* Irma Rose?"

Your Irma Rose? Jonas frowned. "I don't know about that. Maybe it's just a co-incidence."

"Wow." Theo spoke so softly that Jonas barely heard him. "Wouldn't that be something. I didn't think I'd ever see that girl again, but even at fourteen, I knew I'd never forget her." He smiled, and Jonas thought Theo's eyes looked a little misty. "I never knew her last name."

Jonas shook his head. "I doubt it's the same girl, but Irma Rose's last name is Kauffman."

"Only one way to find out."

Jonas raised an eyebrow and waited.

"Ask her if she remembers Theo from Hershey. If she does . . . that's her."

Jonas was having a hard time picturing Irma Rose with the likes of Theo, even as friends, but he nodded. "I will."

The next day, Irma Rose stayed with Missy while Elizabeth took Annie and Mae with her to the hospital. A couple of hours later, Irma Rose was sweeping the living room floor when she heard a car coming up the driveway. She stowed the broom and looked out the window, glad Elizabeth was returning in plenty of time for Irma Rose to meet Jake for lunch. But she was surprised when Sarah Jane stepped out of the backseat of the car at the same time all three girls did.

"Your *mamm* is home!" Irma Rose scooped up Missy from the couch. "Let's go greet her."

Irma Rose pushed the screen door open with her foot, and once on the porch, she set Missy down. The little girl took off barefoot toward her mother, only to be stopped by Elizabeth.

"Easy does it, Missy," Elizabeth said as she kept her hand in between Missy and their mother. "*Mamm* is sore."

Irma Rose listened and watched from the porch, waving to all of them. Elizabeth paid the driver as Sarah Jane spoke softly to Missy while rubbing her head.

"What a wonderful surprise," Irma Rose said as Elizabeth and Annie helped Sarah Jane up the porch steps while Mae lagged behind carrying a small red suitcase. Missy clung to her mother's dress. "How are you feeling?"

"*Wie bischt,* Irma Rose?" Sarah Jane took each step slowly. "I'm doing *gut.*"

Irma Rose held the screen door as they all crossed over the threshold. Elizabeth hung behind, whispering to Irma Rose before she went inside. "I told her Jonas was away on business, but she wanted to know where he was, and eventually I had to tell her where he was. But I whispered it so Annie and Mae wouldn't hear."

Elizabeth walked inside and Irma Rose followed her. Sarah Jane sat down on the couch, Missy beside her. "Annie and Mae, take Missy upstairs with you. I need to talk to Elizabeth and Irma Rose alone. In a little while, I want to hear all about your Bible learning and anything I've missed while I was away, *ya*?"

Sarah Jane waited until the girls were upstairs before she spoke. "Irma Rose, Elizabeth tells me how much you have helped her and the girls the past couple of days, and I'm so appreciative." She paused, frowning. "She also told me that Jonas is in jail." She reached into her purse and pulled out a wad of money. "I can't stand to think of him in such a place, and I stopped at the bank on the way home." She looked up at Irma Rose. "I'm so sorry to ask this, but can you go get my *sohn* out of jail? I'm just not up to the task, and I'd rather as few people as possible know his circumstances.

225

It's an awful thing to ask you to do, but Elizabeth said you've been to see him a couple of times." She raised her shoulders and dropped them slowly. "I can ask someone else if you'd like."

"*Nee.* Of course I'll do it." Irma Rose took the money.

"We are all in your debt. Elizabeth said she didn't know what she would have done without your help."

Irma Rose felt herself blushing. "It was no problem for me." She wondered how she would get word to Jake that she wasn't going to be able to go to lunch with him. And how was she going to get out of lunch without lying? She didn't want Jake to know she'd been visiting Jonas at the jailhouse.

Jonas grinned as Theo eyed his breakfast. "It won't kill you," Jonas said as he shoveled a nasty forkful of eggs into his mouth.

Theo continued to stare at the plate, then finally looked up at Jonas. "You got any of that shoofly pie left?"

Jonas nodded to the pie plate on the floor by his bed. "One piece. But I thought you didn't like molasses."

"I'll take it over this mess." Theo tossed the plate in a nearby trash can and picked up the pie plate. After peeling back the

226

plastic wrap, he picked up the last slice and took a giant bite. When he was all done, he surprised Jonas by thanking him.

"You're welcome." Jonas bit into his toast, not quite as burnt as the day before. From the moment he'd woken up this morning, all he could think about was Irma Rose going on a lunch date with Jake today.

After breakfast, Jonas was glad that Theo fell back asleep for a while. Although, in the silence, he couldn't shake loose the vision of Jake and Irma Rose together. Maybe Irma Rose deserved someone like Jake, a man who was well respected in the community. A man who hadn't gone to jail. He bowed his head in prayer, vowing to stay away from fast cars and other *Englisch* hobbies that might get him in trouble again. Jonas accepted that this life lesson was part of the Lord's plan for him, but he didn't see how any good could come out of this experience.

He looked up when he heard footsteps. It was Peter. He unlocked the cell, smiled, and said, "Jonas Miller, you just got sprung."

CHAPTER EIGHT

Irma Rose was hoping to quell the butterflies dancing in her tummy as she and Jonas rode home from the jailhouse. Sarah Jane had insisted on paying for a driver there and back. Jonas was as quiet as Irma Rose had ever seen, but he could also barely keep his eyes open, nodding in and out. Finally, he laid his head back against the seat and lightly snored. She latched onto the opportunity and watched him. Even during his sleep, she could see the hint of a smile. He didn't nap long, though, and when he opened his eyes, he turned to her and grinned.

"Sorry you missed your date with Jake."

"*Nee*, you're not." She folded her hands in her lap as she cut her eyes in his direction. She'd left a note on Jake's mailbox, just saying that she couldn't go to lunch today.

Jonas grinned. "*Nee*, I'm not." He

squinted as he looked at her, and his expression stilled into a look of distress. "Irma Rose . . ."

She held her breath and waited.

"I'm so hungry, I feel like I might die without some food. Do you care if we stop and eat somewhere?"

Relief washed over her, and she laughed. "I'm quite sure you won't die, but that's fine." She put a hand on the seat in front of her and leaned forward. "Sir, would it be possible for you to take us somewhere to eat? I'd be happy to pay for your meal as well."

"I've already eaten, but thanks," the driver said before he glanced over his shoulder. "I hear the Burger King has something new. It's called a Whopper. How does that sound?"

Burger King had come to their town about three years ago, and it was always a treat to go there. Irma Rose nodded, and a few minutes later, they were pulling in the parking lot off the main highway. The driver dropped them off, saying he had an errand to run and that he would return in forty-five minutes.

As they walked to the entrance of the burger place, Irma Rose noticed a sign advertising a movie that would be played in the *Englisch* theaters in November. *Jailhouse Rock* starring Elvis Presley. Giggling, she nudged Jonas.

"Very funny," he said, grinning.

Irma Rose couldn't stop her smile from spreading, but as they neared the sign, she stared at it for a few moments. She'd never been to a movie. She was barely into her *rumschpringe* and hoped one day to be able to. But it wouldn't be anything with Elvis Presley. *Mamm* said he wasn't fit for young girls to watch, and that some television stations only filmed him from the waist up because of the inappropriate way he danced.

Glancing at Jonas, she wondered if he'd ever been to a movie. Probably, she decided. She couldn't imagine seeing *Jailhouse Rock* with him. *I'd be so embarrassed.*

Cool air met them when they entered the restaurant, and after they ordered and sat down, Jonas thanked her repeatedly for everything she'd done for him and his family.

"I would have found a way to come up with the money if I'd known *Mamm* would be in the hospital so long." He paused. "How did she look? How mad was she when she found out I was in jail?"

"She looked tired, but otherwise okay. And I don't think she was mad, more worried, it seemed."

Jonas just stared at her, which only fueled the dancing butterflies in her stomach.

"Why are you staring at me?"

He smiled. "Because you're so pretty. The prettiest woman I've ever seen."

She covered her face with her hands for a couple of seconds. "You're embarrassing me."

He gently lowered her hands from her face. "It's true, Irma Rose."

She thought about what Elizabeth had said, how Jonas always talked about her and told stories. Maybe the warmth she felt around him wasn't to be feared, but embraced. Maybe what made her uncomfortable was that he looked at her with such stark admiration. She wasn't used to being the center of attention, nor had anyone made mention of her outer beauty. It wasn't their way.

They were quiet as they unwrapped their burgers.

Jonas wasted no time biting into the burger. Irma Rose took a small bite, feeling self-conscious about eating in front of him.

"Do you like it?"

She was relieved he'd changed the subject. She finished chewing and swallowed. "I think it's very good. I'm not sure if thirty-seven cents isn't a bit much, though."

"You're worth it, Irma Rose." He grinned, but his expression quickly shifted. "I need to ask you something." He leaned back, his eyes locked with hers.

"Okay." She sipped her Coca-Cola from the straw.

"Before you came here, you lived in Hershey, right?"

She nodded. "*Ya*. I was thirteen when we moved here. Why?"

"Did you ever know a boy named Theo? It's probably a coincidence that my cell mate . . ." He paused, hung his head for a moment. "I hate the way that sounds, cell mate. Anyway, the *Englisch* man that was in my cell said he knew a girl named Irma Rose while he lived in Hershey. I think this guy is seventeen. Is that a coincidence, or did you know someone named Theodore? His parents owned some type of hotels there."

Irma Rose's breath hitched in her chest. She'd always wondered what happened to Theodore.

Jonas waited for Irma Rose to answer, but every time she opened her mouth to say something, she couldn't seem to get her words in order.

232

"I-I, um . . ." She took several gulps of her soda, then looked up at him. Then more soda.

"You *did* know him, didn't you?"

She stared back at him with a blank expression.

"It wonders me why you look like you've seen a ghost."

Blinking her eyes a few times, she opened her mouth, but still nothing came out. As badly as he wanted to know the connection between the woman he loved and his crazy cell mate, he could see that the conversation was bothering her. "We don't have to talk about it, if it makes you uncomfortable."

"Okay. *Gut. Danki.*" She took another sip of her soda.

"I told you that I'd make it up to you, remember? What can I do to show my thanks?"

She swallowed as she shook her head. "Jonas, you've told me *danki* a dozen times. That's enough."

"Let me take you on a proper date to a fancy restaurant." He didn't know how he'd get the money for that, but he'd figure out a way if she would agree to go with him. Lots of the fellows in their district had side jobs, but it took all of Jonas's time to take care of the farm. He didn't have time for anything extra. Even when it wasn't planting season or harvesttime, there were always outdoor chores. Repairing fences, tending to the animals, painting, and most recently leveling gravel across the driveway in an area that held water when it rained.

"*Nee.* That's not necessary." She dabbed her mouth with the napkin from her lap before she lifted a French fry to her mouth.

"Is it Jake? Is he courting you now?" Jonas held his breath, willing it not to be so. "Or you just don't want to date a *convict*?" He grinned, thinking how that sounded.

Irma Rose giggled, which was nice to hear. "I think you like hearing that word roll off your tongue," she said in a whisper.

"And I think that Jake Ebersol will never be exciting enough for you, Irma Rose. You have a fire in your belly, a sense of adventure."

She laughed again. "And Jonas Miller, you have way too much adventure to suit my liking."

"Then I'll change." He gazed into her eyes. "Who do you want me to be? Tell me three things you'd change about me if you could." Chuckling, he added, "then I'll tell you three things that I'd change about you."

"*Ach,* really?" She smiled. "And what

makes you think I'd like to hear what you'd change about me?"

He shrugged. "You go first."

She tapped a finger to her chin. "I wish you didn't smoke cigars."

Jonas chewed on a French fry, nodding. That didn't seem too hard. "That's one," he said after he swallowed, "I'll try to change," he added, winking at her.

"Actually, I don't think a person should change for another person. That doesn't seem right."

Jonas pointed a finger at her. "You can't think of anything else that you'd like for me to change."

"That's not what I said. I said that any changes a person makes should be for himself . . . or for God."

He sighed. "Okay. But I had a really long list of things you need to change."

Her eyes rounded as she halted a French fry between her mouth and her tray. After she put it back down, she scowled at him. "Then let's hear your list." She was so cute when she pouted.

"First and foremost, you need to change your dating circumstances and not date anyone but me."

"That's not changing something about *me.* That's just doing something you want

235

me to do." She leaned against the seat of the booth. "What else?"

"You need to sell your baked goods at the market. That shoofly pie was the best I've ever had." He was telling her the truth. The woman could cook. "You could make money from the tourists."

"I'm listening." She straightened, raising that cute little chin of hers.

"I've heard folks talking. More and more *Englisch* people are coming here to visit and shop. The local vendors are talking about forming something called the Pennsylvania Dutch Tourist Bureau. All the shop owners would work together to attract people to Lancaster County."

"Don't you think it's touristy enough here?"

Jonas shrugged. "I think that Lancaster County is going to become a place that people all over the United States will know about. The *Englisch* seem real interested in the way we live, and I don't think there's any gettin' away from them. You've heard the saying, 'If you can't beat them, join them.' " He smiled at her. "And you're a real *gut* cook, Irma Rose. You could even have a bakery in the heart of Paradise, maybe even right off Lincoln Highway."

"I think I'd rather be married, stay home

236

and have *kinner,* and tend to *mei* family."

That was music to Jonas's ears. "If you were my *fraa,* I'd want you to do whatever made your heart sing."

Irma Rose was speechless as her entire being filled with warmth. She folded her hands atop her napkin, surprised they weren't clammy. And as they eyed each other across the table, she had to rethink why she kept fighting the attraction she felt for Jonas. She'd thought it had been simple, that he just wasn't right for her. Anyone who unnerved her in such a way couldn't possibly be the person God intended her to be with.

She thought about how comfortable she was around Jake. But then she thought about their kiss and wondered if safe and comfortable would ever be enough. What would walking a little bit on the wild side with Jonas Miller be like? Would life be filled with his desire to live more adventurously than Irma Rose would like? Or would she saddle up next to him, love the ride, and not worry about the destination? And all these thoughts were reasons why Jonas upset her stomach. He constantly tipped the balance of her applecart, tempting her with a life she hadn't planned. "What else would you change about me?" she finally asked.

"Irma Rose, if the truth be told, you are perfect in every way. I wouldn't change one thing about you. I've loved you since the day I saw you sitting under that tree. I could tell you were nervous, and you were real young. But I've watched you become a woman, and there isn't anyone else I'd rather spend my life with. And I feel like I need to tell you this because life is short. *Mei daed* is gone, and *mei mamm* gave us all a real scare." He paused, and Irma Rose could feel herself trembling. "And I know in my heart that you feel something for me too."

Irma Rose swallowed back the knot in her throat, and in the distance, she was sure she heard angelic singing again. It wasn't real. It couldn't be. "I-I think we need to go."

Jonas's expression dropped instantly, and Irma Rose had a strong urge to reach for his hand across the table. But until she could corral her feelings, she couldn't tell him how she felt.

Jonas picked up their trays and deposited them in the designated area, and Irma Rose offered again to pay for her half of the meal. Jonas shook his head, and they were quiet as they walked outside. The driver was waiting curbside, and Jonas opened the door for her. They rode silently to Irma Rose's house, then politely said good-bye. She stood in the grass, the afternoon sun blazing down on her, and watched the car until it was out of sight, tears filling her eyes.

God, I need a sign from You. What should I do?

CHAPTER NINE

Irma Rose stayed to herself for the next couple of weeks. When she wasn't busy cooking, sewing, or tending to the farm animals, she read books her mother had approved for her. She craved anything that would take her away from her own thoughts. She'd waited a long time to be old enough to date, but now the prospect of marriage and making lifelong decisions overwhelmed her. What if she didn't choose correctly? Would the wrong choice land her on a path that wasn't the one God intended for her? People married young in her community. *But I'm only sixteen years old.*

She was sitting on the couch reading a book, the warm breeze wafting into the living room and mingling with the aroma of oatmeal cookies baking in the oven. Not even the battery-operated fan on the coffee table did much to counter the August heat that had settled upon them like a dense fog.

She tried to focus on the book she was reading, but her mind kept drifting.

"Are you okay, *mei maedel*?" Her mother walked into the living room, a kitchen towel draped over her shoulder and an oatmeal cookie in one hand. She smiled. "Because I don't think there is anything an oatmeal cookie can't cure."

Irma Rose closed the book. She'd considered talking to her mother about the confusion swirling around in her head, but she felt like even the decisions she might make at sixteen years old should be based on her own thoughts and feelings. Once she got them figured out. "I'm fine, *Mamm*. Do you need me to do anything this afternoon?"

Her mother shook her head. "*Nee*. It's too hot to do more than get by today. I shouldn't have baked in the middle of the day, but I couldn't stop thinking about *Mammi*'s recipe." She handed the cookie to Irma Rose, and the moist, warm treat melted on her tongue. Her grandmother on her mother's side had been the best cook Irma Rose had ever known, a thought that made her think of her conversation with Jonas a couple of weeks ago.

Mamm sat down on the couch next to her. "I ran into Mary's mother at the market yesterday. She asked me if you were all

241

right. She said you haven't been to the malt shop with Mary and Hannah in two weeks." Her mother nudged her gently with her shoulder. "And I know how you feel about strawberry shakes. And you didn't feel up to church service last weekend either."

Irma Rose again considered talking to her mother, but decided against it. Again. "It's so hot outside. I guess I'm just being lazy after I get my chores done. But I really didn't feel very well the day of worship." It was a partial version of the truth. Mary and Hannah would ask about Jake, if they were going steady, as the *Englisch* would say. Irma Rose was afraid of getting pulled into a conversation about Jonas, and she didn't want to lie to her friends. She'd avoided Jake too.

Mamm patted her on the leg. "Since we're ahead this week on some of our chores, I think I'm going to take a nap." *Mamm* stood up, yawned, and headed toward her downstairs bedroom, but she stopped and faced Irma Rose. "*Ach,* next time you go outside, can you fetch the mail?"

Irma Rose nodded. "Have a *gut* nap." She thought about Sarah Jane Miller and wondered how she was doing, if she was fully recovered from her time in the hospital.

She opened her book, a sweet tale about

two childhood friends who reconnected after years apart. She'd read the book before — it was a favorite of hers — but try as she might, she just couldn't keep her mind on the story. Setting the book aside, she decided to face the heat and get the mail.

It was a fair hike down their long driveway to the mailbox, and by the time she got there, she was dripping with sweat. She reached into the box for the mail. A flyer, one regular-sized envelope, and one larger package stuffed so tight she had to yank on it a couple of times to get it out. The flyer was an advertisement for a new Kenmore twelve-speed mixer that was on sale for thirty-two dollars and ninety-five cents. She eyed the special features, wondering what it would be like to use such a fine electric appliance. *The Englisch spend lavishly,* she thought as she walked back to the house.

The second envelope was addressed to her father, and Irma Rose recognized the return address as a cousin's from Ohio. The large envelope was addressed to Irma Rose, and at first glance she assumed it must be from a relative also, but she stopped abruptly when she read the return address:

Theodore Von Minden III
32 East Willow Road
Chicago, IL 60004

She'd thought about Theo ever since Jonas said he'd shared a jail cell with him. But she'd also promised never to speak about what happened. She'd kept her word.

She opened the envelope and pulled out a white sheet of paper, along with a book. A Bible. Her heart flipped in her chest, and with shaky hands, she read the letter.

Dear Irma Rose,

Once I found out what your last name was, and that you lived in Paradise, it was easy to track you down. You probably know that I spent some time in jail with your Amish boyfriend, Jonas. He said he wasn't your beau, but I know he sure wants to be. I've thought about you often over the past three years, and your words on that day stayed with me. Jonas told me something that reminded me of something you'd said. It seems like more than a coincidence, and I hope that you'll consider what I'm saying as both appreciation and hope for a bright future for you.

Irma Rose paused as she recalled the three

hours she spent with Theo, both of them hiding in a broom closet in one of his father's small hotels — "inns," he'd called them. She'd just finished changing sheets in one of the rooms when she set out to find a mop and broom. She'd opened the closet to find Theo crouched in the corner, crying. They'd both heard footsteps approaching, and Theo had begged her to hurry inside and to stay quiet as a church mouse. So she'd done what he asked since he was so upset . . . and bleeding. She pulled herself from the memory, a recollection that was painful and life-changing at the same time.

Jonas said the fruit of the Spirit is love, joy, peace, patience, kindness, goodness, faithfulness, gentleness, and self-control. Do you remember telling me that, Irma Rose? Do you remember what else you said that day? You told me that one life could make the difference in a thousand lives and that I had a purpose. Holding hands, we whispered a prayer together, fearful that my father might hear us. You ripped the pocket from your apron and held it against my bleeding ear, and you cried along with me that day. You saved my life.

For the next week, I looked for you.

When I finally tracked you down, it was to learn that you had moved away. No one would tell me where. But for the next year, I prayed, I secretly went to church with a neighbor kid, and I forgave my father . . . for a while. I had hope. But the abuse didn't stop, and over time . . . I fell back into the dark place I'd been before. By the time I landed myself in jail with your Jonas, I'd decided that I couldn't go on this way. I treated him rather badly. When you talk to him, please tell him that I'm sorry. I was lonely after he left, and I spent another week in that cell with nothing to do but read. The only reading material was the Bible that Jonas left behind. I read it cover to cover and took it with me when I left.

I'm sending it to you, knowing that life is filled with coincidences, but to me, the events that have unfolded aren't coincidences, and once again, I have hope. I left Lancaster where I was living with my father and made it to Chicago. I'm broke, working in a diner, and renting a fairly trashy room over the place. But I'm safe. I'm finally working toward happiness. And I'm going to turn my life around. Hearing about you from Jonas, reading the Bible, and remembering our time together has lifted me out of the darkness yet again.

I think you must be an angel. Maybe Jonas is your messenger, I don't know. But open this Bible to page forty-six. There's a letter folded between the pages that Jonas was writing you, but he didn't finish it. I hope you will let me know how the story ends.

Sending you thanks and blessings from Chicago.

Theo

Sweat was pouring down Irma Rose's face and mixing with her tears as she stood in the middle of her driveway, the searing sun blasting down on her. But her feet were rooted to the ground as she thumbed open the Bible and found the letter.

Dear Irma Rose,

What does the future hold for us? Will we be together or apart? I'm writing this from a jail cell, so that's probably not a *gut* start. But I know I have enough love for you in my heart to get me through any situation. I have time to think about things in here, and I want to be a better man.

Irma Rose paused. *You are a gut man, Jonas.* The thought breezed through her mind easily and without hesitation.

I want to raise a family with you. I want to love you for the rest of our lives. I want to hold and protect you. I want to cherish you. And most of all, I want

The words stopped, and Irma Rose stiffened. *And most of all you want what? No, no, no!* It couldn't just end like that. What did Jonas want most of all? She sat down in the middle of the driveway, reread Theo's letter, then reread Jonas's letter three more times. She stood up, hugged everything to her chest, and started running as fast as she could.

Jonas pressed his heel on the auger, then threw his weight onto it, struggling to break the dry dirt to put in a new fence post. He'd waited until after the supper hour, but the setting sun to his west was having no mercy on him. There were still six posts he needed to get into the ground, so he forged ahead, hoping to finish before dark.

He hadn't seen Irma Rose since their burger, and he was trying to imagine a life without her since she didn't have much of a response to his laying out his soul to her. But he was wise enough to know that he couldn't force her to love him, so he'd been working on readjusting his thinking about his future. If it were God's plan for them to pursue a future, He would lead them to each other. Jonas couldn't continue to lay all of his hopes on a dream that might not ever turn to reality.

After several more attempts, he'd dug deep enough for the post, so he set the hole digger aside, hoisted up the piece of redwood, and dropped it into the hole. Breathing heavily, he used his handkerchief to swipe sweat from his forehead, wishing for the umpteenth time that the Lord could have seen fit to give him a brother or two for times like this. If nothing else, maybe He could just send some rain to cool him off.

After he gulped from his thermos of water, he glanced at the setting sun, knowing he didn't have time to dillydally if he planned to finish tonight. He picked up the auger again and moved a few feet to his left. Distracted by a movement in the distance, he noticed someone running up his driveway. A woman. He put down the tool and starting moving in that direction. The closer she got to him, the faster he made his own stride, until he was running toward the girl who had his heart.

"What's wrong?" He grabbed both her shoulders to hold her up since she was completely out of breath. "What is it? One of your parents? What's wrong?"

She shook her head repeatedly and finally caught her breath. She handed him the Bible and the letter he'd written. Jonas reread what he'd written that day. He'd left the jail so fast, he'd forgotten about the letter. He never would have had the nerve to give it to her. He was just writing down his thoughts, mostly for his own benefit.

"Theo read your Bible," she said, still breathing hard. "It's a long story about Theo, but I think he'd want me to tell you about it." She wiggled out of his hold. "But first . . ." She pointed to the letter in Jonas's hands. "I need to know what you were going to write, what it is that you want most."

Jonas was sure his blood pressure was dropping and he might pass out. If ever there was a time he wanted to lie, it was now. He remembered exactly what he was thinking at that moment, and since he'd had no plans to give her the letter, he remembered even chuckling about what he was going to write next. Then the guard came, and his time in jail was done.

"Tell me, Jonas. What is it you were writing? What did you want the most?"

Jonas was sure she was waiting for him to say something that would make the earth move beneath their feet. But he was still trying to understand why she was here.

"Why are you here, Irma Rose?"

Her eyes filled with tears. "I want to be with you, Jonas. I want us to date."

He cupped her face, but she took a step backward.

"I'm only sixteen years old though. I'm not ready to decide my entire future today, next week, next month, or maybe not even next year. But I know that I feel different with you than I do with anyone else. And I think there is something to that, but it scares me. I think I love you, and I'm so confused." She covered her face, and Jonas wrapped his arms around her.

"Oh, Irma Rose . . . I'm not scared at all, and someday you won't be either." He kissed the top of her head. Then when she looked up at him, his lips met hers. The earth definitely moved beneath them.

Irma Rose lingered in the kiss, and before Jonas even pulled away, she was certain she would spend the rest of her life with this man. *So this is what kissing is all about.* She let him kiss her two more times, each time better than the last, and somehow she knew that if she was with Jonas, that's how it would always be . . . each day better than the last. She forced some distance between them and asked, "What was it in the letter that you wanted the most?"

"I'm going to assume that I need to tell the truth."

Irma Rose squinted at him. *"Ya.* The truth would be *gut."*

"I, uh . . ." He paused, stood taller, and looped his thumbs beneath his suspenders. "I wasn't going to give you the letter. I was just writing my thoughts."

She smiled the sweetest smile Jonas had ever seen. "That's okay. What you wrote is beautiful, and I can't wait to hear what you wanted the most at that very moment."

He hung his head and sighed, then looked back up at her and grinned. "I wanted a cigar."

Irma Rose's lips parted. "Are you teasing me, Jonas Miller?"

He wrapped an arm around her. "Now, now, Irma Rose . . . let's walk over to the bench near the garden." Moving slowly with his arm around her, he added, "I probably need to tell you about a certain situation that involved some bullet holes in my buggy . . ."

Irma Rose laughed. Being married to Jonas was going to be one adventure after another, but she was excited to see what God had in store for them both.

EPILOGUE

Many years later, Jonas and Irma Rose had a daughter named Sarah Jane and a grand-daughter named Lillian. Jonas's love for speed never dwindled, even after forty-eight years of marriage. Nor did his love of cigars.

"Let's kick up some dirt, Lilly! Let ol' Jessie stretch his legs. Give a gentle flick with the reins. Jessie will do the rest."

Doing as her grandpa suggested, Lillian carefully maneuvered the buggy down the dirt lane to the main road. Then she looked at Grandpa again. He grinned and nodded.

"Ya!" she yelled, which thrust Jessie forward so fast Grandma fell backward against the seat.

"Thata girl, Lilly! A *wunderbaar* day to feel the wind in our face," Grandpa said as Jessie got comfortable in a quick gallop.

"Jonas, the Good Lord will still be there when we arrive!" Grandma yelled, regaining her composure as she adjusted her *kapp.* "This is Lillian's first time to drive the buggy. She might not feel comfortable moving along so fast."

"Sure she does. Pick it up, Lilly! Another gentle flick of the reins."

Lillian glanced at her grandma, who was preparing herself for another increase in speed. But when she smiled in Lillian's direction, Lillian took that as the go-ahead and did indeed pick up the pace.

"Yee-ha!" Grandpa wailed.

Suddenly his face took on a fearful expression and he stuffed the cigar into the coffee cup. "Quick! Start fanning the room! Dump this out!" He handed Lilly the coffee cup. "My hearing must be off too! I usually hear Jessie's hooves before he hits the dirt drive. Look at that! They're already in the yard!"

She grabbed the coffee cup and dumped the contents as instructed. Grandpa moved faster than she'd seen him since she arrived, waving his arms about, pushing the smoke toward the open windows. She watched with amusement at his wholehearted effort to keep his secret.

Then, shaking her head, she said, "I'll go outside and try to stall Grandma. I'll show her the flowers I'm going to plant today."

With her grandpa still flailing his arms wildly around the room, she moved toward the open screen door. "I still think you shouldn't smoke," she whispered before she walked onto the porch.

"Hurry, child! Or Irma Rose will have my hide!"

— FROM *PLAIN PERFECT,* BOOK ONE IN THE DAUGHTERS OF THE PROMISE SERIES

The complete story of Jonas, Irma Rose, and their family and friends can be found in the Daughters of the Promise series:

- Plain Perfect
- Plain Pursuit
- Plain Promise
- Plain Paradise
- Plain Proposal
- Plain Peace

DISCUSSION QUESTIONS

1. Irma Rose is interested in Jake because she thinks he is "right" for her. We all know it takes more than logic to attain true love. Do you think that Irma Rose could have been happy with Jake if Jonas hadn't made his intentions known? Or would she have always longed for more?

2. Irma Rose thinks Jonas is wild and reckless, but what are some of the qualities in Jonas that Irma Rose overlooks early on, and which parts of Jonas's character shine toward the end of the story?

3. My mother was the same age as Irma Rose when she married my father. My parents were married fifty-four years, and Irma Rose and Jonas were married almost that long. Do you think marriages back then were more apt to last, especially when marrying so young? Or are young people today just as likely to have a long-lasting marriage when they commit at

such an early age?

4. If you could have written Irma Rose and Jonas's love story, would you have done it differently? If so, discuss with the group.

ACKNOWLEDGMENTS

God continues to bless me with stories to tell, and I loved writing this novella about Jonas and Irma Rose. All of the characters in the Daughters of the Promise series are special to me, so it was like revisiting old friends.

Many thanks to Larry Knopick for his friendship and continued support along this amazing journey. Larry, you've been an ambassador of the Amish genre, and it's an honor to dedicate this very special story to you. Peace be with you and Jolene, my friend.☺

To my family and friends — I couldn't do this without you. And I have a fabulous publishing team at HarperCollins Christian Publishing.

Thank you, Natasha, for all you do to guide my career and for your friendship.

PATCHWORK
PERFECT

To Kiki and Katie

PENNSYLVANIA DUTCH GLOSSARY

ab im kopp — off in the head; crazy
ach — oh
bruder — brother
daed — dad
danki — thank you
Englisch — non-Amish person
fraa — wife
gut — good
haus — house
kapp — prayer covering or cap
kinner — children
maedel — girl
mamm — mom
mei — my
mudder — mother
nee — no
rumschpringe — running-around period when a teenager turns sixteen years old
sohn — son
Wie bischt — How are you?; Howdy

wunderbaar — wonderful
ya — yes

CHAPTER ONE

Eli walked toward a group of men gathered in the front yard. He'd met several of them over the past couple of weeks, but he was having a hard time remembering names. Back home, there weren't nearly as many people to keep track of. Then he reminded himself, *This is home now.*

Amos Glick extended his hand when Eli joined the men. Amos was an easy name to remember since it was his father's.

"It was a fine worship service today," Eli said as he greeted the other men with a handshake. Amos introduced everyone to Eli. Some were repeat introductions, but Eli was grateful to hear their names again.

"For those of you who haven't met Eli before now, he comes to us from a small church district near Bucks County." Amos stroked his beard, a mixture of brown and gray streaks, though Eli suspected the gray was premature. Amos looked about Eli's age, early thirties, and couldn't be over five foot five. He'd also met Amos's wife, Sarah, who towered over her husband. One thing Eli liked right away about Amos was that he smiled a lot. Eli remembered a time when he smiled often, and he wondered if he'd ever be that man again.

"What brings you to Lancaster County?" one of the other men asked, an older fellow with a big black mole above his left eye. Eli had already forgotten his name.

Eli had practiced how he would respond to this question. "More opportunities for work here." He forced a smile, content that he'd told the truth, even if it wasn't the entire truth.

"Do you farm?" The same man squinted one eye, still stroking his beard.

"*Ya,* mostly farming." Eli tipped the brim of his hat to block the sun that had reached its midday peak. This was his favorite time of year, when the foliage shifted into soft hues of amber and crimson. His former home was only an hour and a half from here, and they'd enjoyed the same type of Octobers in the past. Not only was the shift in seasons a feast for the eyes, but cool breezes drifted beneath the brilliant blue skies. Soon they could expect low clouds that floated like billowy cotton overhead.

Best of all, it signified that the fall harvest would soon be upon them. It was always a lot of work, but following the harvest there would be time for rest. And weddings. Almost everyone waited until the fall to get married.

"Eli bought the old Dienner place," Amos said as he looped his thumbs beneath his suspenders. "And Gideon had already done all the planting, so it'll be ready for harvesting in a few weeks."

Eli was grateful to the prior owners of his new farm, though Gideon had planted alfalfa before he knew he'd be moving away. The kindly older man had met with unfortunate circumstances of the financial type. That was all Eli knew. It was the only reason Eli had been able to buy the Dienners' farm. It was worth more than he'd offered Gideon, but it was all he could afford. Eli had been surprised when Gideon had accepted his bid, but somehow it seemed like a win-win situation for both men. A chance for Gideon to relocate with his wife to a smaller house now that their *kinner* were grown and living in a different district, and a fresh start for Eli, Ben, and Grace.

The men began to disassemble when the ladies starting bringing out trays of food, placing them on tables set up in a shaded area. But Amos lingered behind with Eli until they were alone.

Amos's smile grew as he nudged Eli. "*Ach,* let's get down to business." He pointed toward the group of women and lifted up on his toes, closer to Eli's ear, so Eli leaned down a bit. "See that woman in the maroon dress, the one carrying the tea pitcher? She's a widow."

Eli nodded, grinning. He'd told Amos that he lost his wife two years ago in an accident. Eli would always miss Leah. But he was ready to find a wife and a mother for his children. He'd been ready for the past year, but with no more than twenty Amish families in his area, his choices had been limited.

"Her name is Elizabeth," Amos whispered as two men walked past them. "She's twenty-five, no *kinner,* and her husband passed a few months ago."

Eli stretched his neck to have a better look at her. She was a petite woman with dark hair, but he couldn't make out her features.

Amos tapped him on the arm. "Let's walk that way."

Eli fell in step beside Amos, who slowed down as they approached the crowd. Most of the men were finding seats at the tables as the women delivered pitchers of tea and glasses filled with ice. "She's pretty," Eli said as he studied her. He could tell by the way she moved around the table carrying glasses of ice that she was graceful and feminine, flowerlike. Her eyes were dark brown, set against an olive complexion, and when she smiled, Eli instinctively smiled too.

"*Ach,* and not only is she pretty, but she might be the best cook we have around here." Amos raised his chin as he also looked at Elizabeth. "I'll introduce you to her after the meal."

Eli wondered if Elizabeth was too young for him. Probably no one would think so, but eight years was stretching it. He had been married at seventeen, widowed at thirty-one, and now was raising a fifteen-year-old and an eleven-year-old. He felt older than his thirty-three years. And would someone Elizabeth's age want to step into a family with older children? He scratched his chin as he watched her.

Amos cleared his throat, then whispered again. "Sarah told me that Elizabeth is in a hurry to get remarried. She wants *kinner.* Her husband died of cancer." Amos shook his head. "A real shame. He took sick not long after their wedding. He had lots of treatments in the hospital. I don't think they ever had a chance to think about starting a family. Elizabeth took care of him for their entire marriage, right up to the end. I think everyone was surprised at how strong she was, and what a *gut* caregiver she was to John." Amos turned to Eli and sighed. "We're all praying Elizabeth will find a nice fellow. There are several vying for her affection, but if the truth be told, I don't think a one of them is right for her."

Eli was seeing Elizabeth in a new light. Taking care of someone like that lent her a maturity that was uncommon for her age. *Pretty, can cook, graceful, and wants more children.* Eli wanted more children too. "I'd like to meet her." He took a step forward, but Amos tugged on his shirt.

"Hold on there, fellow." Amos nodded to his left. Almost everyone was seated now, and Eli could feel several sets of eyes on them. Amos must have, too, because he was whispering so softly that Eli had to ask him to speak up a little.

"We have one other widow in our church district that I'll point out to you as soon as I find her. Her name is Ruth." Amos turned to Eli. "There are plenty of younger women who are available, but . . ." He grinned. "They got their eyes set on the young bucks. You'd be an old man in their eyes."

Eli took a deep breath and blew it out slowly. He knew Amos was right. But at least there were two widows in his new church district. It would be nice if he was properly suited to one of them and didn't have to travel outside of the community to find a *fraa*.

Amos scanned the tables looking for Ruth. Eli's stomach rumbled, and his need to eat was becoming more important than being introduced to anyone. But when he heard a screen door slam in the distance, he turned his attention to the tall woman floating down the front porch steps as if she had angel wings on her back. Even from a distance, Eli was mesmerized as she strode across the yard. The closer she got to him, the more her beauty shone, and he had to force himself to breathe. From beneath her *kapp* wisps of red hair blew against her rosy cheeks. But it was her green eyes twinkling in the sunlight that kept Eli from being able to look away. He'd been taught that pride and vanity were sin, and most of the time he did his best not to let them dominate his choices.

"She's a beauty, isn't she?" Amos said as they finally started making their way to two empty seats. "That's Ruth."

Eli nodded, finally pulling his gaze from Ruth. After he was seated, he bowed his head in prayer, then reached for a slice of bread. He was glad to see Ben two tables over talking with two boys who looked to be around his age, maybe ten or twelve. But as his eyes traveled from table to table, he didn't see Gracie. He took a bite of bread, assuming his daughter must be inside. Maybe the bathroom. Or maybe just sitting in the living room avoiding everyone. His fifteen-year-old hadn't been happy about the move and leaving her friends behind. But Eli was certain a fresh start was just what they all needed.

Grace loved kissing as much as chocolate pie, a warm bath on a cold winter's night, and reading *Englisch* magazines on the sly, the ones she kept hidden between her mattresses. But Wayne Huyard was interested in a lot more than just kissing, and she was having a hard time guiding his hands away from places they needn't be. They'd barely been in Lancaster County a week when she'd met Wayne at a Sunday singing. He was sixteen, a year older than Grace, and with his dreamy blue eyes and blond hair, he was cuter than cute.

"*Mei daed*'s going to come looking for me," she said, latching onto one of Wayne's roaming hands. Actually, she doubted that was the case. The only thing her father was

274

looking for was a wife. She'd met Wayne behind the far barn on the property. As everyone was getting ready for the meal, they'd slipped away as planned.

"I love kissing you," he said as his mouth covered hers again. She loved the way he cupped her cheeks in his hands, thankful to know exactly where those hands were for the moment. But within seconds, they wandered again.

"I can't," she said as she eased her lips away from his, stepping back until his hands finally fell to his sides.

Wayne gently touched her cheek with the back of his hand. "You're so pretty. I *really* like you."

Grace felt herself blush as he slowly inched forward, kissing her again. She tried to relax. Wayne had kissed her one other time, after the singing the night they'd met. Maybe he thought she was easy, as the *Englisch* girls would say, since she'd allowed him to kiss her that first night. But his roaming hands could get them both into trouble. She'd seen it happen with other girls.

Grace put her hand on top of his, hoping she wasn't going to make him mad. She was grateful to have met someone so cute not long after moving here, and she'd only kissed one other boy; that was about a year ago. He'd been shorter than her and didn't seem to know what he was doing. Wayne was a take-charge man. Handsome. And he knew what he was doing. Grace had never had anyone like him take an interest in her.

"I want to spend time with you," he said between kisses. He pushed away a strand of hair that had fallen from her *kapp,* a gesture that caused her to shiver. "Some of us guys play baseball in a big field at the Lantzes' *haus* on Saturdays." He kissed her tenderly on the lips. "I want you to come watch." He pulled her closer and whispered, "As my date."

Grace felt herself relaxing a tiny bit and she wasn't as quick to latch onto his hand. She'd never had a boyfriend, and for the first time in two years, she wondered if maybe she could be happy again. But no matter how good looking and sweet Wayne might be, some things were just off-limits. She grabbed his hand again, but he didn't leave the area. She eased him away.

"I'm sorry, Wayne. I just can't." She took a deep breath and held it, knowing that some boys — even *gut* Amish boys — wanted a girl who was willing to go further than just kissing.

"It's okay," he whispered in her ear. "I

like you so much, I don't mind waiting. I think you're someone I could really fall for."

Grace was sure the clouds were opening up and raining down blessings on her, and for a brief second, she considered giving him some freedoms that went against what she believed was right, but at the last minute, she took his hand and repeated, "I can't."

Wayne trailed his kisses down her neck, and Grace wasn't sure what was happening to her. She was a bit weak in the knees, but a rustling in the leaves to their right caused both of them to stop and turn. Grace's heart was beating hard, but she quickly thanked God that it wasn't her father.

"Wayne Huyard, what are you doing back here?" A woman a few years older than she and Wayne walked toward them, stopping a couple of feet away. Grace remembered meeting her earlier that morning before the worship service. Her name was Miriam, and Grace was pretty sure her last name was Fisher. The woman didn't look as old as Grace's father, but she had those feathery lines women get when they start to age. Miriam had a smudge of dirt on her chin.

Scowling, Miriam put her hands on her hips. Grace was pretty sure this woman was going to haul them back to the group, and her father would know she'd been alone with a boy. And so would everyone else. She swallowed hard, wondering exactly how much Miriam had seen.

CHAPTER TWO

Miriam felt like punching Wayne, even though it wasn't their way, and she'd never hit anyone in her life. But why was it that some boys felt the need to welcome the new girls in a way that wasn't appropriate? Especially on a Sunday.

"Miriam, this ain't none of your business." Wayne shrugged. "We weren't doing nothing anyway."

Miriam rolled her eyes as she folded her arms across her chest. "If that's what *nothing* looks like, I don't need to see *something.*" She'd known Wayne since he was born. She'd been about twelve when she used to babysit him. And at sixteen, he'd already grown into the type of young man that mothers feared.

She glanced at the girl, who appeared to be quaking in her loafers, her big brown eyes as round as saucers. Miriam wasn't sure Wayne's prey was even breathing.

"Have we met?" Miriam squinted one eye as she tried to remember. She knew a new family had moved to their church district, but she didn't recall formally meeting any of them.

The girl let out a breath. She was a cute little thing, but she was no match for Wayne.

"*Ya*. We met this morning. I'm Grace Byler. My family moved here a couple of weeks ago."

Miriam recalled being introduced to the girl early this morning. "You have a *bruder*, too, right?"

Grace nodded. "*Ya*. Ben."

That morning, Miriam had left the house before having a cup of coffee, something she tried never to do. But she'd overslept, tripped over the threshold between the kitchen and den, and landed on her right knee. By the time she'd cleaned up her wound, she was late for worship and ran to her buggy, bypassing her cup of coffee. She glared at Wayne, wanting to give him a good talking-to, but Miriam didn't want to embarrass Grace even further. And it wouldn't do any good.

"Are you going to tell *mei* father?" Grace blinked her eyes a few times and her lip was trembling.

"Did I meet your father too?" Miriam

280

frowned, vowing never to start her day without coffee again. She should have just been late. Relief washed over her when Grace shook her head.

"*Nee.* I don't think you met him yet. He wasn't with us when Ben and I were introduced to you."

"*Nee,* I'm not going to tell your *daed,*" Miriam finally said. She was wise enough to know that Grace and Wayne were going to do whatever they wanted, but she wasn't sure she could live with herself if she didn't try to warn Grace. She turned to Wayne. "You go join the others. If Grace goes back with you now, it will be obvious you two snuck off together."

Wayne nodded, picked his straw hat up off the ground next to him, and quickly disappeared around the corner.

Miriam thought for a few moments. She wanted to warn Grace about Wayne without making him sound like the resident bad boy. Even though he was.

Miriam sighed, thinking *bad boy* was probably too strong a description. Wayne was a teenager finding his way into adulthood, like a lot of other young men here. But he seemed to have an overabundance of cuteness, hormones, and confidence. A dangerous combination when it came to the teenage girls. Miriam knew of two girls who hadn't been able to resist Wayne's charms, and they'd both been left brokenhearted after he'd won their affections and then tossed them aside later for reasons Miriam could only speculate about. Miriam didn't want to see that happen to the new girl.

"Grace, I know you're new here, so I'm going to tell you about Wayne." She paused, wondering how to structure her words in a way that Grace would understand, without Miriam having to spell it out. "Wayne is . . . well . . ." She blew out a breath, then scratched her chin. "Wayne is probably not the best person for you to spend time with right now. Maybe get to know the other young people before settling on the first boy who shows interest."

Miriam hoped the other girls would talk to Grace about Wayne soon, but just in case they didn't, Miriam wanted to walk away with a clear conscience. Some of these boys seemed to swoop in on the new girls like vultures, even before they had time to make close girlfriends. Not many new families came into their community, but those with teenage daughters needed to be warned about this particular teen boy.

Grace raised her chin as she lifted one shoulder, then let it drop slowly. "We really weren't doing anything, and I can handle boys like Wayne."

Miriam stifled a grin. It was a very *Englisch* thing to say, and Miriam doubted it was true, but she just shrugged. "If you say so. I tried to warn you."

"Well, I don't need a warning, but *danki* anyway." Grace folded her hands in front of her and stiffened.

Miriam stared at the girl for a few moments, but her eyes hadn't deceived her. Grace could have used two extra hands to ward off Wayne during their little kissing extravaganza. If Grace allowed Wayne to kiss her like that, how long before she allowed him to go further? Maybe things were different in the district Grace came from.

"*Ya,* okay," Miriam finally said. "I guess we can go join the others now."

Eli was relieved to see Gracie coming across the front yard. He would ask her later where she'd been, but for now, he was just glad she was okay. After breathing a sigh of relief, he noticed the woman walking next to his daughter.

"Don't get any notions," Amos said, then snickered. "That's Miriam Fisher, and she ain't the woman for you."

"I just assumed she was married." Eli had

noticed Miriam earlier in the day, mostly because she had blood seeping down her leg. He'd been about to ask her if she needed help when another woman handed her a paper towel. "You said there were only two widows in this district."

"There are." Amos grinned. "Miriam has never been married."

Eli opened his mouth as Gracie and Miriam took seats at different tables. "But she looks like she could be close to thirty."

Amos whispered, "*Ya.* She's our resident old maid. She's twenty-eight."

Eli watched Miriam reach for a slice of bread, thinking she was pretty. Not beautiful, like Ruth, but pretty. "What's wrong with her?" he finally asked.

Amos chuckled. "The list is too long to recite, *mei* friend. Just take my word for it and keep your eyes focused on Elizabeth and Ruth. Either of those two ladies would make a fine *fraa* and *mudder* to your *kinner.*"

Eli nodded, but he couldn't stop wondering about her. "Is she . . . sick? Or maybe *ab im kopp*?"

"*Nee,* she's not sick that I know of or off in the head. Miriam grew up here, and for as long as I can remember, she's been . . ." Amos grinned. "Strong willed."

"That is *gut,* a strong woman." Eli pulled his eyes from Miriam and put another slice of bread on his plate, then lathered it with church spread and took a bite, savoring the flavor. Nothing in God's perfect world was better than marshmallow and peanut butter mixed together and swiped across a piece of homemade bread. It had been Leah's favorite too.

"Miriam isn't just strong willed," Amos went on. "She's different. I ain't been in her house in years, but rumor has it that she can't host worship service because the *haus* is barely fit for living in. Sarah says Miriam don't cook, have a garden, or know how to sew." Amos raised his eyebrows. "Does that sound like a woman you'd want to be married to?"

Eli stole another look at Miriam. "Doesn't she want to be married? You would think she might work on some of those skills to marry a *gut* man."

"She's a mystery." Amos tapped a finger to his chin. "Although . . . I recall her dating someone a long time ago. She was barely of age. But the courtship seemed to end before it really got going." He pointed a finger at Eli. "And another thing. She plays baseball with the young people when they gather on Saturdays, and most think she's a

285

mite too old to be doing that. And she's got cats . . . lots and lots of cats."

Eli had loved playing baseball as a boy, but Amos was right — there comes a time when a person must put the joys of their youth behind them in order to work, marry, and raise a family. But for a few moments, Eli imagined hearing the crack of the bat when it collided with the ball and the adrenaline of running with all he had. And he loved cats, although he hadn't been around many since finding out he was allergic to them.

Amos was still talking when Eli said, "Who is that?" Eli pointed to where Gracie was standing with an Amish boy who looked to be around her age. His daughter was grinning as the boy whispered in her ear. It was still hard for him to believe that his daughter was old enough to be interested in boys. But he reminded himself that he and Leah had gotten married at seventeen. Most Plain people married young, but Eli hoped Gracie would wait awhile.

"That's Wayne Huyard," Amos said as he glanced up before grabbing the last pickle on a nearby platter. "He's a *gut* boy, a hard worker. I ain't heard nothing bad about him. His parents are fine people. They've raised the boy well."

Eli was glad to hear that, but he remembered being Wayne's age, and he planned to keep a close eye on his daughter, no matter what. He stood up and eased his chair back. "I think I'll go introduce myself to Wayne." He pushed his chair in and began making his way toward his daughter and her new friend. While walking, he took the opportunity to catch a better look at Elizabeth and Ruth, both of whom were busy cleaning tables with the other women. He wasn't sure which one of them he might like to ask out, or if they'd even accept his invitation, but he couldn't help but feel hopeful that he might find love again.

He was several yards from reaching Gracie and Wayne when Miriam crossed in front of him carrying at least six empty plates, three glasses piled on top, and a half full pitcher of tea. Some of the tea was sloshing over the side as she struggled to keep everything balanced. Eli reached for the pitcher. "Here, let me help you." It was customary for the women to serve the men and children, then they'd eat, and after the meal, the women cleaned up. But Eli couldn't help but think it was a bit unfair. Over the past two years, he'd been forced to learn to cook, and he realized he enjoyed cooking almost as much as eating.

"Danki," she said as she got a better grip on the plates and glasses. "If you'll put that pitcher on the table, someone will get it, or I'll come back for it." She smiled at Eli, and when she did, tiny dimples indented her cheeks, which deepened even more when Eli smiled. Eli couldn't tell if her rosy cheeks were sun kissed or windburned, but either way, it made her dark eyes stand out even more. And when her long eyelashes swept down over her high cheekbones, Eli thought she might be flirting with him. He recalled everything Amos had told him about her, but Eli believed in forming his own opinions.

"I'm Eli Byler," he said. "We just moved here a couple of weeks ago."

"Wie bischt." She set the stack of plates and glasses on the table and brushed back a strand of dark hair. "I think I met your *kinner.* But, um . . . oops. I can't remember their names."

Eli grinned. "I'm not *gut* with names either. Grace is my daughter. She's fifteen. And Ben, my son, is eleven."

She nodded. "Welcome to Paradise; it's *gut* to meet you."

Shrugging, Eli said, "I don't have a *fraa."* He felt his face turning red. *Why in the world did I say that?* He felt silly when she grinned at him.

"I hope you find one." She picked up the plates and glasses again. "I'd better get these inside and help with the cleanup. Again, nice to meet you."

"Nice to meet you too." Eli told his feet to stay where they were, that Amos had made it perfectly clear that Miriam was not someone he should pursue, but within seconds, he'd sauntered up beside her.

"Would you like to go to supper with me sometime?"

Miriam didn't even slow down or look at him. "*Nee,* but *danki* anyway. It's kind of you to ask."

"Wait." She was almost to the porch steps when Eli gently touched her arm.

She turned to face him. "*Ya?*"

She wasn't smiling anymore, and maybe that should have been his clue to walk away, but something outside of his own thoughts seemed to be controlling his movements. "I could, uh . . . cook for you. I like to cook." He grinned. "And I heard you don't cook. I like to," he repeated. Eli held his breath as he waited, wondering who had taken over his brain. *What a dumb thing to say.*

Miriam's expression softened. "So, you are asking me to come to your *haus,* and you will cook for me?"

Eli looped his thumbs beneath his suspenders, feeling a little bit taller all of a sudden. He nodded, smiling. "*Ya,* I am."

"Aw," she said softly as she took a step closer to him, so close he could have kissed her. "I guess it's pretty well known that I'm not very handy in the kitchen. And I've never had a man offer to cook for me. Are you any *gut* at it?"

"*Ya.* I am. After *mei fraa* died — Leah — I had to learn how. Grace was thirteen, but she was still in school, and she tended to cook things that weren't all that healthy, so I started spending some time in the kitchen and realized . . . I enjoy it." He chuckled. "And I'd be happy to cook for you."

Miriam looked down at her feet for a few seconds, then back up at him. She flashed him a thin-lipped smile. It was an expression he recognized. Leah used to give him the same look when she was irritated, before she scolded him for something. *Uh-oh.*

"Eli . . ."

He waited, feeling hopeful by the gentle tone of her voice. Maybe he'd read her expression wrong. *"Ya?"*

"I can't come to your *haus* for you to cook for me. And I will never go on a date with you. But I wish you God's blessings and a happy life here for you and your family." She turned and headed up the porch steps, and this time, Eli's feet remained rooted to the ground beneath him.

CHAPTER THREE

Grace sat on the makeshift bleachers that faced the baseball field at the Lantzes' place the following Saturday. The bleachers were six logs lined up in a row behind home plate. Bases were marked with large bags of rice. There were eight boys and . . . *Miriam?*

Grace was sitting next to three girls she didn't know very well. She'd tried to talk to them the couple of times she'd been around them — once at the singing when she'd met Wayne, and then again after worship service. They were friendly enough both times, but when they saw Grace and Wayne walk up together today, the girls met her with a stony expression and hadn't said much. Jealousy was a sin, but that was clearly the girls' problem. Grace had never wanted to move here. Their former community was small, but at least she'd had a couple of close girlfriends she'd grown up with, even if the shortage of available boys was disappointing.

Grace turned to the girl sitting to her right, Rachel. "Why is Miriam playing with the boys?" She waited until Rachel finished whispering to Naomi and Linda. Hopefully they weren't talking about Grace.

Rachel pulled her sweater snug as she turned to face Grace. The first cold front had blown in, and it was starting to feel like fall. Grace was wishing she'd brought a sweater too. "The boys all think she plays to show them up." Rachel grinned. "We don't think that's it." She pointed to Naomi and Linda, who had leaned forward to hear. "Miriam babysat all of us when we were young, and since she's not married, she seems to make it her job to look after us."

"More like spying," Naomi added. "I think she reports back to our parents if she sees us with a boy, doesn't approve of something we're doing, or finds us somewhere we aren't supposed to be."

If that was the case, why didn't Miriam tell Grace's father that she'd been kissing Wayne? Or maybe Miriam cared about these girls since she'd known them so long.

"We're in our *rumschpringe*," Linda said. "So it's really none of her business what we do."

Grace nodded, recalling that Wayne had said the same thing to Miriam: *none of your business.* Grace couldn't wait until she turned sixteen in a few months. Then she'd be able to enjoy her running-around period too. In a way, she already was — with Wayne. Her father hadn't even missed her on Sunday when she'd snuck off. He was too busy identifying the widows in the community. *Daed* could say whatever he wanted, that they'd moved for more work opportunities, but Grace knew the truth. *Daed* was on the hunt for a *fraa,* and there hadn't been much to choose from back home.

"She looks old not to be married," Grace said as Miriam pitched the ball to the other team. Her arm was as good as or better than the boys'.

"That's what she is, an old maid." Rachel chuckled. "It probably has something to do with the fact that she can't cook, her house is always a mess, she doesn't garden, and she's a tomboy."

Linda leaned forward until she met eyes with Grace. "Don't listen to Rachel. Miriam is a *gut* person." She shrugged. "She's just different than most of the grown-ups here. But she'd do anything for any of us." Linda glared at Rachel. "Shame on you, Rachel."

Linda leaned back, and they all went back to watching the game. Naomi and Linda cheered the loudest each time a boy named Jessie made a good play. Grace couldn't help but smile when Wayne hit a double and slid into second base, but when she glanced to her right, Rachel was glowering in her direction.

Grace knew it would take time to make friends. But at least she had Wayne. She smiled again when he winked at her from second base. And she didn't bother looking over at Rachel.

Eli sat down in the rocking chair in his bedroom and thumbed through the cookbook he'd bought last week. It was his guilty pleasure, and after the day he'd had, he deserved some downtime. He and Ben had repaired a long stretch of fence along the back of the property, and then they'd cut enough firewood to last most of the winter. Ben was as exhausted as he was, and last he saw his son, he was napping on the couch. Eli glanced down at his paint-splattered clothes at about the same time he got a whiff of himself. Next stop, bathtub. But he'd allow himself a few more minutes to skim the cookbook. He ran a hand through his beard, a gesture that made him think of

Leah and the way she'd playfully yank on his whiskers to get his attention.

Eli lifted the bottom of his beard. Tiny threads of gray had emerged over the past year, and he found himself checking it often. Sighing, he refocused on his book. A moment later, someone knocked on his bedroom door.

"*Daed,* there's a lady here to see you," Ben said as he rolled his eyes.

Eli wondered if Ben made the gesture because he'd been disturbed while napping, or if he was just irritated because a woman was visiting. Neither of his children had made a big secret about not wanting Eli to date and therefore stayed suspicious about all females close to Eli's age. Eli got another whiff of himself and grimaced. "Who is it?" he whispered as he lifted his stinky self from the rocker.

"She said her name is Elizabeth." Ben yawned. "And she's carrying a pie."

Eli put a finger to his mouth, narrowing his eyebrows at his son. "Whisper," he said. "And where is she?"

"On the porch." Ben closed the door, and Eli made a mental note to speak with his son about manners.

He couldn't just leave her on the porch while he got cleaned up. Shaking his head, he hurried into the living room, and when he didn't see Ben, he assumed his son must have gone upstairs to finish his nap. Eli had briefly been introduced to Elizabeth and Ruth last Sunday after worship service, but he still hadn't decided whom he might be interested in courting. He'd ruled out Miriam right away, since she'd ruled him out before he'd even put his best foot forward. He opened the wooden door and saw Elizabeth through the screen.

"*Wie bischt,* Elizabeth." He eased the screen door open and motioned for her to come in, noticing Ben's almost-empty plate on the coffee table; just one half-eaten cookie remained. "I apologize for my son leaving you on the porch." He nodded to the coffee table. "And please forgive the mess." Although the biggest mess was himself.

"*Nee, nee,*" Elizabeth quickly said. "Not to worry." She handed Eli a pie, and the aroma of freshly baked apples swirled in the air. "I wanted to bring your family a welcome present, so I made this apple crumb pie." She smiled as she lifted up on her toes for a second. "My own recipe."

Amos had told him that Elizabeth might be the best cook in the community. She seemed mighty young to have earned that title at twenty-five, but Eli loved apple pie. "*Danki.* It's so nice of you to do this." He looked down at himself. "Please don't take notice of the way I'm dressed. Ben and I repaired the fence and chopped wood today."

"I feel awful for just dropping in like this, but I felt a proper welcome was in order, and I didn't have a shanty number . . . or cell phone number, if you happen to have one."

Eli was pretty sure that was a hint for his phone number, and as a warm and flattering feeling wrapped around him, he pondered what to say.

"I-I think I'm going to go now. I caught you at a bad time." She gave him a quick wave, then turned to leave.

"Wait."

She turned to face him, her hand on the doorknob.

"I *never* eat pie alone. It's a rule I have. So you have to stay and have a slice with me. I'll get some coffee percolating too."

A full smile swept across her face as she folded her hands in front of her. "I would love to."

"This way." Eli motioned for her to follow him into the kitchen, and once he had the percolator on the stove top, he pulled a knife from the drawer, along with two plates.

"Allow me," Elizabeth said as she gently took the knife from him. "You sit down and let me serve you." She pulled out a chair, and when Eli didn't move, she added, "I never let a man serve me. It's a rule I have."

Eli grinned but shook his head. "*Nee,* you are in my home. Please let me —"

"I insist. It is obvious you have done a hard day's labor, so you rest."

After hesitating a few more seconds, Eli sat down. His own exhaustion had won that argument.

"This is the best apple pie I've ever had," Eli said a few minutes later. And he meant it. "Where did you learn to bake like this?" He shoveled another piece in his mouth, fully aware that his manners weren't any better than his son's at the moment. "You said it's your recipe?"

She nodded, taking tiny bites of the small slice she'd cut for herself. "I like to play around with recipes. If I see one that looks *gut,* I'll usually make it as written, but then I make a list of things I'd like to try to make it better. Sometimes it takes two or three times before I get it exactly the way I want it."

Eli swallowed and sat taller, tempted to tell her that he loved to cook, but he wasn't sure if that would sound unmanly, so he chose another version of the truth. "I've done a lot of cooking since *mei fraa* died two years ago."

Elizabeth gazed at him from across the table. "I bet you miss someone cooking for you. I met both your *kinner* last Sunday; they are lovely. Does Grace do most of the cooking?"

Eli swallowed the last of his pie, then chose another safe version of the truth, since he did most of the cooking. "She does some of the cooking, but she stays busy keeping the *haus* clean, doing laundry, and mending Ben's clothes. I think my *sohn* is growing so fast that he's popping buttons. It seems like Gracie is always letting out hems or sewing on buttons."

"That is a lot for a young girl to do." Elizabeth shook her head. "My husband passed recently. I miss him very much, but I also miss having someone to take care of. I bet you miss being taken care of?"

"I did in the beginning. Leah — that was *mei fraa*'s name — did all the cooking, and there wasn't a day that I didn't come home to a hot supper." He paused when he saw that Elizabeth had a faraway look in her eyes. "I know it hasn't been long since you lost your husband. I'm sure you've heard this a hundred times, but it does get easier."

She seemed to force a smile. "It's lonely sometimes."

Eli nodded as he recalled the months following Leah's death. Even in a roomful of people, he'd never been lonelier in his life. "I heard that your husband had a long battle with cancer. I also heard that you took very *gut* care of him."

"*Danki* for saying so." Her cheeks took on a rosy hue as she tipped her chin down.

"Leah died instantly." Eli took a deep breath, remembering the heavy steps he took to the morgue to identify his beloved wife. "She was in her buggy when a car hit her." As much as Eli missed Leah, he'd thanked God every day that Ben and Grace hadn't been with her. Elizabeth's eyes locked with his, and Eli had to wonder which was worse — losing someone unexpectedly or watching them suffer month after month.

Elizabeth shook her head, still watching him. "I'm very sorry for your loss."

Eli nodded. "*Danki.* And I'm sorry for yours. What kind of cancer did your husband have?"

"A brain tumor. When we found out about John's cancer, he was already in a bad way, and . . ."

Eli listened to Elizabeth for the next hour, detailing every phase of John's battle. He commented when the conversation called for it, but it was clear that Elizabeth was in a different place than he was in the grieving process. The first year is the hardest. Amos had obviously thought Elizabeth was ready to move on, but Eli wasn't sure. But they did have two things in common. They both liked to cook, and they'd both endured a terrible loss. Elizabeth was also easy on the eyes. Just the thought made him think of Ruth and her incredible beauty. But pretty on the outside didn't always mean pretty on the inside, and he was going to keep an open mind about his possibilities.

When the room grew silent, Eli snapped back to the present.

"I am so sorry," Elizabeth said as she covered her face with her hands. "I have spent the past hour boring you with details about a man you didn't even know."

Eli reached over and lightly touched her arm until she uncovered her face. "Elizabeth, if anyone understands, I do." He offered her a tender smile and held it until she smiled back.

"*Danki,* Eli." She eased the chair back and stood up. "I have overstayed my welcome, but please let me know if there is anything I can do for your family. If your daughter Grace needs help with anything, I'm a stone's throw away. I live alone, and I'd welcome the company." She winked at Eli. "Tell her I'll even cook, if she'd like."

"That sounds *gut.*" Eli said a quick prayer asking God to forgive the lie. Grace was worse than Ben when it came to Eli finding a wife, and he doubted his daughter would enjoy spending time with anyone who might be vying for her father's attention. Eli had never approved of courting more than one person at a time, so if he asked out Elizabeth, he would be passing on Ruth. At least for now.

Elizabeth moved around the table and stopped in front of Eli, then touched him on the arm. "Please call on me for anything you or your family might need," she said again. She exhibited such sincerity, mingled with a loneliness Eli remembered well.

"Would you like to go to supper with me next Saturday night?" Eli filled with warmth when Elizabeth's face lit up, but when she frowned after that and shook her head, Eli felt his heart drop.

"*Nee,* I am not going to let you take me to supper. You are going to come to my *haus* where I can make you a proper home-cooked meal." She gave her head a taut nod.

"You deserve that."

Eli smiled. "It's a date then."

CHAPTER FOUR

Miriam ran her hand across sweat beaded on her forehead. The crisp October air was refreshing.

"You played *gut* today, Miriam." Wayne brushed by her, smirking, as he made his way to where Grace was sitting. The other girls had already left, but when Wayne leaned down and kissed Grace, Miriam's stomach churned. A tasteless show of public affection. Once again, she found herself wanting to smack that boy. But instead, she glared at him as she walked by, then nodded at Grace, whose face immediately flushed.

As Miriam untethered her horse, she glanced at Grace again. Even though she didn't know the girl, it was hard not to worry about her. She kept hearing a tiny voice in her head, asking if she'd really done enough to warn Grace about Wayne Huyard. But Wayne had been right about one thing. She'd played *gut* today — even hit a home run. They'd been taught not to keep score, but Miriam knew that every person on that field was tallying points, and today Miriam's team had won.

When she pulled up to her small *haus*, Kiki was waiting on the porch.

"*Wie bischt*, sweet girl." She scooped up the orange-and-white tabby, scratched behind her ears, and opened the door with her other hand. A pungent odor met her, and she carried Kiki with her until she found the source. The trash can in the kitchen.

Pinching her nose, she bundled the trash and headed for the door. She was almost down the steps when she heard horse hooves. She spun around, still holding her nose, and peered down the road. It wasn't until the buggy got much closer that she recognized the driver. The new guy. She couldn't remember his name.

Miriam hurried down the remaining steps, dropped the bag next to the house, and met him before he even got out of his buggy. "*Wie bischt*," she said as he stepped down. *What could this man want? Is he going to ask me out again?* She was pretty sure she'd made her answer clear. Miriam didn't date. She couldn't. What was the point? She'd accepted God's plan for her years ago.

"Wie bischt," the man said. "We met briefly after worship service. Eli Byler."

Miriam folded her arms across her chest. "*Ya,* I remember. You asked me out. You're not here to do that again, are you?"

He held up both palms, grinned slightly, and shook his head. "*Nee.* I think you made it perfectly clear that taking you out was never going to happen."

Miriam stifled a smile as she took in Eli's appearance, wishing things were different. Eli had a gentle smile that crooked up on one side, and his dark hair and beard were specked with gray, even though his features suggested he was in his thirties. "Then why are you here?" she finally asked.

"I'm looking for *mei* daughter, Grace." Worry lines creased his forehead. "She said she was going to the Lantz *haus* to watch her friend Wayne play baseball, but she didn't come home when she said she would." He paused, shrugged. "Anyway, Amos told me that you play baseball some-times, and I wondered if you saw her there. I drove by the Lantz *haus,* but all the play-ers had left."

"She was there. And I saw her and Wayne leave together." Miriam took a quick breath. "How old is Grace?"

"She's fifteen. And very responsible. It's not like her not to come home when she says."

Miriam squinted as she stared at Eli. "She's not even in her *rumschpringe,* but you let her date?"

Eli frowned. "She's not dating. She just went to watch a friend play baseball." He looped his thumbs under his suspenders and stood taller. "Besides, she'll be sixteen in a couple of months. She's had such a hard time with this move, I guess I've given her some liberties a little early. And Amos said Wayne is a *gut* boy, a hard worker."

Miriam rolled her eyes. "*Ya,* he's a hard worker all right."

"What does that mean?" Eli folded his arms across his chest like Miriam's.

She wasn't sure whether or not to spill the beans about Wayne. All the girls already thought she was a snitch, but she loved those girls and felt a certain responsibility. She didn't even know Grace.

"I'd just keep a close eye on your daughter," she said. "Boys that age . . ." Biting her bottom lip, she watched the furrows of Eli's brow deepen. "I'm sure she's fine," she added, trying to backtrack, but it was too late. She'd already set the stage, and she could tell by the way Eli was scowling that she'd said too much. But Eli was a man. Surely he remembered what it was like to be a teenage boy.

"I'm sure I'll find her, or she'll show up at home. I'm sorry to have bothered you." He got back into his buggy.

"Eli, wait." Miriam took a few steps until she was right next to the buggy. She was pretty sure she knew where Wayne and Grace had gone, but when she opened her mouth to tell Eli, the words didn't come out. Grace would be horrified if her father caught her in an inappropriate situation with Wayne. But maybe that's exactly what needed to happen so Eli could keep his daughter safe. She thought about it for a few more seconds, then said, "I'm sure she's fine, and if I should happen to hear anything, I'll make sure she knows you are looking for her."

"Danki."

Miriam stood in the yard until she saw Eli turn the corner, then she let out a heavy sigh and huffed back to the side of the house to grab the trash. It would have been nice to curl up on the couch with Kiki and bury her head in a good book. But now she was going to have to go tell Grace that her father was looking for her.

Grace wiggled free of Wayne's tight hold as he kissed her in a way that was making her uncomfortable, and his hands were traveling again. "I can't, Wayne."

He eased away, breathing hard and frowning. Cupping her cheek gently in his hand, he said, "I know it might seem wrong, but when two people really like each other, it's just natural to want to be closer."

Grace's breathing was ragged, and alarms were going off in her mind, but Wayne spoke with such tenderness. And he was so cute. If he really cared about her, maybe there was no harm in letting him take things a little further. But she quickly tossed the thought aside as her mother's face flashed in front of her, and the thought of disappointing her was too much to bear, even if *Mamm*'s view was from heaven. She shook her head, and Wayne dropped his hand.

"I think you'd better take me home. I'm already late." Grace doubted her father had even noticed, but if she was gone much longer, he might. Or maybe not. From her seat next to Wayne in the buggy, it was easy to see why he had chosen this spot. From the highway, they'd turned onto a dirt road, followed wagon-wheel ruts across a pasture, and arrived at this cluster of trees with barely enough room for a buggy. There was an overlook about fifty feet away and a creek below. Secluded and pretty. The perfect make-out spot.

"Fine." Wayne twisted in his seat, and Grace was startled by his gruff tone.

"Are you mad?" She reached for his hand at the same time he grabbed the reins, so she slowly returned her hand to her lap.

"*Nee.* I'm not mad." He dropped the reins and sighed. "It's just . . ." He turned to look at her and pressed his lips together, and for a moment, she thought she saw his lip tremble. "I've never felt this way about anyone before. I know we haven't known each other long, but I'm feeling something I've never felt before. And it wonders me if you are feeling the same way. I'm worried that you're not." He hung his head, and this time Grace reached for his hand and latched on.

"*Ach,* Wayne." Her words sounded dreamy, but she felt like she might burst with emotion. "I *am* feeling something. I really am." As he turned to face her, she leaned over and kissed him on the mouth, and as he returned the kiss, Grace knew that it was going to take more than just a few kisses to hold on to someone like him. But they both jumped when they heard a buggy come up the path.

"You have got to be kidding me," Wayne said as he abruptly pulled away from Grace and stepped out of the buggy. "This is *ab im kopp,* you following us around."

"I'm not off in the head, Wayne. I don't want to be here any more than you want me here." Miriam spat the words as she approached them. "But Grace's *daed* showed up at *mei haus* looking for her."

Grace brought a hand to her chest, then stepped out of the buggy. Following a brief thrust of adrenaline that shot through her veins, she realized that even if she got in trouble, her father did care about her. Deep down, she knew he did, but he'd been so preoccupied that it was good to know she'd been missed.

Miriam scowled at Grace before she looked back at Wayne. "And I knew you'd bring her to make-out mountain, or whatever you boys are calling it these days." She pointed a finger at him. "You'd best get Grace home. Now!"

Grace couldn't get back in the buggy fast enough. She wasn't sure who she was more scared of, Miriam or her father.

Surprisingly, Wayne didn't respond to her.

He just hurried back to the buggy and stayed quiet on the ride home.

Grace sat on the couch, staring at the floor as Eli paced the living room. He wasn't sure how strict he should be with Gracie. He wanted her to make friends and to be happy here, but too much freedom could also lead to trouble at her age. And how much had Leah talked to Grace about boys?

"I was worried about you. When you didn't come home, all I could think about was . . ." He stopped pacing and locked eyes with Gracie when she looked up. "You know, your *mamm.* What if there had been an accident?"

She pulled her eyes away, leaned back on the couch, and folded her arms across her chest. "Sorry."

You don't sound very sorry. Eli stroked his beard, thinking and praying he was saying the right things. Grace had already told him that Miriam had gotten word to her that Eli was looking for her. He was grateful to Miriam for that.

"Can I go upstairs now?"

Eli stared at his beautiful daughter, and in his mind's eye, he could still see her as a little girl, running into his arms. Now he couldn't recall the last time Gracie had initiated a hug, and it was hard for him to acknowledge that his little girl was growing up.

"There's someone here anyway," she said, standing up.

Eli looked out the window, and sure enough, a buggy was heading up the driveway. "All right. We can talk more about this later."

Grace padded across the living room in her socks, then scurried up the stairs.

"See what Ben's doing up there," Eli hollered before he walked onto the porch. When he saw who his visitor was, he couldn't keep the smile from his face. Two female visitors in one day.

Ruth floated her way to him in total perfection, like the angel he'd made her out to be the moment he'd laid eyes on her.

"Please forgive my unannounced visit, but I wanted to welcome you and your family to Paradise." She handed him a pie. "I've brought you an apple crumb pie."

When Ruth smiled, Eli went weak in the knees. *"Danki,"* he managed to say, even though he felt tongue-tied. "How nice of dooo . . . I mean, you." He nervously chuckled. "Um . . . would . . . would you like maybe to come have a chunk?" He blinked his eyes a few times. *What is wrong with me?* "I mean a *slice.* Not a chunk."

Ruth laughed, and Eli felt like his body was lifting off the ground when she said she'd love a slice. So together they floated into the house, and Eli had never been more grateful to be freshly bathed and dressed in his Sunday blue shirt. He hadn't realized until this moment that he'd grabbed his newest shirt reserved for worship service. He invited Ruth to sit in the living room, and he fetched two slices of pie, then two cups of coffee. The pie wasn't nearly as good as Elizabeth's, but it was merely a passing thought.

"I met your precious *kinner* last Sunday, Grace and Ben. I'm guessing Grace is fourteen or fifteen, and Ben . . . maybe ten?"

Eli nodded from his spot on the couch next to Ruth. "Close. Gracie is fifteen, almost sixteen, and Ben is eleven."

"How wonderful," Ruth said, setting her plate on the coffee table after only a couple of bites. "I have four *kinner.* Stephen is six, Carolyn is seven, Eve just turned eleven — same age as your Ben — and Mary is thirteen."

"Aren't big families *wunderbaar?* Together we have six *kinner.*" Eli felt his face turning fire-engine red, since he apparently already had them married off and raising their six

315

children together, but when Ruth smiled, Eli smiled too. Then he hung on Ruth's every word for the next thirty minutes.

"What is wrong with *Daed*?" Ben whispered to Grace from the top of the stairs. "He don't sound right."

Grace rolled her eyes. "He's trying to impress that lady."

"What's that mean, imperess?"

"Not imperess, impress. It means he's trying to put on a *gut* show for her so that she'll like him."

Ben grinned. "I don't think he's doin' too *gut* a job. Sounds like he can't say his words right."

Grace had to put a hand over her mouth to keep from laughing. She'd never heard her father stutter before, or sound so nervous with a woman. She held a finger to her lips before whispering to Ben. "Listen, that lady just asked *Daed* if he wanted to come over for lunch next Saturday. Guess she wants to be our new *mamm,*" Grace said as she rolled her eyes again. Maybe it wouldn't be so bad. With six kids, Grace could just stay lost in the crowd; lost with Wayne. She smiled.

"I don't know. Maybe the other woman will be *Daed*'s *fraa.*"

316

Grace scowled. "What other woman?"

"A lady named Elizabeth was here earlier. She brought *Daed* a pie, too, and before she left, I heard *Daed* say he'd see her for Saturday supper."

Grace heard the door shut and the house go silent. "What is he doing? Someone needs to explain to him how dating works." She tromped down the stairs, Ben on her heels.

Ben laughed. "Uh, you gonna explain it to him? Like you'd know anything about it."

When they hit the landing, Grace spun around. "As a matter of fact, I do. I have a boyfriend."

"You're as bad as *Daed*. You didn't waste any time either. But you ain't old enough to date."

"Well, *Daed* is letting me go out with Wayne."

They were quiet when the front door opened and their father came in. Grace walked to the middle of the living room and slammed her hands to her hips. *Daed* was grinning in such a way that he looked like a little boy. Grace lifted her chin.

"*Daed,* please tell me that it isn't true . . . that you have a date for lunch next Saturday and a date for supper? Don't you think that's a bit much? I've heard you say that you never date two women at the same time, that it isn't right."

"I . . . I did say that." *Daed* scratched his forehead. "But these aren't really dates." He smiled as he shrugged. "Just friends having a meal."

"It's still dates." Grace shook her head. "You need to go to dating school or something. I know you didn't go out much back home, but you need to use some discretion." Grace had recently learned that word from Rachel, who liked to throw big words around. She nodded to Ben. "You have a young child at home."

"Hey!" Ben said, scowling. "You ain't much older than me."

"Dating school?" *Daed* stroked his beard, grinning. "Is there such a thing?"

"Be serious, *Daed*. You made two dates that could overlap. Dinner at noon and supper at four. Do you know what they call that in the *Englisch* world?" She waited, lifting her chin higher. "It's called double-booking, *Daed*. That's what they call it. You've double-booked."

Grace clicked her tongue, then turned and went upstairs, certain that her father was going to embarrass her by acting like a silly schoolboy.

CHAPTER FIVE

Eli tucked his shirt in and pulled his suspenders over his shoulders. He'd spent all week looking forward to his lunch with Ruth and supper with Elizabeth, even though he was guilty of breaking his own rule. Double-booked, Gracie had called it.

Thirty minutes later, he was knocking on Ruth's door, praying that he wouldn't stutter or act stupid. But when she opened the door and gazed into his eyes, his knees got that weird feeling again, and he wished he'd brought her flowers. As it were, she might as well have been holding his heart on a platter. Eli knew Leah would want him to be happy, but he couldn't help but wonder if she was frowning from heaven and saying, "*Ach,* Eli. Pick up your jaw before you slobber on yourself." Eli was well aware that looks shouldn't play a part in his decisions, but Ruth was an exception that he'd never been faced with before.

"Come in, Eli. Welcome to our home." Ruth stepped aside, and Eli walked into the living room, surprised at how fancy it was. She had green shades covering the windows, which he'd learned was customary in Lancaster County, but she had ivory lace valances as well. Above the fireplace were several decorative figurines and even two pictures hanging on the wall. The rug atop the wood floor was colorful and looked expensive. As he took a deep breath, he could vaguely smell something cooking, but mingling with a meaty aroma was a lemony scent, like the kind of cleaning solution Leah used to make. Eli couldn't recall a time when his home was ever this clean, even when Leah was alive, especially after Gracie and Ben were born. And Ruth had twice as many *kinner* as he did.

"Your home is very nice," he said, proud of himself for speaking clearly this time.

"Danki. So nice of you to say so." She motioned for him to sit down on the couch, and he noticed how quiet it was. "I'm anxious to meet your *kinner."*

Ruth sat down in a rocking chair across from Eli. She crossed her legs and cupped one knee with her hands. "I was looking forward to them meeting you, but they aren't here today. *Mei* sister has them for the day, and they love going to their aunt's *haus* since she has young *kinner* too." Ruth smiled. "I just couldn't tell them no."

Eli swallowed hard and nodded as he shifted his weight on the couch, wishing he wasn't so nervous. And when Ruth got up and walked to the couch, the knot in his throat grew to the size of a walnut. She sat down beside him. So close that her black apron brushed against his blue slacks.

"I don't date much, Eli, so this is a little awkward for me." She tucked her chin, then looked up and batted her eyelashes at him. "But when I saw you after worship service for the first time, I felt like you were someone I wanted to get to know."

"It is a little awkward for me too." Eli swallowed twice, then coughed. "I dated a little back home, but never anyone — anyone . . . as pretty as you."

Ruth's lashes swept down over her high cheekbones as she bit her bottom lip, then she looked up at him and smiled. "What a nice thing to say."

"And . . . and I would like to get to know you too."

"Are you ready for dinner?"

Eli nodded, then followed Ruth into her kitchen where two white china plates were laid out at opposite ends of a table for six.

In addition to the green blinds, green-and-white-checked valances hung on the windows, and cool air blew through the screened windows. The lemony smell had faded, replaced with the aroma of roast. There was another colorful rug on the floor underneath the table, and several kitchen gadgets on the counter, along with a set of green canisters. It was a large room that was painted light beige. Eli had sought information about the bishop before he chose to move here, and he'd learned that the man was lenient. *Very lenient, apparently.*

After they ate, Ruth insisted Eli wait in the living room while she cleaned things up and started some coffee. A few minutes later, she joined Eli on the couch with two cups of coffee. Eli thanked her for the meal. She twisted to face him, tucking one foot underneath her, and even though her cooking skills weren't the best, he could overlook that.

"Tell me everything about you, Eli," she said as she leaned her shoulder against the back of the couch.

Eli gave her a condensed version of his life thus far, anxious to hear about her. She listened intently when he got to the part about Leah dying.

"That must have been so hard." She

touched his arm and hung her head for a few moments.

Ruth's life story was similar to Eli's. She'd married young and started having children right away, and her husband had died a year and a half ago, six months short of how long Leah had been gone. Cancer had taken him, too, like Elizabeth's husband. Ruth was in a much better place emotionally than Elizabeth, but time made loss more bearable. Eli knew he would never forget his first love, and the pain was still present, but he was learning to live again. And for the first time in a long time, he was excited about his future. As Ruth started talking to him about the kind of books she liked to read, her favorite foods, and how important it was to her that her children stay in the community, they fell into a comfortable conversation. He shed his nervousness, and eventually he surprised himself by sharing his love for cooking with her.

Miriam wasn't surprised to see Grace watching the baseball game again since Wayne was playing. But she was surprised to see the girl still sitting there after everyone had left the Lantzes' house, including Wayne. Miriam got in her buggy and started to back up when she noticed there weren't any other buggies left, except those belonging to the Lantzes. She glanced at Grace, whose head hung low, her shoulders moving up and down.

As she backed the horse up, she recalled how she'd felt called to go find Grace last Saturday, a girl she didn't even know. It hadn't been her responsibility, but Eli had been so worried. Today, she was going to do what she'd planned to do last Saturday, curl up with Kiki and read a book. But she hadn't even made it off the Lantzes' property when she turned the buggy around, grumbling to herself. She tethered the horse and walked to Grace.

"Do you need a ride?" Miriam silently prayed that Grace hadn't already done something she regretted. "Your *haus* isn't that much out of the way, and I'd be happy to take you home."

Grace sniffled as she stood up, then pulled her sweater around her. "*Nee,* I can walk."

"That's a far piece to your place from here." Miriam studied Grace's tearstained face, and for the third time in the past two weeks, she felt like smacking Wayne. But where were the girls she'd been sitting with? "Did your girlfriends just leave you here?"

"They aren't my girlfriends," she snapped back. "And I didn't ride here with them

324

anyway. I came with Wayne." Glaring a little, she added, "But you probably know that."

Miriam had been late today, but she had assumed Grace had come with Wayne. She cringed a bit when Grace continued to shoot daggers at her. Nothing worse than a hormonal teenager who had been wronged by a boy. *Walk away, Miriam.*

"*Mei maedel,* I tried to warn you about Wayne. There are lots of nice boys here, and —"

"I don't want to talk about this with you." Grace took long strides toward the driveway, continuing to swipe at her eyes.

Miriam glanced up at the dark clouds overhead, the reason they'd cut the baseball game short. "Did Wayne just leave you here?" she asked as she scurried to catch up with Grace.

"Just leave me alone. I hate it here. I wish we'd never moved here." Grace stopped and faced Miriam, her eyes red and swollen. "The only reason we're here is so *mei daed* can find a *fraa.*"

"I gathered that." Miriam bit her lip, trying not to grin, but when a smile broke through anyway, Grace grunted and started walking away. "Grace, wait!"

When Grace didn't slow down, Miriam ran to catch up to her. She grabbed her by the arm. "Please wait."

"What do you want, Miriam? You were right. I wouldn't give Wayne what he wanted, and he left me here. When I said I needed to go straight home today, he said he was going to town to visit two girls he knew, *Englisch* girls."

Relief washed over Miriam, but she knew Wayne wouldn't give up that easily, and Grace didn't have a mother to confide in, or apparently anyone else. Miriam wouldn't have gone to her mother about something like this when she was Grace's age anyway.

"Just let me take you home. A storm is coming, and I can't let you walk all the way to your place."

"*Ach,* well, you're not my boss, so you can't stop me." Grace folded her arms across her chest.

Miriam smiled broadly. "Really, Grace? You sound like a five-year-old. *You're not the boss of me,*" Miriam mimicked as she waved her hands playfully in the air, although it was apparent by Grace's blazing eyes that she wasn't amused. "I'm taking you home. Come on." Miriam looked up at the sky as thunder rumbled in the distance. "Please. We don't even have to talk."

"Fine," Grace huffed as she headed toward Miriam's buggy. It was everything

Miriam could do not to say something about her smart mouth and lack of appreciation, but the important thing was to get her home safely, so she bit her lip again. It started drizzling not five minutes after they got on the road. She didn't dare tell Grace that Mr. Ed got spooked by thunder, but when he whinnied and tried to pick up the pace, Miriam had to pull back on the reins.

"Whoa, Mr. Ed." She eased him back into a steady trot, hoping to beat the storm that was fast approaching.

"What kind of a name is Mr. Ed?" Grace spat the words at Miriam.

"It was the name he had when I got him. He was put out to pasture after he was no *gut* on the racetrack anymore. Things like trains, thunder, and the fire alarms in town tend to spook him, but I've learned how to handle him."

"I hope so," Grace said under her breath as she leaned out the window and looked up at the sky.

Miriam only had one buggy, and she was glad it was covered. "He wasn't treated very well where he was, and someone got word to me, and I took him in." She glanced at Grace and smiled. "He's a lovable fellow."

"The *Englisch* don't always treat their

animals very *gut,*" Grace said as she kept her eyes on the road. Big drops of rain had started to slam against the windshield.

"I got him from an Amish farmer, not *Englisch.*" Miriam had to pay twice as much as the horse was worth, but after seeing the whip marks across his flanks, she wasn't leaving without him.

They were quiet until the horse reared up in response to a loud clap of thunder, and it took a little longer for Miriam to get him settled down.

"I think I would have been safer to just walk," Grace said as she clutched the dashboard.

"That's my *haus.* I think we'd better wait out the storm there. It's still a ways to your place."

"*Ya,* okay."

Miriam was a little surprised that Grace was so agreeable. Miriam would have kept going if it was just herself in the buggy, but she had Grace to think about.

"Do you have a cell phone?" Miriam asked as she pulled into her driveway. Grace nodded. "Call your *daed* and tell him that I'll bring you home after the weather gets better."

"I doubt he'll be too worried." Grace finally let go of the dash when Miriam

328

pulled back on the reins and Mr. Ed was stopped in front of the barn.

"Of course he will be worried. I could tell he was concerned when he was looking for you last weekend."

"Well, he's on a date, so I'm sure he's pre-occupied interviewing a new *mamm* for me and Ben." She paused, turned to Miriam, and held up two fingers. "Actually, he has *two* dates today."

"Busy man," Miriam mumbled as she wondered whether or not Eli had asked her out first, second, or maybe even third. "Who is he out with?" *Not that I care.*

"His dinner date at noon was with someone named Ruth."

"Ruth Zook?"

"I think so. And the other one is someone named Elizabeth Petersheim."

Miriam was quiet for a few moments. She knew Elizabeth wanted to get remarried and start a family, but it seemed that she might not be ready. Elizabeth still cried a lot. Ruth, on the other hand, easily lured men in. She was beautiful. But the few she'd dated hadn't worked out. "I wonder who the lucky lady will be. He asked me out too." Miriam said the last part under her breath, although Grace must have heard.

"Ach, nee." Grace had her hand on the

329

door handle, but she threw her head back and let out an exaggerated sigh. "Please tell me that you are not trying to be our new *mamm* too."

Miriam glared at Grace. "I assure you, I want nothing to do with your father in that way, so you'll never have to worry about me being your new mommy." She thought this news would make Grace happy, but the girl just sat there staring blankly at her.

"*Mei daed* is a wonderful man." Grace's tone was defensive.

Touching. "I'm sure he is. Now let's get Mr. Ed settled in the barn and make a dash for the *haus* before this weather gets worse. Then you can call Mr. Wonderful and let him know you're safe." She grinned, and surprisingly, Grace did too.

CHAPTER SIX

Eli pushed his horse harder than ever through the downpour, wondering if he could blame the rain as his excuse for being so late to Elizabeth's house. *"Ya, ya!"* he yelled. When he'd realized what time it was, he'd made a mad dash out of Ruth's house, promising to call her later. He'd already made his decision about whom he wanted to date. Ruth was everything he wanted in a woman, aside from just being beautiful. But he owed it to Elizabeth to be polite, and he was angry with himself for being so late.

When Elizabeth opened her front door, she handed Eli a towel to dry off. Eli took the towel, but he'd never felt like such a heel in his life. Elizabeth's eyes were red and swollen. "I'm so sorry." It had to be nearly five thirty by now, and he was due at Elizabeth's house at four.

"It's no problem." Elizabeth waited on the other side of the threshold, and for a few moments, Eli wasn't sure he was going to be invited in, but once he'd finished drying off, she eased the screen door open and stepped aside. "Supper is cold, but I can reheat everything if you'd like."

"Nee, nee," he quickly said. "I'm sure it will be wonderful like it is." Shivering, he followed her into the living room, a much plainer room than at Ruth's house, more like what Eli was used to. "It sure smells *gut* in here."

Elizabeth didn't say anything but motioned for him to follow her.

When Eli walked into the kitchen, he'd never seen such a spread laid out, especially for just two people. There must have been ten different offerings, including two pies. Elizabeth's table wasn't as big as Ruth's, to be expected since she lived alone. There was seating for four and two place settings, which barely fit amidst all the food. Eli pulled out a chair and sat down. He wasn't all that hungry since he'd eaten a heavy meal a few hours ago, but he planned to force himself to eat generous portions since Elizabeth had gone to so much trouble. "*Ach,* Elizabeth . . . this looks *gut* beyond words."

She smiled, but there was something not quite right about the way she pressed her lips together. Eli knew that look. "I hope you like it. I worked on it all day."

Ouch. He deserved that. Worst of all was that she looked like she'd been crying, and Eli felt like a louse. "I can't apologize enough for being so late. There's no excuse. I was busy and lost track of the time."

"It is fine." She took a seat across from him, then they both bowed their heads in prayer. After Eli filled his plate, he took a bite of chicken casserole. And that was all it took for his appetite to return. He'd wondered if the pie was a fluke, just her best recipe. But after trying a little bit of everything, he had to admit — she was a better cook than Leah. And certainly better in the kitchen than Ruth. Eli had jokingly thought, *If I marry Ruth, I'll have to do the cooking,* and it was an idea he liked. But first he was going to get through this meal.

As they ate, the silence grew awkward. "How was your day?" Eli scooped up a forkful of mashed potatoes. Even the potatoes were better than most, with just the right amount of butter slightly browned on top.

"I cooked all day," she said again, barely picking at her food and not looking at him.

Eli needed to do something to redeem himself, even if he had no plans to pursue Elizabeth in a romantic way. He was sorry for being late, but he couldn't help but think maybe she was overreacting a little. This situation didn't seem to warrant tears, but just the same, he wanted to cheer her up. But visions of his time with Ruth were distracting him. He couldn't wait to see her again.

"You have a very pretty home." Eli was getting full, but he accepted a slice of coconut pie when Elizabeth inched the pie closer to him. "Coconut pie is a favorite of mine." He took a bite. "And this is surely the best I've ever had." The truth. But Elizabeth stayed quiet.

When they were done eating, they moved into the living room. There was no mention of coffee, and the brittle silence was even worse now that they weren't busy eating. Eli decided to break the ice.

"I can tell you're upset about me being late, Elizabeth. It wonders me what I can do to make you feel better. I'm usually punctual, so I apologize to you again." They were each sitting in a rocking chair, a small table between them with a lantern on top, a box of tissues, and several books.

"It's fine, really," Elizabeth said with a stone-faced expression that Eli knew meant trouble. *Fine* never meant fine when a woman said it like that, accompanied by that look. Eli used to be able to talk his way out of trouble with Leah.

Eli picked up the book on top of the pile, a Christian devotional guide for women. "I love to read when I have the time," he said, casually thumbing through the pages. He put it down, smiled, then picked up the next book, a novel with a woman on the front cover, a prairie in the background.

"I have plenty of time to read," she said as her voice cracked a little bit. Eli had a strong urge to hug her, to comfort her, but in a fatherly sort of way. But he just nodded as he put the book back.

"*Danki* for supper. It was the best meal I've had in a very long time. But I reckon it's best to get home. Gracie went to watch the baseball game at the Lantzes' *haus,* and I'm anxious to make sure she got home safely." Eli stood up, but Elizabeth remained seated, kicking her rocker into motion as she folded her hands in her lap. Eli should have already called his daughter, but Grace was the worst about leaving her cell phone lying around or not answering it. He was glad the use of cell phones was acceptable in Lancaster County.

"*Danki* again," Eli said when it appeared that Elizabeth wasn't going to walk him to the door. "See you soon." He forced a smile and moved toward the door, but when he heard a whimper, he turned around. Elizabeth had covered her face with her hands. Eli suspected this was going to be a long evening. He needed to call Gracie. Ben was spending the night at his new friend's house, so he just needed to make sure his daughter was okay before he tried to make amends with Elizabeth, whose whimpering had turned into full-blown sobs.

Grace lagged behind Miriam and stayed on the porch to talk on her cell to her father, then walked into Miriam's living room and closed the door behind her.

"*Daed* is with date number two, and he'll pick me up in a little while," she said as she looked around Miriam's house. "No wonder you're not married," Grace mumbled as Miriam started a fire in the fireplace. It wasn't very cold, but the fall afternoons and evenings were cool enough to enjoy a fire, and within a few minutes, orange sparks shimmied up the chimney. Grace tossed her sweater on the couch, which was filled with . . . stuff. There wasn't even room to sit down.

"Okay, now we have warmth." Miriam brushed her hands against her dress. "Now, what did you say?"

"I said . . ." Grace twisted her mouth back and forth but didn't have the heart to come out and tell Miriam that this place was a wreck. Newspapers, books, and empty plates were piled high on the coffee table, and a further inspection of the couch revealed laundry that needed folding, more books, and . . . a cat. "Aw, who's this?" Grace picked up the orange-and-white tabby. "I love, love, love cats. But *Daed* is allergic, so we've never had one." She held the kitty close and stroked her ears, and within seconds she purred.

"That's Kiki."

Grace recalled hearing someone say that Miriam had lots of cats, like a crazy cat lady. "Where are the others? Don't you have more cats?"

Miriam shook her head. "*Nee,* it's just me and Kiki." She gave the fire another poke, then turned to Grace. "Are you hungry?"

Grace had figured she and Wayne would eat after the baseball game, but his only suggestion had been to go back to the same place as last Saturday to make out. When Grace had said no, that she better get home, there was no mention of food or even a ride home. *Jerk.* "*Ya,* I'm a little hungry."

"Come on." Miriam motioned for Grace to follow her into the kitchen, so she set

Kiki back on the couch. They both had to step around three big boxes on the way.

"Did you just move here?" Grace walked into the kitchen behind Miriam. Dishes were piled in the sink, but otherwise, it wasn't too bad. Kind of pretty. Plain and simple, but with just a little color here and there.

"*Nee,* I've been here about four years. My parents moved to Colorado after both of my grandparents died. Some of the Amish folks here have been moving out there. Land is cheaper, and there's more of it. My two younger *bruders* went with them, but I chose to stay here." She shriveled up her face. "It's cold there." Then she shrugged. "Besides, I couldn't imagine leaving here. But they are all happy and that's what counts. Both my *bruders* got married in the past year, and one of my sister-in-laws is expecting. But I miss them all." She opened the pantry and pulled out a box of macaroni and cheese. "This okay?"

Grace was speechless. She'd never had boxed macaroni and cheese. "Okay," she said hesitantly as she pulled out a chair at the small kitchen table and sat down, briefly wondering how her father's two dates had gone. She wanted him to be happy, but it was unsettling to think about anyone besides their mother living with them. "Why aren't you married?"

"I'm not planning to get married," Miriam said as she turned the gas up on the burner before placing a pot of water on top.

"Why?" That was unheard of to Grace. Everyone wanted to get married and have children. "Um . . . are you sick or something?" Maybe Miriam didn't want to burden a man if she wasn't well.

"*Nee*, not that I know of." Miriam turned to face Grace and leaned against the kitchen counter. "I know those girls you hang out with call me an old maid." She smiled. "They can be a bit rude sometimes, but I think once you get to know them, you'll find that they really are *gut* girls. I know it's hard to make friends at your age, but give it some time. All of those girls have grown up together. It will just take awhile for them to warm up to you."

"But why aren't you married? I don't understand." Grace propped her elbows on the table, then cupped her cheeks as she and Miriam locked eyes. "I mean, you're . . . um . . . pretty."

"For an old maid, huh?" Miriam chuckled. "I just choose not to get married. I spend my time trying to do for others, trying to live a *gut* life, and worshipping my heavenly

339

Father as often as I can."

"But lots of people do all those things and still get married and have *kinner.* I don't understand," she said again.

Folks in their community had stopped asking these questions a long time ago. It was just accepted that Miriam planned to live her life alone. But every time a new single man came along, the questions started again. Miriam was tempted to tell Grace the truth, that she wished more than ever that she could share her life with a wonderful man, and why that wasn't possible anymore. But this was a teenage girl she barely knew.

"You don't have to understand," she finally said. "It's just the way I choose to live my life."

"It's weird."

That wasn't the first time Miriam had heard the popular *Englisch* word used to describe her. "*Ya,* you are correct. I am a weird old maid." Miriam had grown used to laughing at herself. She wished things were different, but this was the path God had chosen for her, and she made do, trying to stay focused on the positives. But sometimes, late at night, in the darkness when no one was around, she'd allow herself a good cry.

"Do you date?"

Miriam sighed, hoping Grace would move on to something else soon. "*Nee,* I stay busy doing other things."

"Like what?" Grace nodded toward the sink full of dishes, then strained her neck to look into the living room. "You don't stay busy cleaning *haus.*"

Miriam folded her arms across her chest and raised an eyebrow. "Anything I want to do. How many people can say that?"

"Do you work? I noticed you don't have a garden. What do you do?"

"You are a curious creature, are you not?" Miriam grinned, tempted to make up a fun story to tell Grace, but instead, she dumped the noodles in the boiling water before motioning for Grace to follow her. They walked down the hall to Miriam's extra bedroom that she'd turned into a sewing room after her parents left for Colorado. She pushed the door wide and kept her eyes on Grace, not wanting to miss her expression.

Grace's jaw dropped as she walked into the spacious room toward the quilting table, then took in the dozens of quilts on racks around the room.

"Did you do all of these on your own?"

Grace took another look around, then gingerly touched the project on the table, a quilt filled with bold colors, a special order that Miriam was almost done with. "Or do you have quilting parties in here?"

"*Nee.* I've done all of these myself." She picked up an old red suitcase and set it on a nearby chair. "This suitcase is filled with scraps from Widow Hostetler's life. I've been piecing them together for weeks, until the patchwork is just perfect." She eased closer to where Grace was standing and pointed to the square in the middle. "This piece represents Widow Hostetler. It's a scrap from her swaddling cloth when she was born." Miriam touched each of the six squares surrounding the center. "Each of these scraps represents what Widow Hostetler believes to be the most important events in her life. Her baptism into the faith, marrying her husband, and the birth of her four children."

She pointed to the next eight larger squares. "These squares represent things to do with her baptism, husband, and children, things relevant to them. Then it branches out from there, until the quilt becomes her entire life story." Miriam smiled. "I love doing these story quilts. I know more about Widow Hostetler than I ever would have

342

known otherwise." She walked around the table and pointed to a maroon square. "This was the dress she was wearing when she packed up and left the community. She was shunned for doing so." She glanced at Grace. "She was sixteen when she left."

"But she came back?" Grace was still running her hand along the tightly sewn patches.

"*Ya.* But not for six years." Miriam touched the square with the white cross etched in the middle. "This represents her return to Christ."

"What's this one?" Grace touched a square with a cross-stitched pie in the middle.

Miriam smiled. "Against the bishop's wishes — it was a different bishop back then — Widow . . . Annie Hostetler . . . entered her key lime pie at the county fair. And she won."

Grace smiled. "This is the neatest thing." She looked up at Miriam. "Are all your quilts like this? Do they all tell a life story?"

"*Nee,* some people just order a regular old quilt. But these are my favorites to make. Annie plans to write up a list of what each scrap means, then she'll give it to her *kinner.* She has arthritis, so it's hard for her to do any type of quilting these days. But most of my orders are from the *Englisch.*"

"So . . . I guess someone wouldn't do this until they were old, right?"

Miriam shook her head. "*Nee.* I do them for all different reasons." She walked to a rack on the far wall and pulled down a small quilt. "I just need to finish the edges on this, but each scrap represents a child's life — when she was born, when she took her first step — see the picture of baby shoes sewn in? And it goes all the way until she starts her first day of school, represented by the book in this square."

"These are the most beautiful quilts I've ever seen." Grace lifted her eyes to Miriam's again. "Beauty goes so much deeper than what our eyes can see, and the beauty in these quilts isn't just on the outside."

Miriam smiled, warmed by Grace's mature comment. "*Danki,* Grace."

Her eyes lit up. "Where's yours? Surely you've started one for yourself?"

This was the bad part about showing newcomers her quilting room. It was the question that ultimately came up. She didn't want to lie to Grace, but she'd never shown anyone her quilt, and she doubted she'd ever have anyone to hand it down to. "It's not very far along, a work in progress," she finally said.

Grace opened her mouth to say something, but they both looked toward the hallway when they heard a buggy coming.

"Probably *mei daed*," Grace said softly. "*Danki* for showing me this, Miriam."

"You're welcome. Ready for mac and cheese?"

Grace smiled and nodded, so they headed back to the kitchen. Miriam supposed she would have to ask Eli to stay for supper. She smiled to herself. *Unless he's too full from all his dates.*

But when Eli walked into the house, Miriam had to ward off the sadness that threatened her sometimes in the presence of someone she might have been interested in. *Oh, how I wish things were different.*

CHAPTER SEVEN

Eli was sure he'd never eaten so much in one day, and he'd surely never had noodles and cheese that came from a box. Gracie had tapped him on the arm and nodded to the empty box when Miriam wasn't looking. Eli forced himself to take a few bites. It was awful, but Grace ate most of her serving.

"I'm sorry it's not a better meal, but I didn't know I'd have company for supper," Miriam said, smiling. Eli wondered if her house was tidier when she was expecting visitors.

"*Danki* for asking me to stay." Eli would have preferred to go home, but Gracie wanted to stay. And now that he was here, he was having a hard time keeping his eyes off of Miriam. He'd never had a woman shoot him down so fast. Eli knew he was no expert when it came to dating, but her rejection had left him wondering if there was something outwardly wrong with him. He tried to clear his thoughts. It had gone from a wonderful afternoon with Ruth to a terrible time with Elizabeth. But when Eli had finally left Elizabeth, she'd stopped crying. They'd both decided she wasn't ready for any type of courtship yet, a decision that would make it easy for Eli to move forward with Ruth, especially since they'd set another date before saying good-bye earlier. Ruth wanted Eli to come for lunch again next Saturday. And he would meet her four children.

Grace laughed out loud, which caught Eli's attention. She and Miriam had been chatting about quilts, and Eli hadn't heard most of what was said. But as he eyed his daughter, such merriment shining in her eyes, he tuned in to their conversation.

"So the *Englisch* lady wanted the entire quilt to have shoes on it? All different ones?"

"*Ya*. She loved shoes and she had many, many pairs." Miriam shook her head. "Can you imagine? So wasteful, but she paid a *gut* sum of money for me to make her the quilt."

Grace chuckled again. "*Nee*, I can't imagine. I wish I could have seen that."

Miriam tapped her finger to her chin for a few seconds, then she glanced at Eli before excusing herself. "Be right back."

After Miriam was out of earshot, Grace raised an eyebrow and said, "How were your dates?"

Eli shrugged. "One was *gut.* The other . . . not so *gut.*"

"So, who was the winner? Elizabeth or Ruth?"

"*Ach,* it's not really about being a winner because neither one of them is a loser."

"You picked Ruth, didn't you?" Grace slouched into her chair.

"It's not about picking, but *ya,* I think Ruth and I are better suited to each other. And Elizabeth isn't really ready to date. She wants to be ready, to get on with her life, but she is still grieving."

"If you're going to insist on dating, it's too bad you can't date Miriam." Grace stretched her neck and looked around the corner, apparently to see if Miriam was coming. "I like her," she added.

"You'll like Ruth too." Eli set his fork on the plate still half filled with the cheesy noodles from a box. "And besides, I *did* ask Miriam if she would like to go out, and she said no." He kept his eyes on Gracie's, curious how she'd react. She slouched even deeper into her chair.

"Don't take it personally. She doesn't date

348

anyone because she says she is never getting married."

"Maybe it's because she has a dozen cats, a messy *haus,* and eats noodles from a box." Eli realized he hadn't sneezed once since he got here.

"She only has one cat, and her name is Kiki." Gracie narrowed her eyebrows at Eli. "Why aren't you sneezing?"

Eli shrugged. "I don't know."

Gracie sat up tall in her chair and smiled. "Maybe you're not allergic anymore." She pressed her palms together. "Maybe we can get a cat?"

"We'll see. I imagine if I was around a cat all the time, I would take to sneezing again." Eli wanted to follow up on Gracie's earlier comment. "Why is Miriam never getting married?"

"I'm not sure." Gracie paused, then opened her mouth like she had more to say, but quickly closed it when Miriam came back into the room holding a photograph.

"This is our secret," Miriam said as she handed the picture to Gracie. "It took me awhile to find it. The *Englisch* woman took pictures of the quilt, and she gave me one. I've never shown it to anyone. We have a very *gut* and lenient bishop, but the one thing he frowns on is photographs of any kind. The younger folks are using their mobile phones to take pictures, and the bishop *really* dislikes that."

Eli had heard of phones taking pictures, even though his and Gracie's phones flipped open and didn't do such things. Eli was all for embracing certain technology that was necessary, and cell phones had become a necessity. He could recall several emergencies back home when folks could have died if they hadn't had a phone with them. Even though it didn't help Leah. But phones that took pictures were just too much luxury for Eli.

"I wish my phone took photographs," Gracie said as she glanced at Eli.

"Nee." Miriam spoke up before Eli had a chance to tell his daughter no. "It's not *gut.* We're all forced to move forward, to be more like the *Englisch* in many ways. But I think we need to remember the second commandment: 'Thou shalt not make unto thee any graven image, or any likeness of any thing that is in heaven above, or that is in the earth beneath, or that is in the water under the earth.' " She frowned. "I probably should not have even kept this photo, but . . ."

"I'm glad you showed me the picture. It's odd, but pretty." Gracie giggled, which was music to Eli's ears. "What a strange *Englisch* woman."

"Her shoes were like her *kinner*," Miriam said softly as she eased the picture from Gracie's hand. "She loved them all. She didn't have a husband or any *kinner*."

Eli kept his eyes on Miriam's. Such sadness in her voice, like regret. Possibly at her own situation? He waited until they'd left before he asked Gracie about it again.

"Um . . . so Miriam is never getting married — why?"

"I told you. I don't know." Gracie shrugged, then turned to him and grinned. *"Daed,* I can't believe you asked her out *too."*

Eli maneuvered the buggy around a pothole in the road filled with water, thankful it had stopped raining. "*Ya,* well, I did." They were both quiet for a while, then Eli said, "Next Saturday, I'm going to Ruth's again to meet her *kinner,* and I would like it if you and Ben would come too."

Gracie didn't respond.

"Will you do that for me?" Eli glanced at his daughter, and in the darkness, he saw her nod.

They were quiet again, until Gracie cleared her throat. *"Daed?"*

"Ya?"

"Who did you ask out first? Elizabeth,

Ruth, or Miriam?"

Eli turned into their driveway. "I didn't ask Elizabeth or Ruth out. They both asked me to their homes for dinner and supper." He paused, thinking. "The only one I asked out was Miriam."

"Why?"

Eli slowed the horse to a stop in front of their barn. It had been a spontaneous gesture asking Miriam to dinner, but he knew what prompted him to do so.

"She's pretty," Gracie said before Eli answered.

"*Ya,* she is. But she's different, and that interests me." He met Gracie in front of the buggy and they walked toward the house.

"I really like her," Gracie said as the glow from the propane light lit Gracie's features. Eli smiled, knowing Miriam had won Gracie over. Not an easy thing to do.

Monday morning, Grace shivered as she pinned a towel on the line, not realizing until today that she'd left her sweater at Miriam's. Maybe Miriam had found it and taken it to worship service, but Grace had no way to know since her family hadn't attended the service yesterday. *Daed* was sick with a stomach bug, and it was raining, so he didn't want Grace and Ben going alone.

Her father had tried to blame his stomach troubles on the boxed noodles and cheese, but finally admitted that it could have been any dozen of things he'd eaten on Saturday. Ben woke up this morning complaining of an upset stomach, so *Daed* let him stay home from school, but Grace wasn't sure that Ben didn't just want the day off.

Grace was picturing her mother next to her, showing her the best way to hang clothes on the line while they sang songs. *I miss you, Mamm.*

She looked over her shoulder when she heard footsteps. "You could help me, you know."

Ben sidled up beside her. "That's girls' work. But I'll do it if you'll go clean the barn."

Grace shook her head, clipping another towel to the line. "*Nee.* I don't think so."

Ben pulled a wet towel from the basket anyway and pulled two clothespins from the bag. Grace smiled. "You seem to be feeling better."

"Um . . . *ya.* When's *Daed* going to be back?" Ben dropped one of the clothespins, leaned down to pick it up, then the other pin came loose and the towel landed in the grass. "See, girls' work." He grimaced but set to hanging the towel again.

"He's opening an account at the bank and said he had some other business to take care of in town. He shouldn't be much longer." Grace's teeth chattered as she hurried to finish. "Did he tell you about wanting us to meet his new *friend* next Saturday, and her family?"

"*Ya.* I hope whoever he picks to replace *Mamm* is nice."

"No one can replace *Mamm.* And I don't want anyone living with us."

Ben was quiet. "Maybe . . . maybe . . ." He shrugged. "Maybe it wouldn't be so bad to have a replacement *mudder.*"

Grace dropped the towel she was holding into the basket and put her hands on her hips. Ben had always said he didn't want their father to remarry. "What are you saying? And no one can replace *Mamm.*"

"I'm just saying . . ." Ben threw his hands up. "You have a lot to do. Cleaning, sewing, laundry, and other things. Don't you want some help?"

"*Nee.* I don't need help. I thought we both agreed that we like things the way they are."

Ben stared at Grace until his eyes filled with water. "*You* like things the way they are." Then he ran to the barn. Grace called out to him and started toward the barn, wondering how long her brother had felt like this. She reminded herself that Ben was only eleven. Grace had done her best to nurture him when he seemed to need it, but she could also recall trying to bandage his knee before they'd moved here, and how he kept telling her she was doing it wrong. He'd also mentioned how their mother used to read to him. And now that Grace thought about it, she wondered how much her own opinions had rubbed off on Ben. Did he need a mother figure in his life?

She'd slowed her pace and was trying to organize her thoughts before she went into the barn. A buggy turned in, so she waited. Maybe it would be best to let her father handle this, father to son. But as the buggy got closer and the driver came into view, she realized it wasn't her father returning from town. She draped an arm across her stomach, took a deep breath, and walked across the yard toward the approaching buggy.

CHAPTER EIGHT

"What are you doing here?" Grace asked Wayne as he stepped out of the buggy.

"You weren't at worship service yesterday, and it wondered me if you were okay."

"We're fine." Gracie glanced toward the barn, then looked back at Wayne. "I've got to finish getting the clothes on the line." She nodded over her shoulder. "*Danki* for checking on us."

Wayne stared at her. "I can tell you're mad at me."

Shivering, Grace looked down at the moist, dewy grass, then back at him. "You left me at the Lantzes'. Just because I didn't want to . . ." She swallowed back the lump in her throat.

"Your teeth are chattering." Wayne took off his jacket and put it around her shoulders. "Please don't be mad. It's just . . . you scare me."

Grace's jaw dropped. "Scare you? What

are you talking about?"

Wayne sighed, shifted his weight, and stuffed his hands in his pockets. "I've never liked anyone as much as you, so when you don't want to be closer to me, it makes me feel like you don't like me as much as I like you."

Grace locked eyes with him. "I do like you, Wayne. I'm just . . . not ready for . . ." She could feel her cheeks flushing, and she forced herself to recall how she'd felt Saturday. "If you like me so much, I don't understand why you'd leave me to go be with *Englisch* girls."

"I had to go," he said, sighing again. "My feelings for you are so strong, and when I'm around you, I just want to show you."

Grace glanced at the barn again, then met Wayne's gaze, wanting to believe him. "I like you, too, Wayne . . . but . . ."

"Why do you keep looking at the barn?" Wayne looked over Grace's shoulder.

"*Mei bruder* is in there. I'm a little worried about him."

"What's wrong?"

Grace scratched her forehead as she wondered how much to tell Wayne. "It's just . . . well, it's hard for me to think about our father possibly marrying someone. And I always thought Ben felt the same way. But we just had a conversation that makes me think otherwise, like he might actually want and still need a mother. But no one can replace our *mamm*."

Wayne touched Grace lightly on the arm, then pulled the coat snug over her shoulders. "Poor guy. At his age, he probably does need a *mamm,* but I bet he feels guilty for even thinking that way." He paused, looking toward the barn again. "Do you want me to talk to him?"

"Um, I don't know."

"Come on. Let's go together." Wayne put an arm around her, and Grace got in step beside him. He opened the barn door for Grace to go first. Ben had hoisted himself up on *Daed*'s workbench and was kicking his legs back and forth.

"This is my friend Wayne," Grace said to Ben as they walked toward him. "I think you met him at worship service."

Ben nodded, but didn't say anything.

"*Wie bischt,* buddy." Wayne sat on the stool near the workbench. "Whatcha doin'?"

Ben shrugged as he kept his eyes on the floor. "Nothing."

"Grace, I'm a little thirsty. Could you maybe get me a glass of water or tea?" Wayne winked at Grace. She glanced at Ben, then back at Wayne, who gave a nod.

358

"Um, sure. *Ya.* Ben, do you want something to drink?"

Her brother still didn't look up as he shook his head. Grace hesitantly left, got a glass of tea for her and Wayne, and hurried back to the barn, but when she heard voices, she stopped outside and listened.

"I know how you feel," Wayne said. "When *mei mamm* died, it was real weird for a long time."

Grace froze. She'd seen Wayne with his parents, and she'd just assumed that the woman he called *Mamm* was his mother. She leaned her ear closer.

"And when *mei daed* married someone else, I was confused. I wanted *Daed* to be happy, and he married a real nice woman, but I felt a little bad, like *mei mamm* was being replaced and forgotten about. But I wanted a mom, someone to look after me."

"Grace doesn't want *Daed* to marry anyone else," Ben said softly. "But I miss things. You know, those things a mother does. But it ain't like I want to replace *Mamm.*"

"I know what you're saying. And I think that your *mamm* would want your *daed* to be happy. She'd want you and Grace to be happy too."

"I know all that," Ben said a little louder. "It's Grace that doesn't want anyone living with us. And she gets mad about *Daed* dating anyone."

Grace's eyes filled with tears. Why hadn't she given more consideration to Ben's needs? And her father's.

"Do you want me to talk to her?" Wayne's voice was filled with tenderness, and this was a beautiful side to him that she didn't know about. She sniffled, then leaned her face to Wayne's jacket still around her shoulders and blotted her eyes on it.

"Here's tea," she said as she walked into the barn. "Everything okay?"

Wayne stood up and accepted the glass. Grace set hers on the bench near Ben. Her teeth were still chattering, and a cold drink didn't sound all that good. But Wayne chugged his down, then put his glass on the workbench. "Everything is *gut,*" he said to Grace, winking again.

"I gotta clean the barn." Ben jumped down from the workbench, the hint of a smile on his face.

"Someone's coming." Grace nodded toward the driveway. "Probably *Daed.*"

Wayne walked out of the barn. Grace lagged behind, but when Ben started putting away tools that had been left out, Grace followed Wayne.

As her father stepped out of the buggy, he

shook hands with Wayne, and after pleasantries about the weather turning cooler, Wayne said, "I know Grace isn't quite sixteen yet, but I would like to ask your permission to take her to eat pizza next Saturday for dinner. We're not having a baseball game at the Lantzes' because the womenfolk are having a baby shower that day."

Grace held her breath. She'd just assumed that Wayne wouldn't want anything to do with her anymore. And that had started to be okay. But maybe he'd realized that there were other ways for a couple to be close, besides what he had in mind. And after hearing him with Ben, and now so politely asking Grace's father to take her out . . . Grace would go crazy if her father didn't say yes.

"Wayne, I'm told you're a fine fellow," Grace's father said as she continued to hold her breath. "But we have plans next Saturday. Maybe another time, though."

Daed." Grace locked eyes with her father, willing him to change his mind. "Please, *Daed.* I'd rather go eat pizza."

Her father frowned as he stroked his beard. Grace shouldn't face off with her father in front of Wayne. "Please," she added, glancing at Wayne and hoping she

361

didn't sound too desperate.

"I was hoping you'd be able to go Saturday." Grace's father scratched his cheek, glanced at Wayne, then back at Grace. "I guess it will be okay."

Grace let go of the breath she was holding and smiled.

"Pick you up at noon?" Wayne smiled, and Grace took off his coat and handed it back to him.

"See you then," she said.

Thank You, God. And thank you, Daed.

Eli felt all warm and fuzzy, as Leah used to say, watching Gracie clean the kitchen later that evening. She was humming and had been chattier than usual during supper, which she'd also prepared. A beef and potato casserole, her mother's recipe. Eli rarely made the casserole, but it was Ben's favorite, and the boy had enjoyed two generous helpings. Eli was well aware of the source of his daughter's joyful mood, and his name was Wayne Huyard.

"*Daed,* I have something to tell you." Gracie tossed the kitchen towel over her shoulder, then pulled out a chair at the table, across from Eli. Ben had already excused himself to go feed the pigs and get the other animals secure for the night.

362

"You're welcome," Eli said, grinning.

Grace sat down, smiling herself. "I am grateful that you are letting me go with Wayne next Saturday, but I want to tell you something else."

Eli leaned back in his chair, then picked up his cup of coffee, a little concerned about the serious tone of his daughter's voice. "What is it?"

"I haven't really wanted you to remarry." She crinkled her nose as she pressed her lips together.

This wasn't news to Eli, but he just nodded.

"I've been worried about replacing *Mamm*. It just didn't feel right."

Eli swallowed his sip of coffee and put the cup on the table. "No one can ever replace your mother."

Grace put her palm up for a couple of seconds, then laid both hands on the table as she sat taller. "I know that now. And I want to let you know that it's okay with me for you to find someone to spend your life with." She smiled. "I won't always be living here anyway. And I think Ben really needs a mother figure. He's still at a tender age."

Eli was watching his daughter grow up before his eyes, and it was lovely and terrifying at the same time.

"I'm sorry I won't be going with you to Ruth's on Saturday. I briefly met her *kinner* at worship service, but it would have been nice to get to know them better."

Eli had been praying that Gracie would feel this way, but hearing her talk in such a mature manner about a subject so close to their hearts was giving him a lump in his throat. He knew good and well that he didn't need his daughter's permission to remarry, but he'd always wanted hers and Ben's blessing. He nodded. "I'm sure there will be other opportunities to spend time with Ruth and her family."

Gracie got up, walked around the table, and kissed Eli on the cheek. "I'm sure there will be." Then she left Eli sitting at the table, knowing that God was giving his family a second chance at happiness.

He couldn't wait to spend some time with Ruth. Saturday wasn't going to get here soon enough.

CHAPTER NINE

"You look very nice," Grace told her father the following Saturday, before turning to Ben. "And you clean up pretty *gut* too."

Her father slipped on his jacket and his Sunday black hat. "I hope you and Wayne enjoy the pizza." Frowning, he said, "Don't be late."

Grace wasn't sure who'd been looking forward to Saturday more — her or her father. "I won't."

Once they were gone, Grace ran upstairs and found her lip balm. Since seeing a different side of Wayne, she felt sure he'd be better about respecting her boundaries. But kissing was on her "okay" list. She ran downstairs, pleased to see Wayne out the window, right on time.

Wayne was all worked up about some chores his father wanted him to do later in the afternoon, so he talked about that most of the way to the restaurant. Grace felt warm inside despite the cool temperature.

At the pizzeria, Wayne chose the booth in the far corner, and they shared a pepperoni pizza and each had a soda.

"*Danki* again for talking to Ben. I had no idea that your *mudder* had passed. How long ago?"

"When I was little, about four. I don't even think about it anymore." Wayne took a drink, then reached for the last slice of pizza.

"I still miss *mei mamm* all the time." Grace pictured her mother looking down from heaven and seeing her with the cutest boy in their community, out on a real date.

"You ready?" Wayne wiped his mouth. "I've gotta get going so I have time to do all that stupid extra work for my *daed.*"

"*Ya,* sure." Grace stood up when Wayne did and glanced at the clock on the wall. She was going to get home way before she'd expected. Maybe she would surprise her father and walk to Ruth's house since it wasn't too far.

They were about halfway home when Wayne turned off the main highway. It took Grace a few seconds before she recognized where he was heading. "I-I thought you needed to get home?"

Wayne looked her way. "I do. But now that we're back together, I thought we could spend some time by ourselves."

Grace swallowed hard. She didn't want to make Wayne mad, but she didn't want to lead him on either. "Wayne . . ."

He glanced her way again. *"Ya?"*

"I-I just need you to respect my boundaries."

Wayne chuckled. "That sounds very *Englisch,* the way you said that."

Grace felt her cheeks turning red as she grinned. *"Ya,* I guess it does." But at least she'd said it before any kissing started. That way, Wayne wouldn't have expectations.

Eli glanced at the empty chair at Ruth's table for eight, wishing Gracie were here, but hoping she was having a good time with Wayne. Ben was quiet. Ruth's only boy, Stephen, was only six, and the girls — Carolyn, Eve, and Mary — chatted among themselves at one end of the table. Eli cleaned his plate and laid his fork across it. It hadn't been a bad meal, although he had thought about Elizabeth's mashed potatoes. And he would have seasoned the roast more than Ruth had. But all in all, things were going well. Ruth's *kinner* were polite and well behaved.

"Eli, are you ready for dessert?" Ruth pointed to the stove. "Shoofly pie."

"*I* am," Stephen said. "And I ate all my roast," he added, sitting up taller.

"Let's serve our guests first." Ruth stood up to get the pie, then brought it to the table, along with a stack of small plates.

"*Danki* for a wonderful meal, Ruth." Eli allowed himself to envision the seven of them — eight with Gracie — as a family. He knew it was way too soon to be having such thoughts, but he loved the idea of having a large family. He and Leah had wanted more children, but it just never happened after Ben came. Eli and Ruth hadn't discussed whether or not either of them wanted more children.

When Ruth's three daughters finished their pie, they asked to be excused, leaving Ben and Stephen. Eli's son was starting to fidget, and he was glad when Ruth's oldest daughter, Mary, asked if he'd like to go with them to the barn to see a calf that had been born two days ago.

"Don't you want to go with the other *kinner,* Stephen?" Ruth began to clear the table, and when Eli stood up and picked up a plate, she said, "*Nee, nee.* You sit. Let me do this."

Eli sat back down across from Stephen, who was shaking his head. "I would like another piece of pie, please."

Ruth walked to the pie plate. "Just a small piece, Stephen." She looked over her shoulder. "What about you, Eli? Another slice of pie?"

Eli put a hand across his stomach. "I don't think I can eat one more bite. It was all very *gut.*"

"So, Stephen," Eli said to the boy, "is this your first or second year of school?"

"He's six, so this is his second year," Ruth said as Stephen took another bite of pie.

Grace had been out of school for almost two years, but he could still remember her first day at the one-room schoolhouse back home like it was yesterday. Ben's first day was just as memorable.

"What is your favorite thing to study?" Eli said to Stephen as Ruth scurried around the kitchen.

"Anything but my numbers," Stephen said with a mouthful. "*Mamm* says I'm stupid when it comes to my numbers."

"Stephen!" Ruth spun around and walked toward him, her face as red as the beets still in a bowl on the table. "I didn't say *stupid.*" She looked at Eli and smiled. "He has a hard time with math; it's not his favorite subject."

"I hate math, so that makes me stupid." Stephen shrugged, and for a few tense moments, everyone was quiet. Eli could tell that Stephen's behavior was embarrassing Ruth as her face turned even redder.

"I disliked math as a young scholar too," Eli finally said. "But it's important to know. You'll use your numbers in many ways for the rest of your life."

Ruth cleared her throat. "Stephen, don't you want to go join the other *kinner* and check on the new calf?"

"Nee." The boy eyed his empty plate. "I would like another piece of pie, please."

"No more pie, sweetheart." Ruth turned to Eli. "Coffee, Eli?"

"I would like one more piece of pie, please," Stephen repeated as he slammed his fork down on the plate. Eli stifled a grin. He remembered this age with both of his children, a time for testing the boundaries.

"If you eat another piece of pie, you might turn into a pie," Eli said, winking at Stephen. He glanced at Ruth, but she wasn't smiling.

"No pie, Stephen. Now, do not ask me again." Ruth cleared the beets and a bowl of chowchow from the table as Stephen slouched down in his chair until he was barely still in it.

"But I ate all my dinner, and my second piece of pie was small. I want another one."

He eased his way back up the chair. "You're mean," he grumbled under his breath, but after a quick glance toward Ruth, Eli knew she'd heard.

"Eli, can you excuse Stephen and me for a minute?" Eli nodded, and Ruth walked to Stephen's side, then pointed to the doorway in between the living room and kitchen. "March," she said to her son.

Stephen slowly stood up, and before he even hit the threshold, Ruth grabbed his shirt and pulled him along at her side. He'd tell her when she got back not to be embarrassed. *Kinner,* especially at that age, could make a parent want to pull their hair out at times. And they always seemed to put on the best show in front of visitors.

After a few moments, Eli decided to find the bathroom, then maybe he'd go have a look at the new calf. He'd seen plenty, but he mostly wanted to see how Ben was interacting with the girls.

He turned down a long hallway, thinking maybe the bathroom was at the end, like at his house. But when he heard muffled voices, then what sounded like a slap followed by crying, he stopped in his tracks.

"Stop crying."

It was Ruth talking to Stephen, but she spoke to the boy in a deep whisper, almost

371

like it wasn't even her. Eli knew better than to eavesdrop, but his feet were rooted to the floor as Stephen's sobs got quieter.

"I told you that you would be in trouble if you didn't act right in front of *Mamm*'s friend, didn't I? You stay in this room and don't come out. If I hear one peep out of you, I will give you much more to cry about."

The door flew open, and Ruth ran right into Eli. She brought a hand to her chest as her jaw dropped. "Eli?"

"I-I was looking for the bathroom."

Miriam eased the pile of clean clothes over to make room for Kiki, who had joined her on the couch. She opened her book and settled back into the love story she was reading, hoping Landon would ask Mary Beth to marry him in this chapter. Ever since she was a teenager, she'd chosen to read Christian fiction because those books always had happy endings.

She jumped when she heard a ruckus on the front porch, then hurried to the front door when someone started knocking.

"I forgot my sweater," Grace said, breathless, gulping in air.

Miriam pushed the screen door open. "*Ya,* you left it here." She closed the door behind

Grace and took note of her red, swollen eyes. "Did you run here?"

"Ya." Grace pushed back several strands of hair that had fallen from her *kapp.*

Miriam walked to the couch and dug around the clean clothes until she found Grace's black sweater and handed it to her.

"Danki." Grace slipped it on and didn't seem to notice the orange cat hair that clung to it. She waited for Grace to do or say something, but the girl just stood in the middle of the room.

"Um, do you want to stay for a while? Need a glass of water?"

Grace was still catching her breath when she nodded, so Miriam left her in the middle of the living room and brought her back a glass of water, deciding that she wasn't going to find out if Landon proposed to Mary Beth today.

Grace chugged the water and handed the glass back to Miriam, but the girl still didn't move.

Miriam put the glass on the table. "Grace, what's wrong?"

Grace didn't say anything for a few seconds, then she tearfully recounted the time she'd spent with Wayne.

Miriam's blood was boiling. "He did *what*?"

"I can't say, I can't say." Grace ran into Miriam's arms, and Miriam held her tightly as she also started to get teary eyed. This was so similar to her own experience when she was Grace's age, the day that changed everything for Miriam. She eased Grace away and cupped her cheeks with her hands. "First, are you okay physically? Did Wayne force himself on you?"

"I'm okay, and *nee,* he didn't force me to do anything. But when I wouldn't do what he wanted, he got really mad and said ugly things to me."

Relief washed over Miriam as flashbacks of her and Luke filled her mind. Luke hadn't forced Miriam to do anything either. Miriam had made that decision on her own, and now she lived with the consequences. She was thankful that Grace had the courage to walk away — or run, as it appeared.

"He told me he could have any girl he wanted, girls that were prettier than me. Like Rachel. He said he'd been pursuing Rachel before I came to town, but had put her on hold for me." She sniffled. "And that if I didn't grow up, I was never going to have a boyfriend here."

"That's all rubbish. Boys can be jerks." Miriam guided Grace to the couch, hoping Rachel wouldn't fall for Wayne's charm. Ra-

374

chel wasn't the sweetest girl in the community, but Miriam didn't want to see any of them get hurt. "And if Wayne was trying to get you to do something you're not comfortable with, then you did the right thing, no matter how much he says he cares about you, and no matter what kind of ugly things he might have said."

"If he liked me so much, he shouldn't even ask me to go further than kissing," Grace said between sobs. "And then he was so mean about it and didn't talk to me all the way home. *Mei daed* is at Ruth's *haus,* and I couldn't have talked to him about this anyway. I don't have any girlfriends here, and I'm just so mad at myself for believing that he really liked me when all he really wanted was . . ." She covered her face with her hands.

Miriam sat down, put an arm around her, and let Grace bury her face in her shoulder. "I'm glad you came here, Grace." She kissed the top of Grace's head, knowing she was going to have a little chat with Wayne.

CHAPTER TEN

Eli sat alone on his couch. He could hear Ben upstairs tinkering, probably digging in his closet looking for a book his mother had given him. The subject had come up on the way home, and Ben was frustrated that he didn't know where the book was.

Sighing, Eli was wondering if this move was a good idea. Miriam had left a message on Eli's phone saying she would bring Grace home in a little while. When Eli had asked if his daughter was okay, Miriam told him that she was fine. But Miriam said she needed to talk to Eli, which caused Eli's stomach to sour.

He recalled the abrupt way he and Ben had left Ruth's house. Children needed discipline, and Eli was all for that, but his and Ruth's way to reprimand their *kinner* wasn't the same. On the ride home, he'd asked Ben if he had a good time, but his son had only shrugged and said it was okay.

Eli wasn't sure he could afford to move again, and a month really wasn't long enough to give Lancaster County a chance.

Gracie walked into the house, and Eli stood and went to her. "Gracie?" Her cheeks were red, eyes swollen. "What happened?"

"*Daed,* I don't want to talk. Can I please be excused?"

Miriam walked in behind Gracie and nodded to Eli. Eli told Gracie that was fine. Once she was upstairs, he motioned for Miriam to sit down. Eli sat down beside her on the couch. "What happened?"

Miriam's cheeks were flushed, and her eyes were a bit swollen as well, which caused Eli's stomach to roil even more.

"Eli, I don't have any *kinner,*" she said softly. "And I would never try to tell you how to raise your children. But I would strongly suggest that you not allow Grace to spend any more time with Wayne."

Eli's hair prickled against the back of his neck. "Did that boy hurt Gracie?"

"Not physically." Miriam kept her eyes down as she spoke. "But he's . . . pressuring her to do things that aren't right, things that would cause her regret later on, things that aren't right in God's eyes."

Eli started to tremble as anger boiled to

377

the surface. Amos had told him Wayne was a good lad from a good family. He wanted to grab that boy by the shirt collar and throw him to the ground, an unfamiliar emotion that went against everything Eli believed.

"Wayne isn't a terrible person," Miriam said. "But he isn't respectful of the boundaries that girls set for him. I've seen this with other girls. And I know about boys that age." She lifted her eyes to Eli's. "I care about Grace, and I just thought you should know. I'm planning to have a talk with Wayne. It probably won't do any *gut,* but I'm tired of watching him pursue these young girls like an animal on the hunt."

"*Nee,* you don't need to do that. I will take care of him."

A hint of a smile crossed Miriam's face. "I thought you might say that, and maybe Wayne would heed a man more than me."

Eli stared at Miriam for a few moments. Too long, apparently, since her face took on a pinkish glow as she pulled her eyes from his. "*Danki* for bringing Grace home," he said.

Miriam looked up at him again. "Sometimes young girls are so smitten with a cute boy that they eventually give in, believing that the boy loves them and they will be

378

together forever. But that isn't always the case. And sometimes the girl isn't strong enough to walk away and she does something that leaves her feeling unworthy for the rest of her life, undeserving of a husband." Miriam paused as she looked away from Eli, blinking her eyes a few times. "And it's those choices that we make as young girls that we have to live with."

Eli was quiet, knowing they were no longer talking about Grace. "But God forgives our sins the moment we ask Him to," he said softly, moving his head to search her eyes, but she wouldn't look at him. "Many times, the challenge is to forgive ourselves."

Miriam finally lifted her eyes to his and took a deep breath. "I must go." She stood up abruptly and smoothed the wrinkles from her black apron. "Do you mind if I go upstairs and say good-bye to Grace?"

Eli stood up, too, and as he looked at Miriam, he had a strong urge to hug her, so he did. It took her several seconds before she embraced him as well, and when she tried to pull away, Eli gave her a final squeeze and whispered, "*Danki* again."

Miriam hurried up the stairs after Eli told her which room was Gracie's. And once she was up there, Eli tiptoed up the stairs. He wanted to believe that Miriam's intentions were all good, but he'd been so wrong lately — about Ruth . . . and Wayne. He listened outside Grace's door, feeling guilty, but not enough to walk away. This was his daughter, one of the two greatest gifts the Lord had blessed him with, and he'd do whatever it took to keep her safe.

Miriam and Gracie spoke softly to each other, but Eli could hear every word.

Miriam tried to choose her words carefully. She and Grace had talked for a while before Miriam had carted her home, but she wanted to make sure Grace was going to be okay. Miriam understood teenage heartbreak, and at Grace's age, it could seem like the end of the world.

"You are strong and did the right thing, Grace," Miriam said. "And don't be mad, but I talked to your father about this."

Grace hung her head. "How mad is he?"

Miriam cupped her chin and smiled. "He isn't mad at you, but I do think he might have a little talk with Wayne."

Grace swiped at her eyes. "I really liked him. And I've never had anyone that cute want to be my boyfriend."

"You are a beautiful *maedel*, Grace. The right boy, one who truly loves you, won't

380

pressure you to do things you aren't comfortable with, things that should be saved until marriage. You are special, and you must always remember that."

Grace stared at her long and hard. "You are special, too, and you deserve to be happy."

Now it was Miriam who feared she might cry again. Maybe she'd said too much to Grace while they were still at Miriam's house. She knew she'd said too much to Eli just now, and she was wondering why that was. Something about Eli made her feel safe, and she was growing fond of Grace. But now she was embarrassed to even face Eli, fearful he'd read between the lines.

"*Danki* for saying that," Miriam said as she reached for Grace's hand and held it for a few moments before she stood up. "I should go. I just wanted to make sure you would be okay." She turned to leave, feeling the need to go home, curl up with Kiki, and have a good cry. Landon and Mary Beth weren't of much interest to her at the moment.

"Miriam?"

With her hand on the doorknob, she turned to face Grace. "*Ya?*"

"Everything is going to be okay."

Miriam forced a smile. "*Ya, mei maedel.*

381

You will be just fine."

Grace stood up and walked to her. "*Nee,* that's not what I meant. What I meant was . . ." She smiled. "*You* will be just fine." Grace wrapped her arms around Miriam and hugged her as genuinely as Eli had downstairs.

This is a gut family, she thought as she went back downstairs. Eli was standing in the middle of the room, and Miriam needed to leave before she burst into tears, the events of the day catching up with her. But she couldn't stand the question dancing around in her mind.

"How did things go with Ruth? Grace told me she was cooking for you and Ben. I hope things went well." Miriam cringed, knowing that wasn't entirely true. She'd never deny Eli and his family happiness, but she wasn't sure Ruth was the right person for them.

Eli walked up to her, standing entirely too close, and softly said, "It's not going to work out for me and Ruth."

Miriam avoided his eyes. "*Ach,* I'm sorry to hear that. Maybe Elizabeth?"

"*Nee,*" Eli said softly. "Not her either."

Miriam rushed around him, mumbling about how she had to get home. She didn't stop when he called her name.

■ ■ ■ ■

A week later, Grace walked into Ben's room. "Are you ready?"

Ben rolled his eyes, but the smile on his face let Grace know he was happy. "*Ya, ya.* You've asked me that three times. I'm coming."

"Okay. Be downstairs in five minutes." Grace ran down the stairs, excited and nervous about what she was about to do. She'd prayed hard about her decision, and she was glad Ben was excited too.

Grace scribbled out a note to her father, turned the oven off, and picked up Ben's gloves from the kitchen counter, as he was sure to forget them . . . again.

"Ready?" she yelled upstairs.

"*Ya.* But it's cold outside," he said as he hit the landing. Grace handed him his gloves.

"It's not that cold outside yet, and next week is the harvest, so you'd best get used to the cold."

They both bundled up, then moved to the porch when the blue van pulled up. Grace knew her father would be upset if she and Ben ventured out on foot this time of day, with darkness almost upon them.

"Come on," she said, almost pulling Ben along. "We've got to go before *Daed* gets home."

Eli had spent the first part of his day readying up the plows for the fall harvest, greasing the parts and going through a safety checklist since his two most prized possessions would be helping him next week. Then he'd given the mules an extra helping of feed and reminded them that hard work and nurture of the land was a God-given blessing, and he prayed over the horses. Talking to his animals wasn't something Eli would want a living soul to see, but it was a common practice for him.

Earlier in the afternoon, he'd visited the bishop, a courtesy he'd been meaning to get around to in an attempt to get to know the man better. And now it was time to visit Wayne. As he pulled up to the boy's house, he quickly asked God to give him the right words and help him control the urge to sling the lad onto the ground. Wayne swaggered toward Eli's buggy as if he didn't have a care in the world.

"*Wie bischt,* Eli." Wayne looped his hands beneath his suspenders. "What brings you this way?"

Eli took in a deep breath as he stepped

out of his buggy and reached for the reins, not planning to tether his horse or stay longer than he had to.

"I need to speak to you about my daughter."

Wayne stood taller as he pulled his hands from his suspenders and folded his arms across his chest, but he didn't say anything.

Eli stared at him for a few moments, then forced himself to shake the images from his mind that were probably far worse than what had actually happened. Just the same, he moved closer to Wayne. Close enough to be able to take a swing at the boy and knock him to the ground. He inhaled another deep breath but kept his gaze fixed on Wayne's eyes. Eli wanted to see fear in the boy's eyes when he was done speaking.

"My Gracie, and every *maedel* is this community, deserves to be treated with respect." Eli spoke in a whisper, but he could feel himself trembling. "We can have a long conversation about what this means, or you can take me at my word when I say that I will be watching you. And if I hear of you behaving inappropriately with any of these girls, I won't be coming back here to talk."

The knot in Eli's throat pulsed. He'd never hit anyone, but if Wayne didn't heed

385

his warning, he might be tempted to do something he didn't believe in. He clenched his teeth and watched Wayne's eyes for any sign of fear, but the boy didn't flinch, still remaining quiet.

Eli took a small step closer to the boy, close enough to poke Wayne's chest. "Do you understand what I'm saying?"

Wayne stumbled backward, blinking his eyes a few times. *"Ya, ya,"* he said, his eyes widening.

Eli stared at him, wondering if what he'd said would make a bit of difference, and not feeling proud of himself for resorting to physical intimidation, even if it was just his finger. He'd ask God for forgiveness later, but for now, he wanted Wayne to understand that Eli meant business. When he saw a hint of fear in Wayne's eyes, Eli left.

It was almost dark when he pulled into his driveway, and he was surprised to see another buggy parked out front. And Miriam sitting on the porch.

"I'm a little early," Miriam said when Eli walked up the steps. She stood up. "I knocked on the door, but there was no answer. But Grace said it was urgent."

Eli's stomach flipped as he threw open the door and rushed inside. He picked up a note on the kitchen table as Miriam followed him in. "Is everything okay?" she asked.

Eli read the note, eyed the table set for two, and inhaled a heavenly aroma of what smelled like pork roast. Smiling, he handed the note to Miriam and looked over her shoulder, rereading what Grace had written.

Dear Daed,

Me and Ben went to Naomi's haus. She and I went shopping at the market this week, and I think we are becoming friends. She has a younger bruder Ben's age. I knew you wouldn't want us to walk, so we took our money and hired a driver Naomi's mamm said was a nice Englisch lady. Don't be mad. We love you and want you to be happy. Miriam might be mad, but tell her not to be mad either.

Supper is keeping warm in the oven. There is a salad in the refrigerator and a pecan pie on the counter.

Love,
Gracie and Ben

Eli walked to the oven and eased the door open, realizing he'd been wrong about the roast. He slowly closed the oven and took his time turning around, but when he saw Miriam smiling, he said, "How do you feel about meat loaf?"

"I love meat loaf," she said, still grinning.

Eli pulled out a chair for her, and after she sat down, he lit the two candles that his daughter had put in the middle of the table, then he lit the two lanterns on the counter, knowing it would be dark soon. He put the salad on the table, then the meat loaf, potatoes, and carrots that had been keeping warm in the oven. Sitting down, he was having trouble keeping the smile from his face. "I'm not mad at all," he said as he glanced at Miriam, encouraged by the fact that she was still smiling.

"I'm not mad either," she said.

They both bowed their head in silent prayer, and afterward, Eli stared at the woman across from him, the flicker from the candles creating a glow on her face that Eli had always seen. But it seemed to him that maybe for the first time, Miriam was seeing for herself the life she was meant to live.

The life Eli had seen the first time he'd laid eyes on her.

EPILOGUE

Miriam had settled into her new life almost effortlessly, and there was no reason to regret that she'd waited until she was twenty-eight years old to do so. If anything had happened differently, she might not be exactly where the Lord had always intended for her to be.

She'd moved into Eli's house after they were married the following fall. Forgiving herself for past choices hadn't come easily, but over time, she realized that harboring such ill will toward herself was just as much a sin as the inability to forgive others. She had Eli to thank for that. And God. Eli led by example. He was a loving man who forgave easily — most of the time. But when he'd said he was having trouble forgiving Wayne for hurting Grace, Miriam found herself explaining all the reasons God wants us to be forgiving. When she was done, Eli kissed her on the cheek and lovingly told her to follow her own advice. From that moment on, Miriam began to shed the sins of her past and started to let go of burdens that weren't hers to carry, discovering that God was ready and willing to take over the job.

Grace hadn't shied away from boys completely. She still attended the Sunday singings, but Miriam was glad to see her focusing more on new friendships with some of the kinder girls in the community. And Ben had his first crush on a girl. Grace teased him unmercifully at times, but Miriam suspected that when the time came, Grace would be his coach on how to treat the young ladies.

Eli was everything Miriam had always dreamed of. Kind, gentle, forgiving, a wonderful parent, and Miriam's inability to cook a decent meal didn't bother him. He'd tenderly told her not long into their courtship that he didn't think he could eat noodles and cheese from a box. Luckily, Eli loved to cook.

Miriam hadn't heard about any problems with Wayne, and although no one spoke of it, Miriam assumed that had something to do with the visit Eli had paid Wayne not long after the incident with Grace.

Miriam was motivated to keep their home

tidy, and with Grace's guidance, she'd become a pretty good housekeeper. But her most important role, aside from being a good wife to Eli, was mothering Ben. He was at a touchy age where he wanted to be grown up but in many ways was still a boy.

Today was a special day. Eli had added a room onto the back of the house not long after they'd married, a sewing room much larger than Miriam had at her home, and she'd asked Grace to meet her here this afternoon to see a quilt that Miriam hadn't shown anyone yet.

"Are you ready?" she asked when Grace came into the room.

"I've been ready." Grace folded her hands in front of her, smiling. "Do I need to close my eyes?"

Miriam watched as Grace closed her eyes, even though Miriam didn't tell her to. She marveled at the beautiful woman Grace was becoming, both inside and out.

"You can open your eyes," she said once the quilt was spread on the table. "What do you think?"

Grace ran her hand gingerly across the colorful squares and tears pooled in the corners of her eyes. She looked at Miriam. "It's you."

Miriam nodded. "And look." She began

pointing to all the squares, explaining what each one meant. The day she fell in love with Grace's father was represented by a red heart. There was a piece of her wedding dress, along with many other symbolic squares, some from her life before she found her family, but mostly ones she'd added over the past year. Recently, she'd added a square with an orange cat. Her sweet Kiki had passed not long after she'd married Eli; curiously, no one ever understood why Eli wasn't allergic to the cat, the way he'd always been of other felines. And Miriam had also quilted in a square with a baseball mitt. She'd given up playing on Saturdays, even though Eli had encouraged her to continue. But her happiest times were now at home with her family.

As Grace studied the quilt, Miriam peeked her head out the door and called for Eli and Ben to join them. Eli was grinning ear to ear. Ben was yawning, probably thinking this was girls' stuff. And as Miriam had hoped, Grace found the one square that was going to make her quilt patchwork perfect.

"What's this one?" Grace asked, pointing to a yellow square with a rattle.

Eli put his arm around Miriam. "What do you think it is?"

Grace tapped a finger to her chin as Ben

walked to Grace's side, then his face lit up. "A baby!"

"Ya." Miriam couldn't imagine a better moment in life than when Grace and Ben ran into her and Eli's arms. But deep down, she knew there was a lifetime of happiness waiting for all of them. She touched her stomach, acknowledging the tiny life growing inside her, feeling overwhelmed by the love and gratitude she felt for her new family. And for God's love and divine providence.

DISCUSSION QUESTIONS

1. When Eli was introduced to Elizabeth and Ruth in the beginning of the story, whom did you hope he would choose? Did you like one woman better than the other? Were you relieved when Miriam came into Eli's life? Did you root for her?

2. Miriam doesn't cook, clean, or have a garden. She's an untraditional Amish woman who isn't interested in marriage, so she doesn't hone in on those skills to attract a husband. But later in the story, we find out that Miriam can't forgive herself for a choice she made when she was young. Do you think that her inability to get past that is part of the reason Miriam lives the way she does? Do you think she was depressed?

3. From the beginning, Wayne is pushing Grace beyond her comfort zone when it comes to affection. Did you feel like Wayne only wanted Grace for his own

reasons, or did you think he really liked her and was just being a boy? As you think about this, remember the kindness that he showed to Ben in the barn.

4. Amos tells Eli that Miriam is their "resident old maid" at the age of twenty-eight. While this might sound harsh, it is common for Amish folks to get married at a young age. Do you think Eli and Miriam will be happier because they are both older when they got married?

ACKNOWLEDGMENTS

This was a fun story to write, and I happily dedicate this novella to Kiki and Katie — my precious kitties who were with me for seventeen years. I miss you girls.

My heartfelt thanks to my family and friends, and also to my amazing team at HarperCollins Christian Publishing. And Natasha Kern, I appreciate you as my agent, but even more so as my friend.

God's blessed me abundantly with stories to tell, and I am grateful for the opportunity to serve Him.

WHEN CHRISTMAS COMES AGAIN

To Karla Hanns and Joan Main

PENNSYLVANIA DUTCH GLOSSARY

ab im kopp — off in the head; crazy
ach — oh
bruder — brother
daadi — grandfather
daed — father
danki — thank you
Englisch — non-Amish person
gut — good
kapp — prayer covering or cap
kinner — children
mamm — mom
mammi — grandmother
mei — my
mudder — mother
nee — no
Ordnung — the unwritten rules of the Amish
***Pennsylvania* Deitsch** — the language spoken by the Amish
rumschpringe — running-around period when a teenager turns sixteen years old

wunderbaar — wonderful
ya — yes

CHAPTER ONE

Katherine Zook fell into step with two *Englisch* women who were crossing the parking lot toward the Bird-in-Hand market. Normally, she would avoid the chatty tourists, but the tall man with the shoulder-length salt-and-pepper hair and a limp was following her again.

"It's a lovely day, isn't it?" The middle-aged woman walking next to Katherine was a little thing with short red hair and wore a blue T-shirt with *Paradise, Pennsylvania* on the front. Her friend had on the same T-shirt, but it was red.

"*Ya,* it is." Katherine glanced at the dark clouds overhead. There wasn't anything lovely about the weather. Frigid temperatures, and the snow had just begun to fall again. She picked up the pace and hoped the women would speed up too. She looked over her shoulder, glad they were gaining some distance on the stranger. She'd first seen him a week ago, loitering outside the Gordonville Bookstore, and she hadn't thought much about it. Then when she saw him at Kauffman's Fruit Farm and Market, she'd thought it was a coincidence. She'd also spotted him outside Paradiso's when she'd stopped to pick up a pizza as a treat for the children. But this was becoming more than a fluke.

Katherine could feel the women staring at her, but she kept her eyes straight ahead and hoped they weren't about to ask a string of questions. *Do you have a telephone? Can I take your picture? Is this where you do your shopping? How many children do you have? Are your people Christians?* And Katherine's personal favorite: *Do you know where I can get an Amish pen pal?*

It wasn't that she held ill will against the curious *Englisch* tourists, but she often wondered what their reactions would be if the situation were reversed. They'd most likely run from her or summon the police.

"Ma'am, can I ask you a quick question?" The redhead spoke loudly, as if Katherine might be hard of hearing, making it impossible to ignore her. She looked over her shoulder again, but she didn't see the man anymore. She stopped a few feet from the entrance when the two women did. "*Ya.*

What can I help you with?"

"I-I was wondering . . ." The woman blushed as her eyes darted back and forth between Katherine and the other lady. "My friend and I were wondering . . ." She pulled her large black purse up on her shoulder. "We — well . . ."

Katherine waited. She was anxious to get in and out of the market, then back on the road. She'd left her two youngest *kinner* home alone. Linda was old enough to babysit five-year-old Gideon, but he could be a handful even for Katherine. She pulled her black coat snug, looking forward to a brief reprieve from the weather once she got inside the market.

"Do Amish women shave their legs?" the woman finally asked. Luckily, she hadn't spoken as loudly as before.

This is *a first.* Katherine closed her gaping mouth and tried to find the words for a response. Before she could, the other *Englischer* spoke up.

"And . . . you know . . ." The woman was a bit taller than her friend with short gray hair that was slightly spiked on the top of her head. She raised one of her arms and with her other hand pointed under her arm. "Do you shave here too?"

The first woman touched Katherine lightly

on the arm. "We can't find the answer to that question online, and it's been an ongoing argument during our book-club gatherings." She stood taller and smiled. "We only read Amish books."

Does that fact make it okay to ask such questions? Katherine considered telling the women that they were very rude, but changed her mind. She folded her hands in front of her and glanced back and forth between the ladies.

"Only when I've planned for my husband and me to be alone. But he died six months ago, so . . ." Katherine smiled and shrugged. *That will give you something to tell your book club.* Both of the women's eyes went round as saucers. "Have a *wunderbaar* day," Katherine added before she walked into the market. She looked back once to make sure neither of them had fainted. She didn't know any Amish folks who used the word *wunderbaar,* but the *Englisch* seemed to think they did, so she was happy to throw it in for good measure.

She held her laughter until she was inside the store. On most days, it was a challenge just to get out of bed in the morning, much less to find humor in anything. But as she made her way to the back of the market, she thought about Elias. Her husband would have gotten a chuckle out of Katherine's response. *I miss you, Elias.*

She dropped off some quilted pot holders for Diana to display in her booth. Katherine tried to make several per week for her *Englisch* friend to sell. The market in Bird-in-Hand catered to tourists mostly, and Diana had a permanent booth. Katherine and a few other local Amish women provided Diana with items to sell. And occasionally, when Katherine had time, she and Diana would sneak away and grab lunch and then split a dessert. They both suffered from an insatiable sweet tooth. But those times were getting more infrequent since she bore the entire responsibility of caring for the family.

Making small craft items used to be more of a hobby for Katherine, but now that money was tight, Linda and Mary Carol had been putting in extra hours sewing, knitting, and crocheting. Katherine hadn't told the children that they might have to sell their house, or at least part of the fifty acres that surrounded their home. That would be a last resort because the land had been in her family for three generations. She grabbed the last thing on her list, and as she made her way to the checkout line, she caught sight of an *Englisch* couple walking hand in hand. She missed having someone to bounce the important decisions off of. Her oldest, Stephen, was sixteen and trying hard to assume the role of head of the household, even though it should have been a time for him to be enjoying his *rumschpringe.*

As she made her way toward the exit, she saw the two women from the parking lot. The ladies actually bumped into each other as they scurried to avoid Katherine, but Katherine smiled and gave a little wave before she walked out the door.

She stuffed her gloved hands into the pockets of her coat. The snow was beginning to accumulate, and the wind was biting. It was colder than usual for December. Somehow, Katherine and her children had managed to get through Thanksgiving, but this first Christmas without Elias was going to be hard.

When she felt the tears starting to build in her eyes, she forced herself to think about the two *Englisch* women, and it brought a smile to her face. She was going to bottle that memory and pull it out when she felt sad, which was most days.

As she hurried toward her buggy, she tipped the brim of her black bonnet to shield her face from the snow, but every few seconds, she scanned the parking lot for signs of the tall man with the gray hair. Katherine didn't see him.

She stowed her purse on the seat beside her and waited for two cars to pass before she clicked her tongue and pulled back on the reins. She said a silent prayer of thanks when the snow started to let up. John Wayne was an older horse, and like so many others that pulled buggies in Lancaster County, he hadn't fared well at the racetrack. And as a result, he was no longer any use to his owner. Elias had paid a fair price at auction, and John Wayne had been a good horse for a lot of years, but these days the winters took a toll on the animal.

Katherine could still remember when, years ago, she and Elias let Mary Carol name the animal. They'd assumed their oldest daughter must have heard the name on television — maybe at an *Englisch* friend's house. Katherine and Elias had limited visits to the *Englisch* homes when their *kinner* were young since the *Ordnung* encouraged their people to stay as separate as possible from outsiders. But in Lancaster County, it was impossible to avoid the *Englisch* completely. Their district relied on the *Englisch* tourists to supplement their income. With each new generation, there was less land available for farming. More

411

and more, Amish men and women were working outside their homes. The women in their district enjoyed having a little extra money of their own. "Mad money" was what the *Englisch* called it. Katherine had no idea why. But then, the *Englisch* seemed to get mad about lots of things.

It was several years before Katherine found out that John Wayne was the name of some kind of gunslinger. But by then, it was too late to change it. The name had stuck.

She picked up speed to get ahead of another car in the parking lot, and she was almost to the highway when she caught sight of the strange man again. He was standing beside a blue car, staring at her. A shiver ran up her spine. As she passed by him, she allowed herself a good, long look, tempted to stop and ask him why he was following her. But that wasn't always safe with the *Englisch.* Katherine was wise enough to know that there were good and bad people everywhere — even in her small Amish district — but the bad seemed to settle in around the *Englisch.* It was just simple math. There were more of them.

When Katherine locked eyes with the stranger, he hurried into the blue car. Would he follow her? She didn't know who he was, but something about him was familiar.

She turned around several times during her trip home, double-checking that he wasn't behind her. Thirty minutes later, she pulled into her driveway. She got John Wayne settled in the barn before she hurried into the house. She called out to Linda as soon as she walked into the living room. After she hung her bonnet and coat on the rack by the door, she pulled off her gloves.

"Linda! Gideon!" She edged toward the stairs and was relieved when Linda answered. "Up here, *Mamm.*"

"Is everything okay?" she asked from the landing.

"No!"

Katherine sighed as she started up the stairs. Out of her four children, Linda was what her friend Diana described as dramatic. Since no one was crying, she assumed no one had gotten hurt, always a good thing. "I'm on my way up."

"You're not going to be happy!"

Katherine picked up the pace. *I'm already not happy. What now?* She opened the door to Linda's bedroom, and when no one was there, she moved down the hall to Gideon's room.

Linda threw her hands up in the air and grunted. "I don't know what you're going to do with him." Linda stormed past Katherine before she could ask her why she hadn't kept a closer eye on the five-year-old, but right now, she needed to have a talk with her youngest.

She sat down across from Gideon's bed where the boy was playing with his shoelaces. Stephen disliked having to share a room with little Gideon. He would definitely not approve of these new drawings on the walls. Their home was plain. Everywhere except this room. Stephen had begged for a few luxuries when his *rumschpringe* began, and Katherine had given in since he seemed to be taking his father's death the hardest. Posters of hot rods and musicians on the wall, a battery-operated radio by the bed, a pair of earbuds on the nightstand, and a magazine with a fancy automobile on the front. Katherine didn't like all these things being in the same room with Gideon, but she was choosing her battles these days.

"Gideon, we've talked about this. You cannot draw on the walls." Katherine rubbed her forehead as she eyed her son's artwork and recalled how she'd just repainted this room a month ago. Diana had told her that drawing pictures on the walls was Gideon's way of expressing his grief. Katherine hadn't been sure about that, but today's imagery proved Diana was right. However, this was not a time for scolding. "What made you draw this, Gideon? We talked about where *Daed* went, remember?"

Her son hung his head for a few moments before he looked up at her with his big brown eyes. He brushed his blond bangs out of the way. His hair needed a trim but it would have to wait. Maybe Stephen could do it.

Gideon started talking to her in *Deitsch*, but Katherine interrupted him. *"Nee,* when you're at home, talk to me in *Englisch."* It was Gideon's first year of school, so he'd just started learning *Englisch* as a second language. "It's *gut* practice for you."

"Daed is in a box in the dirt. I saw him put there." Her son pointed to his large drawing on the wall. An outsider might not have recognized it as a coffin in the middle of a bunch of stick people, but Katherine did.

"Nee." She leaned forward until she was close enough to gently grasp Gideon's chin, lifting his eyes to hers. *"Daed* is in heaven with God and Jesus and your *mammi* and *daadi."* Why was Gideon so fixated on thinking his *daed* was in the ground? From an early age, all of her *kinner* had been schooled about the Lord and taught the ways of the *Ordnung.* "Only *Daed*'s body was buried.

415

Daed's soul went to heaven."

For the hundredth time, Katherine tried to explain this to her son, frustrated that the other children had accepted this as truth by the time they were Gideon's age. But maybe it had been easier for the others because they didn't have to apply it to the death of their own father.

"Mom!"

Katherine stood up and got to the bedroom door just as Linda blew into the room carrying a box wrapped in silver paper with a purple bow. Her face was red and her teeth chattered.

"You don't have to yell." She touched her daughter's icy cheek. "Were you outside?" She nodded to the box. "And what's that?"

"I saw a man in the driveway. By the time I got outside, he was in his car driving away."

Katherine rushed to the window in time to see a blue car going down the road. She rested a hand on her chest.

Linda joined her at the window. "This was on the rocking chair on the front porch." She handed the box to Katherine and smiled. "It has your name written on it." Her daughter bounced up on her toes. "Your first Christmas present!"

CHAPTER TWO

Mary Carol didn't think she'd ever get tired of kissing Abraham Fisher. She just wished that she didn't feel so guilty about it. Everyone in her house — except maybe Linda — was still mourning the loss of their father. Mary Carol heard her mother crying softly in her room sometimes. Stephen wouldn't say much to anyone. And Gideon had taken to drawing all over the walls, something he'd never done before. Mary Carol missed her father so much it hurt, but she was trying to give herself permission to find happiness again. And she was doing that with Abe. She'd known him all her life, but they'd only been dating for a few months. He'd just recently gotten baptized, something she hoped was the first step in what would lead to a marriage proposal.

Abe kissed her again, then pulled away. "I can tell you're distracted."

"What?" Mary Carol twisted the tie of her

kapp between her fingers and tried to still her chattering teeth. Now that she was in her *rumschpringe,* they were spending more time together, but this was the first time they'd come to the abandoned farmhouse off Black Horse Road. Mary Carol was afraid the structure might collapse on them, but it was much too cold to sit in the buggy. The battery-operated heater in Abe's buggy had quit working earlier in the day.

Abe reached for her hand and squeezed. "You're feeling bad about being happy."

She'd done her best not to let it show. "Sorry."

"It's okay. I can just tell when your mind goes somewhere else." Abe blew a cold fog as he spoke.

Mary Carol snuggled up against him on the couch. The blue-and-red-checked fabric was faded, and the cushions sagged in the middle. The house had been vacant for years, but from the looks of things, they hadn't been the only ones seeking privacy and a little relief from the weather.

"I wonder who else is coming here." She pointed to an empty Coke can on a TV tray next to an old tan recliner.

Abe got up and walked to the chair. "Maybe this has been here for a long time." He lifted the can and smelled it. Mary Carol giggled. "Do you think smelling it will tell you how old it is?" She stood up and walked toward him.

"*Ya*, maybe, smarty-pants." He grinned as he tossed the empty can back and forth, his teeth chattering like hers. "Let's look around."

"Not upstairs," she said quickly. "I'm already worried the second floor is going to fall in on us, or we're going to step on a loose board down here."

"Nah." Abe pushed back the brim of his straw hat. "These old farmhouses were built sturdy, probably by *gut* Amish folks."

Mary Carol hugged herself to keep warm as she followed Abe into the kitchen. "*Nee*, Mr. Porter lived here until he died, and he wasn't Amish."

"I know, but he was in his seventies. I heard *mei daed* talking about this house once. He was telling *mei mamm* about three men who were staying here, but he stopped talking when he saw me, and I didn't hear the rest. But I think he said it was about a hundred years old. So it could have been one of our ancestors who built it before Mr. Porter lived here." He pointed to an electrical outlet to the right of the sink. "Mr. Porter probably had it wired for electricity." Abe opened one of the cabinets, which was empty, then he shuffled sideways and opened the rest.

"Ew," Mary Carol said when she saw the skeletal remains of a small mouse. She took a step back, and Abe came to her and wrapped his arms around her waist.

"I was warmer when we were on the couch." He towered over her as he pressed his lips to hers. In thirty years, would kissing Abe still give her this heady feeling?

She eased away from him and shivered. "It's much colder here in the kitchen."

Abe pointed to the window above the sink. "When I was looking in the cabinets, I felt the cold air blowing from here. Needs caulking around the panes." He latched onto her hand and they returned to the living room. The only furniture was the couch, the recliner, and the tray. She wanted to see the second story, but one of the steps was missing a piece of wood, and part of the handrail was broken off about halfway up. They were about to sit when Mary Carol noticed something in the corner of the room.

"Look." She pointed to a roll of silver wrapping paper, a reel of purple ribbon, a pair of scissors, and some tape. "Someone's been wrapping Christmas presents." She sat down beside Abe on the couch. "Maybe we shouldn't be here."

Abe cupped her cheeks in his hands, and she decided not to worry about it. After a few more minutes, she eased away. Abe's breathing was ragged, and she could feel her heart pounding. These were indicators that it was time to stop. She wondered how many other couples — *Englisch* or Amish — had made out on this very couch. "I probably need to get home."

Abe took a deep breath and blew it out slowly. "*Ya,* probably so." He stood up and offered her his hand. Mary Carol trusted Abe not to go too far with her, but it was getting harder and harder to keep tabs on his roaming hands. Sometimes she was tempted to give herself to him, but she'd made a vow to God that she would wait until she was married. She was only eighteen, but that was a fine marrying age. Mary Carol planned to be baptized soon, so maybe Abe would ask her before too long. Her parents had been eighteen when they got married. But every time she thought about a wedding, she thought about her father. Maybe it was too soon to be thinking about celebrating such things.

A blast of cold air met them when Abe opened the front door, and they rushed to the buggy. Mary Carol had told her mother she'd be home in time to help with supper. She hoped she wasn't late.

Katherine sat down on her bed and stared at the gift. Luckily, Linda had gotten distracted shortly after the package arrived and hadn't pestered her about it.

She turned up the lantern on her bedside table and took a deep breath. What if this man was a threat to her family? It was an additional worry she didn't need.

She slid the purple ribbon from the package, then slowly peeled back the silver paper to reveal a saltine cracker box. She gave it a gentle shake before she turned it end over end and listened to the contents shift. *A strange choice for a gift box.*

The box opened easily at one end. She peeked inside before she dumped it on her bed. Photographs. Dozens of them. All of Elias. And a few of Katherine and the children.

She tried to blink back the tears that rushed to her eyes.

There was a photo of Elias at an auction not long before he died. Another was of Katherine and Elias outside the pizza place. She picked up a snapshot of Elias holding Gideon and could no longer stave off her tears. She brought it closer to her face, and it took her a minute before she realized it had been taken just two days before the accident. She quickly glanced at the rest of the pictures, but fear was catching up with her other emotions. She unfolded a yellow piece of paper that was mixed in with the photographs.

Katherine wiped her eyes and put on her reading glasses. The penmanship was shaky, barely legible.

I know pictures are not allowed, but following the loss of a loved one, photographs can bring much comfort. I think the bishop — and the Lord — would think it's okay for you to have these. I hope they will bring you a little bit of happiness.

I'm leaving this on your front porch because I haven't gotten up the nerve to talk to you. I don't know if you're even going to want to talk to me, but I know you've seen me around. I'm not a stalker or anything. I won't cause you any troubles. I'm just an old man with a borrowed camera who enjoys taking pictures of your family. Or I should say, our family.

I will be at the coffee shop on Tuesday morning at nine o'clock if you would like to meet. The coffee shop where you and Elias used to go sometimes.

Katherine held her breath as she reread the last couple of lines.

Kindest regards,
James Zook

Katherine was a little girl the last time she saw James. Even back then, he walked with a limp, although she didn't know why. Like the other Amish men in their community, he'd grown a long beard following marriage, and Katherine remembered him being a deacon in the church. He no longer had a beard, and his dark hair was now long and peppered with gray.

She stood up and paced the length of her bedroom, trying to decide what to do. Part of her wanted to meet Elias's father because it would give her back a piece of her husband. But why had the man disappeared all those years ago? And why was he sneaking around? The thought of him taking pictures of the family was disturbing. And why were so many taken shortly before her husband was hit by a car?

James Zook had abandoned his wife and only son over thirty years ago. And to Katherine's knowledge, no one had heard from him since. Had he been living right here in Paradise?

She sat down on the bed and flipped through each picture again. Whatever his intentions, her father-in-law was right about one thing. Pictures were not allowed by their people, but seeing them made her feel something she hadn't felt in months: comforted.

CHAPTER THREE

Katherine arrived at the coffee shop early and ordered a black coffee. As she waited at the table, she prayed that the Lord would bless her with the right words today. Elias had rarely talked about his father, but his departure had left scars. Over the years, the pain had been mostly replaced by anger and resentment. She wasn't sure her husband would approve of this meeting. She'd chosen not to say anything to the children. Not yet.

James came in the door and walked directly to her booth. He stood in front of her for a few moments before sliding into the booth across from her.

Katherine cleared her throat. "Hello." She noticed right away that he and Elias both had the same nose, long and narrow. Her husband had also been blessed with incredible blue eyes that he had obviously inherited from his father. The most noticeable difference between Elias and his father were the lines of time feathering across James's face, and whereas Elias had been gifted with a lovely set of straight teeth, this man's bottom teeth crossed in the front.

"Am I late? I hate to be late." His eyebrows drew together in an agonized expression, his eyes fixed on her as he waited for her response.

"Uh, *nee*. I-I don't think you're late." Katherine's stomach churned. "Would you like some coffee? You have to order it at the counter."

"I don't drink coffee, but *danki.*" He folded his hands on top of the table. Katherine noticed a stain on his wrinkled blue shirt. He wasn't wearing a coat. She studied his face, noticing he looked a bit disheveled and needed a shave.

"Do you still speak Pennsylvania *Deitsch*?" Maybe Elias's father had left his family but resumed his Amish lifestyle within another district.

"I remember a few words." His face split into a wide grin. He was missing a couple of teeth toward the back. "Did you like the pictures?" Katherine swallowed hard, wishing her stomach would settle down. *"Ya,* I did. *Danki."*

"I have lots more."

"Mr. Zook . . . why didn't —"

"Just James," he said as he sat taller. "We're family."

Katherine took a deep breath and wondered if Elias was watching from heaven. "Why didn't you make yourself known to Elias before he died? And why the pictures?"

James's eyes darted around the room as he blinked his left eye a few times. Then he locked eyes with her. "I'm being followed, so I can't be too careful."

Katherine looked around the small coffee shop, then back at him. "Who is following you?"

He tapped a finger to the side of his face. "I'm not sure. But I think it's the FBI. That stands for Federal Bureau of Investigation."

"Uh, *ya*. I know." She recalled a horrific crime that had occurred in the area when she was very young. Even though her parents had kept the details from Katherine, she remembered hearing that the FBI was in Paradise. She took a sip of her coffee and kept her eyes on him.

"I used to be one of them. That's why I don't drink coffee. Got burned out on it." He leaned back against the booth and folded his arms across his chest. "I'm privy to a lot of top-secret information, so they keep a tail on me. But I have no intention of telling them what I know until I'm safely behind the pearly gates." He leaned forward and folded his hands atop the table again. "How old are you?"

Katherine tried to find her voice, relieved that Elias wasn't here to see his father like this. "I'm, uh . . . thirty-eight." She forced a smile. "James, can you tell me why you're taking pictures of my family?"

He sighed, and Katherine got a whiff of his breath. She struggled not to cringe. She prayed that James wasn't dangerous, just crazy.

"I came here to see Elias, but I was nervous to meet all of you." His eye fluttered again before he went on. "I took a bunch of pictures in case Elias sent me packing, figuring I'd at least have pictures to look at sometimes." He shrugged. "But that car hit him not long after I got here." Frowning, he started counting on his fingers. "Six or seven days. No . . . actually it was twelve days after I got here. Possibly a week." He sighed. "It could have been three days."

Katherine wasn't a drinker, but she'd seen Widow Kauffman adding brandy to her coffee on more than one occasion. Katherine didn't think that sounded like a bad idea right now. She took another sip of coffee as she wondered what James had been doing

429

for the past thirty years. "So are you living here in Paradise?"

"For now. The Lord sent me here. The same way He sent me to Michigan to work with the FBI." He hung his head for a few moments before he looked back at her with sad eyes, one of them beginning to twitch again. "We can't question the Lord." He shrugged and grinned. "Why would we, right? He's God." Then he chuckled. Loudly.

Katherine moved her eyes about the room. Two elderly couples on the other side of the shop chatted, not seeming to notice James's outburst. Katherine nodded. "*Ya*, you're right. We don't question the Lord's will." She paused. "James, did you continue practicing our faith after you left here? Did you live in another Amish community?"

He stared at her with a blank expression. "Of course not."

"Oh, it just wondered me if you might have."

Leaning forward, he put his palms flat on the table and spoke to her in a whisper. "They don't take Amish people at the Federal Bureau of Investigation."

"*Ya*. Of course not." Katherine smoothed the wrinkles from her dress. "James, I need to ask you not to take any more pictures of me or *mei* family. It is very unsettling. And can I ask you to please stop following me? I'm happy to meet you here for coffee from time to time."

He leaned back again and waved a hand in her direction as he grunted. "No worries. I won't be here long." He shook his head. "To tell you the truth, I thought I would have been gone long before now. But our Father extended my stay."

Katherine hoped she didn't have to get the *Englisch* authorities involved. "Where are you staying?"

"I'd rather not say."

Katherine inhaled a slow, steady breath, and as she released it, she willed herself to stay calm and sympathetic. She had a great-aunt who was mentally ill. "Okay. But you will stop following me, right?"

"I will."

Katherine drank the last of her coffee. "I should go now. It was nice to see you after all these years." *Forgive the lie, Lord.* "I'm sorry you weren't able to visit with Elias while he was alive."

"I didn't really care for that funeral your people threw for my son."

Katherine's breath caught in her throat. She tried not to think about the funeral and how difficult it had been to say good-bye to

431

Elias's earthly body. "You were there?"

"Only at the grave site, and I stayed under the patch of trees at the back of the cemetery. I couldn't hear what was said." James frowned. "But it was clear that there wasn't near enough fanfare for my son. No flowers or music."

"Have you forgotten that Amish funerals are plain? We don't do those things."

James stood up. "I know I have to go now." He scanned the room.

Looking for federal agents? Katherine kept her seat, just in case he tried to hug her. Instead, he put a gentle hand on her shoulder. "I wish that Elias was still here."

Her eyes clouded. "Me too." Katherine forced herself to stand.

"Don't worry. I won't hug you. I know your people don't like that."

She nodded, thankful that he spared her the awkward moment. "Hey. It's almost Christmas, huh?" He smiled. "A celebration indeed." After he looked around the room again, he turned and left. Katherine stood there for a few moments, then she walked out the door and saw him on the sidewalk. *He must be freezing.* She watched him for a few moments and tried to fight the strange feeling settling over her. She called out to him. He turned around and walked back to her.

"I can't stay at your home if that's what you were going to ask me. And I'm not ready to meet my grandchildren either."

"I, uh . . ." Katherine stared at him, tongue-tied for a few seconds since neither of those thoughts had crossed her mind. Inviting him to her home was out of the question, but she had a lot of questions for James Zook. "Would you like to meet here next Tuesday?" She could bring him some of Elias's things. A coat, for starters.

He walked a few steps closer to her, and a smile lit up his face.

"I know you're not going to like this, but . . ."

Katherine tensed when he threw his arms around her, and her initial reaction was to push him away. But then he rubbed her back, the way a parent lovingly rubs a child's back, and he said, "Elias loved you very much. He talks to me in my dreams sometimes. He understands why I couldn't be with him when he was growing up. But I gotta say, I sure am excited to go see him after Christmas." He eased himself away. "He said they are really going to roll out the red carpet when I get there."

Then he abruptly withdrew from the hug.

"See you Tuesday." He turned and headed down the sidewalk.

Katherine tried to ignore the rush of grief that came over her.

And then she made her way slowly toward her buggy.

CHAPTER FOUR

Mary Carol waited as Abe put batteries in the new heater. He had also brought a heavy blanket for them to use at the old farmhouse. She huddled beneath it on the couch while Abe got the heater set up on the floor a few feet in front of them. Everything looked about the same as the last time they'd borrowed old Mr. Porter's house, except now six Coke cans were on the TV tray by the chair.

"Can you feel the heat?" Abe put a hand in front of the blower. Mary Carol nodded. It wasn't very powerful, but it was better than nothing. Abe joined her on the couch and she raised the cover so he could get underneath it.

"I missed you," he said as he cupped her face and kissed her. As much as she enjoyed these Saturdays with Abe, she was becoming more and more distracted from her effort to keep things from going too far. As he

435

eased her down on the couch, he lay beside her. "And I love you," he added, his breath ragged, his hand traveling. She gently pushed him away and sat up.

"I love you, too, but . . ." She bit her bottom lip as she lowered her chin. "I feel like we're doing something wrong."

Abe sat up, got out from under the blanket, and wrapped it around both her shoulders. Then he kissed her on the cheek. "I don't want to do anything that makes you feel like that."

Mary Carol was trying to decide if he was upset or mad. She'd only known one girl who had gone all the way before marriage, and not only had Lena regretted it right away, but she'd also gotten pregnant. They were quiet as the heater hummed, blowing a warm breeze their way.

"I just want to hold you." Abe wrapped his arms around her. After awhile, she invited him to share the blanket with her again, and they resumed kissing. But it took even less time for Abe to start breathing hard as he pulled her closer.

"I can't," she whispered as her body reacted to his touch in ways she didn't understand. "I'm scared."

"Don't be. I won't do anything you don't want me to do." Abe trembled, and Mary

436

Carol wanted to trust him, but she wasn't sure she could trust herself.

"No," she said in a louder voice, but she didn't push him away as she closed her eyes and returned his kisses.

A noise from upstairs made them both jump, and when they heard footsteps, Mary Carol gasped as she squeezed Abe's arm. "What do we do?"

They both stood up, shedding the blanket, and moved quickly toward the door, but they were still a few feet from it when they heard a man's voice. "Hey!"

Mary Carol turned around when Abe did, and as the old man walked toward them, she held her breath. He walked with a limp and wore tattered jeans and a blue shirt. His hair was matted on one side like he'd been lying down. He stopped in front of Abe. He squinted his eyes and leaned forward. His left eye seemed to have a mind of its own, or was he winking at Abe?

"What's going on in here?" The stranger's voice was gruff. He held up his first finger, then poked Abe in the chest. "I don't know what you're doing down here, but I'm sure I heard that girl say no." He glanced at Mary Carol. "Are you okay?"

She nodded, but her feet were rooted to the floor. The man took a step back as he

eyed them both. His left eye blinked ran-
domly. "Sit down. Both of you." The man
pointed to the couch as he backed into the
recliner by the TV tray.

Abe cleared his throat. "We're sorry, sir.
We didn't know anyone lived here. We'll go."

Before Abe even had time to take a step,
the man pointed to the couch. "Sit."

Mary Carol glanced toward the door, and
she hoped Abe would grab her hand so they
could make a run for it. But instead, he
walked to the couch and sat down, and once
Mary Carol found her feet, she followed.
Abe didn't even realize he'd sat down on
his straw hat.

The man rubbed his chin, squinting again.
"Did you know that in sixteenth-century
Naples, people were hung for kissing? I'm
going to guess you probably didn't."

Mary Carol looked to Abe, whose eyes
were wide as he shook his head. "No, sir. I
didn't know that." His voice trembled when
he went on. "Please don't kill us."

"Wait here." The man abruptly rose from
the chair and limped toward the kitchen.
Mary Carol pictured him returning with a
gun. But before he'd even gotten out of the
living room, he turned around to face them.
"I have a soda every four hours. I do this
because I enjoy it. And because I can." He

paused and studied them for a few seconds. "Wait right there."

"Let's go," Mary Carol said the moment he was out of sight. She tugged on the sleeve of Abe's black coat.

"What if he comes after us? What if he has a gun or something?" Abe looked at Mary Carol, then toward the kitchen as the man walked back into the living room carrying three cans of Coke.

"I have over a hundred guns, but I'm not planning to shoot anyone." His teeth were crooked when he smiled. "Not today anyway." He handed a soda to each of them. "Who are you people?"

Mary Carol swallowed the lump in her throat. "That's Abe Fisher. I'm Mary Carol Zook." She turned to Abe, but she wasn't sure he was breathing.

The man popped the top on his soda and took a long swig.

Mary Carol opened her cola too. Despite the circumstances, the Coke was a treat. Her mother never bought sodas. She took a sip and swallowed, enjoying the tingle from all the bubbles.

"Are you any relation to Katherine Zook?" The man shivered as he talked, but every few seconds he took another gulp of Coke.

Mary Carol nodded. "*Ya.* I'm her daughter."

"Ah, yes." He pointed a finger at her. "I thought you looked familiar, but sometimes you all look the same in those clothes."

Mary Carol reached for the string on her *kapp* and twirled it in her fingers. Then she glanced at Abe before looking back at the man. "Do we know each other?"

"No." He finished the soda, crushed the can, and put it next to the others on the tray. He pointed a finger at Abe. "The next time this girl tells you no, what will you do?"

Abe sat taller. "I-I will listen to-to her."

Mary Carol hung her head as she felt her cheeks heat up. When she looked up, she saw the man's teeth chattering. She picked up the brown blanket from where it had fallen on the floor and offered it to him.

"Danki." He quickly covered himself with it, and she returned to the couch.

"Do you speak Pennsylvania *Deitsch*?" She took a sip of her cola. Abe hadn't opened his.

"A little. My name is Paul, by the way." He slapped himself upside the head and rolled his eyes. "I mean James. My name is James. And I don't live here. I'm just borrowing the place, if you know what I mean. Kinda like the two of you, I guess." His left

440

eye started to twitter again. "So tell me about your life."

Mary Carol glanced at Abe and waited for him to go first. "I-I am the son of John and Elizabeth Fisher. We are —"

James grunted loudly. "Not *you*. Her." He pointed to Mary Carol. "I want to know about you."

"Uh . . ." She wasn't sure what he wanted to know. The man couldn't even keep his own name straight. "I have a sister named Linda who is twelve. I have two brothers named Stephen and Gideon, and they are sixteen and five."

James raised his eyebrows. "And?"

"And you know that my mother is Katherine." She paused. "How do you know my mother?"

"I don't really know her. Go on. What else?"

"Um . . . my father was Elias. He passed on six months ago." She locked eyes with James. "I miss him very much." She glanced at Abe again, but he was tapping one foot and turning the full can of Coke over in his hands. She hoped he didn't plan to open it anytime soon.

" 'A time to weep, and a time to laugh,' " James said, pausing to sigh. " 'A time to mourn, and a time to dance.' "

"Ecclesiastes," she said softly.

James nodded. "Yes. And the Beatles." He scratched his chin. "Or was it the Byrds?"

Mary Carol had no idea what beetles and birds had to do with the Scripture verse.

"Can we go now?" Abe put his unopened can of Coke on the couch next to him. "Are you going to tell our parents you found us here?"

James shook his head. "Kid, you aren't the sharpest tool in the shed, are you? Why would I tell your parents when I'm not supposed to be here either?"

Abe scowled as he stood up. "Come on, Mary Carol. Let's go."

She slowly lifted herself from the couch as she studied James. There was something about him that seemed familiar. She was thankful he'd come down the stairs before she and Abe did something they would have regretted.

"I'm the most interesting person you'll probably ever meet, but go ahead and leave if you want."

Abe picked up his squashed hat from the couch and motioned to Mary Carol for them to move toward the door, but she sat back down. "I'd like to hear about you," she said as she set her soda can on the floor near her feet.

Abe glared at her. "Come on, Mary Carol. Let's go."

James folded his arms across his chest and glared at Abe. "Well, you can't leave her here with me. I'm a stranger. So you might as well sit back down."

Mary Carol looked up at Abe, then said in Pennsylvania *Deitsch,* "Let's just stay a little bit longer."

Abe huffed, but he sat down beside her.

James pulled the blanket snug, then smiled. "Before I begin, let's pray together."

Mary Carol chewed on her bottom lip but finally nodded. Abe lowered his head when she did.

"Dear heavenly Father, please bless these children." James paused, and when Mary Carol glanced up at him, she caught him eyeing Abe before he shook his head and continued. "And help young Abraham to behave like a gentleman."

Mary Carol bit her lip again and stifled a grin. Abe didn't look up, but she could see his face turning red.

"I pray that Mary Carol and what's-his-name will walk the right path and stay on track toward a life that pleases You. I pray for Bonnie. You and I know why. And I pray for a chocolate cake, that someone will bring me one. Loving Father, I will see You soon. Amen."

Mary Carol opened her eyes, not sure what to make of this man. But for the next two hours, she and Abe listened to him talk about his life. And James had spoken the truth earlier.

He really was the most interesting person she had ever met.

CHAPTER FIVE

Mary Carol shivered as Abe guided the buggy toward her house. A light snow was falling.

"Well, you can call him interesting all you want," Abe said as he picked up speed. "But he's *ab im kopp*."

"*Ya,* he might be a little off in the head." Mary Carol recalled the stories James told. "But I still find him interesting, and I like him."

"He told me to shut up twice." Abe shook his head.

Mary Carol laughed. "That's because you interrupted him twice. My favorite story was when he told us about staying at the White House."

Abe turned onto Mary Carol's road. "*Ya,* but I don't believe any of it. I don't think the president's wife had a sister that no one knew about named Bonnie, or that she made him chocolate cakes every week." He turned to her, eyes wide. "And I'm sure I don't believe that he saved eighty-six lives while he worked for the FBI. Tall tales. He's an old man who likes to tell stories."

Mary Carol smiled. "I like him." She'd laughed more than she had in a long time.

"We are going to have to find somewhere else to go on Saturdays so we can be alone."

"Didn't you hear me tell him that I would see him next Saturday? He seemed happy about that. And I'm going to surprise him with a chocolate cake."

Abe pulled back on the reins until the horse slowed to barely a trot. "You meant that? What about us? Don't you want to spend time by ourselves?"

"Abe, we need to be smarter about the time we spend alone. The last couple of times have been close." Mary Carol didn't want to hurt Abe's feelings. She knew he loved her, and she loved him too. But they'd been treading in dangerous waters the past few weeks. "There will be plenty of time for us to be alone after the holidays. Christmas is in a couple of weeks, and James was excited that we were going to visit him again." She shrugged as she looked out the window of the buggy. "You don't have to go if you don't want to."

Abe grunted. "*Ya,* I do. I'd never let you

go there by yourself."

He pulled into Mary Carol's driveway. "He doesn't like me though." She smiled, tempted to agree with him. But James had been very nice to her. When Abe stopped the buggy near the gate in the front yard, she looked around to make sure her mother or siblings weren't outside, then she leaned over and quickly kissed Abe good-bye.

"See you Saturday?" she asked, still smiling. Abe frowned as he nodded. "*Ya*, I guess."

"I love you."

"I love you, too, Mary Carol." He hung his head, sighing before he looked back up at her. She'd known Abe for so long, sometimes she felt like she could think his thoughts. He was about to apologize. "I'm real sorry if I did anything to upset you. I never want to hurt you. Not ever."

"I know. I just think maybe things were moving a little too fast." She was thankful for their new friend. Today, for a couple of hours, she hadn't thought about her father, about how much she missed him. But as she got out of the buggy and hurried through the snow to the house, she knew any sense of joy she'd felt would turn to guilt when she saw her mother. When Mary Carol was around her family, it seemed wrong to be anything other than sad.

Katherine stayed quiet while her oldest son voiced his opinion about Gideon drawing on their bedroom walls. "It's bad enough that I have to share a room with him, but now you are *letting* him draw on the walls?" He waved a hand toward Gideon's stick people and coffins. Just that morning, Gideon had added more people . . . and another coffin. When Katherine had questioned her youngest son about the extra coffin, he'd just shrugged.

"Your *bruder* is having a hard time coping with your *daed*'s death, and he is just expressing himself." Katherine wanted to ask her older son how he was coping. He'd closed himself off from everyone. He hadn't gone to any of the singings on Sunday afternoons since his father died. And sometimes he refused to go to worship service.

"*Ya,* well, I wish he'd find some other way to do it." Stephen shook his head, then began to walk out of the bedroom.

"Stephen, can you wait a minute?" Katherine didn't want to bring this up right now, but the boy was out of the house so much, she needed to catch him while she could. "I'm sorry to have to ask this, but would you please find some time in the next few days to winterize the pipes in the basement?" She considered it a small miracle that a pipe hadn't burst, given that December had been colder than usual. If Stephen handled the pipes, it would give her time to give Gideon a trim.

Stephen turned, and before he was out of earshot, she heard a faint, "Fine."

Katherine was tempted to follow him, but maybe this wasn't the best time to get him to open up about his dad's death and the added responsibilities.

She went to her own bedroom where she'd laid out all the items she planned to take to her father-in-law. She still wasn't sure if she was doing the right thing by befriending the man who'd hurt his own son so deeply, but it was the holidays, and she was going to do what she could for him. She picked up the brown coat she'd bought Elias only two Christmases ago, and she buried her face in it, breathing in his scent. Fighting the urge to cry, she gathered up some of Elias's shirts, two pairs of shoes, and some other toiletries she thought James could use. She packed them in an old red suitcase that Elias had used when traveling to out-of-town auctions.

She wondered if James was homeless, and it worried her where he might be living since

449

he wouldn't tell her. *But how does he have a car and how does he afford to put gas in it?*

An hour later, she walked into the coffee shop. James sat at the same booth they'd sat at a week ago. He wore the same clothes. Katherine put the suitcase on the floor next to him.

"I put together a few things for you. They were Elias's. I thought you might like to have them."

"Why?" James stared at her, a blank expression on his face.

"Because I . . . well, I thought you might want them." She looked down at two cups of coffee already on the table. "There's a coat in there too." She touched the white plastic lid on top of the Styrofoam cup. "Is this for me?"

"Yeah." He picked up the cup in front of him and took a large swallow.

Katherine tried to recall if she'd told James she drank her coffee black. She didn't think so, but as she took her first sip, she was glad he'd guessed right. "I thought you didn't like coffee."

James laughed. "Are you kidding me? I love coffee."

Katherine tapped a finger to her chin. "Um, what about your time as a federal agent? I thought you said you got burned out on coffee."

His expression went flat. "Oh dear." He pushed the cup as far as he could to one side of the table. "You're right."

Did he even remember their last conversation? "If you want the coffee, you should drink it." She wondered how he'd paid for it.

"I hope there is coffee in heaven." He shook his head. "I've asked the Lord about that a dozen times, but He doesn't ever tell me."

Katherine wondered if establishing a relationship with James was going to be worth it, but she pulled the cup back in front of him. "Drink the coffee. It will warm you up."

He stared at her for a while, but eventually he took another sip. "I had another dream about Elias this past week. On Thursday, I think. No . . . wait. It was Friday." He shook his head. "No. It was last night." He pointed a finger at her. "He said you aren't handling his death very well with your youngest son. You need to do something different. He told me what you need to do." He picked up his cup of coffee, put it back down again, then pushed it to the side.

Katherine was startled that James was

451

bringing up something he'd have no way of knowing — or maybe it was simply a co-incidence. She had cherished the few dreams she'd had about Elias over the past six months, but was her husband really trying to communicate through James? She doubted it. *I'll humor him.* "And what am I supposed to do differently?"

He scratched the top of his head. "For the life of me, I can't remember what he said."

That figures.

"So, how are you handling Gideon's grief?"

Katherine was surprised that James remembered his youngest grandson's name. "I'm letting him express his feelings by drawing on the wall. It seems to help him."

James burst out laughing. "Boy howdy. He's pulled the wool over your eyes. He probably just likes to draw on the wall. What does he draw?"

Katherine stiffened, clenched her jaw, and reminded herself whom she was dealing with. "He draws stick people standing around a coffin, and he doesn't understand how his father's body is under the earth, but his soul is in heaven." She sat quietly for a few moments, but when James didn't say anything, she said, "He added an extra coffin to the drawing this morning."

James rolled his eyes, the left one fluttering for a couple of seconds, and pulled his coffee back in front of him. "Well, it doesn't take a brain surgeon to figure that out, about the extra coffin."

"Well, I'm no brain surgeon, so maybe you can explain it to me." Raw curiosity brought on the question that she was sure he couldn't answer.

James took several gulps from his cup. She could see the steam rising from the opening of the lid, and she wondered how he wasn't scorching his mouth. "The extra coffin is Gideon's."

"What?"

James sighed. "The boy is afraid that he is going to die and that you'll bury him in a box too. If you keep letting him draw on the walls, he'll probably draw more coffins. One for you, then his brother and sisters. The kid is afraid of dying and worried everyone else he loves will die too." He grimaced. "Wow. You've got four kids. I'm surprised you didn't figure that out."

Katherine forced herself to ignore his last comment. She wondered if maybe he was right. Was Gideon afraid of everyone around him dying, himself included? "That might be true. But he doesn't understand that his father isn't actually in the ground, that he is in heaven. So even if he is worried his family might die, he doesn't understand what we believe."

"Then you're not explaining it right. Like Elias said, you need to do something different."

She let her hands fall into her lap, then clenched them together. "I've explained it to him the same way I did with *mei* other *kinner,* and all of them had a *gut* understanding about heaven by the time they were Gideon's age."

He drummed the fingers of his left hand on the table as his mouth twitched from side to side. Katherine finished her coffee while he pondered the situation for a minute. She jumped when he slammed his hand on the table.

"Okay. I know what you should do."

Katherine waited, but James just stared at her. At this point, she was willing to try anything to help her youngest. "Is it a secret, or are you going to tell me?"

He frowned. "Tell you what?"

Katherine took a deep breath. How could anyone be so together one moment, but totally lost the next? "Are you going to tell me what I should do about Gideon?"

"Oh, sure." He nodded. "I'm going to assume that the boy has been taught the basics about Jesus, that He died for our sins, and so on." He raised an eyebrow.

Katherine nodded. She was skeptical that a man like James could tell her anything helpful. A nutty man who had spent very little time raising his own son.

"Kids are visual little creatures. They have to see something to understand it. Gideon saw his father lowered into the ground, so he needs to *see* heaven too."

Katherine brought a hand to her chest. "I don't want him to *see* heaven. He's only five."

James grunted. "Good grief, woman. Hear me out. He needs to see it in his mind's eye as clearly as he saw his father's body go into the ground."

She looked at him and nodded slightly. "How do I help him to do that?"

"We all see heaven differently. Gideon's heaven won't look like the pictures you find in books about this subject. He won't envision it the way your other children do, or the way any other person on earth does. Gideon needs to see and feel all the beauty and love in heaven, and you need to walk him through it until that light shines brightly, until he can see his father enjoying life in our Father's house."

Katherine tried to hold her tears at bay. "I

don't know how to do that."

James smiled. "Yes. You do. Now . . ." He reached over and patted her hand. "I have to go. I will see you here next Tuesday at the same time. And I will be praying that you bring me good news about Gideon."

Katherine had no idea how James got out of bed and dressed himself without getting lost in his home, or wherever he was living. How in the world did he keep track of his days? The man could barely hold on to his own thoughts. But his explanation about how to help Gideon had left her speechless.

He picked up the suitcase she'd brought him, gave a quick wave, then walked out of the coffee shop. And this time, he wasn't limping.

CHAPTER SIX

Mary Carol knocked on the farmhouse's front door as she and Abe shivered on the porch. James opened it dressed in a pair of black slacks being held up with suspenders, and he was wearing a long-sleeved blue shirt. Clothes just like her father and most Amish men in their community wore. And he'd gotten a haircut. He stepped aside so they could enter, and she handed him the chocolate cake. "Bonnie, you shouldn't have," James said, holding the cake. "But your chocolate cakes are the best, and you know how much I will enjoy this."

Mary Carol glanced at Abe before she turned back to James.

"Um . . . I'm Mary Carol, not Bonnie."

James put the cake on the TV tray by the chair, then he popped himself in the side of the head, hard enough that Mary Carol cringed.

"I'm so sorry! Of course you are. You're

Katherine's daughter." She looked at Abe in time to see him roll his eyes.

"Do you feel like company right now? Or we can go. I just wanted you to have the cake."

James sat down in the worn recliner. "I would like for you to stay." He looked at Abe, frowning. "So I guess you have to be here also. Sit. The both of you."

Mary Carol sat down, and after a few seconds, Abe did too. "Tell me, Mary Carol, how is your brother Stephen?" James crossed one leg over the other. "Stephen?" He smiled. "Yes."

"Um, he's okay, I guess." The truth was, Mary Carol worried about Stephen. He had detached himself from everyone, but people handled grief in different ways. "He's having a hard time with our father's passing. We all are, but Stephen stays to himself most of the time. He didn't cry at the funeral either."

"Hmm . . ." James stroked his clean-shaven chin. "Sounds like Stephen is keeping his emotions bottled up. Someone needs to pop that cork." He pointed a finger at her. "And that person is you. You need to get Stephen to open up to you."

She shook her head. "*Ach,* you don't know my *bruder.* He was cranky even before our father died. He snaps at everyone, yells at our *mudder,* and refuses to go to worship service sometimes. I'm not the one to talk to him."

"Okay." James looked at Abe. "Then you do it." Abe stiffened on the couch next to her. "Huh?"

"You heard me. You talk to Stephen. Get the boy to talk about how he is feeling. Maybe he'd be more comfortable talking to you." James scowled again. "Although I don't know why." This time it was James who rolled his eyes, and Mary Carol tried to hide her grin.

"I'm, uh, not really very close to Stephen. He's a couple of years younger than me, and we've never hung out or anything."

"Do you ever think about anyone but yourself?" James clicked his tongue, shook his head, then locked eyes with Mary Carol. "What do you see in this guy?"

She smiled as she elbowed Abe. "*Ach,* he's a *gut* man. You just have to get to know him."

"Fine. I will talk to Stephen," Abe said.

"Wonderful." James clapped his hands. "I bought some plates today." He stood up. "And some forks. I prayed and prayed that someone would bring me a chocolate cake." He looked up. "Thank You for that, Lord."

Then he picked up the cake. "I'm going to get us all a piece of this."

"He is crazy. We shouldn't be here," Abe whispered.

"I told you before, I like him." Mary Carol giggled. "But he doesn't like you. That's for sure."

"Are we going to have to come back here again?"

She shrugged. "I don't know. I'd like to. I think he's —"

"I know," Abe said. "You think he's *interesting.* I just hope he isn't dangerous or anything. He might go nuts, kill us, and bury us in the backyard."

Mary Carol slapped him gently on the arm. "Don't say things like that. He's just an old man whose memory is failing."

Abe raised one eyebrow. "That's an understatement. He's out of his mind."

"I'm going to try to find out more about him."

James walked into the living room and handed them each a plate with a wedge of cake.

"You're not limping," she said as he headed back toward the kitchen. He returned with his own slice. He set it on the TV tray and turned to them, looping his thumbs in his suspenders.

"Ain't that the craziest of things? I've limped for my entire life, since I was a boy. I'm missing a bone in my leg." He stood even taller. "And I feel better than I've felt in years, since before I got shot." He walked to the chair and sat down.

"Shot?" Abe had just put a large piece of cake in his mouth.

"Yes, shot. In the head." James took a bite of his cake. "By a bad guy."

Mary Carol wondered if this could be true. Maybe that's why he was a bit . . . off. "That's terrible. When did that happen?"

"When did what happen?" James frowned.

"You just said you got shot," Abe said loudly.

"Kid, I'm forgetful, not deaf." James shook his head as he stabbed at another piece of cake. Mary Carol decided to let the shooting incident go.

"You've told us stories about your job with the FBI, but you haven't told us about your family. Do you have children? Maybe grand-children?"

James put the empty plate on the tray. "I had a son." He paused with a faraway look in his eyes. "I really loved him. But that's all I have to say about that."

She wasn't getting very far in her effort to know him better.

"When you were telling us stories about your FBI adventures, you never said how long you were employed with them."

James hurried to the window. "Did anyone see you come here? Someone might be following you, trying to find me." He turned to Abe. "Did you see anything? They are usually in a red car, which is mighty ridiculous since everyone knows you don't use a red car to follow someone."

"I didn't see any red car following us," Abe said.

"Keep an eye out for them. Two men. One of them, the older one, is always wearing a black suit. The younger guy is always wearing a white jacket." He walked back to his chair and settled into it. "I don't know who trained them. I see them everywhere. They blend in about as well as a tiger swimming in the ocean."

Mary Carol smiled when she pictured that, even though it was an odd comparison. "We will keep an eye out for them."

James nodded. "Good. They aren't dangerous, just pesky." He snapped a finger. "Hey, did I tell you about the time I got shot in the head?"

Abe spoke up. "You started to, but you didn't finish. What happened?"

James sighed. "Well, it was a really long

time ago. I was in a witness protection program. I had to leave my family behind for their own safety."

"I thought you were an FBI agent," Abe said as he glanced at Mary Carol, grinning.

"Kid, try to keep up." James narrowed his eyebrows as he stared at Abe and shook his head. "First I was in protective custody, then moved to the witness protection program. Six years later — or maybe two or three — the feds begged me to become one of them."

"I'm sure they did," Abe said.

"I'm not sure you're sure of much of anything." James pointed to Abe. "But yes, that's what happened. I didn't want to join them at first. I was raised in a home that didn't believe in violence of any kind, and I knew that I might be called to handle dangerous situations that could lead to me using a gun."

"Did you ever kill anyone?" Abe took off his straw hat, still a little misshapen from his sitting on it the other day, and placed it on the couch beside him.

James stared long and hard at Abe, and Mary Carol was afraid to hear the answer. She wasn't sure she could be friends with someone who had taken another person's life.

"Don't you know that you're not supposed to ask a person something like that? Just like you never ask a soldier if they killed anyone in battle."

Mary Carol swallowed hard. That sounded like a yes to her. James looked at Mary Carol. "Don't look so scared," he said softly. "I've been blessed. I never killed anyone. I was directed onto that path to save lives. Eighty-six to be exact."

She smiled. "Tell us more."

James broke into a story about how he saved a sixteen-year-old boy from committing suicide. Mary Carol listened, but her mind was somewhere else. *Stephen.*

Katherine wasn't one to spy on her children, but she was curious why Abe had come to see Stephen. As she passed by Stephen's room with freshly folded towels in her arms, she slowed down and listened.

"I don't want to talk about this." Stephen's voice was so loud that Katherine almost opened the door to make sure everything was okay between the boys. But as she tucked the towels under one arm and reached for the doorknob, she stopped.

"I know you don't, but you gotta face your grief. Mary Carol is really worried about you."

"I knew she put you up to this."

Katherine held her breath.

"Mary Carol didn't put me up to this. A friend suggested that I talk to you."

"Who?"

Katherine stayed still and listened.

"It doesn't matter," Abe said. "The point is, it might help if you talk to someone. And if it's not me, then maybe you should talk to someone else."

"I ain't talking to no doctor, if that's what you're suggesting."

It got quiet, and Katherine heard Abe's voice, but she couldn't make out what he was saying.

"Get out of here, Abe! You have no idea how I feel!"

Katherine latched onto the doorknob, but before she turned it, her grieving son went on.

"I hurt! I hurt every day. It's a kind of pain that I don't even know how to explain. But I'm the man of the house. I can't be crying all the time. And that's all I want to do! I just want to run into my mother's arms, bury my head on her shoulder, and cry. I want her to rub my back and tell me that everything is going to be okay! I'd be just like a big sissy baby! So get out of here, Abe."

Katherine dropped the towels on the floor, turned the knob, and rushed to where her son was sitting on the bed. Both boys froze at the sudden interruption. Stephen huffed and started to rub his forehead. She inched closer to him, motioning for Abe to let himself out. Stephen wouldn't look at her, just kept rubbing his forehead and looking at the floor. She saw the muscles in his cheeks shift, obviously from him clenching his teeth. "Stephen." That was all she said, and when the boy stood, she swiftly pulled him into her arms. When he tried to push her away, a fierce strength overtook Katherine, and she held him firmly until finally, he buried his head against her shoulder. At first he just held on to her tightly. Then she heard what sounded like a hiccup. His body heaved as he released the breath in his lungs and a torrent of sobs followed. She found it impossible to focus on her own pain while her son was in such agony. She continued to hold him, patting the back of his hair and telling him it was all okay.

She was thankful for whoever it was who had encouraged Abe to talk to Stephen. She would pray for this person.

And thank you, Abe, for having the courage to follow through on the task.

CHAPTER SEVEN

Katherine was ten minutes late to the coffee shop, and she prepared for a verbal lashing from her father-in-law, but instead he broke into a big smile when she joined him at the table.

"You have the light," he said.

"What?" She took off her black bonnet and put it on the booth beside her, then she tied the strings on her *kapp.*

"Let me rephrase that. You've always had the light, but today it is shining extra bright. I think you have good news."

Katherine smiled back at him. "*Ya,* I do. I think my family is starting to heal."

James pushed one of the coffee cups toward her. She took a sip and nearly spit out the hot liquid. "What is this?" she asked, wishing she had a glass of water. It wasn't coffee. It was . . . sweet.

"The waitress asked me if I'd like to try the vanilla latte, so I figured, why not?"

"But you didn't try it. I did."

"I never touch that whipped-up stuff." He waved his hand dismissively.

She wasn't sure how to politely refuse the drink, so she moved it to the side.

"So does part of that healing have to do with Gideon?"

"*Ya,* I spent some time with him a few days ago and we talked about his vision of heaven. I told him I imagined heaven was full of all of our favorite things and people. It was fun to hear him describe what his heaven would look like. Lots of games, trees with candy instead of leaves, children playing tag and hide-and-seek. I told him to imagine his father was there, waiting for him." A warm feeling washed over her. "He spent the next few days drawing his heaven on the wall. Then last night he told me I could repaint the wall if I wanted to. I think I'm going to wait a little while before I do that. Every time I see that wall, I smile." Katherine realized that working with Gideon on this had made her truly happy, something she hadn't felt in months. "He seems to be getting better. And I'm grateful to God for that." She held up a finger. "*And,* we had another breakthrough. Apparently, someone encouraged Abe — that's my daughter's boyfriend — to talk to Stephen.

Remember, he is my sixteen-year-old son?"

James was still smiling. "Yes, I remember."

"Well, whoever suggested this might have saved my son's life. Stephen finally opened up to me. Some of the things he said . . . well, they were hard to hear." Katherine looked down, then back up at James, whose smile had faded. "Stephen admitted to me that he had been having thoughts of killing himself. His grief over his father's death was worse than any of us realized. We all miss Elias, but Stephen's grief was manifesting itself in a dangerous way. The good news is that he agreed to talk to a grief counselor."

James put his hand on hers. "This is the best news." He smiled. "And just in time for Christmas next week."

"We know that this is a process and things won't be fixed in a day, but at least he'll talk to someone and maybe the counselor can help him work through his feelings. I also called the bishop and asked him to talk with Stephen soon. It's important for Stephen to have a strong male role model, especially at his age." They were quiet for a moment, their hands still touching. "Speaking of next week, on Christmas Day we will be having worship service and a large meal. And as you probably remember, we celebrate Christmas for two days. Most years, on Second Christmas — the day after Christmas — we visit shut-ins and elderly friends who might not have family nearby, or whoever we would just like to spend extra time with during this blessed time of year. But this year, we have decided that on Second Christmas we will stay home and share memories about Elias." Katherine moved her hand out from under James's and gently laid it on top of his. "Would you like to come to our home on Second Christmas? I think it's time the children meet their grandfather."

James blinked back tears. "And hear about my son? About all that I missed?" He dabbed at his left eye, which hadn't twitched once. "And meet my grandchildren?"

Katherine nodded. "Would you like that?"

James squeezed her hand. "It would be the best gift a man could receive."

She gently took her hand back and smiled. "*Gut.* Then it's a date." She grabbed her cup and took a sip, forgetting that it wasn't black coffee. After getting over the initial shock of sweetness, she had to admit it tasted pretty good.

James watched her and then nodded toward the cup. "Not as bad as you thought, huh?"

Katherine smiled. "Might take some getting used to, but I like it better than I thought I would."

He swiped at his eyes again. She was doing the right thing. She could feel the Lord's approval shining down on her. And Elias's.

Mary Carol couldn't thank Abe enough for talking to Stephen. She smothered him in kisses as he drove them to James's house the following Saturday.

"*Danki* so much. Whatever you said to Stephen, it helped him open up to *Mamm.* He has an appointment to talk to a doctor who helps people with grief. And we're thinking maybe all of us might go."

"Aw, I didn't do much. But I'm loving my reward." He grinned before he returned one of her kisses.

"I know you're not thrilled to be visiting James again, but next week is Christmas. He probably doesn't have anyone to spend the day with, so I at least wanted to visit him today to wish him Christmas blessings." She nodded toward the backseat. "And to give him another cake."

"*Ach,* just admit it. You like the old guy."

She pulled her coat tighter, hugging herself. Paradise was having a hard winter so far, and the temperature today wasn't supposed to get above freezing. She was glad that they'd left the small heater for James. And he'd mentioned that a friend had given him a coat. "*Ya*. I do like him," she said after a moment. "Who knows if anything he says is true. But there is a kindness about him that seems genuine." She paused and sighed. "He's familiar. I wonder where I would know him from."

"I don't know." He turned the horse onto the gravel road that led to the farmhouse. "Who does your *mamm* think you're making the cake for? Have you told her about James?"

"*Mamm* left early this morning with Gideon, so she didn't see me baking. I've been lucky about that both times. I don't want to lie, but I know that once *Mamm* finds out, she's going to forbid me to go there since he's a stranger. And *Englisch*."

"*Ya,* you're probably right."

"*Mamm*'s been staying up late working on quilted items to sell at the market. I know it's because we are short on money, even though she won't admit it. But she did say that the bishop was insistent that she use the community health fund for any grief counseling any of us might need. We're lucky we have a lenient bishop."

After Abe tethered the horse, Mary Carol jumped out of the buggy and grabbed the cake pan, and they trudged through the snow to the farmhouse. James opened the door before either of them knocked. He wasn't well groomed like last time, and Mary Carol wondered if he'd forgotten that he had invited them over today. He was wearing a wrinkled white shirt, his hair was flattened on one side, and he was barefoot and shivering. But he stepped aside so they could enter.

"Goodness, it's cold in here. Where is the little heater we left for you?" She scanned the living room. All the empty Coke cans were gone. "And what about the blanket?"

James walked to his chair and sat down. "What heater and blanket?"

"Did you maybe take them upstairs so you would be warm when you slept?" Mary Carol was still holding the cake.

James shook his head. "No. I don't know what happened to them. Is that chocolate cake?"

"Yes. Should I put it in the kitchen?"

James nodded. Mary Carol walked to the counter and set the cake down. She wondered what else James ate. She peeked in some of the cabinets, and just like last time, they were empty. She walked back into the living room and sat down on the couch beside Abe. They were all shivering.

"James, do you have food to eat?" Mary Carol gave him a quick once-over. He had a small belly and didn't appear to be undernourished.

"Oh yes. Lots of food." He pointed to the kitchen. "And sometimes I eat out."

Mary Carol made a mental note to bring something more than cake next time. She doubted James had money to eat out. "Do you have plans for Christmas?"

He sat taller, ran a hand through his hair, and smiled. "Yes, I do."

Mary Carol doubted that was true either. "That's *gut.*"

They were all quiet. James's left eye twitched again. He was rubbing his forehead.

"It was a *gut* idea for me to talk to Mary Carol's brother Stephen. I think it helped." Abe took off his hat and set it on the floor.

"I know it helped." Mary Carol waited for James to comment, but he just kept rubbing his forehead. "James, are you okay?" she asked after a moment.

James put his hands in his lap. "Some days my head hurts. Other days it doesn't." He scowled. "I think I got shot once."

Mary Carol was going to have to get her mother involved after the holidays. If *Mamm* knew how this man was living, she could

474

contact the *Englisch* authorities for help. Mary Carol wasn't sure who to call.

She glanced at Abe, then said, "We can't stay today, James. But we wanted to bring you the cake." They both stood up, and James did too.

"I love cake. Chocolate cake. Thank you for bringing it to me." He walked them to the door. Abe extended his hand to James.

"Merry Christmas, sir."

Mary Carol held her breath as she waited to see if James would shake Abe's hand. She smiled when he did. Then she hugged James. "Merry Christmas," she said.

He gave a quick wave and closed the door behind them.

"We're going straight to the market," Abe said once he got the buggy going. "I've got enough money to get him a few things."

Her heart swelled at Abe's generosity.

Mary Carol opened her purse and dug around. "I have fourteen dollars. That will buy a little bit."

After they loaded up at the market, they went back to the farmhouse and knocked on the door. When James didn't answer, they left everything on the front porch. A new heater in the box, blankets, and as much nonperishable food as they could afford.

"He's not in there." Mary Carol was peeking in the living room window. "Do you think he's lying down upstairs?"

"Probably."

They knocked one more time, and when there wasn't any answer, they headed back to Abe's buggy.

God, please make sure that James eats plenty today and that he stays warm.

CHAPTER EIGHT

Christmas morning, Katherine knew that she wasn't the only one feeling the void, but they were all going through the motions in an effort to remember the reason for the season. As she'd done in the past, she had colorfully decorated gifts for the children and placed them around the house. She knew a few Plain families who put up a Christmas tree, but it was kept secret from the bishop, and mostly it was for the benefit of relatives who weren't Amish. Katherine had never put up a tree, but she did have holiday candles, sprigs of holly, and festive bows on the mantel.

"Do you like the gloves, Gideon?" Katherine had handmade all the gifts this year. In the past, she and Elias had shopped for one store-bought gift for each child, but that wasn't practical this year. In addition to farming, Elias had worked for a construction company part time, but they didn't have much of a nest egg built up.

Gideon put the gloves on his tiny hands. *"Danki, Mamm."*

Katherine giggled to herself at Gideon's new haircut. Stephen had kept his word and wrapped the pipes in the basement with some foam that Elias had in the shed. He'd also surprised Katherine and trimmed his brother's hair. Gideon's bangs were noticeably crooked, but she decided to let them be instead of fixing them. Delegating some of her responsibilities meant some things weren't going to be done up to her standard, and she was going to have to be okay with that.

Stephen kept the fire going, and generally, things were going better than Katherine would have predicted a month ago.

And James Zook got credit for speeding up the healing process. Despite his odd ways, memory loss, and bizarre stories, he seemed to have a gift — an ability to understand the human spirit better than most.

Mary Carol ripped through her gifts with lightning speed, and Katherine knew it was because she was in a hurry to spend part of the day with Abe and his family. Katherine had invited Abe to tomorrow's Second Christmas. The smile on her daughter's face had been a gift in itself.

"Slow down, Mary Carol. You have plenty of time, and the meal is keeping warm. You can head to Abe's right after we eat."

"I love everything!" Linda said loudly as she put on a black sweater Katherine had knitted for her. Katherine had asked Linda if she might need to talk to the counselor, but Linda had frowned and told her no. "*Daed* is in heaven. And I miss him, but I know he is with Jesus having fun." Linda's maturity surprised Katherine, but she was thankful for her daughter's positive spirit. Katherine could learn a thing or two from her.

After lots of hugs, they made their way to the kitchen, and once everyone was seated, they bowed their heads and prayed silently.

Katherine looked up just as Stephen pointed to the sweet potatoes.

"*Daed*'s favorite. And you didn't put the pecans on top."

"*Nee*. But I will if you all want me to," she said while she grabbed the pot holder to handle the hot dish. Her children shook their heads. Elias had never liked nuts.

"I'm just glad you always make the paprika potatoes too," Linda said, "since those are my favorite."

After Katherine had served Gideon, she held up the pot holder. Her hand burned because a portion of the material had worn thin from years of use. She normally wouldn't consider pulling one out from the stash to sell at Diana's booth, but she thought about it for a moment. *Why not? It's okay to do for yourself sometimes, Katherine.*

Most of the families in their district enjoyed a traditional meal of turkey, dressing, potatoes, peas, casseroles, cranberry sauce, and way too many desserts. Katherine's family was no exception. Katherine and Mary Carol had been cooking since early that morning while Linda kept an eye on Gideon. Despite the knot that kept trying to form in her throat, it was a blessed day.

After the dishes were washed and put away, she brought the box of craft items to the kitchen table. She lifted up a pretty sage and burgundy pot holder and turned it over in her hands. Yes, this would do. She smiled, surprised at how much she was looking forward to celebrating Second Christmas tomorrow. And following a good night's sleep, she awoke with an unexpected bounce in her step.

"You're next, Linda. What fond memory of

Daed do you want to share?" Katherine asked.

Linda clapped her hands a few times from where she was sitting on the floor. "I have a *gut* one! Remember when the family played volleyball? Me, Mary Carol, and *Mamm* were on one team, and *Daed,* Gideon, and Stephen were on the other?"

Stephen laughed. "That was so unfair. Gideon was only four. That's the only reason you girls won."

"*Nee,* we won because we were better than you!" Mary Carol said, nudging Linda's shoulder in a loving gesture.

Linda laughed. "You're just not used to losing to girls, Stephen." While the kids continued to tease each other, Katherine snuck a glance at the clock on the mantel. She hoped James remembered to be here at noon. She'd already put the homemade bread, chowchow, jams, and jellies on the table. She'd poured a glaze over the ham and was keeping it warm in the oven, and green beans were simmering on the stove. She was planning to make a batch of brownies, but for some reason they were almost out of their powdered cocoa. She'd just bought the canister a couple of weeks ago. She'd have to ask Mary Carol about that later.

Stephen would be the most excited to see the large bowl of potato salad in the refrigerator. Katherine added bell pepper to her potato salad and Stephen loved it. *Elias loved it as well.* She wondered if he was watching them from heaven, listening to them recall their favorite memories of him.

She eased herself off the couch when she heard a car coming up the driveway. The last time they'd met, she had questioned James about where he'd gotten the car and how he put gas in it. He'd told her, "I got it the normal way people get a car. I bought it. And I put gas in it so it will run."

She watched him park and walk around to the trunk. He took out a large box. Katherine's heart started to pound as he got closer, and she could see that inside were smaller wrapped gifts. She didn't want her children having any more worldly items than necessary. There were enough electronic gadgets lying around with Stephen and Mary Carol in their *rumschpringes.* And where did he get the money for presents?

She forced the thoughts aside, deciding to focus on the bigger issue. Her *kinner* were about to meet their grandfather. She'd never heard her husband speak poorly about his father in front of the children, so she was hoping the *kinner* would welcome this new family member into their lives.

Mary Carol couldn't believe her eyes when her mother escorted James into the middle of the living room. He was carrying a box full of wrapped gifts and looking spiffy in a long-sleeved maroon shirt that was freshly pressed, black slacks, and shiny black shoes. He had on a brown coat that was similar to the one her father used to wear.

She grabbed Abe's arm. "What is he doing here?" she whispered. "I don't know," Abe said as he kept his eyes on James. "Your *mamm* must know him."

Mary Carol watched James as he set the presents down. She noticed that once again, he wasn't limping, nor did his eye flutter.

"Hello to all," he said as he looked at each of them.

Mamm walked to his side, smiling as she gently touched his arm. "Children, I'd like for you to meet James." She paused as she looked around the room. "James Zook."

Mary Carol realized that she'd never asked James his last name.

"Isn't that the name of your father's father?" Abe whispered in her ear.

She nodded. "I'm sure there are a lot of James Zooks in this area." Even as she made the comment, it struck her why James had always seemed familiar. Finally, he looked at her and smiled broadly. She wanted to run to him, to throw her arms around him, but she was already going to have some explaining to do later.

"James is your grandfather," *Mamm* said after a moment passed. "He is going to have dinner with us. So I trust you will use your best manners." Her mother's expression turned from joyful to stern, which led Mary Carol to wonder if her mother knew James as well as she and Abe did . . . well enough to know that anything might come out of his mouth.

Her mother made introductions. Mary Carol swallowed hard and wondered if James would acknowledge knowing her already. But he just smiled and shook her hand.

"A pleasure to meet you."

Her palms were clammy from this unexpected situation, but a warm feeling settled over her to know that James was her grandfather. "Your mother told me that you would be sharing memories about your father today, so I've brought gifts for each of you with that in mind." He smiled as he took presents out of the box, handing one to each of them. Even Abe. Mary Carol was as nervous as she could be. James looked and sounded perfectly normal. But she knew how quickly he could change. And how long had her mother known him? Should Mary Carol call him *Daadi* now?

Once everyone had a gift, *Mamm* sat down on the couch next to James while everyone else found a seat. Mary Carol noticed the way her mother was biting her lip and glancing around the room. Maybe she knew James better than Mary Carol thought.

"Young Gideon, why don't you open your present first." James sat taller, his palms flat on his knees.

Please, God, keep him on course.

Mary Carol's little brother tore the silver paper from the small package, then opened the box and pulled out a baseball.

"That was the first baseball your *daed* ever had," James said. "When he wasn't much older than you, he became quite the baseball player. A big group of kids used to play ball at the Stoltzfuses' place."

Gideon turned the ball over in his hands. "*Danki* . . ." He looked at their mother. "What do I call him?"

Mamm looked between James and Gideon. "Um . . ." Her eyes landed on James. "What would you like the *kinner* to call you?"

James smiled. "If I remember correctly,

the word for grandfather is *daadi*. But Katherine, if you would prefer for the youngsters to call me James, that would be mighty fine also."

"Can I call him *Daadi, Mamm*?" Gideon asked from where he was sitting on the floor. Mary Carol realized that Gideon hadn't known any of their grandparents. Their mother's parents had died six years ago — the same year and within a month of each other. And their father's mother had passed right before Gideon was born.

After *Mamm* told Gideon that was fine, Linda lifted her present above her head. "Me next!" She brought it to her lap, ripped the paper off, and pulled the lid off of the shoe box. "Look! Look!" She held up a yellow flashlight. "Was this *Daed*'s when he was a boy?"

James nodded. "I borrowed it the night I left. And I've had it all these years, along with a few other keepsakes."

Mary Carol was sure they could have heard a pin drop in the room. Everyone was wondering the same thing. *Why did you leave your family?* But Mary Carol had spent enough time with James to know he probably didn't understand what he was doing back then.

Maybe her mother knew. She was trying

to speculate how *Mamm* had found their grandfather. *At the farmhouse? Did they write letters over the years?*

After an awkward moment, Stephen asked what everyone was thinking. "Why did you leave when our *daed* was a boy?"

Mamm cleared her throat. "That is a conversation for another day. Today is for sharing memories of your father. Stephen, you go next."

Stephen's box was small, but his eyes lit up when he pulled out a pocketknife.

"I'm afraid that wasn't your father's, Stephen," James said. "It's mine. But I'd be honored for you to have it, to maybe pass down to your own son someday."

Stephen held up the knife. *"Danki."*

Mary Carol gave her box a little shake before she untied the purple ribbon. She recalled seeing the wrapping paper and other items the first time she was at the farmhouse. Inside, there was a children's book with three ducks on the front.

"Your grandmother used to read that to your father. It was his favorite. At least it was back then. He was probably Gideon's age." James got the faraway look in his eyes again. "Maybe you can read it to your children one day," he added.

Mary Carol thanked him. "*Mamm,* open

487

yours," she said.

"Let Abe go first." *Mamm* walked to the fireplace, warmed her hands, then turned around to watch Abe.

James had warmed up a little to Abe, but Mary Carol was still nervous about what he might have given Abe. *A hangman's noose to warn him not to kiss me, maybe? A lump of coal? A bag of switches?* She stifled a smile as she thought about different possibilities. Abe's box was larger than all the rest.

Abe lifted a straw hat from the box. "Did this belong to Elias?" Abe asked with some eagerness in his voice.

Mary Carol held her breath when she saw James scowl. "No."

He didn't elaborate even though everyone in the room was waiting. A moment later, he said, "In case you ever sit on yours or something."

Everyone was quiet, but Abe actually burst out laughing and thanked him. James winked at him.

"I guess I'm the last one." *Mamm* slowly unwrapped her present. It was a box small enough to fit in her hand. She opened it and then pulled out a key. "What's this?"

James stood up and put his hands in his pockets. He wasn't wearing any suspenders today, but he had on a black belt. "It's the key to my heart. For bringing me to your home to meet my grandchildren. I am a blessed man."

"Thank you, James. We are happy to have you here, and glad that you're a part of our family."

They all watched James open two presents that their mother had placed in front of him, and he thanked her repeatedly for the two sweaters she'd knitted for him.

"Is everyone ready to eat?" *Mamm* clapped her hands together the same way Linda did when she was excited.

"Uh, actually . . ." Abe's face turned bright red as he moved toward Mary Carol. "I have something to ask Mary Carol."

"What is it?" She tried to read his expression, but his face just turned a darker shade of red. Mary Carol had been disappointed in Abe's Christmas gift to her. Well, that wasn't entirely true — the quilt his mother made her was beautiful. But it wasn't a personal gift from him. Before she had time to guess what he might be doing, he left the room and returned with a gift bag.

"I wanted to give you this yesterday at *mei* house, but I wasn't finished with it."

Mary Carol had given him several things she'd made by hand, so she wasn't surprised to find inside the bag a beautiful oak box that he'd carved for her. But she was surprised when he dropped to one knee.

"Open the box," he said.

With shaky fingers, she opened the beautiful box and pulled out a piece of paper that read, *Will you marry me?*

She looked at Abe, then at all her family members. As her eyes filled with tears, she thought about her father. But this was a season of hope for all of them, and as she gazed into Abe's eyes, she was certain that she wanted to be with him for the rest of her life.

"Yes," she whispered. Then she looked at James. He rolled his eyes, and Mary Carol laughed out loud.

CHAPTER NINE

Katherine was at the coffee shop a little early, surprised that James hadn't arrived. She decided to be daring and ordered a vanilla latte.

It was nothing short of a miracle that James had behaved so perfectly during their Second Christmas celebration. She'd been worried about her children meeting him since she never knew when he might turn into one of his characters and talk about his federal agent days or tell one of his tall tales. It was bound to happen eventually; she should sit down with all of the children before their next family gathering.

Thirty minutes later, she finished her drink and left. Worry was burrowing into her heart as she thought about where to even look for James. And how easily he could slip out of their lives, the same way he'd slipped in. What if she never saw him again?

By the time she got home, she'd worked herself up even more, picturing him lost, cold, or hungry. She'd asked him if he'd wanted to stay overnight on the couch after the big meal on Second Christmas, but he said he already had plans. Katherine was sure he didn't, so she'd prayed that he would have shelter, warmth, and food.

"What's wrong?" Mary Carol asked when Katherine walked into the house. She took off her black cape and hung it on the rack. "James — I mean your grandfather — is always at the coffee shop on time. We've been meeting there on Tuesdays. Today he didn't show up, and I'm worried." She untied her black bonnet, brushed specks of snow from it, and hung it next to her cape. "I don't think he has a home. I don't know where to find him."

"I know where he is."

"How could you possibly know where he is?" *Mamm* put her hands on her hips. "Mary Carol, what's going on?"

"I'll explain on the way."

Katherine found Linda and asked her to keep an eye on Gideon since Stephen was at work. Linda rolled her eyes but dutifully complied. Her two youngest children didn't start back to school until the following week.

"He stays at the old Porter farmhouse,"

Mary Carol said as they directed the buggy onto the road. Katherine listened to how her daughter had been spending her Saturdays and how she and Abe had gotten to know James.

"I never lied, *Mamm.* I told you I was spending the day with Abe, and that's what I was doing."

Katherine sighed. "You didn't tell me because you knew I wouldn't approve of your visits with an *Englisch* stranger."

Mary Carol hung her head for a few moments. "He tells all kinds of stories, *Mamm.* Do you think he's . . . you know . . . crazy?"

"I don't know. Something isn't right with him, but sometimes he makes more sense than all of us."

Mary Carol gasped as Katherine guided the buggy up the driveway of the old Porter place. Katherine slowed the buggy, unsure whether to keep going.

"There's a red car. Did James tell you that two men in a red car have been following him?"

Katherine pulled back the reins. "*Ya,* but I didn't believe him."

"What should we do?" Mary Carol asked when Katherine brought the buggy to a stop in front of the house.

"I'm going to check on him. You wait here."

"*Nee.* I'm coming too."

Katherine didn't argue as she tethered the horse, then they both hurried across the packed snow toward the door. She knocked. When no one answered, she knocked harder.

"James's car is here." Katherine knocked again.

"Why do you think he has a car but no real place to live? I've asked him, but he always changes the subject."

"I don't know." Katherine had asked him the same thing several times.

Finally, the door opened and an older man, who looked to have many years even on James, greeted them. He was a tall man in a black suit.

"Hello, Katherine. Hello, Mary Carol," he said as he stepped aside so they could go into the house.

Katherine grabbed Mary Carol's arm and held her in place. "How do you know our names?"

The elderly *Englisch* man smiled just as another man wearing a white jacket appeared beside him, extending his hand to Katherine. "I am Dr. Reynolds," he said. "I am James's caregiver."

Katherine kept one hand on Mary Carol's

494

arm, ignoring the doctor's gesture. "And this is how you let him live?" Mary Carol had filled Katherine in on the conditions inside the old Porter place.

"Please come in," the man in the black suit said, not responding to Katherine's comment. "We know you have questions, and the time has come for us to give you answers. My name is Weldon Bartosh. I've been a friend of James's for a very long time."

Katherine still didn't move.

"Come on, *Mamm,*" Mary Carol said softly.

The two men stepped back even farther, and Katherine and her daughter went into the living room.

"Where is James?"

Dr. Reynolds sat down in the recliner. "Please, have a seat on the couch. I will explain everything to you. James is upstairs napping, so this is a good time for us to chat."

Weldon remained standing as Katherine and Mary Carol sat down.

"James has an inoperable brain tumor. I am his physician, and as Weldon told you, he has been a friend to James for many years." Katherine brought two fingers to her lips, unsure what to ask first. She decided

495

to ask Dr. Reynolds the question heaviest on her heart. "Is he dying?"

"Yes. I'm sorry to say that he is. And his dying wish was to see you and his grandchildren. We knew that James would come here, regardless of his condition, so when Agent Weldon told me he intended to follow him, I offered to join him. James and I have been friends for years. My wife died last year and it does me good to have a purpose again." Dr. Reynolds smiled. "We bring him hot meals in the evening, and even though he rarely changes his clothes, he has a closet full upstairs."

Katherine swallowed hard as she glanced at Mary Carol, whose jaw was on the floor. Katherine was still processing the fact that James was dying. "How long does he have . . . to live?" She reached for Mary Carol's hand and squeezed.

Dr. Reynolds looked at Weldon, then back at them. "We honestly didn't think he would live this long."

Mary Carol sniffled. "Is he crazy?"

Dr. Reynolds grinned. "I'm sure he's told you some stories that might make him appear crazy, but no, that is not his diagnosis. His unpredictable behavior is a result of the tumor growing on his brain. You may have also noticed some unusual physical mannerisms, like his eye twitching."

"Or that his limp sometimes goes away?" Katherine said.

"I'm actually unsure what caused his limp to disappear. Especially since he'd had that his entire life."

Maybe God relieved him of the limp, Katherine thought.

Mary Carol was dabbing at her eyes. "He told us he'd been shot," she said. "We didn't think that was true. I guess now I'm wishing that's all it was instead of hearing that he's dying."

"Oh, he *did* get shot," Weldon said. "But that isn't what's causing his confusion."

"When?" Katherine asked as she sat taller. "Why?"

Weldon sat down on the arm of the couch farthest from where Katherine and Mary Carol were sitting. "Back when James was living here in Paradise, he witnessed a horrific crime," Weldon said. "After safely fleeing the scene, he went directly to the police station. He was shaken and fearful. Rightfully so." Weldon paused and hung his head for a few moments. "James led the police back to the scene, and based on evidence in the house and James's descriptions, they had a pretty good idea who he'd seen. These were some bad fellows." He looked back up.

"And once they explained this to James, he was afraid for his family. The police escorted him home, and he gathered a few things. His wife and son were running errands at the time. We put him in protective custody that same day. We encouraged him to leave his wife a note, but he just kept saying to hurry, that she wouldn't understand. We needed him to be safe until the trial. Then he'd be free to return home. Or so we thought. And we did a pretty good job keeping his identity a secret. But on the day of the trial, despite the security we had for him, someone shot him going up the courthouse steps. They must have assumed he was our key witness. I wanted to pay a visit to his wife, to let her know he'd been injured, but she didn't have a phone, and if the criminals had gotten to James . . ." He shrugged, shaking his head. "We just couldn't take a chance that they might be following us, so we didn't notify her. By then, we knew it was a large ring of delinquents we were dealing with, part of the Philadelphia mob. After he recovered, James went into the witness protection program."

"Witness protection?" Katherine took a quick, short breath before she brought her hand to her mouth. Questions were forming faster than she could organize them, but the words wedged in her throat. She felt light-headed, but she didn't move or say anything.

"We assumed he would want to bring his wife and son into the program, but he insisted that he would be the only one to go, as long as we could guarantee their safety, which at that point, we thought we could. If he had waited any longer, I don't know if we could have. It was important to James that his son be raised in this Amish community. And as I said, the goal was to keep him only until the trial ended and all the bad guys were locked up. James didn't realize — nor did we — that when he left, he wouldn't return for decades."

"Why didn't they all just move to another Amish district?"

Mary Carol's voice cracked as she spoke. "Maybe in another state?"

"We offered that to him. We told him that all three of them could start over in a new place with new identities. But he remained fearful that the criminals would find him, and he wanted to be far away from his family if they did."

Katherine dabbed at her eyes.

"The trial was postponed for a while, but eventually justice was served and the crooks went to jail for life with no chance of parole. We didn't get the entire criminal ring, but we at least captured two of the men responsible for the murder that day in Lancaster. The third man remained on the loose."

Weldon was using words that Katherine had never heard, but she was pretty sure that he was saying that the criminals would never get out of jail. She recalled the time the FBI had been in Lancaster County. A shiver ran the length of her spine.

"James made the ultimate sacrifice for his family, and only a few of us know how he suffered by not being able to see his wife and son. He wept for days when he heard his wife had died."

Katherine shook as she tried to stop the tears rolling down her cheeks. She squeezed Mary Carol's hand even harder.

"What — what did he see on that day, the crime?" Katherine's voice trembled and she stole a look at Mary Carol, unsure if she wanted her daughter to hear these details.

CHAPTER TEN

Mary Carol waited for an explanation from the *Englisch* man, feeling nervous and sick and scared. She held tightly to her mother's hand. Her father had rarely mentioned Mary Carol's grandfather over the years, and the little bit of family history that Weldon was filling in was bittersweet.

Mr. Bartosh sighed. "He told us that he was strolling down a side road toward a grove of pecan trees. It was a pretty day. He was not far from here, across the lane, when he said he saw the front door of this house burst open and a man run out into the front yard, a look of sheer terror on his face. Three men rushed out onto the front porch, one holding a shotgun. The young man was shot five times in the back. James said when the man fell in the front yard, the three men had a direct line of sight to James."

Mary Carol gasped. "Here?"

"Yes. Long before Mr. Porter lived here,

501

three men lived in this house. They were involved in some shady transactions and more or less hiding out in your Amish community. This place is pretty secluded, and we found Amish clothes in the house. Apparently they tried to dress the part anytime they traveled away from the house. One of the guys had even grown a beard. After James witnessed the murder, he ran from the scene. It's a miracle he got away from those men. It benefited him to know the woods and surrounding area so well. Somehow he lost them and made it to the station. He admitted that at least one of the men had gotten a good look at him, so we encouraged him to shave his beard and cut his hair, which he did.

"When I first met Paul — I mean James — I saw signs of a man who had obviously grown up in a peaceful environment, who witnessed something so horrific and upsetting, it changed him and he never was the same again."

"What about his wife and child — my *mammi* and *mei daed*? Couldn't this mob group have come after them?" Mary Carol asked in a shaky voice.

Mr. Bartosh lowered his head and was quiet. When he looked up, he grimaced and shifted his weight. "This is where we messed up. We wanted these thugs to get word that Paul Johnson was the man who witnessed the shooting — that he was an Amish man from Ohio visiting friends. We gave him a whole new identity so that he could never be traced back to Lancaster County, so that these men would never find James's wife and son. It was all in an effort to get him back here when it was all over. We knew that the media would eventually find out that Paul Johnson was our key witness. We thought we could keep him safe through the trial until everyone was behind bars." He paused. "That's when the mob in Philadelphia got involved."

Mary Carol had no idea what a mob actually was. She looked at her mother, but *Mamm* shook her head.

"It's a criminal organization. These men would do anything to get to James before he testified and implicated their involvement, so we changed his name once more and relocated him. Again. To Michigan this time, where he lived as James Shelton in a small apartment."

"When it was all over, why didn't he come back?" Mary Carol asked.

"It wasn't all over until a year ago. Remember I said one man was still on the loose? Well, that last man was found living in a nursing home in Colorado. He'd been using a different name all those years. That man was taken to jail like the others, also with a lifelong sentence, but he died soon afterward. James was bitter about that for a long time — that the last holdout got to live almost his entire life as a free man, enjoying his family, while James had been ripped from his wife and child at such a young age. But it was then that James felt it was finally safe to come home. He was making travel plans to surprise his son when Dr. Reynolds diagnosed him with a brain tumor."

The doctor cleared his throat. "James gets very confused sometimes, and he often forgets to take his medication. On the days he remembers, he can be fairly coherent. But even with his pills, he has a hard time due to the pressure in his head."

Mary Carol recalled the headaches James would get. "So he isn't crazy? This tumor in his head makes him tell the tall tales about being a federal agent?"

Dr. Reynolds looked at Mr. Bartosh, and the older man took over. "James stays confused, hopping from one identity to the other. But it's all true. He lived it." He paused as he locked eyes with Mary Carol. "And I assure you . . . James *was* a federal agent. A very good one."

Mary Carol couldn't speak, and her mother just stared.

"It seemed a stretch since I know your people are pacifists," Mr. Bartosh said. "But James knew he couldn't go home and he had an inborn desire to let justice prevail at all costs. He was a young man, around twenty-five, when this all began. He worked hard and saved his money. Then he went on to college, got a degree in criminal justice, and landed a job in law enforcement. To hear him talk about it, he was able to completely separate from his Amish life and become this new man who used the law to right the wrongs of others.

"Six years later, he looked me up, and eventually he came to work for us. It was his mission in life to find the one man left who had been involved in the shootings. And he did. So he was now free to return home to his family."

Dr. Reynolds spoke up again. "James insisted on staying at this farmhouse even though we wanted to put him up at the same bed-and-breakfast we've been staying at since we arrived. We keep an eye on him, even though he hates that we followed him here to Lancaster County."

"We were friends for a long time," Mr. Bartosh said before he looked at her mother.

"I couldn't stand the thought of him dying alone if you rejected him."

Katherine thought about how differently things could have turned out for all of them if James hadn't shown up. But she was having a hard time understanding why these men would spend months of their lives following James, no matter how strong their friendship.

Weldon chuckled. "He's quite capable of giving us the slip when he really wants to. We lost track of him for eight days last month and were really worried about whether or not he was taking his medications. He did fairly well after his initial diagnosis, but he started getting more and more confused and needed someone to check on him daily, so that's where Dr. Reynolds came in. The doctor had known James for years through other circles, and he offered to take over his case and monitor his care." Weldon paused, the hint of a smile on his face. "You know, he was a handsome devil in his younger days, but he never remarried and always said there would never be anyone like his beloved wife, Sarah."

"Is he —" As much as Katherine wanted to care for James, she had her children to think about. She'd been nervous on Second

Christmas. "Is he a danger to himself or others?"

Weldon shook his head. "No. He just stays confused, and that will most likely get worse as the tumor grows."

"We were worried that he wouldn't get here in time to meet all of you, but he has surprised us." Dr. Reynolds's smile was genuine. Katherine believed the man truly cared for James. She silently thanked God for putting these two men in her father-in-law's life.

Katherine recalled James telling her that he would be called home soon. "Can we take him home to live with us for however long he has left?"

Weldon glanced at Dr. Reynolds, then back at Katherine. "We were hoping you would."

Katherine marveled at the wonderful way the Lord worked.

Mary Carol put her head on her mother's shoulder. "I wish *Daed* would have known all of this."

Katherine put her arm around her daughter and pulled her close. She thought about the dreams James had told her about, his conversations with Elias.

Smiling, she said, "Somehow I think your *daed* does know."

Weldon cleared his throat. "There is one more thing. James has some classified information we need. Do you know anything about this? Has he mentioned anything to you? During one of his rants, he said that you were the keeper of this classified information, but it's always difficult to know when James is creating his own version of the truth."

Ah. Now things were making more sense. She didn't doubt that these men cared about her father-in-law, but he also had something Weldon wanted, which explained why he had taken time out of his own life to follow James for months.

Katherine recalled the key James had given her. Her father-in-law had said it was the key to his heart, but had he entrusted her with something else? The more she thought about it, she realized that the key resembled the one to her own safety deposit box in town. She decided to keep her answer vague for now so as to avoid telling a lie. "James told me he was the keeper of top-secret information, but he never said what it was."

Weldon sighed.

Katherine thought about this great man who'd given so much of himself to keep his family safe. She planned to take care of him

508

for the rest of his life, however long that might be. But first thing the next morning, she was going to her bank on the off chance that the key he'd given her was to a safety deposit box.

Weldon stood up and reached into his pocket. "Take this card so you'll always know how to reach me. And can you please let me know if you come across anything that James might have stashed away for me?"

Katherine took the card and nodded.

"Do your people use . . . uh, regular doctors?" Weldon blushed a little.

"*Ya.* We do."

Dr. Reynolds stood up and gave Katherine his business card. "You'll want to have a doctor monitor his medications and probably check on him at least once a week. I can make sure his medical records are transferred here. And he really shouldn't be driving." He shrugged. "We didn't have any luck getting him to give that up, but maybe you will."

"We will help him pack his things and bring him to your house tomorrow if that's okay," Weldon said. "He keeps everything upstairs — the heater, the clothes we got him, and even his food. We eventually bought a small refrigerator for the upstairs bedroom." He shook his head. "We hate him living here, but he insisted. We figured it was better than him sleeping in his car, which he'd done in the past. He doesn't know it, but we're actually paying Mr. Porter's granddaughter rent on this dump."

Katherine's mind was still reeling, but she just kept nodding.

"I have some errands to run in the morning," she said. "Can you bring James to our house in the afternoon?"

"Sure." Weldon extended his hand. "I wish you all the best." He smiled as he shook Katherine's hand. "Gonna miss that man. Please keep us informed. If possible, we'd like to come back . . . uh, when the time comes."

Katherine and Mary Carol walked to their buggy. The sun was shining off the freshly fallen snow, and Katherine thought it was brighter than she'd ever seen it.

The next morning, Katherine arrived at the bank in town just as they were opening the doors. Mary Carol was unhappy that she had to stay at home, but Stephen was working and Linda had stayed overnight at a friend's house. Someone had to watch Gideon. He had a cold and didn't need to be out in the weather.

It took less than a minute for the bank clerk to confirm that Katherine's key was for safety deposit box number 2042, and Katherine was an authorized user. On shaky legs, Katherine followed the woman into a large vault. Even though Elias had kept a safety deposit box for property deeds and legal papers, Katherine had only been in the vault one time, and that had been when the bank called her after Elias died and asked her what she wanted to do about the box. She'd purchased a safe to keep at home.

After the woman left her alone in the vault, Katherine fought the urge to cry. So much had happened, and she wished she had her husband to lean on. She put the key in the lock and lifted the top. There were two envelopes inside. Katherine's name was on one, although Elias's name was scratched out. The other envelope had Weldon's name written on it. She opened her envelope, knowing that it was originally for her husband. She started to sob when she saw the cash and savings bonds inside.

"Oh, James . . . ," she whispered. She wouldn't have to worry about getting good medical care for James, and she was never going to have to worry about taking care of her family. Enclosed was a letter.

Dear Katherine,

If you're reading this letter, I've most likely passed on, or I'm well on my way. I'm told by my doctors that my mental capacity will continue to deteriorate. I thought it best to write to you while I am still somewhat in control of my faculties — and it's hit or miss these days. But by now, you probably know my story, or at least I hope you do. I pray that the legacy I leave behind for my grandchildren will be one of honor and that I won't go down in history as the guy who abandoned his wife and child.

Katherine sniffled as she turned the piece of paper over to continue reading.

There is another envelope for Weldon. You might meet him. If not, here's the address for where to send his letter.

Katherine scanned the address.

Please do not open the envelope addressed to Weldon. It's classified information, and I trust you to get it to him. BUT — AND THIS IS VERY IMPORTANT — if you are in possession of this envelope and I'm still alive, PLEASE do not give this to Weldon until I die. That's

512

all I can say about that.

And if it's not too much to ask, could you please get word of my death to a woman named Bonnie? She wasn't a love interest or anything. Only your mother, Sarah, held my heart. But Bonnie was a special person in my life at a time when I needed a friend. Here is her address, and on the outside of the envelope, you'll need to write this code in the bottom left corner so that the letter will actually get to her. 3891055574-HHG46l.

Katherine brought a hand to her chest as she read the address.

The White House
1600 Pennsylvania Avenue
NW Washington, DC 20500
So, I think that's it. I love you, ~~Elias~~Katherine. So, as the song says . . . I'll be seeing you.

~~Dad~~James

Katherine held the letter to her heart for a while before composing herself and then walking out of the bank.

CHAPTER ELEVEN

James surprised them all by staying around much longer than predicted — long enough to see Mary Carol and Abe get married in the fall. He was in a wheelchair by then. Katherine couldn't help but smile when she recalled the blessing James said aloud before the wedding feast. Over a hundred people were at Katherine's house — as was tradition — for the ceremony and grand meal afterward. James whistled to get everyone's attention. Katherine had told him that everyone would pray silently, but James had insisted on reciting his own version of thanks to the Lord.

"Thank You, God, for this glorious, wonderful, superb, outstanding day! Please bless this couple and encourage them to name their firstborn James. Now, over the lips and through the gums, look out, tummy, here it comes!"

Katherine smiled at the memory as she

watched Gideon sitting on the edge of James's bed. Her father-in-law spoke in a whisper, his eyes barely open.

"Not only is it beautiful where I am going, but there's always chocolate cake to eat." James paused and looked across the room. "Katherine, you should ask Mary Carol for her recipe, by the way. Hers are the best." Katherine looked over to her daughter, who wore a sheepish expression and shrugged. "But the best part, Gideon, is that your father and grandmother are there waiting for me, and I can't wait to see them."

Gideon looked at his grandfather with an expression that seemed older than his years. "Sometimes I'm sad that my *daed* isn't here anymore."

James was quiet for a moment. "When I was gone all those years, I missed your dad something fierce. I thought about him every day. Prayed for him too. Even though he isn't here with you, he still loves you very much."

Gideon hugged James and then made his way over to Katherine's lap. Stephen, Mary Carol, Linda, and Abe were gathered around James. Each of them had privately said good-bye to him earlier in the day. But even though they knew what was coming, it didn't stop the flood of tears. Abe was sobbing even more than the rest of them. Their family doctor had been by that morning and said it wouldn't be long now. Katherine was so thankful to God that James was cognizant of them all as he prepared to take his final breath.

But now, as Christmas approached, they would be saying good-bye to another loved one. A miracle of sorts who'd breezed into their world and changed the way they all looked at life. And death.

Katherine was having a hard time holding back her tears, but she knew that this was a time for celebration. James would finally be reunited with the son and wife he'd left behind so many years ago.

"Tell *Daed* we all say hi," Gideon said softly.

James closed his eyes and nodded. Katherine had turned her small sewing room into her bedroom. There was barely enough room for a twin bed, but she didn't mind. She'd given James her bedroom so that they could all gather here with him for prayers each day. Katherine was sure James had seen and done things that would shock her and the children, but the man had stayed strong in his faith his entire life. She held his hand, hoping he could feel all the love

516

they had for him.

As the clock neared eleven, she encouraged her children to go to bed. And she told Mary Carol and Abe that they should go home. "He is sleeping now. These things can drag on," she whispered as James snored.

Reluctantly, they all did as she asked.

After the door closed behind them all, Katherine grinned. "I can tell when you are fake snoring." It was something he did when he didn't want to talk or be bothered. "But you are stuck with me right now."

Her father-in-law opened one eye and gave her a weak smile, then he slowly opened the other eye. She had to lean close so she could hear him. "I didn't figure you'd want them in here when I took my last breath. I might turn purple or have saliva dribbling down my chin."

Katherine smiled. "Do you realize the joy you have brought into our lives?"

He squeezed Katherine's hand. "You've made this old man very happy. Thank you for sharing your family with me. I have so much to tell Elias . . ." His voice had weakened so that his words were barely audible. She relaxed in the chair next to his bed and held his hand. They sat this way for an hour.

Then suddenly she heard him try to speak again. She stood and gripped his hand.

"They're here," he said, and a broad, luminous smile spread across his face. His eyes grew wider and he focused on the corner of the room.

"It's been a long time. Sarah . . . Elias . . . Take me home." And he closed his eyes for the last time.

Katherine sat there for a while and prayed. Then she slowly lifted herself from the chair and eased her hand from James's. She kissed him on the forehead before she walked to the dresser and pulled open the top drawer. She took out the envelope with Weldon's name on it so that she could mail it first thing in the morning, along with a letter to a woman named Bonnie that she'd written the day before.

She held both envelopes to her heart.

"Go in peace, James Zook." She smiled. "I'll be seeing you . . ."

Katherine was in the living room, looking out the window, when Mary Carol arrived for a visit. James's burial had been earlier in the week and the family was still adjusting to his absence. Katherine was also still getting used to the fact that her sweet Mary Carol was a married woman and living

518

somewhere else. "What's going on, *Mamm*? Are you okay?"

"I'm fine, just received some news this afternoon that made me smile." Katherine was still holding the letter she'd gotten earlier. She looked at her daughter. "Do you remember your *daadi* mentioning a woman named Bonnie?"

"Yeah, Abe and I didn't believe for one minute that the first lady's sister was baking him chocolate cakes. I know that Mr. Bartosh confirmed most of *Daadi*'s stories, but he never said anything about the White House or a woman named Bonnie."

Katherine chuckled. "No, he didn't. But maybe we should have thought to inquire about Bonnie. I mailed a letter to the White House, to Bonnie, after your *daadi* passed on, just like he asked me to. I was doubtful I'd get a response. But I got a letter in the mail today. From the White House." She handed the piece of stationery to her daughter. Mary Carol stared at it with wide eyes for a second before she looked up at Katherine. "No way."

Katherine smiled as she waited for her daughter to read the letter.

Dear Ms. Zook,
Thank you for your letter informing

519

me about Paul's passing (James, as you know him). He was an incredible man, someone I'm proud to have called a friend. I know that it blessed his life immensely to finally be with his family. It's all he ever talked about during his time at the White House, how someday he would get home. He was a great source of strength to me during a difficult time in my life, and I would like to think that in some way, I had a positive influence on his life as well. He will be greatly missed.

Sending you blessings at this difficult time.

All the best,
Bonita (Bonnie) Morgan

"*Daadi* always said Bonnie was the former first lady's sister, but that no one knew. Do you think that's true?"

Katherine was wondering the same thing. "I don't know. Everything else he told us turned out to be true."

"Maybe that's what *Daadi*'s letter to Mr. Bartosh was about."

"I don't know. I didn't open the letter because your *daadi* asked me not to. Mr. Weldon was your *daadi*'s friend, but he was also after some information that James wouldn't share." Katherine walked to the window in the living room, thankful for the bright sunlight. "Maybe it had something to do with Bonnie, or maybe not. But either way, your *daadi* was indeed friends with a woman named Bonnie at the White House."

Mary Carol read over the letter again. "I wish we knew for sure who she was."

"Well, maybe one day we can ask James about this ourselves. But not anytime soon, the Lord willing." Katherine's heart was still heavy at having endured another funeral service for someone she loved. But Bonnie's letter lifted her spirits, and it seemed to do the same for Mary Carol.

She grabbed her daughter's hand and led her to the kitchen. She pulled out the new canister of cocoa and smiled. "I know the perfect thing to do in remembrance of your *daadi.*"

Mary Carol beamed. "Chocolate cake!"

DISCUSSION QUESTIONS

1. James tells Katherine that Gideon must "see" his own heaven to understand where his father is. Have you ever done this — visualized your idea of heaven? If not, take a few minutes to do so.
2. Each family member expresses grief in a different way, as is the case in real life. Who could you relate to the most and why?
3. After James witnessed the crime, he chose to stay away from his family in an effort to keep them safe. Would you be able to practice such unconditional love if it meant that you might not see your loved ones for a very long time, possibly forever?
4. What were your thoughts about James — in the beginning, then later toward the end of the story? Did you believe his tall tales? Did you think he was crazy?
5. At the end of the novella, Katherine keeps her promise and mails the envelope from

the safety deposit box — without opening it. What do you think was inside the envelope? Was it really classified information? Can you speculate as to the contents?

ACKNOWLEDGMENTS

Karla and Joan, you've been with me on this journey from the beginning. You even set up my first radio interview six years ago. What an amazing journey this has been, and I'm blessed to know you both. It's an honor to dedicate this story to such fabulous women.

To my wonderful husband, Patrick — I'm your Annie, and I always will be, lol. You're the best, and I love you with all my heart.

Natasha Kern, thanks for all you do. What a wonderful agent and friend you are. So glad to have you on my team. xo

Many thanks to the folks at HarperCollins Christian Fiction. You all ROCK! It's a privilege to work with all of you.

And, as always, God gets the glory for every story I write, but without the support of family and friends, it would be a challenging journey sometimes. Thank you!

RECIPES FROM *ROOTED IN LOVE*

KATHERINE'S PINEAPPLE CHERRY CRISP

- 1 cup canned crushed pineapple
- 3 tablespoons minute tapioca
- 1 cup sugar
- 2 1/2 cups (pitted) cherries
- 1 tablespoon lemon juice

Combine and cook until clear, stirring constantly.

Mix crumbs together:

- 1 cup flour
- 1/2 cup butter, melted
- 1/4 teaspoon baking soda
- 1 cup quick-cooking oats
- 2/3 cup brown sugar

Put half of crumb mixture on the bottom of 9×13-inch baking pan. Add cherry and pineapple mixture, then cover with remaining crumbs. Bake at 400 degrees for 25 minutes.

ROSEMARY'S CHEESY SALMON CASSEROLE

- 1/4 cup chopped onions
- 2 tablespoons margarine
- 1 can cream of mushroom soup
- 1/2 cup milk
- 1 cup shredded cheddar cheese, divided
- 4 cups cooked macaroni
- 1 (8 ounce) can salmon
- 1/2 cup buttered bread crumbs

In medium saucepan cook onions in margarine until tender. Stir in soup, milk, 3/4 cup cheese, macaroni, and salmon. Pour into baking dish. Bake at 250 degrees for 25 minutes. Top with bread crumbs and remaining cheese, then bake 5 minutes longer.

RECIPES FROM
A LOVE FOR IRMA ROSE

IRMA ROSE'S WHOOPIE PIES
- 4 cups flour
- 2 teaspoons soda
- 1 cup shortening
- 2 eggs
- 1 cup thick sour milk
- 2 cups sugar
- 1/2 teaspoon salt
- 1 cup cocoa
- 2 teaspoons vanilla
- 1 cup cold water

Cream together salt, sugar, shortening, vanilla, and eggs. Sift together flour, soda, and cocoa, then add to first mixture, alternating with water and sour milk. Add more flour if milk is not thick. Drop by teaspoon and bake at 350 degrees for 10–12 minutes. Let cool.

Filling:
- 1 egg white, beaten
- 2 tablespoons flour
- 2 cups powered sugar (or as needed)
- 1 tablespoon vanilla
- 2 tablespoons milk
- 3/4 cup Crisco

Beat egg white, sugar, and vanilla. Add remaining ingredients. Beat well. Spread filling across cooled cookie surfaces.

CINNAMON RAISIN BREAD
- 1/2 cup sugar
- 1 cup lard or oil
- 2 eggs, beaten
- 1 tablespoon cinnamon
- 1 1/2 to 2 cups raisins, cooked 5 min. in enough water to cover, adding water if necessary to make 5 cups liquid.
- 10 to 12 cups flour (more if necessary)
- 2 tablespoons salt
- 1 1/2 cup hot milk
- 2 tablespoons yeast in 1 cup warm water

Mix together. Bake at 350 degrees for 40 minutes. Makes 4 to 5 loaves.

RECIPES FROM
PATCHWORK PERFECT

COCONUT PIE
- 1 1/2 cups sugar
- 3 eggs, beaten
- 1/2 cup buttermilk
- 1 cup coconut
- 2 tablespoons flour
- 1/2 cup butter or margarine
- 1 teaspoon vanilla

Combine sugar and flour in a large bowl. Add butter, eggs, buttermilk, vanilla, and 2/3 cup coconut. Mix well. Pour mixture into pastry shell. Sprinkle with remaining coconut. Bake at 325 degrees for 1 hour or until set.

CHICKEN CASSEROLE
- 1 fryer, cut up
- 1 cup diced carrots, cooked
- 1 loaf bread, cubed
- salt and pepper to taste

- 1 medium onion, chopped
- 2 cups milk
- 1 egg

Beat together egg and milk. Roll raw chicken pieces in flour and fry lightly in butter. Arrange chicken in bottom of roasting pan. Bake uncovered at 450 degrees for 1 hour. Mix the vegetables, bread cubes, milk, and egg together. Spread on top of chicken. Top with dots of butter. Bake half an hour longer.

RECITES FROM
WHEN CHRISTMAS COMES AGAIN

KATHERINE'S PAPRIKA POTATOES

- 1/4 cup flour
- 1/4 cup Parmesan cheese
- 1 tablespoon paprika
- 3/4 teaspoon salt
- 1/8 teaspoon garlic salt (or onion salt)
- 6 medium potatoes
- vegetable oil or cooking spray

Put all the ingredients except the potatoes into a gallon-size plastic baggie. Shake until well blended. Wash the potatoes and cut them into small wedges. Add potato wedges to the bag until one-third full. Shake the bag to coat the potatoes. Place them on an oiled pan and repeat until all the potatoes are covered with the mixture. Bake at 350 degrees for 1 hour.

MARY CAROL'S CHOCOLATE CAKE

- 2 cups white sugar
- 1 3/4 cups flour
- 3/4 cup unsweetened cocoa powder
- 1 1/2 teaspoons baking powder
- 1 1/2 teaspoons baking soda
- 1 teaspoon salt
- 2 eggs
- 1 cup milk
- 1/2 cup vegetable oil
- 2 teaspoons vanilla extract
- 1 cup boiling water

Preheat oven to 350 degrees. Grease and flour two 9-inch round pans. In a large bowl, stir together the sugar, flour, cocoa, baking powder, baking soda, and salt. Add the eggs, milk, oil, and vanilla. Mix for 2 minutes on medium speed. Stir in the boiling water last. Batter will be thin. Pour into prepared pans. Bake for 30 to 35 minutes, until the cake tests done with a toothpick. Cool in the pans for 10 minutes, then remove to a wire rack to cool completely. Frost with your favorite chocolate frosting and enjoy!

ABOUT THE AUTHOR

Award-winning, bestselling author **Beth Wiseman** is best known for her Amish novels, but her most recent novels, *Need You Now* and *The House that Love Built,* are contemporaries set in small Texas towns. Both have received glowing reviews. Beth's *The Promise* is inspired by a true story.